P9-CQD-972

Claudia

Anthony Trevelyan was born in Lancashire. He read English at Trinity College, Oxford, before going on to further studies at Lancaster University. Currently he lives with his wife near Manchester, where he takes part in numerous performance events. He works as a teacher of English and Creative Writing at a sixth-form college in Stockport.

His first novel, *The Weightless World*, was published in 2015 and was longlisted for the 2016 Desmond Elliott Prize.

Anthony Trevelyan

Claudia

SCEPTRE

First published in Great Britain in 2018 by Sceptre
An Imprint of Hodder & Stoughton
An Hachette UK company

1

The extract from 'Hearing Voices' quoted p. vii first appeared, in a different form, in *On Shakespeare's Sonnets: A Poet's Celebration* and is reproduced here with the permission of Mimi Khalvati

A CIP catalogue record for this title is available from the British Library

Hardback ISBN 978 1 473 66477 7
eBook ISBN 978 1 473 66478 4

Typeset in Sabon MT Std 11.5/14.75 pt by Palimpsest Book Production Limited, Falkirk, Stirlingshire

Printed and bound in Great Britain by Clays Ltd, St Ives plc

Hodder & Stoughton policy is to use papers that are natural, renewable and recyclable products and made from wood grown in sustainable forests. The logging and manufacturing processes are expected to conform to the environmental regulations of the country of origin.

Hodder & Stoughton Ltd
Carmelite House
50 Victoria Embankment
London EC4Y 0DZ

www.sceptrebooks.co.uk

To my mum,
Joan Trevelyan

But how you hid when the sky split, the voices came,
Each with a face you drew, wild familiars,
Grotesques that only talking to could tame . . .

Mimi Khalvati

Shock Valley – I

Here they come, the men, striding down the hill as if it's something they own, and they make me so sorry I almost don't want to kill them. One young and one old, one short and one tall, kicking down the trail in long-laced black boots, lashing every twig and branch they pass with the dismembered tent poles they use for whatever (to feel powerful, to feel like men, to feel like their fathers): they believe themselves masters of all they survey and all they don't, and they are masters of nothing. You could break your heart for them. How did anything so stupid wind up so proud?

They leave the trees on the far side of the valley, stand for a while peering at the lake, what's left of it, then start over the track towards me and my house. I've been watching them for the best part of an hour and by the time they pass the log from which strips of pelt hang down in tufted glitters I'm outside, arms folded, waiting for them.

'Hello, madam!' calls the older, shorter man, smiling and hefting the pole he's carrying as he might a silver-topped cane. 'And how are we, this beautiful day?'

'I'm well enough. Not sure there's any "we" I can speak for.'

'Is that so?' He glances at the younger, taller man. 'Forgive my asking, but do you have a husband round about? A son, perhaps?'

'Not even a daughter.'

'You astonish me.' The younger one smirks and looks away. Meanwhile the older unslings his rucksack and drops it on the packed earth at his feet. 'In that case, madam, I wonder if my associate and I may prevail upon you.' His smile widens but does not deepen. 'We find ourselves in need of a place to camp. I only wonder if we may do so here, in sight of your very lovely lake.'

'It's not my lake.'

'A manner of speaking, madam.'

'Not so lovely either, I wouldn't have said.'

'We would inconvenience you no longer than a night. Two at most.'

The older man unzips his anorak, one of those showy all-weather affairs patterned with webs and vents. Meanwhile the younger swings down his rucksack also and places it on the ground next to his associate's.

'There's tea,' I say. 'Might be able to find some bread and butter.'

'And rabbit.' It's the first time the kid has spoken. Instructively he points the pole in his hand at the log with its glittering tufts. 'There's rabbit.'

'There's tea, and there's bread and butter.'

'Most civil, madam.'

They look at me – a little old black lady, in night-nurse cardy and spinster jeans, living alone in her dead sister's house by a dead lake in a desolate valley. Well yes, well no. I go with my folded arms into the kitchen and rootle about in the compost-coloured gloom, thinking only about the drawers and their knives and knives and knives, until I have a tray with two cups of tea and two rough plugs of bread on it then I go outside again and find them fussing in that proud, heartbreaking way they have with groundsheets, pegs, poles.

'A fine pitch, this.' The older man chuckles as I lower the tray to him. 'Do you know, I can't quite believe our luck!'

I bet you can't. And – do you know – I don't believe it either.

At night the lake, or what's left of it, stinks. Probably it does during the day too, only you don't notice it with everything else you have to do (trapping, cutting, salting, roasting the sole shrivelled buck that a week's vigilance yields). At night the heat stops moving and stands over the clayey fissures where the lake used to be and draws out their pox and pong, their sultry pollution. You lie in bed with nothing to do but notice it.

Tonight however there are other things to notice, and I lie alert on my unopened bed, one arm hanging, fingers trailing over the stone floor. I've never been one of those who start in the night at nothing – rattling windows, clicking pebbles. Still I know what I'm hearing when the door clanks first softly, then more forcefully. Then the lock bursts with a splendid roar and again I am sorry for them. Can they imagine I didn't hear that? Then their feet on the kitchen flags, tap tap, undecided. Poor boys.

The door to my room creaks. It's a creaker, but even so. The men push past it into the black air. On top of the bed, fully clothed (cardy, jeans), I lie perfectly still. One of the men mutters something. And there is the snick of a catch, a button unbuttoning, and then the rigid slither of metal on leather.

One of the men shouts. The other grabs at the bed.

The kid is fumbling in the sheet for my ankles and his older associate is looking for somewhere about my person to plant the tip of the hunting knife that he unhappily wields and while they do this I reach under the bed for my hammer which I raise with a momentumless swing and connect to the jaw of the knife-wielder.

Even before I kick away the kid's hands and sit upright I register that the chief consequence of my swing is that the older man's neck is broken. He lets out a sort of shriek nonetheless and crumples himself into the wall, folds and refolds his limbs as if trying to pack himself into any of the large cracks in the wall.

The kid is trickier. Without a sound he tries to run from the room. He runs into the door and rebounds into the darkness on the other side of the bed. I stand and wait. He can't see me, isn't looking for me, is looking only at the door and the problem of getting past it. Teetering, he manages at last to scuttle past the door into the kitchen, which gives me ample time to walk up behind him and float my hammer at the back of his head. Without a sound he kneels on the flags.

I push him over, arrange him on his back and sit heavily on his hip, sucking more strongly at the compost-flavoured air than I'd prefer. I put down my hammer and have a look at him. He wears a distantly concentrated expression: there he is at ten, at eight, assembling some rainy-day Lego masterwork, clicking together the guileless blocks.

'You're making a mistake,' he says.

'Don't think so, sweetheart.'

'We're a word.' He shakes his head. 'We've a word. Come to tell you.'

'Is that so? You break into my house, attack me in my bed, for a word?'

But he doesn't have to say anything (and he can't anyway). It's all there in the stilled glaze of his Lego eyes. They have heard of me: Black Mabel, Bloody Mabel – Mad Mabel. These strong men thought to test my reputation, to see what I'm made of. Well, now they know. I am made of the hammer. And they (poor boys) are made of the nail.

'What word did you come to tell me?'

'Peter.'

I might have known. It even makes a grisly kind of sense. Once upon a time Peter and I had a commercial agreement. That is, once upon a time Peter paid me to kill people. Not in the way these two chancers thought they were being paid to kill people – they are messengers, messenger boys. I was never that. I can't say exactly what I was (disaster-averter, miracle-worker), but I was never Peter's messenger girl. Then Helios changed everything and whatever I had been I ceased to be that, and I came here, to my dead sister's house, and the dead level of the lake.

Over the next ten to fifteen minutes the kid on the floor tells me some other words, too.

When he has finished speaking I straighten on his hip. It feels bony, gristly, under me. 'I see. Thank you.'

'That's it.' The kid tries to smile. His head is shaking but he's no longer doing it: the nerves and muscles spasm of their own ruined accord. 'That's done then.'

'Oh, sweetheart, I wish it was.'

He doesn't understand. These men, these boys – they think they know Peter. They think they see another man in him, but he is not a man. He is an order, with many nuances. One of which, I know, concerns messages and messengers.

At least it doesn't take long. (I am made of the hammer.) Then there's everything else I have to do, the clothes to change, the bag to pack, the last breakfast I eat sitting at the kitchen table with my back turned to the two soft shadows laid side by side on the floor and my gaze fixed on the sun finally rising over the hill and the drained unlovely lake.

Part One

Hello Stranger

1. In the Flesh

She comes out of the lift and it's him. And it's disturbing. Her first instinct is to run and jump into his arms, and that can't be right. She's not six years old any more. And he's not – whatever he was back then. Except of course he is. Timeless man. Every wonk and wisp and snaggle the same.

A visitor, Reception Holly said (not to be confused with Holly from IT or Holly the Moan). *Can you come down, Dia? We have a visitor for you in reception*. Which was weird enough in itself, as the excessive politeness of Holly's telephone voice suggested, and more than enough to have Dia groping through her mental purse of possible bad pennies all the way from her desk to the lift doors. Then on top of that, it's him. Wild Samson. The Aztec, the Sun King. Samson Glaze.

Careful now. Six-year-old instincts in a nearly thirty-year-old body don't flatter anyone. So instead of whooping and running and leaping ecstatic into his mangy grip, she just sort of slopes up and stands in front of him with folded arms and a delighted frown she can do nothing about.

'You know,' she says, 'technically you're trespassing.'

'Old habits.'

They both laugh at that. She sees he does it how he always did, with clamped jaws and raised chin, a trapped hyena snicker.

Then he rolls his eyes and says, 'Look at you. Holy Moses. What happened? You're ancient.'

'While you're such a fragrant young rose.'

'Seriously. Do you have diabetes or something? You look about a thousand years old.' She shrugs, glows. This, she understands, is his way of telling her that he thinks she is very, very beautiful.

'To what do I owe the pleasure, Samson?' Only saying his name is deeply strange. Behind her frown her head swims with it.

'Can you talk? Is this a good time?'

'It's an okay time.'

They leave the building, the glare of the reception coven falling on their backs as they step into the midday sun and the main square of the new Complex development. For years this whole area of Manchester was a mess of building-site barricades and yellow-sleeved scaffolding rigs; then about six months ago the barricades peeled off and revealed an eerie landscape, seashell colours of tile surrounded by towering crystal shapes, a cinema, a theatre, an art gallery and who knows what else sealed away inside these glassy slabs of the New Architecture. Round the sides of the square wooden bench surfaces are attractively sunk into concrete blocks and are occupied, as always at this time of day, by Complex staff and international students. Dia finds a vacant surface and is about to sit when she notices Samson already sprawled on a bench a couple of rotations further down. She shoots her arms from her sides – what the hell? – but he only goes on grinning at her until she slogs across and sits next to him.

'Well, this is new,' he says, inspecting the development with an arch look. 'Very striking, very *Martian-colony chic*. Do you like it? *I* like it.'

'I didn't think people like you were allowed to like places like this.'

'Oh, Dee. Are there any people like me?'

Unfortunately, he has a point. Who ever lived a life like Samson Glaze's? When she was six, seven, eight, he was a red-eyed, stubble-masked wild man, a fantastical traveller who came seasonally with his fantastical traveller friends to wreck every last atom of the patch of green scrub behind the tower block in which Dia lived with her mum at the saddest end of their sad small town. He was the most fun she'd ever known crammed into human form. He told her stories and lies and solemn laughable truths, he picked her up by the ankles and spun and spun her, then made her keep score while he wrestled in the mud with his dogs. Then, when she was nine, ten, eleven, he started to become something else. And by the time she was thirteen he had transformed himself so utterly almost no one but Dia still knew who he was. She did, though. She always knew who he was.

And now he is . . . what? Not quite a reformed character. But a success. No question about it. A self-made man with a fortune in *solar panels*, if you please.

And yet neither time nor success appear to have changed him much. He affects no corporate airs, in T-shirt, jeans, trainers. The chicken-bone arms protruding from the T-shirt may have some gym tone, but chicken bones are chicken bones and she doubts all the spin classes in the world could ever get the druggy scrawn fully out of him. And yes, now she sees it up close, maybe his face has a certain sheen, but under the fancy finish it's the same wreck it always was, with wisping brows, dinged cheeks, snaggled teeth.

One big change is his hair. She used to love his scratty white-blonde mane; its loss reduces him by about a third of a person. But at least this is a change she was ready for. Dia may not have seen him in the flesh for more than fifteen years, but she has fairly often seen him out of it. On TV. Online. In newspapers, magazines. Doing what he does these days, which apparently is make speeches; raise objections; open things and close things; and publicly (and baldly) sneer at, heckle, shout down and otherwise appall the various scoffers and naysayers of the Whitehall elect.

So much she's picked up. Samson Glaze is famous, and everyone knows something about him. Certainly she has not for fifteen-plus years followed with a fanatic's zeal his every public statement and movement – has not spent the entire second half of her life talking to him in her head, inviting his opinion on this or that remark, soliciting his agreement with this or that view, confirming his approval of this decision, this strategy, this look, this scarf with these boots. God, no. Nothing like that.

The only real shock then is his smell. He leans towards her and there it is: aniseed and iron filings. That's what he smelled of, always. He never smelled of dirt, even when he was filthy. He smelled of this, aniseed and iron filings, and she is six years old and the urge to go *wheee* and torpedo into his lap is so preposterously strong it creaks in her gums. Careful now.

'Why are you here?' she says, with heavy severity.

'I wanted to see you. To see how haggard and sickly you'd grown.'

'Fifteen years, Samson.'

'Is it as long as that.' Not a question. He sits back, turns his head as if taking an interest in the man sitting on the next bench surface along, a gesture that briefly alerts her to the presence of another anomaly in this highly anomalous situation (Samson Glaze is sitting in broad daylight in a public space: where are the crowds, the autograph-hunters and selfie-seekers?), then he leans towards her again with his big blue eyes and his big wonky grin and he says, 'Yeah, I've got an ulterior motive. Did you hear I'm opening a new office up here? High ceilings, awesome flow. I'm going for a kind of office-space-cum-illegal-rave-venue. Photocopier in the chillout room, that sort of vibe. You should check it out.'

'So this is a business trip.'

'Did I say that was my ulterior motive?'

'Isn't it?'

'No, Dee. My ulterior motive is Reggie.'

At once she sees a red-haired little boy in halves of two different but equally antique pyjama sets (top half ThunderCats, bottom half Strawberry Shortcake) admiring an unusually cool bit of polystyrene packaging. Samson's boy, the boy Samson had with his wife, Cait. Briefly Dia's head wheels with them, Mama Styx, Pisces, all the Thin Love Collective in one leaping fractal of firelight . . . then she lets out a breath and says, 'What about Reggie?'

And he tells her.

It turns out Reggie Glaze not only lives right here in town, but he has done for some time. He made the move not long after periods spent in London and New York that Samson, with visible pain, describes as 'troubled'. She doesn't press him on it; her unblinking eyes invite no comparison to the troubled periods in her own life that he may or may not already know about. Nonetheless she gets the idea – drugs, low company, stints on metal bunk beds and plumply upholstered couches. The move to town was supposed to be, in the parlance of family discomfiture, a 'fresh start'; likewise Samson fast-tracked plans for the regional office so he could maintain an orbit close to his son's, keep a watchful eye, offer a steadying hand. It turns out further that neither hand nor eye was appreciated. The father was soon accused of being 'a control freak'. The son was shortly afterwards accused of being 'a silly prick'. At this stage dialogue degenerated sharply.

'Fisticuffs?'

'Near enough.' One night at the flat Reggie shares with his new girlfriend (a being dismissed by Samson with an impatient twirl of the fingers), father and son reached a pitch of fury in their relations that culminated in the father throwing the son's phone against a wall. The son then threw the same phone at the father's head. Connection was made. Samson indicates a corner of his dome and Dia thinks she sees the trace of a faint unbloody cut, maybe nothing. 'He told me to get out, and that's what I did, because at that moment I didn't know what else I could do. Since then, nothing. He won't take my calls, won't answer emails, if I go to his building I just stand there with my finger on the buzzer.'

She marvels at the fact that Samson has been able to keep all this quiet – to keep his tribulations out of everyone's newspapers and off everyone's screens. If Reggie's psychodrama had made its way into any corner of the public domain, she would certainly have known about it. Not that she keeps an obsessive's vigil for Samson-related content in her media streams, newsfeeds, timelines (nothing like that). 'You wrecked the boy's phone, Samson. What did you expect?'

'It's been a tough few years. Especially for Reggie. It's still not so long since we lost his mother.'

That's right. In the shock of seeing him she has forgotten, but yes: Cait died. When? Two years ago? Three? This Samson had not been able to keep quiet. She remembers the pictures that for three days spooled through her phone (and everyone else's): the funeral, the humanist chapel in unseasonable sunshine, Samson at the graveside with a seized tremulous look, as if trying to contain a sneeze.

'You heard about Cait? Of course you did.' His expression hasn't changed, but his face looks different: brittle, hollow, a long horn like the decorative head of a shaman's staff. 'At least it was quick. She was fine, she was ill, she was gone. I think that's what Reggie found so difficult. No time to prepare.'

It is awful. She remembers the pictures, but for the first time she feels the weight of Cait's death. A woman she recalls in terms of an unbounded laugh, sombre brown eyes, heels of hands like mother of pearl.

'He'd been struggling for a while. I should've seen it, but I didn't, and I went barging in and . . . well. What happened happened and I've tried everything I can think of, and now I'm left wondering. Will you do something for me, Dia?'

She frowns at him, annoyed. She seems to have sucked her lips to a hard dot. Will she do something for him? Since she was in single digits it has been the profoundest wish of her heart to do something for Samson Glaze. Preferably to save his life, hoist his limp body from a burning building, but she'll take what she can get. It is stupid of him not to know. Will she do something for him? She will do anything for him.

'Let's have it,' she says.

'I know Reggie's always thought highly of you.'

'What do you want me to do, Samson?'

'He'd talk to you. He'd open the door to you, at least. If you could go round, check he's all right, see what's on his mind . . . it would mean so much to me.'

'I'm not saying I won't.' Because she will. She will do anything he asks of her. 'The last time I saw Reggie he was a little boy. Now he's, what, twenty-two? If I just rock up at his door, he won't have a clue who I am.'

'Oh, he'll remember you.' Slowly, deliberately, underlining the point, Samson nods. 'People remember you, Dee. You're the type of person people remember.'

She stares at him, to make sure he knows that this is not too much, that she can bear it. 'What's the address?'

He tells her, and she snorts derisively. For almost a year Reggie Glaze has lived less than a ten-minute walk from her flat on unglamorous Granby Row.

'This girlfriend have a name?'

'Ugh, some bogus hooray diminutive – I think Tilly . . . ?'

'I'll go round tonight. Should we exchange numbers?'

'At present I'm "between phones". How about you give me your number and I'll catch up with you in a couple of days?'

Tight-lipped, she stands and recites her phone number, which he salutes. She waits for him to stand also, but he shows no sign of coming out of his sprawl on the bench surface. She waits, stepping from foot to foot. At last she jabs a thumb in the direction of her office.

'I should get back.'

'I can't tell you what this means to me, Dia.'

'Don't blame me if he goes mad.'

'He'll remember you. You'll see.'

She is halfway across the square when she turns back, mouth

opening to call to him, to say she doesn't know what, to vent the torrent of everything she's been saying in her head to him for fifteen-plus years. And he is sitting where she left him, only not watching her walk away, as she was sure he would be, but engaged in conversation with the man seated next to him, the one he found so distracting earlier: a thin man in a black suit and sunglasses, with black hair, a strangely puckered and withery white face.

And now she realises where the crowds were, the Samson fans, the Glaze enthusiasts. Because for the first time she sees that the square is discreetly populated by men in identical black suits and sunglasses, and these men comprise a loose perimeter round Samson through which no one is choosing to pass. Which means that every second of her intimate conference with him was superintended by this formal guard, and more especially by the thin man with the black hair and withery face stationed beside him throughout . . . Samson looks at her and the thin man looks at her also. She raises a hand in farewell. After a beat Samson raises a hand too. She stands there, her hand raised, waiting for the thin man to raise his hand also. He does not raise his hand. She shouldn't care, but she does. If it's ridiculous, so she's ridiculous. And she stands there, her hand in the air, waiting for the thin man to raise his hand also.

It's been years since Dia has woken up feeling like she's died in the night and become her own zombie, shuffling left, shuffling right, struggling to make sense of wholly unfamiliar surroundings and acquaintances, by and by finding out little curiosities like she's broken all the fingers of her left hand, or she is in a police van in an English shire she's not previously heard of. That time has never been further behind her, but as she rides the lift back up to the office where she now resignedly passes four days out of each week, there stirs, like the gusts of Samson's smell, the hectic vestige of an old brilliance, some flash, some spark . . . 'Billy Zane's going to kill you,' Val Mather says as she arrives back at her desk.

'Good for him.'

They are talking about their team leader, who is not called Billy Zane (he's called Neil Sneed), who does not in any way resemble Billy Zane (he looks like a small, sorry teapot), but who everyone in the office refers to as Billy Zane for some reason.

'No, he's *properly* pissed off,' Val says. 'He reckons you're being headhunted.'

'Does he now.'

'Well, you were talking to Samson Glaze, weren't you? The solar-panel bloke off the telly. Bloody hell, Claw. How do you know Samson Glaze?'

'I was renewing an acquaintance. Don't see what that's—'

'We saw you. Talking to *Samson Glaze*.' Val beams at the starriness of it all.

'Who's "we"?'

'Oh, just everyone.'

'Is that a fact.' Dia slots herself in place at her keyboard. 'Actually Billy Zane's right. Samson Glaze the solar-panel bloke is headhunting me. I'm only here to clear out my desk. In a minute I'm going to tell Billy Zane to kiss my arse then I'm off to work for Samson Glaze off the telly. Making solar panels.'

'Properly, Claw?'

'No of course I'm not. Told you. I was catching up with a pal.'

Val slumps towards her computer. 'Shame.'

'Yeah.' She is sitting at her desk but all at once again they wheel past her: the flashes and sparks of an old mirrorball brilliance. 'Shame.'

That night she leaves the office and the precincts of the Complex early and walks quickly along Oxford Road, following the tides of students and the four-square brick arches that uphold the railway track into crosscurrents of traffic then on towards her flat. She reaches Granby Row and stands for a full minute in the street outside her building, wondering whether or not she can be bothered to go up to her flat (eight floors, against the grain of a broken lift) and get changed before heading on to Reggie's place. She decides not.

Important to keep up momentum. Nonetheless she knows she is charging at a hornets' nest. Judging by the little Samson has told her – and it's only now that she sees how little it is – this is a father-son cockfight she might have been wiser steering clear of. Best she gets it over with: finds the boy, tests the clarity of his speech and eyes, then goes on her merry way. Besides, she struggles to reconcile her image of Reggie as a child in mismatched PJs reverently fashioning a polystyrene pickaxe with the anthology of rich-kid problems described by Samson. How bad can things be?

At the same time she knows Samson. He couldn't ask her but he didn't have to: she knows what he wants. He wants his son back. And if Samson Glaze wants his son back, she will bring him his son back. Never mind this weak stuff about seeing what's on Reggie's mind. She'll drag him through the street by his hair, if she has to.

Why? Because Samson is her first memory of shelter. When she was a little girl and had nowhere else to go (not her mother's flat, nine floors up in Sycamore House) and no one else to go to (not her mother; not Lila) there was always Samson finding a deckchair for her next to his scrabble-sided fire. Samson with his hyena laugh and his chicken bones, a mug of orange squash and a plate of ragged sandwiches and all the time in the world. Throughout her life since every instance of comfort and safety has aspired to the perfect encompassing shelter of that scrabble fire, that mug of squash, that plate of sandwiches, and has fallen short. He was refuge before she knew what that was, or understood that she needed it. He was her friend, her first ever friend.

She passes the old UMIST building with its picturesque observatory poking out of the top and crosses onto Aytoun Street. The address Samson gave her is a building on the corner with Chatham Street, for Dia's money another fine example of the New Architecture, with its unsensually contoured metal façade and weird-angled, sand-coloured pillars. She finds the buzzer panel and is still squinting for Reggie's flat number when someone says 'Hi', and with a scratch of keys yanks open the front door right next to her. Dia looks up to see a young blonde woman with a nose piercing and a kaftan grinning and holding the door for her. She steps in after the woman.

It's a nice place, or at least a swanky one, with everything rendered in glass or steel and reduced to its purest elements. The atrium is like a place of worship on a space station; the lift is basically the Great Glass Elevator. She steps out on Reggie's floor into a channel of sunlight that keeps making more room for itself. In pin-drop silence she walks along, counting down the flat numbers. Odd this is how she first experiences it: the reality of Samson's money. And this, she has to remind herself, isn't even where he lives. This is where *his son* lives.

And now here's a comic moment, because as she approaches

Reggie's door she hears footsteps behind her and turns to see the woman who held the door for her, flyers but no actual post gripped under her arm while she jangles her key ring and makes, unmistakably, for the same door. Dia steps back to let the woman pass, and here it is, that comic moment, the woman scratching her key in the door while Dia stands next to her as if in a supervisory capacity. Then the woman smiles at her and says 'Hi' again.

'Hi,' Dia says. 'Tilly?'

'Yeah, hi, I'm not Tilly, I'm Mel. I think Tilly's inside?'

Just what she needs. Posh new girlfriend breathing down the neck of everything.

'Can't promise she's decent, she's such a slut,' Mel says pleasantly, in a way that makes clear i) her poshness, and ii) her fondness for controlled substances. 'See what we can't do though, joint effort, er . . . ?'

'Dia. Dia Talwar.'

Mel leads her along a short hallway into a large pale sitting room on which the flat's residents have made scant impression. There's the garish street debris you have to expect of a clan of posh potheads, along with a slew of expensive-looking vinyl covering the floor by the windows, and yet the room's ice-cave atmosphere is largely intact. Mel yowls something encouraging about a coffee machine then trots away up a staircase. But Dia is not alone for long. Mel has hardly left her when a young fellow with damp black hair and a swishy silk dressing gown shuffles through an archway at the back of the room and comes up to her with a baffled grimace.

'Do I know you?'

'I'm a sort of friend of Reggie's.'

'Oh, *right*,' he says, with a mild sceptical air.

Mel reappears with another woman, also blonde, also pot-scattered, carrying an unlit cigarette and wearing the rugby shirt and checked shorts she clearly employs as nightwear. This, Dia supposes, is Tilly.

'You see,' Mel says, 'here's Dia.'

'Do I know you?' Tilly calls from across the room.

'She's a "sort of" friend of Reggie's,' the man calls back. 'Whatever that means.'

Tilly's eyes flicker. 'You know Reggie?'

'We used to be pals. Back in the mists of.' With what she hopes comes off as a bright look, Dia peers at the room's two or three visible doorways, as if expecting to catch a glimpse of him. 'Is he knocking about?'

'He isn't, no.' Sleepily Tilly focuses on her cigarette. 'Do you have a light, Dia?'

'I'm afraid I don't. Any idea where he is?'

'Where Reggie is? Oh, well, Reggie went with them.' Tilly glances at Dia. Her glance is anything but stable. 'He had a horrid fight with his horrid father and then he went with them.'

'Went where . . . with who?'

Tilly opens her mouth. For a while she seems about to say something. Then her lips start to quake. She clamps them together but they go on quaking.

It is awful. You look at this soft and rosy Tilly and you think: pony trials. Gymkhana. Haberdashers' Aske's and Centre Court and strawberries. But still she's hurt. Still somehow she suffers. In the high white air her face quakes and it's awful.

Then Tilly turns, not quite in time to hide the full collapse of her glance, and croaking that she needs a *bloody* light lurches from the room.

'I'd better . . .' Mel tips her forehead in the direction in which Tilly has miserably fled. 'Sorry. Hold the fort, Dan, will you?' And she too trots out.

An airless interval passes during which Dan stands with his hands in his silky pockets and Dia stares curiously at a patch of white wall, trying to fathom the precise means by which the day led her to this room, these walls, these tightly vacuous seconds.

'Tills is in rather a poor way,' Dan says eventually. 'All this business with Reggie has been something of a shock for her.'

'Which is what? Can't say I was following.'

'The Ranters.' He gives a mild, sceptical smile. 'I suppose you've heard of them?'

In fact she has; even thinks she's seen them, once or twice, through the oil prisms of the city at dusk, men and women marching in mute single file . . .

'What's Reggie got to do with the Ranters?'

'It's like Tills said. He went with them. About a fortnight ago. They were here, four of them, with that bizarre Ranter look they all have. They talked in his room for an absolute dog's age then they came out and he said he was leaving and he wasn't coming back. There was a rather grim scene. Poor Tills was inconsolable. And then he left with them. Or they took him. Depending on your point of view. But that's the essence of it. The Ranters took Reggie away.'

2. Save My Life

Next morning is Thursday, her day off, and Dia goes to see her professor at the university, first to talk about her dissertation with him, then to have sex with him. The first part of the arrangement they conclude sitting in uncomfortable wicker chairs on either side of his office in the School of Arts; then they cross the street to the second-floor flat in which he's lived since the early dithering days of his divorce, and they complete the second part.

Sex with Professor Andrew Evert, she's discovered, is a lot like conversation with him: fun while it lasts. He is a sweet, youthful forty, grey at the temples with a choirboy face stuck inside a bewildered mesh of wrinkles; his body is swimmer-slim, as probably it always has been, with moronic pink nipples, the odd jet-black hair fizzing out of somewhere, a grainy thinness or slackness at the shoulders and neck that is probably new. She likes him, does not idolise him, occasionally worries about him. After all, what's the poor prat doing sleeping with his students?

Afterwards he pads off between the stacks of unopened boxes that are the flat's only decoration and she lies on her side wondering why she is here. Why is she here? Because she has a degree. This in itself continues to dismay her. But she has one, though not a single person she knew growing up had one, and though she spent her teens cycling from troubled period to troubled period. Then abruptly at twenty-two she cleared the headspace for study. Six years and a string of waitressing gigs later, she had it: her dismaying degree. After graduation she took a job at Sonata Office Supplies – 'Bulk Order? Sonata Problem!' – and the next year enrolled on a part-time MA course, by then having realised that if she had nothing but work to look forward to for the rest of her life she would either slip into a coma or go on a killing spree. She met Andrew at a party for the new students, made a vague remark about Ali Smith to which he replied with an endearingly full-of-himself monologue on Eimear McBride. They did not on that occasion have sex; they did that the following Christmas, at a similar blowout at the Midland Hotel, where, entirely at her behest, they found a vacant bathroom and drunkenly screwed in it.

Andrew was mortified. When she went to see him in his office the next day he looked and behaved exactly as if he'd gone blind. The light, the little light, did not return to his eyes until she interrupted the drone of his remorse to assure him that he had not taken advantage of her – just barely doing his pride the kindness of not saying she was pretty sure *she* had taken advantage of *him*. That was the second time, there and then in his office. The third time was in his flat, in his blank-space bed. And that, for some reason, is where it has been every time since.

It would be nice to think their relationship is as gratifying academically as it is in other ways, except it isn't. Since they started sleeping together, Andrew's supposed supervision of her dissertation has dropped to near nil. At first he was keen to get her working on Kathy Acker, Giannina Braschi, someone like that; she wanted to work on Faulkner. He persisted – Marilynne Robinson, maybe? – but so did she. In the end they compromised and drafted a title about the representation of women in

Faulkner's late novels. The problem is she doesn't care about the representation of women in Faulkner's late novels, and nor does Andrew (and nor did Faulkner). And so for both of them now the tart little talks in his office are mere preludes to their crossing the road, coming here, doing this.

He returns with the tea tray and once it is grounded between them she says, 'Have you heard of the Ranters?'

'In what context?' Because he can't just say no, he hasn't heard of them.

'They're a group. You see them marching.'

'Do I.' He chuckles, head down in the chemistry-set intricacies of his tea preparation: timer, strainer, secondary teapot; practically the only things he's troubled to disinter from the taped stacks. 'Where do I see this?'

'In town. Not on Market Street, out in the hustle and bustle with the obvious nutjobs. Just around. Portland Street, maybe. Some further cranny of the university.'

He chuckles over the cream jug. 'Young chap I taught this year was a Ranter. That's what it said on his form, in any case. Must have done, because I remember observing at the time that he was far from ranty. In fact he was extremely quiet.'

'They are.' And she thinks of them, on Portland Street or wherever, in the late urban glower, their eyes with their low, unarrogant sightline, their mouths calmly closed.

'Never made any fuss. No glaring religion or ideology or suchlike. Not much of one for meeting my gaze, but they're all like that now. Eyes screwed into their phones, even while you stand there talking to them. Except he didn't have a phone. Ha, there you go. The weirdo. Nineteen years old and he didn't have a phone. The pervert.'

'What was his work like?'

'Wholly unexceptionally, he never did any. Dropped out after the first month.'

'What did he do then?'

'Returned to the happy-clappy communal bosom, would be my guess.' Smiling in a way that brings out the grey bits above his ears, he passes her a teacup in whose contents he is plainly delighted. 'What's got you turned on to the Ranters?'

'Oh . . .' She has never talked to Andrew about Samson. She has hardly talked to him about anything beyond books, ideas, arguments. Is this how she wants to start doing that? 'Someone I know is thinking of joining.'

'Are they? Who?'

'A pal. Not even that.'

'Well, tell them from me to think again.' He takes a long suck of tea. 'Something else I remember about my Ranter friend. Wouldn't say boo to a goose, but he did speak once. I asked him what he made of Alice Walker, put him on the spot, and after much anxious gurning he said, "She loves the world." That was it. Couldn't get another word out of him. "She loves the world." And he evidently did not think this was a good thing. Oh no. He thought it was a bad thing.'

'Creepy.'

'I was quite pleased when the little psycho dropped out.'

'Well, yes.' Frowning, she takes a sip of her tea. 'I can see why you would be.'

She is walking back to Granby Row when her phone starts to ring. It is him – it can only be him. She has been on hooks for Samson to call since she left the poshos' building last night. In a freezing sweat she stands by a lamppost, clawing her phone from her bag. Traffic chops by. Her hair flies, her nails click and snap. It can only be him.

It is not him. It is Sumi at Greenflowers, with the weekly update.

'Hey Dia, you ready for story time?'

'Sitting comfortably and everything,' Dia says, walking on up the sunny, icy street.

On Friday morning she arrives at Sonata early, settles at her desk, opens everything up and does what she promised herself she would not do, and asks the internet what it knows about the Ranters. For two nights she has resisted, kept her fingers clear of the touchscreens that make up the innermost curve of her life. Because what's the point? Once she has talked to Samson, he can do this for himself. But that's not the only reason. Her resistance to posing this simplest of virtual questions has obtained some other quality, some voodoo itch or gnaw, like the fear of the abyss that scribbles up from stepped-on pavement cracks, of whirring playground ropes whose touch will not merely sting her leg but slice it clean off . . . kiddie crap, in other words. Grow up, why don't you, Dia.

It's soon clear she may as well have not bothered. Her search returns nothing that is not fragmentary, third party, and primarily recreational. Look, here's a picture of me, thumbs-up, in front of a bunch of crazy Ranter dudes! Look, a crazy Ranter dude falling over! Then the soberly authoritative overviews, all contradicting each other. The Ranters are a religious organisation. Have no connection to religion. A recent phenomenon. An ancient tradition. Branches worldwide. A single-cell organism. Anything that resembles a link to an official website redirects her to a shopping cart for hair-removal cream or whatever.

She is already losing interest, thinking about opening her work area, when Val Mather sways up to her desk and says, 'Save my life.'

Val has that wind-tunnel look she gets when she's cocked something up. Dia is a lot more familiar with this look than she'd like to be. Val is all right, a tolerable deskmate, for the most part a repository of bland cheer and salacious anecdote, though on a fairly regular basis her free interpretation of the job spec gets the better of her and she commits some outrageous gaffe then spends two days crying in the toilet with precisely this white and breathless aspect. Dia has a suspicion Val does it on purpose, cocks things up simply to bring a spike of drama into the humdrum chart of her week. She further suspects Val has no idea she does this, and would meet any such suggestion with honest disbelief. As if there are two Vals, sharing the same cow-eyed almost-prettiness, one the victim, the other the victimiser.

This time she's bungled a delivery note. 'So I'm there and it's pure boxes, God knows how many, and the bloke he's there, the bloke who it's his *job* to know how many and I say, "Is this twelve?" and he says, "It's twelve if that's what you ordered," and I don't know, I didn't make the order, so I sign for twelve and, you see, then I check the warehouse, and . . .'

'It's not twelve.'

'It's not twelve.'

'It's eleven.'

'It's eight.'

'Fuck's sake, Val.'

'I know. And I didn't get a countersignature, so if Billy Zane checks it's going to look like another Val cock-up . . .'

'But it *is* another Val cock-up.'

'I know.' Val holds still among her private blasts. 'Save my life, Claw.'

'You want me to countersign.'

'Last time ever in the history of the universe.'

'Why? The missing boxes won't magically reappear.'

'But if you countersign the note looks legit. If Billy Zane checks it he sees your name, your one-hundred-per-cent trustworthy name, and he turns his attention elsewhere.'

'He blames the lads in the warehouse.'

'And everything's hunky-dory.' Val flattens the delivery note out on Dia's keyboard. Glancing at her screen, she says, 'Mad bastards.'

'You've heard of the Ranters?'

'If I tell you will you countersign?'

'I'll countersign. Just tell me.'

'They meet in a bar.' Pertly Val straightens the note. 'In town. I know because my cousin saw them, and our Sal may be a slag and an inbred, but a liar she is not.'

'Which bar?'

'Ah well, it's a secret bar.'

'What's it called?'

'It's called The Secret Bar.'

'Your cousin didn't say where it was?'

'She didn't know. Sort of stumbled on it last Saturday night. Mind you, she was in one of those tinky, rough-bird hen parties, so . . .'

'The Northern Quarter.'

'That'd be my guess.'

A secret bar called The Secret Bar. Where could it be but the Northern Quarter? Dia shakes her head. This town.

'Any chance of that scrawl now?'

'I tell you what, Val,' Dia says, plucking at the note and looping her signature into the appropriate blank box, 'one of these days you're going to be the death of me.'

That night Samson calls.

'Do you have plans? Because if you do, cancel 'em.'

She doesn't, but still. 'There's going to be a lot of disappointed people. Sorrowful stares into soup bowls and whatnot.'

'I'll send a car.'

Half an hour later, after no fewer than ten full or partial costume changes, the result of which is black bag, black ankle boots, black jeans and a black blouse with fractionally more detailing on the shoulder than she'd prefer, her phone rings again, an unfamiliar number, and when she answers it an unfamiliar voice asks if she is ready to come outside. She is, and eight liftless floors later she exits onto the street to find waiting for her not a Bentley or a Rolls or even a Jaguar, but a boxy black people carrier. At least it matches her outfit.

The driver steps out and of course it's the thin man she saw talking to Samson outside the Complex. He may even be wearing the same black suit. So he matches her outfit too.

Pausing on the steps, she raises a hand in greeting. His expression is unreadable inside his sunglasses, but after a second he seems to get it and raises a hand also.

'What are you,' she says to the man, 'Samson's butler?'

'I'm not a butler.' He opens a door for her: it is like a chunk of fighter plane falling out of the sky. She climbs into a reinforced cockpit that seals about her with a thunking of hydraulic locks. She barely has time to wonder where the man has gone when the back of his black-haired head wags into view in a hatch in front of her. He glances round, showing bladed bones, withered rippled cheeks that suggest he wasn't always so thin and that at one time there was very much more of him, and then suddenly very much less, and his voice says, with a faint intercom hiss, 'Make yourself comfortable.'

'Are we going somewhere nice?'

'I'm taking you to Mr Glaze's house, so . . . I'd say fairly nice.'

This actually is news. She expected a classy ride through the city to the base of the Beetham Tower and a night of Prosecco and asparagus shoots in some super-elite executive suite. The idea that they are going to his house calls for adjustment.

The next time she looks she sees through bulletproof glass that they have already left town. The big vehicle cuts a rapid swathe through traffic. They come to the motorway, the hopeful dots of suburbia, then the Tower, its domino height so ingrained on her senses that the sight of its retreat causes her an instant of panic. And then, too soon, the dead level of fields, the inhuman acres of England.

She feels the not-butler waiting for her to ask where they are. Let him wait. She keeps staring until she makes out the leafy outlines of Alderley Edge. Then they're surging on into the green dimness beyond.

Finally the car pauses. She hears some muttered intercom talk then the car starts forward past ambiguous, vane-like presences. Raised barriers? Gates?

For a moment it's as if they are flying. They seem to skim the fields, to rise and glide through the summer air. Then the car emerges into a shocking spill of tall light and here it is – Mr Glaze's house.

It doesn't matter what she knows; as far as Dia is concerned Samson Glaze lives as he has always lived in a 1972 blood-in-the-urine-red Dodge Ram campervan with a dissolved exhaust pipe, an unfixable curtain rail and sticky, foot-seizing carpet, a brave small wreck called Genevieve. The first time she saw the vehicle, she assumed it had recently been gutted by fire; in fact it just looked like that. And she soon learned that the quickest way to call down Samson's ire was to refer to Genevieve as '*it*'. 'Snotnose like you couldn't imagine what this lady has got me through. This angel, this *goddess* . . .'

'It's a van, Samson.'

'I've misjudged you, Dee. I honestly thought you had more about you than that.'

He wasn't joking: to Samson Genevieve was alive. And over the years Dia came almost to believe it too. Somewhere among the flaked fittings of the interior, below the slipped-hinge overhead locker but above the yellowing paperbacks that lined the foot space, there seemed to reside a watchful intelligence. Stately, imperial, protective, not altogether kindly: this, perhaps, was the fascia spirit that Samson called Genevieve.

Except the house standing in front of her now is about as far away from Genevieve as it's possible to get. In fairness, it is quite a long way away from most houses. A cliff-face of arches and lintels, of columns and buttresses, of – essentially – the Old Architecture, it is lit by a battery of hooded lamps laid out at intervals across a vast razored lawn through which a white gravel path self-consciously pours. And along this path comes Samson Glaze.

Has he gone to any trouble over his appearance? The recurrence of T-shirt, jeans, trainers implies not. But there is a burnish about him, something more than the streaming lamplight.

'Tell me you think this place is *unconscionable*.'

'It's not not unconscionable.'

Laughing, he catches hold of her fingertips. He spreads their arms, then lets their fingers pull apart and says, 'Come on. Let me give you the tour.'

She does her best. But right from the start it's too much and soon she tunes out and allows the drawing rooms, the libraries, the studies to revolve past her.

She knew he was rich. But there's rich and there's this. And still some idiot part of her keeps thinking the next door is going to open onto a bare and candle-haloed room containing only the antique saintliness of Genevieve, and he is going to urge her forward saying, 'Obviously this is where I sleep . . .'

Instead the tour pauses in a bright attic room with the atmosphere of an especially barbarous modern-art gallery. 'And here's my baby,' he says, directing her attention to what looks at first like a large table covered with rolls of tinfoil. Then she looks more closely and sees it is a model of some kind, the starred dazzle populated with racks, pods, dishes: the Newer Architecture. 'Little something I've got in the works. A solar plant, and not any old solar plant, this is cutting-edge utility-level stuff. Let's just say it: solar's a joke. Solar's bullshit, right? Everyone thinks that, you think it, half the time I think it, and I'm *me*. Well, no more. My guys on the Glaze gerbil wheels have come up with a very cool new concentrator system, totally game-changing, though bless your sweet diminished attention span . . . This is the breakthrough, yawny girl. Solar for the masses. Solar for all.'

'Dream that anarchist dream, Samson.'

'This one's almost built. Eight square miles of experimental concentrators in a field in Warwick. Couple of holdups, but it's looking good.' He makes a sad face. 'I hear there are concerned noises coming out of the Grid.' The Grid: it takes her a second. Then she remembers those shaggy-dog speeches in which he used to explain how his bit of eked-out solar self-sufficiency was his way of sticking it to Big Electric, the Masters of Dirty Power, the Coal and Oil and Isotope Man: the Grid. 'Why wouldn't there be? This tender lambkin is going to mess with their shit. *Look* at it . . .'

At last he relents and leads her to a sitting room that is mostly empty space and two flabby armchairs pushed up against a frankly camp ornamental fireplace, all but throws her into one of the armchairs and comes back a few minutes later with a tray of sandwiches so raggedly cut he can only have made them himself. Well satisfied, she takes a deep bite.

'So,' he says, contending with his own greedy mouthful, 'you went to see Reggie.'

'I did.' She did. She'd almost forgotten.

His hopeful look makes her pause. She thinks how nice it would be to be able to give him some good news, and how unfortunate it is that she has no news that is not bad, weird, and likely to be the occasion of parental alarm. Someone else would know how to present the facts in a way that made them, if not painless, at least endurable. But she is not that someone else, and she has no idea how it is done.

So she just tells him – about the girlfriend waving her unlit cigarette; about the ludicrous posh pals; and then about the Ranters. As she talks, she watches his face in the living light, living shadow of the frou-frou fireplace, examines it for signs of pain or alarm, though after a while finds herself only considering again the effects of illumination on Samson Glaze's face. Whether the campfire of the Thin Love Collective, finding him with one ear completely full of mud and a headscarved Mama Styx howling as she swats at him with a tea towel and Pisces snickering from within his stubble-headed, leather-creaked aura, or the frilly blaze of this snob grate . . . He shakes his head. 'I don't get it. These "Ranter" types – you say he "left" with them or they "took" him. What does that mean?'

'Wasn't clear to me either.'

He chews thickly then says, 'I mean, fine. If Reggie's made a choice and this is what he wants to do, for however long, fine. But I don't like the sound of someone "taking" him.' He is alarmed; pained, also; but maybe not so overwhelmed as she was expecting. Already there is a sense of flurrying strategy about him: what to do, who to call . . . 'And we don't know *where* they've taken him?'

'No.' Living light, living shadow. She understands with bitter clarity that this could be the end. If she keeps quiet now, eats her sandwich, gives him time to say whatever he's going to say next, all this will end. They will stand, he may embrace her, in his mangy grip she will be six years old again – and that's the reason, to make sure he doesn't embrace her and turn her six years old again, that's why she says, 'I know where they meet, though.'

'Oh yeah?'

'There's a bar in town. I could pop in. See if he's there.'

'You'd do that?'

'It's a bar. I still go to bars now and then.'

He sits back. After a moment, improbably, he smiles. 'Do you remember what I used to say about you?'

'I'd see the inside of a prison cell before I reached twenty.'

'The other thing I used to say.'

'I don't remember any other thing.' It's not true. She does remember – if she forgets her whole life she will remember the other thing he used to say about her.

'I said you're here for a great reason. I said other people I don't know about, but you, you're here because you have a great work to perform. I'd put my ear to your head and say I could hear it, your great work, buzzing inside your skull, like a hive. And I said one day when you perform this work of yours, you'll change everything. Change the world.'

She gives a queasy laugh.

'I'm grateful, Dee. You know that, don't you?'

'Buy me a couple of speedboats and we'll call it quits.'

'You'll be careful? These "Ranters" sound . . . If you go to this bar, you'll take someone with you?'

'Don't worry about it.' She takes another gulp of ham and cheddar and says through her full mouth, 'As it happens, I've already got someone in mind.'

3. All or Nothing

Suzy Poorman. Because who else?

Not only because Suzy is Dia's best and oldest friend; also because she is a resident of and an authority on that swirling maze, that vanishing corridor, the Northern Quarter.

They meet for lunch in a restaurant on the ground floor of Suzy's building, a unit that the last time Dia looked was a hairdresser's, or hair boutique, or gallery of hair art or whatever. Now it's a bare-bulb, jam-jars-on-school-desks urban eatery called Shop. All very hip, if not for the fact that the clientele this sunny Saturday lunchtime is largely middle-aged parents monitoring pushchairs full of tablet-jabbing tots.

'Here you are, honey!' Suzy says. 'What's it like being back on the old stomping ground?'

'I never stomped here. Once in a while tapped a foot, maybe.' True, there was a time when, like so many new arrivals in town, Dia succumbed to the hodge-podge allure of the Northern Quarter and spent her weekends arm in arm with Suzy Poorman, careering from club night to DJ set to private drinks party to underground performance event; but even then she rolled her eyes at the DJs and shrieked with laughter through the events. Now she thinks about it, Suzy rolled her eyes and laughed too. But where for Dia the aching cool of the place soon became merely an ache, for Suzy it never did. And so she stayed, and here she still is.

At least she looks the part. With her pierced lips and inked arms, in her floral-print frock and Aunty-Vera specs, Suzy today resembles a prototypical SVB, or Sour Vintage Bitch (a designation they jointly formulated in the twilight of some poetry reading or other). You'd think she must do what people round here do, build animated instruction manuals for a tech start-up on Church Street, make quinoa burgers for a vegan pop-up on Dale Street, but there you'd be wrong. Suzy is a nurse, and she works at the hospital.

'Right,' she says, clapping her hands together with a down-to-business air, 'we're looking for a secret bar, are we? What's it called?'

'It's called The Secret Bar.'

'A-ha.' Unfazed, Suzy scoops up her phone and begins artfully modelling its screen with her thumbs. 'And is there a reason why we're looking for it?'

'If I told you, it'd spoil the lovely surprise.'

Dia already knows there are countless websites, chat rooms and information streams dedicated to the vagaries of Northern Quarter nightlife; even so, The Secret Bar brings out a fresh nicety. Suzy shows her. If you want to find The Secret Bar, you have to download an app from a hard-to-find and password-protected app store, enter another password (acquired where, from whom?), then wait for a series of clues to the bar's location that night, in text, picture or other form, to download to your phone.

'The Secret Bar moves round?'

'Allegedly. That's what they want you to think.'

'So now we wait for these clues to drop?'

'By no means.' Suzy claps her hands back together. 'Now we go shopping.'

*

So they head out into it: afternoon in the zone of hipster bohemia that pools unsteadily out from the silver-branched flea market of Affleck's Palace. Everything is as Dia remembers it, though also completely different. Each of the bars and boutiques she used to visit has gone, replaced by another exactly like it. Suzy warns her not to be deceived:

'Most places still go for that lackadaisical, we-made-it-all-up-this-morning feel, but it's a con. Everything along here' – she sweeps her arm at a vista of pleasingly clashing outlets – 'is owned by the same investment group. They just don't let on, pretend they're each still a unique countercultural snowflake.'

'Which investment group?'

'Don't think there's an app for that yet.'

They settle on a clothes shop called Clinic, full of aluminum racks and the disdain of the young assistant, Suzy methodically looking at everything, Dia blithely looking at nothing, when Suzy says, 'Remind me. Why do we want to go to this place?'

'I'm looking for someone.'

'Ah. Things on the turn with Andy?'

'Things are fine with Andy.'

'By definition, honey, things are never fine with Andy.' Despite looking like the sort of person usually portrayed by mainstream media as an urban grotesque, part Devil-worshipper, part sex robot, Suzy has a deeply conservative moral streak, inoffensive for the most part but exhausting on the subject of carnal relations with university staff. Dia recalls that the last time she and Suzy argued, their contention was Andrew. Their climactic couplet: 'I wish you knew you're worth more than some manchild saddo who can't do his job without getting his kecks off.' / 'Well, too bad, Suze, because I *don't* know that, do I?'

'I'm looking for a particular someone,' Dia goes on quickly, 'to be precise, a twenty-two-year-old ginger nut called Reggie.' And then, skirting the shop assistant's disdain perimeter, she gives Suzy a brisk overview: Samson, the Ranters, the whole story so far.

'Blimey,' Suzy says, with deliberate banality, 'don't you know some fun people.'

'Headcases more like.'

'And you old chums with Samson Glaze, no less. Kept that a bit dark, didn't you?'

'I've not seen him since I was *thirteen* or something . . .'

'Seems a bit rich, him popping up now and putting you to so much trouble.'

'What trouble? It's a *hoot*.'

'If you say so. Did your mum know this bloke? Sorry, does she?'

'They didn't get on.'

'And what does she think about this?'

'My mum doesn't think anything about anything.'

'Oh.' Suzy touches her shoulder: urgent, purposeful strokes, as if applying a layer of something, or removing one. 'No change?'

'No change.'

'Honey . . .'

'Yeah, yeah.' Dia forgets too. Does it all the time. Whenever she hears something funny her first thought is her mother standing by the sink with a glass of water in her hand, narrating the day she's had – wherever: all Lila's work was temporary work – and evoking this or that canteen dullard or back-room shit-for-brains with such inspired cruelty that Dia would screech until she felt like her insides were coming out. Whatever else she was (and she was lots of things), Lila was funny. Her set-pieces – wielding that glass of water – were onslaughts, annihilations. Their unvarying import: everyone's stupid except you and me. Dia believed it. Maybe still does. She doesn't believe one other word her mother ever spoke, but it's possible she still believes that: *everyone's stupid except you and me*.

Suzy buys a couple of bag-loads of musty tat then they head back to her building, past Shop and the tall, narrow door opening onto the atrium of the residential inner cavity. Some days, with rain pounding the skylight and the foliage of the common areas chopped back to sand, Suzy's building can resemble a dully optimistic open prison; but today, with sunlight dripping on green leaves, it is island-paradise serene, and maybe for an instant Dia feels again the languid pull of the Northern Quarter . . .

In her flat – an archly anachronistic shrine to comfy-cosiness, all crumbled brick and scented candle – Suzy hunts through her purchases for a complete outfit while Dia happily watches her, hugging the pink-painted pillar that pierces the room, a memory of the building's former life as a department store: the cranium or hardwire of that not-quite-vanished mercantile existence. When she loses interest she wanders over to the window, perches on the edge of the couch and peers out. As usual she notes with pleasure the historic venues across the way, the awnings and entrance pits that immediately summon for her nostalgic recollections of thunderous all-day live music, the staggering stabbers and shootists of the NQ's murky pre-revitalisation life.

'Do you still spy on the gangsters in Dry Bar?'

'There are no gangsters in Dry Bar. There haven't been gangsters in Dry for twenty years. Those are accountants. The yowly ones are rough sleepers.'

'Accountants and rough sleepers.'

'That's the Northern Quarter, honey. All human life.'

After zero discussion (they both know better), Suzy composites an outfit: burly boots offset by a sleeveless green tea dress. It shouldn't work, but Dia has grudgingly to concede that Suzy knows what she's doing, because no two ways about it, she looks *fantastic*. Aware of this too, and appropriately emboldened, Suzy begins the labour of cajoling Dia into some of her overpriced charity-shop shite – 'Think of it as a disguise, like we're spies going undercover to infiltrate a terror group . . .'

'Not exactly my ideal scenario,' Dia says, but already it's a failed effort and sooner than either of them expects she's facing an unfamiliar version of herself in the hallway mirror: primrosey gown, Doc Martens, clip-on nose piercings, water-soluble transfers of a Jolly Roger on one shoulder, duelling pistols on the other.

'You look *gorgeous*,' Suzy says. 'It goes so well with your skin tone . . .'

Which triggers the metallic little *eek* this sort of vocab always does; but she runs a scan and, reassured, skims it off.

Suzy joins her in the mirror. Tonight her friend is dark-bright, austere, with that neck, those arms. The first Suzy she knew, the form-group frenemy with 'issues' and 'challenges' that had her dramatically excluding herself mid-lesson every other day for a stroll down the corridor to the counsellor's office – that Suzy never showed her arms. It was only years later, when their trouble cycles resynchronised and they hooked up again, that Dia found out for sure why. By then Suzy was routinely and even aggressively bare-armed, and the sleeves of ink were densely established. And Suzy just said it: she was a cutter. From nine to nineteen she couldn't get through a day without feeling like her face was going to run off her skull unless she raised a line of blood on her forearm with her dead brother's penknife. 'The weird thing is it didn't hurt. I didn't even experience it as pain. It was pleasure. Pure, Delphic ecstasy.'

Suzy's phone pings. The first clue has dropped.

And she's barely looked at it when she says, 'That's almost insulting. Well, it is what it is. Let's go.'

'Don't we have to wait for the next—'

'These halfwits have no idea who they're dealing with. Come on. I know where it is.'

Saturday night in the Northern Quarter was always a lively prospect, but as they re-enter the street Dia at once feels the difference. There are the same crowds she remembers, the overdressed pavement traffic, the spilling lines outside bars, the rough sleepers with their gentle entreaties, and yet it's as if the mass hallucination that always possessed this scene has grown poisonous. At any moment there is the sound of glass breaking from three separate directions. A topless man crawls over the cobbles on all fours. A woman in a cocktail dress, no relation, falls over him, landing heavily. A very young girl somewhere sings 'Nothing Compares 2 U' over and over, with what sounds like professional-quality amplification.

Suzy leads the way back onto Thomas Street, round the corner onto Oak Street then on past warehouse shapes of decreasing familiarity into a darkness from which the crowds thin and on which quantities of brick converge. After several further corners, each bleaker than the last, she halts in an empty alleyway. The light of her phone's screen flashes skeletally into her face.

'A-ha!'

Not raising her eyes from the screen, she walks to the wall on their left-hand side and knocks on it. After a moment she walks forward a couple of steps and knocks again. She is still doing this when someone says, 'Evening, ladies.'

There is a man standing in front of them, behind him an open doorway so feebly lit it is hardly distinguishable from the surrounding darkness. Suddenly and strategically girlish, Suzy trots up to him, is asked for and furnishes what must be another password, then turns back to Dia as if dipped by a dance partner. 'We're in.'

Edging past the doorman, they enter an enormous derelict factory lit only at the far end by a few twists of fairy lights. In isolated spots there are heaps of scrap that someone would probably want to call sculpture. The bearded doorman, one of those topknot fellows who look like they could cut down a forest for you but in fact couldn't open a pickle jar, points out an entrance about halfway down the length of the room, an aperture opening onto a short hallway then a steep plank staircase down into more fairy-lit gloom. Single file.

So this is The Secret Bar. A murky cellar coated and bolted with the usual relics of the Industrial Revolution (studded wheels, engine parts) surrounding a hastily improvised scatter of seating areas made up out of mismatched picnic benches and tables. Dia looks for the bar, but true to its name it remains secretive. Prodding the controls in Suzy's back that only she knows about, she directs them to the least health-risk-looking of the unoccupied seating areas and lowers them both onto a bench.

'Here we are then,' Suzy says, with a lilt of mock excitement that may not be wholly mock. 'Any sign of your Ranters?'

'Not sure.' The place is far from empty – on every side glum twentysomethings nod at each other over their glasses – but there's nothing you could mistake for an atmosphere. At first she thinks there is not even music, then it starts to filter through, zithery off-tempo plinks and plonks. She looks for the inevitable DJ and is surprised to find instead an alcove with a live musician in it, a small, earnest elderly man drawing a violin bow across a cat's cradle of steel wires.

Negotiating the table's uneven edge, Suzy gets up to look for the bar. Dia turns to call a request after her, and she sees them.

Two men and two women, mid-twenties, sit together at the other end of the cellar. And she sees what she's seen before: the common Ranter element. When they marched along Portland Street the Ranters weren't wearing smocks or cassocks; they were wearing normal clothes, drab stuff, dark woolly jumpers, baggy blue jeans. Still, in addition to their equable silence Dia was sure the marchers shared some other element, only at the time she couldn't identify it. Now she identifies it: a square of black cloth. The people across the cellar are all dressed in accordance with the drabness aesthetic – a grey sweater here, a brown T-shirt there – but what makes them a group is the black cloth. They wear it each in their own way: one of the men has tied it round his wrist; the other round his waist; one of the women has looped it into her hair; the other has spread it shawl-like over her shoulder.

What else? They are sitting quietly, but not silently. Not staring zombified into space but talking cheerfully among themselves. One of the men leans against the back wall, an arm curled over his head. One of the women speaks to the other, who shakes her head, laughing.

By the time Suzy returns with their drinks Dia has come to a radical conclusion: 'They don't seem weird. Look.' She flicks a finger at the Ranters. 'They don't seem like a cult. More like a band. A folk band. And not nu folk, either. *Old* folk.'

Suzy hunkers forward. 'So now we prepare. Blend in, loosen up, smile, though what am I saying, you've never smiled in your life.'

'I smile.'

'You do not. Ever. Smile. Oh well. At least we should get incredibly bladdered.' Which they achieve with some dispatch, a process accelerated when Dia finally lashes her legs out from under the splintery table and goes stalking round the cellar until she bumps into the lightless prow of the entirely lightless bar, after which development she is able to buy drinks too. For the next hour or so she and Suzy work a relay between bar and seating area, practically tagging each other as they pass.

Right, Dia tells herself: one more drink and I'm going in. Circling to the bar, she notes in pleasant drunken passing that it was not always the case that she needed a lungful of alcohol before she could contemplate approaching strangers in a bar. Not too many years ago there was a Dia Talwar who would think nothing of approaching anyone anywhere, for any reason: a night-bus berserker, a street-corner chaoticist who lived for the flash of her own brilliance, the sparking light of a ravaged mirrorball only she could see. Was that ever really her? It really was. She has forgotten; it has been possible for her to do that. But now, deep in the depths of Samson's commission, she can't pretend she hasn't at times felt the shuddering proximity of that other Dia, hasn't glimpsed on walls and ceilings faint swipes, migrant sparks from some wrecked and unseen source . . .

'It's like there are two of you' – is how she remembers Suzy put it, one night round at the comfy-cosy flat not too long ago – 'there's nice, polite Dia, who pays her rent and buys groceries, but she's like . . . a secret identity, because there's also another Dia who is this total danger woman, this all-or-nothing woman.'

'This what woman?'

'All or nothing. Do or die. It's like you're one of those people who need something to believe in, something more than just people. And if you can't have it, you go apeshit. You either want to build up this one perfect thing or smash everything to pieces. And you can't decide which. All or nothing. Maybe both.'

'Maybe neither,' Dia said on that occasion, though now she's thinking: all or nothing. Do or die. Is that what she's doing here? And if so, do what? And, for that matter, die why?

She circles back from the bar to find their seating area empty. And squinting across the cellar she sees Suzy, making friends with the Ranters.

A drink in either hand, Dia walks up in time to hear Suzy say, 'Such a statement.'

The two Ranter women are looking at Suzy. The two men are looking at the women. Then there's a general rustling adjustment of scrutiny and everyone looks at Dia.

'Hello,' Dia says.

'Don't you think?' Suzy asks her, with the rattling fierceness that is often the only sign that she's completely wrecked. 'The black armband thing these pretty people are wearing, isn't it fascinating?'

'It's not an armband,' says the Ranter man who is leaning against the wall.

'Well, it can be,' says the Ranter woman who is wearing her cloth in her hair. 'If you want it to be an armband, it's an armband.' She shrugs at the man, who shrugs back.

'That's so interesting,' Suzy says, a line that should kill the whole encounter dead, though it doesn't, and somehow instead leads the Ranter women to pull up another picnic bench for her and Dia to sit on, then while one of the women goes to the bar the other one starts explaining who's who.

The man leaning against the wall is called Marc. He is twenty-six and half-French. The other man is called Jon, he's twenty-four and he's three-quarters English, one-quarter Welsh. The woman who is talking to them (the one with the cloth in her hair) is called Annette. She is twenty-four and English. The other woman (the one with the cloth on her shoulder) is called Fiona, styled Fee. She is twenty-four and English too.

'I'm Suzy, I'm twenty-nine, and I'm, let's see, this much Scottish, this much Turkish, this much Scandinavian . . .'

The Ranters look at Dia.

'I'm Dia,' she says.

'As in "expensive" or as in "beloved"?' This is Marc.

'As in Claudia.'

Suzy raises a hand. 'And did I hear you guys belong to a "group", or . . . ?'

'We're friends.' Annette's tone is not icy, not quite. 'But we also belong to a group.'

'That's so cool,' Suzy says, continuing smoothly, 'so what kind of a group would you say it is? Religious, or . . . ?'

'It's hard to explain,' Jon says, leaning across Annette with a gallant air of helping her out.

Either this is the world's best sales pitch, Dia thinks, or they don't want to talk about it. Don't want to evangelise. Don't want to convert.

'Try me.' Suzy widens her eyes.

There is a pause, crossed only by the atonal plinking and plonking of the earnest live musician. Then Marc calls from his wall, 'It makes more sense if you see it.'

'How would we do that?'

'You'd come to one of our visitor weekends.' He taps the table, which is heaped with many copies of the same muddily colour-photocopied flyer. And this flyer is familiar, Dia realises, because every one of the seating areas in The Secret Bar, including the one at which she and Suzy sat for longer than an hour, is also heaped with it. She assumed it was promoting a band night or something. Embarrassing. But she manages to reach a hand to a copy and slip it into her bag before the conversation moves on, Fee asking Suzy about her tattoos and Suzy delightedly extending both arms and beginning her narration.

Time passes. How drunk is everyone? Surveying the group, Dia sees that both women are still absorbed by Suzy's tales of self-illustration, while Marc, head back against the wall, at least appears to be concentrating on the music. Maybe he has that pestered air of someone whose friends have trapped him with people he has no desire to socialise with. Maybe he's just really into the music.

Jon sits unengaged. Sandy-haired, pink-faced and tubby, with a genial round-shouldered look, he is likely the best chance she's going to get. And before she can stop herself she leans forward and says to him, 'A pal of mine joined your group, I wonder if you know him? Reggie Glaze?'

'I know Reggie.'

'Is he here?'

'Oh, no. Reggie's at the farm.' Jon winks knowledgably.

'Where's that?'

'You know Hastings? Near there.'

Reggie is at a farm – a farm near Hastings. 'Which is . . . ?'

'East Sussex. You can read about it on the flyer you took. It's where we have our visitor weekends.'

Dia takes the flyer out of her bag and looks at it. On its reverse is a map, showing her where the farm and Hastings and East Sussex are. 'It's the other side of the country.'

'Bit of a trek. But worth it. Beautiful scenery down there.'

'I'll bet,' Dia says. Thinking: well, that's that. The other side of the country is my limit. If the choice is all or nothing, I choose nothing. I'm out.

'Actually,' Jon is going on, 'Hastings is where we're based most of the time, we're only up here for a recruitment drive. We do regular stints all over the country. But I always really enjoy Manchester.'

'Is that right?'

'Really enjoy it.'

'So, Jon.' Floundering somewhat, she returns the flyer to her bag then says, 'This may sound like a funny question, but why do you guys call yourselves Ranters?'

For the first time he seems uncomfortable. His lips twitch, his eyes are all lid. Then he says, 'We don't.'

'You don't call yourselves Ranters?'

Repeated, the word makes him wince. 'It's not a term we use. Like calling a gay person "queer", or a black person . . . you know. It's basically a hate term.'

Now Dia winces. That morning at Sonata, when she skimmed those webpages – didn't she read about this? The name, and the other name: but it wasn't clear, the sources conflicted, it was too long ago, she can't remember, she's too drunk.

'I didn't realise. I thought it was just what you were called.'

'It's derived from that, but no. It's not what we call ourselves.'

'So what do you call yourselves?'

'We call ourselves what we're called.' And Jon lifts his chin, and smiles sweetly, and says, 'We're called Tarantula.'

4. The Common Fund

If there were another way to do it – softer, slower – that's how she would do it. Instead next morning with the rocks of her hangover just starting to connect she asks the internet what it knows about Glaze Energy's new regional office, locates the building in a jagged aerial view of Mosley Street, snaps her hair into a rubber band and heads down to the pavement before second or better thoughts can diminish her sense of purpose.

By the time she reaches the place her hangover rocks are already grinding, cracking. Doesn't matter. She's going to leave a message then crawl back to her duvet. Not like he's going to be about on a Sunday morning. And she made doubly sure by allowing herself to come down here looking like crap.

She pushes through the canister of the rotating door, approaches the reception coven – the same wherever you go – and asks the first headset she sees if she can leave a message for Mr Glaze. Headset girl nods then carries on tapping at her keyboard for so long Dia or her hangover starts to take exception. Midway into her rant she gets that dogwalker-over-the-grave spine squiggle and turns to find Samson's thin not-butler standing so close to her she's pretty sure he was trying to look down her top.

'Please don't shout at the staff,' he says.

'I need to leave a message. Can you tell him?'

'Tell him yourself.'

He escorts her to a lift, along a channel of corporate carpet tile and on into a room of such cavernous and manifestly steam-age proportions that Dia's hangover gives a filmy start: where is she? The poshos' flat? The Secret Bar? Or has she merely lived in town so long everywhere has started to blur into everywhere else?

'You came!' Samson appears from behind a stack of networked desks. 'What do you reckon?' Turning on the spot, he spreads his arms. 'I'm thinking the Haçienda without the body count. Ideal base for what I'm seriously considering calling "the northern invasion".' He is elated, gleeful, somewhat unstoppable: full of that whirling look she knows is half the reason why people (some people) call him a genius, a prophet. 'And don't say it, Dee, don't say what every bastard and his monkey seems to feel obliged to say to me right now. I *know* setting up a northern base – a northern "hub"? – is *muchos* work. I *know* I have lots of ambitious projects already in play, top, middle and bottom secret, and some even public knowledge. Don't even say it. Because this is how I like to do things, do you see? This is the Samson Glaze way.'

'I'm not going to say it.'

'Good. Well. Don't.'

'I bring news.'

'Oh yeah?' At last he seems to see her, to register that she is actually here. 'Are you okay? You seem . . .'

'I went to that bar last night.' Only now she realises she has no idea how the night ended. Her last memory contains black pavement, Northern Quarter sound effects (disconsolate yowling) and either her hands pressed urgently to Jon's face or Jon's hands pressed urgently to hers. Could've gone either way. 'Rocks in the head,' she says.

'Well then, let's get this wounded soldier a chair – Weland, you couldn't be a dear and find Miss Talwar something to drink?'

The not-butler withdraws. A Weland, are we.

They sit – facing swivel chairs with the plastic still on – and she tells him. Everything she knows. It takes almost no time. Reggie is at a farm near Hastings. She takes the flyer out of her bag and passes it to him. For the first time she notices the image on the flyer's front, a murky Photoshop job of a city street infiltrated by vegetation, accompanied by the text: 'WHY THE NEXT WORLD DOESN'T NEED YOU . . .' 'There's a map on the back. Shows where you can find him.'

He takes the flyer but doesn't look at it. Stares into space.

Because she has said it: Where *you* can find him.

Because this is her limit. She's out.

Because it's the other side of the country. Because she has a life and a job and a flat and if she even thinks about going to a farm in East Sussex she doesn't know what any of that is any more. Because she's not six years old, and it's no longer her deepest desire to save Samson Glaze's life.

He knows all this. His staring eyes know.

But do they know that she is a danger woman, an all-or-nothing woman? That if he were to ask her, look at her and ask her – 'Dee, I need you to do this for me' – she has no idea what she would say? All or nothing, do or die. Maybe both, maybe neither. She has no idea.

'Thank you, Dee.' And only then he smiles.

If he were to ask her.

'No problem. Glad I could help.'

He stands. She stands also. She waits for him to approach her, embrace her, do to her whatever it is necessary for him to do to her, but he just stands there. The not-butler – Weland – comes back carrying a bottle of water. Seeing them, he halts in the doorway.

'It's been good to see you, Dee.'

Look at her, ask her.

'Yeah,' she says, confused. 'We should stay in touch or something.'

'Good to see you.'

There's nothing else to say. She walks past Weland out through the doorway, hair swaying behind her with that fleshy glimmer of rubber band he remembers at once, the happy impatience of it, the function-over-form provocation, even when she was six years old and grimly resisting Lila's intermittent but insistent efforts to make a mantelpiece figurine of her: 'Don't you have clips, or "scrunchies"? Maybe a ribbon, or a band?' 'Lend me yours, Alice in Wonderland.' 'Now see, *I* don't have . . .' 'Then why the fuck should I?'

The mouth on that girl! He loved it, but even so there's wild and there's wild – the wild that sings and the wild that snaps – and D always had both kinds roaming inside her. Partly it was Lila's doing: if Lila Robinson wasn't tying ribbons in her daughter's hair, she was falling down in the bathroom, falling down in the post office, falling down in the pub. Partly too it was the dad, whoever he was. And partly it was just D, just the girl herself.

'Didn't go well,' Weland says.

'She's a handful, that one.'

'Let me guess. Reminds you of yourself.'

Does she? He steps back into the swivel chair, with its crinkly protective material. What was it he had said to her: *Are there any people like me?* A joke, but also not. And yet he knows it will be a loss, and a terrible one, if he genuinely starts believing he's the only one, that there are no other people like him.

Early on he formed the habit of answering questions about his background with literally the first thing that came into his head: 'We were jewel thieves, the whole family. The best in the biz.' 'Circus people, that's what we were.' 'Carny folk.' The truth is hardly less dreadful: his mother was a suburban watercolourist who once chased him round the garden with a kitchen knife, his father an insurance clerk whose idea of being in the world was a game of statues that lasts your entire life. One blink and you're dead.

Samson learned two things from his father: that people come in types; and the sun was his master. The first lesson he gained at the dinner table one evening when he asked his father if he could invite a boy in his class called Keith Fish to come to play. At the name, Neville Glaze's face became even more sealed and statue-like.

'Fish? I'm afraid not, Sam. The Fishes are not our type of people.'

At first he had no idea what his father meant. He never imagined that people came in types; he assumed they were all just different ones. And yet sitting there at the dinner table he vaguely but intensely understood: people rise into life in clusters. They form layers and blocks – types. He further grasped that he did not belong to the same type as his mother and father, and should take trouble to find out which one he did.

The other lesson started as a punishment. A poor end-of-year report inspired Neville Glaze to fill his son's summer holiday with household chores: lawn-mowing, hedge-trimming, window-cleaning, gutter-clearing. And Samson loved it, the gutter work more than anything. He climbed the ladder, crawled onto the hot roof tiles, spread his limbs, closed his eyes. The sun beat and beat into him; the web of flame blanching under his eyelids appeared to him as spirit lines, spirit threads, weaving willy-nilly between the sun and his own essence. And by summer's end he knew what he was: the sun's servant, its vassal or bondsman.

'More than my dad ever gave me,' said Keith Fish. 'My dad just gives out grief.'

'He does that as well,' said Samson.

Keith looked dubious. 'Your dad gives you grief?'

'Constantly.' It was true and not true. When Keith said 'grief' he meant physical harm – he meant his father lashed him with a soaked bath towel. Samson's father didn't do that; still he knew in some way the statue game was hurting him, hardening things inside him into patterns like grief, and in the end that was enough. Almost as simple a decision as it must have been for Keith, with all that wet-towel horror to sharpen his thoughts.

Nonetheless it took them until the last year of school to quit their suburb and head together into the city, Samson wreathed in tie-dye and a rock-opera blonde bouffant, Keith sporting the shorn scalp, bum-fluff beard and leather waistcoat that later evolved into his post-apocalyptic sorcerer's-apprentice look, with new rucksacks and new names. By this time Keith was calling himself Fish, or the Fish, or Pisces. Samson was now the Aztec.

After a false start in a squat in Crouch End, they ended up where it seemed the drift of the day was collecting London's free wheels – that is, in the dreamy collective on Prince of Wales Crescent in Kentish Town. On their first morning, dead of winter, ice cladding the street, Samson came out early at the urging of the ginger-bearded hippy who kept things rolling in their house and joined a line of yawning and bobble-hatted young people being issued with spades, shovels, brooms and other scraping implements by a tiny headscarved imp, a child barely in double figures, with a woodbine smouldering on her lip. The girl gave him a potato-masher. He sat on the front step, started grinding away the ice at the top of the path, and when he looked up there was a grammar school's worth of youth bent to the common task of making the street safe and usable. Crazy-looking kids shuffling together to do a good and useful thing; to clear ice from a street, not because someone told them to, not because they thought they owned the street (they knew they didn't); not even because they felt a 'sense of community' in that tired old shackling way; but merely because it was the right thing to do, and when it was done they would go back to being crazy-looking kids, until the next thing needed doing, and the next, then the next . . . Tired, unbreakfasted, with fingers he'd stopped feeling long ago, he realised he had found it: the type he belonged to.

Such was the origin story of the Thin Love Collective. Years before they thought to call themselves that, the founding members were enrolled: Samson the Aztec; Pisces; and the snooty imp girl, Constanza le Styx, who everyone called Mama. For years they were the blowy scraps of Prince of Wales Crescent, scouting for lumber after nights of wind, rinsing greens in this kitchen, beating rugs on that doorstep, sleeping on whichever couch or chair they fell down on when tiredness overcame them. All they lacked to make them what they later became was the wreckers' balls that swung through time into the Crescent and its busy makeshift warren, bringing also crowds, shouts, fists; those and the name.

In fact they were ready. By the time the final dust clouds sifted down he had acquired Vieve, and on her spanking new wheels they hit the road together.

'Where now?' Mama wanted to know.

'Where?' he said. 'Here. Us. You, Pisces, Vieve, and me. If others want to come along, them too. For as long as we can.'

It was that weak promise – not 'forever' or 'until the end of days' but 'for as long as we can' – that supplied the name. Certainly it was love between them, but no one was saying it was love eternal. A joke, but also not.

They made mistakes, learned the ill wisdom of outstaying a welcome; of putting down too close to where you put down last; of putting down in cities rather than in towns, where the tensions are fewer and less; of putting down anywhere where every face is white. Learned not everyone who claimed to belong to their type truly did, and their collective could no more than any other social organ endure junkie thieves, escaped psychopaths, or itinerant bigots of every slow-exposing stripe. 'Sometimes feels like the thin love on this charabanc really is thin,' muttered Pisces one night, passing an unsteady hand over his prickly scalp, after he had been left with no choice but to direct another tragic needle-head to the side of the road.

But there were things they got right, too. Cait was right: every inch of her. They put down on a park in Lyme Regis where they'd put down any number of times before, and there she was, as if waiting. A wicker picnic basket over her arm, chestnut hair down to her waist, standing by a tree that seemed to be a part of her. When she saw him she flung her head back and laughed.

That great big laugh that gently reared English girls still did until the end of the Eighties, a laugh that could be all the conversation you needed.

And Reggie was right. On the sober hospital ward on which Cait had firm views ('None of your traveller balls; this is happening somewhere with strip lights'), he doubted he had ever seen anything so right. The sprig of hot red hair so fine it was hardly more than the protractor swirls of glancing sunshine; eyes sticky with infant erudition . . .

And the dogs. Why had they not had dogs before? Then they came, Buttercup and Tara, Snowflake and Annie, Ronnie and Tula, and for days he was so dejected with thinking of the years he'd wasted not consorting with dogs only the dogs themselves could cheer him up. The dogs were so right it hurt, with the bowel-deep grip of love unchanging he had never promised any human.

After that shivering winter night when they adopted every stray they could find on the streets of Cirencester (Pisces' idea: they just rounded them up), the dogs had a place in everything Samson did. They pawed at his sleep, slobbered his breakfast off the plate, flung back his shower water in whiplash oscillation. Later he maintained that his inspiration for the first solar panel he ever built came to him one afternoon out of the sun-sizzled eyes of Buttercup, at whom he gazed often as at a voluptuous lover. That's how you work, he thought, sitting back in his deckchair to admire the lovely creature in his lap, trembling with sheer surplus of life: you run off the sun. You're a sun battery.

And it was Tara and Annie leaping at his crotch in their flirtatious way, dividing his attention as he laid out what was by then a fairly sophisticated panel-array on the bit of scrub where the collective had settled overnight: a small raucous town called

Ainscough they'd not visited before, and where he already doubted they would come again. If not for those playful snouts nudging up at his man-quarters he'd surely have noticed her earlier.

'What are you doing?'

He looked round and there was a little girl standing behind him. Black hair, dark eyes, complexion that could have been a bottle tan. Given the look of the place – chip shop, bookmaker's, job centre – he wouldn't have been surprised.

'I'm doing what any decent fellow does,' he said. 'Bringing power to the people.'

'To these people?' He followed the girl's gaze to the rest of the Thin Love Collective, who were indeed a scrappy-looking bunch that morning: pocked, pilled, milled, monged.

'All God's children, I assure you.'

'Why are you here? You weren't here last night.'

How to explain? It was September: the beginning of the lull season after their frenetic summer-festival circuit, rigging mics and lugging sound systems. They had come north for northern opacity, northern inconspicuousness, as well as rumoured grunt work in the building trade with an – as-yet-unconfirmed – amenable foreman, the usual friend of a friend of a friend. Only rather than mention any of this, he said, 'Do you ever go on holiday?'

'No.'

'You know how some people go on holiday? That's what we do, except we do it year-round. We go from a holiday in one place to a holiday in another place.'

'If you're always on holiday, what are you on holiday from?' Which made him take another good glance at the girl. The eyes, made of pure stubbornness.

'Maybe when you're older.' He stepped back from the array

– six three-metre panels built partly to a design he'd copied out of a manual in Bristol Central Library, partly to his own trial-and-error recipe – and said, 'Want to see if it works?'

'You're going to anyway.'

'That's absolutely true.' He dropped the electric torch he'd cabled up into her hands then headed for the switch. 'Keep an eye on that.'

Always an exciting moment – finding out if last night's potholes had shaken loose anything that might not respond to hot solder and coaxing. But the array behaved beautifully. He flipped the switch and the girl twirled a watery torch beam over and over on Vieve's side.

'Not bad,' she said.

'You live near here?'

'There.' She pointed out a tower block on the road that bounded the scrub. A grey concrete giant that had once squatted and never stood straight since. 'Sycamore House.'

'Okay with you if we hang out round here for a while?'

Eventually it was, though the girl required a full account of the Thin Love Collective both in its generality and its individual membership, and after most of a day spent sorting that out, over a mug of squash and a plate of sandwiches by the fire with the other guys, she returned to first principles: 'I still don't see why you live like this.'

'Because we're the type of people who live like this.' He waved at the circle of faces round the fire: 'Every one of us, we belong to that type. And people want to live with people who belong to the same type as they do.'

This answer did not please the girl. The eyes, with their stubborn floes.

Maybe that's why the next thing he said was: 'It's late. Don't want anyone saying we kidnapped you. Come on, I'll walk you back. Back to Sycamore House.'

But she did not move. 'No one's going to say you kidnapped me.'

Which was the first time D referred, however indirectly, to Lila Robinson. It took him most of that autumn to learn more, but by the time they were packing up, he knew what he needed to know. Lila would not come looking for her daughter. And her daughter could bear it. Some afternoons she would come stalking over the scrub with shadows under her eyes or a pinched transparent look but never without her icy determination to find out what could be done before nightfall, which panel tweaked, which dog scrubbed.

'Will you come back?' she said, when he slammed Vieve shut that last day.

'Same time next year.' He didn't expect her to believe him; indeed he was prepared for a glare of arctic chill. She astonished him with a little-girl smile. Never much of a smiler, D wasn't, so it meant something. It meant she knew it was true.

It was. They came back to Ainscough the next September, then the September after that, which was the September Lila Robinson made liars of them all. One evening he and D were discussing solar-panel kites, he trying to explain why they wouldn't work, she insisting they would, when there came a noise of waterfowl disquiet from somewhere and they looked up to see a woman stumbling towards them in slippers and dressing gown, one arm raised, one finger accusingly extended, softly hooting. Lila.

'You people should be ashamed,' she called in fretful tones.

'Don't worry, ma'am, we are.' Samson stood. 'Can I help you?'

'Help me.' Lila's head trembled, but with a brave effort she kept her eyes on his face. The twisting mouth showed her courage too. 'Give me back my daughter back.'

'All yours, ma'am. Didn't take her, never wanted her.' In fact D had already gone to her mother, though she stood facing towards him, bug-eyed with horror.

'You people shouldn't be allowed,' Lila Robinson said.

'I'm sure you're right. Sadly we are.' But there were no points to be won sparring with Lila. *Give me back my daughter back*. Dark patches on the dressing gown showed she had already fallen, more than once, in the muddy scrub. 'Safe night, ma'am.'

The D who raced into camp next morning was a D he hadn't seen before: cartoonish, two-dimensional with remorse. 'Never again, I promise. I'll lock the cow in if I have to.'

'Be cool, D. Your mum's fine. You should bring her round more often.'

'Not funny. She's disgusting. *She's* the one who shouldn't be allowed.'

He opened his mouth then shut it again. There was nothing he could say. But he felt it painfully, that absence where he should have had something to say.

It stayed with him. Night after night and day after day that year, he looked at the dogs (his beautiful dogs), and he looked at Reggie (his beautiful boy), and he thought of D and the fact he'd had nothing to say when she called her mother disgusting – and his mind filled with questions that started with such words as: *in what world . . . ?* and *with what future . . . ?*

Was that the start of it? At the festivals that year, when the usual keen beans came to admire his panels, rap on the issues, compare right-onness levels, he heard a new quack of urgency in his voice – a clatter, a red-faced hurry of explication. It took a guy with smoke-stained dentures and a sinister black combover to reveal to him what it was.

'That's some sales pitch, my friend.'

'What? Oh no, I don't sell . . .'

'You should.' The guy told him to think about it, even left his card, though it turned out to be a dead end (not a city-slick investor at all, just a fantasist with a photocopier), but only his bothering to follow up the invitation told Samson there had been a change in him.

'I thought you made them for us,' Cait said quietly, when he told her his scheme.

'I do make them for us. If I sold them, that would be for us too.'

'No, Samson, it wouldn't. It would be for *them*.'

She was wrong. But he couldn't explain it to her. He knew if he tried he would sound ridiculous. How could he explain that he wanted to make and sell panels for Reggie, and for D – for their future? The dogs didn't need a better world; they already romped and rolled and snuffled and snoozed and twitched their ears and dangled their tongues in their best reality. But he knew, knew, a better world was possible for Reggie and D, a world whose curves and cambers matched more exactly their own, whose every landmass and skyscape tapered to the humid whorl of the little boy's scalp, to the ice-pack pellicle of the little girl's eye . . .

'I just want to know how it feels, you know? To sell something.'

He had never saved in his life. From place to place he generally found enough work to pay his share of the collective's expenses, but this was the first time he set out to obtain money he wasn't going to spend or hand to someone else as soon as he got it. For a year he collected notes in a jar, like insect specimens. When they rotated through Ainscough that September, he showed it to D.

'You need a bank account,' she said.

'Who says?' But she was right. That afternoon he walked into a high street bank, gave his parents' address, and opened a savings account.

He made his first sale to a regular from the festival circuit, a young geography teacher called Dale Wood. Dale wrote his address on Samson's arm in felt-tip during White Zombie's Reading encore, and one sunny morning a fortnight later Samson rolled up in Vieve outside a semi-detached house in Kent. Dale came out, grinning. 'Have you got them?'

With shaking hands and thudding heart he lifted the six panels from Vieve's interior and laid them in a row against her flank. 'Want me to set up?'

In the end they did it together, passing hammers back and forth, Dale wandering off for minutes at a time to change the record and blast another chunk of commemorative White Zombie through every rattling window of the house.

By early afternoon it was done. They went out in the street to appraise their work.

'Wow,' Dale said. 'Cheque good?'

'Cheque great.' Throughout the day's conviviality, Samson had not forgotten that someone was going to give him money for something he'd made.

'There you go. Cheap at half the price.' And Dale handed him the cheque and they bumped fists and then Samson got back into Vieve and with a final salute drove away.

He had sold twelve more panel sets, one for each month, by the next time he saw D.

'I don't recognise you,' she said.

'Not you as well. If I've not got Mama going on about how I'm not paying my way . . .' It was true he had missed payments to the common fund. But orders were coming in at such a rate there was no other way he could keep up.

'I meant your beard. When was the execution?'

'Couple of weeks ago. You can't imagine what a hassle it is getting these bank types to talk to you if you have so much as a whisker on your face. What do you think?'

'You look like a forehead.'

He honestly believed they would last longer. Even when the bank allocated him what they called a 'unique investment consultant', a curly-haired, fresh-faced article called Jeff who he was sure he'd never get on with, and with whom in the end he got on very well, even when it was clear he needed a fixed base of operations, an office, a production line, even then he thought they would go on as they always had. Mama Styx tried to be reasonable (and Mama was a mama now, with a kiddie of her own running about – little Scylla – though she would happily twist a knife in your neck sooner than tell you who the father was); Pisces, however, soon lost the knack of his reasonableness.

'We're not giving you an ultimatum,' Mama Styx said in the van where they were all supposedly having a nice cup of tea.

'Oh yes, we are,' Pisces said. 'It's us or Microsoft.'

'I was thinking "Glaze Energy" . . . ?'

'Isn't this kind of what we're talking about?' There was pleading in Mama's look but something else too – a dullness, a rind or skin. And how in the world had he not noticed that getting in there? '"Glaze" this, "Glaze" that. What happened to the rest of us?'

'Oh, we *know* what happened.' Pisces stepped heavily across the van and put his face in Samson's. Under a flashbulb of sweat he was more furious than Samson had ever seen him. Pisces, the Fish, Keith Fish: his oldest friend, the calmest man alive, sanguine even at ten years of age when his shit-bastard father striped his arms and legs with a wet bath towel; now reduced to stress patterns of glinting scalp and eyes vibrating with outrage. 'Make a choice, Samson. Thin love or no love.'

'I'm doing this for all of us . . .'

'You're doing this for yourself,' Pisces suddenly roared.

'Shut up, you prick,' Cait said, with a smiling sneer. 'What do you know about love? Samson will always be loved. While Reggie and I are on this earth, he will be loved.'

He went to see D one last time. She looked like she was twenty-five or something, though apparently she was thirteen. 'They wouldn't let me take the dogs.'

'The dogs are still part of the collective. You're not.'

He was not. And nor was Cait, and nor was Reggie. The three of them flung out on a centrifuge of rage that was part Pisces', part Cait's. As they walked away he tried to take Reggie from Cait's arms, but she only clutched the boy tighter, her face set.

'They'll miss me. Will you miss me, Miss Robinson?'

D bared her teeth. 'Talwar. Took my dad's name. Won't be official until I'm sixteen, but still. It's Miss Talwar, if you please.' She frowned at him. They were sitting side by side on the steps of Sycamore House. 'Why will I miss you? Aren't you coming back?'

'Maybe not for a while. You'll see.'

Looking down, he sees his fingers have dug holes in the plastic sheet draped over the brand-new swivel chair. Not one or two but dozens, a compulsive thready mesh.

Weland hands him the water bottle he's been carrying. 'I'll call Dr Lau.'

'Why will you do that?'

'You look like your head's about to come off.'

He takes a sip of the water. 'I'm fine. Just thinking.'

'Never the best sign.'

'I'm thinking we may have to reconsider our position on Miss Talwar.'

'Oh yes?'

'Yeah. Oh yeah.'

5. Bang to Rights

On Monday morning Dia is still thinking about Sunday evening when Billy Zane comes up, hesitates, then calls across her, 'Val. Got a minute?' Staring at her screen, Val grunts, taps her keyboard, clicks and swishes her mouse, then unhurriedly rises from her desk and goes off with Billy Zane.

Dia, meanwhile, goes on thinking. Sunday evening: film night with Andrew. Not a success. After the unsuspected stresses of her encounter with Samson earlier in the day, and with the head rocks that continued grinding all afternoon, she should have known better and cancelled. But it had been so difficult getting Andrew to agree to meet her at her flat and eat a salad and watch a film with her at a particular time, she was reluctant to waste her hard work. So she gobbled aspirin and stood turning round and round in the shower for half an hour then went ahead with the whole thing anyway. Bad idea.

It wasn't just the way he came through the door with a look that said he was fairly sure he was the unwitting star of a hidden-camera show. Nor the way the good professor lowered himself into her couch as he would into cold bathwater. Nor even the way he went on to spend most of the evening in her bedroom, on his phone, talking to his ex-wife in what sounded altogether too much like the tones of ordinary conversation while she sat staring at a single gripped frame of *Chinatown*, Faye Dunaway in a black veil and sanguine expression, for so long she began to feel she had passed a lifetime imprisoned among its textures, blurred background diners, red leather, wood panelling.

No. The real nadir of the evening came later, after they had abandoned the film but before Andrew left, with an explanation that amounted only to the words *well so I'd better um*, at quarter past ten. They were sitting on the couch, talking about Ben Lerner or someone, when he said, 'It doesn't matter what men have to say. At this juncture in history, what men have to say is simply beside the point. For a generation at least men should shut up. In the literary arena as in every other arena. White, bourgeois, heterosexual men, and all the other sorts of men too. Just shut up.'

More amused than anything else, she said, 'But you won't, will you?' – and he looked at her with an expression of startled affront. For an instant Andrew seemed insulted that she included him in the category of 'men'. After that he had some trouble meeting her eye and, she supposes now, his not-really-explained early departure seemed inevitable. But still – can you believe that? Who would do that? Would *you* ever do anything like that? No, forget it. You, I bet *you* would . . .

She barely registers that she's still doing it, or doing it again. For the short while that it seemed he was back in her life, she had stopped it, broken the habit of fifteen-plus years; but now she's doing it again. She is talking to Samson in her head. Though of course she's doing nothing of the sort. What was it Lila said? 'There's not any such thing as "your self". "Your self" is just a great big hole.' Typical Lila cynicism, though maybe there was a time when Dia believed that too, when concentrating as hard as she could, lying on her bed or sitting inside a tent of newspapers at the back of the living room in Sycamore House, blocking out everything that was not her, narrowing in on and isolating the sensation of her self, suggested she was no more than a pair of eyes – a pair of eyes with the wiring not yet done, still in its plastic, still in its box. But that was before Samson. Even when she was a little girl Samson in the shelter of his scrabble fire always spoke to her as if she were a real person and expected her to speak back as if she were one, and when she did, and she heard her real-person voice, she knew that the hole Lila described was not a hole at all but a globe, a luminous, unventured planet . . .

So no; she is not talking to him in her head. Not after she met him in his fancy new office on Mosley Street and did the wise and necessary and grown-up thing and drew the line where it had to be drawn, showed him the limit where he had to be shown it, fully aware that doing so meant she might never see him again. And so she is not doing it. Not really, not like really to you, not *to* you . . .

'Dia. Got a minute?'

She looks up. Billy Zane is standing over her desk. She glances to either side of him but there's no sign of Val.

'I thought you were talking to Val.'

'I am. And now I'd like to talk to you, too.'

She stands into a mist of unease. Looking at Billy Zane for reassurance, she doesn't find any. His expression, usually somewhere between mild-mannered and beaten dog, is as abject as she has ever seen it.

Doesn't take a genius to work out what this is about. Following Billy Zane to his office, a flimsily partitioned cubby at the end of the main workspace, she feels inside herself the rise of a familiar seething, with a familiar object: Val Mather.

Who, seated in one of the chairs facing Billy Zane's desk, at least has the decency to look as if she is about to throw up quietly into her hand. Hardening her jaw, and making a bit of a performance of smoothing her skirt, Dia sits, complacent in her certainty that this fuddled lump is going to be buying her after-work drinks for the next three months.

Billy Zane sits behind his desk. He faces them with visible trepidation; his weak eyes strain at their sockets. He always looks like this, when he has to bollock someone. And, as always, she pities him. Billy Zane is not cut out for management. Small and round, shiny and teapot-like, he is the sort of man who should have abjured human company altogether and spent his days mending fishing nets on a remote Scottish coast.

'Dia,' he says. 'I take it you know why we're here.'

She does: Val's forged delivery note. But she also knows honesty never did anyone the least good. 'Sorry, Neil. Not a clue.'

'Let me explain.' He laces his fingers together and points a thumb at each of them. 'We run an office that supplies office supplies to other offices. Long have I contemplated the spectacle of that particular snake swallowing its own tail . . . But let me be clear. At the heart of what we do is trust. Sometimes known also as faith.'

Dia shifts her legs. One thing you have to allow Billy Zane is he understands these explanations of his are themselves a punishment. He's not one of those managers who take up an hour of your life telling you what you did wrong, then impose a penalty on top of that. In his entire career he has not so much as docked pay. He talks you into a tight little capsule of despair then kicks you back to your desk. She is not sure he even expects you to listen, so long as you keep sitting there. She glances at her feet, shifts her legs again.

'Does that sound right to you, Dia?'

'Sorry, Neil. Does what sound like what?'

'I was describing my disappointment at discovering Val here failed to notice that last Thursday's delivery was short by a count of four.'

'Is that what she did?'

'That is what she did. That is four boxes we do not have, but four boxes for which we must nonetheless pay the supplier, because we now have no way of demonstrating that they did not supply them. Do you know what was in those boxes, Dia? Tablets. And I don't mean aspirin, I don't mean . . . antihistamine tablets. I mean tablet computers. High end. Top of the range. Twenty-five per box.'

One hundred tablets. Even assuming he's exaggerating the quality (and he probably isn't), you're looking at three hundred quid a unit. Holy shit. They've lost Sonata thirty grand.

'Mr Sneed,' Val is saying.

'Sorry, Neil.' Dia arranges the many fronts and planes of her most scalding frown. 'How do we know Val did this? It's no secret she can be . . . scatty at times, but that's no reason to assume she did this.'

'She just told me she did.'

'Did she?'

'She did. She just told me she miscounted the boxes then signed the delivery note anyway and got you to countersign it.'

Dia nods. It is an office reflex: an unavoidable part of office life is that you are always nodding, expressing silent and unsolicited agreement. She glances at Val, who seems to be unaware that Dia is even present. No pleading glance, no mouthed 'Sorry!' Raptly Val stares at Billy Zane's face as if attempting to divine some hidden truth in it.

'It's a bad business,' Billy Zane says.

'It is,' Dia says.

Val only nods, quickly, eagerly.

'I don't know what to say,' Billy Zane says. It is almost a howl. 'I could say "my hands are tied", and that would be true, but it would in no way console us. I could remark, Val, that you have made many mistakes during your time with us. You have taken countless sick days. You . . . this is right, isn't it?'

Val nods, nods.

'And now – well. "My hands are tied."' His eyes weakly strain. 'I'm going to have to let you go, Val.'

Dia laughs. Good one! She turns to Val, who has somehow missed the joke and started to cry. Then she turns to Billy Zane, to Neil Sneed, and sees his face is deathly.

'What?' Dia says. *'What?'*

'I assure you, if the decision were mine—'

'Don't give me that.' She leans forward, all sympathy for him gone. 'Val's rubbish at her job, so what? She's Team Billy Zane. She's *blood*.'

'I'm sorry.' Neil Sneed's head wobbles on its stalk. 'Orders from above.'

'Oh, from who?'

'Above.' He lifts stiff shoulders. 'There's nothing I can do.'

'She'll appeal,' Dia says.

'As is her right.'

'She'll fight you. We all will. Believe me, when this gets round, there are going to be some very pissed-off people in that office.'

'I don't believe that's the case.' Wretchedly he chews his lips. Each part of him seems weighed down by a slightly different kind of helplessness. 'I'm sorry, Dia. You're going too.'

She frowns. Total incomprehension. He must mean some practical contingency, but what? Emptying Val's desk? Walking her to the bus stop?

'It's gross misconduct,' he says tenderly. 'It's not the money, it's the . . . misconduct.'

She stares at it – at the damp meat of Neil Sneed's face. And she listens to it: the coarse pinging that underlies the world's silence.

'You have to go too, Dia. I'm so sorry. I can't keep you.'

Briefly misery descends. It fills the room, glares in their faces. She realises something else – Val's error, the company's money prerogative – is putting them all through this. Then she sits back. With sweeping intensity the new reality assembles itself. And then it is simply reality, neither new nor old.

'Oh no, you don't,' she says.

'No?'

'You're not sacking me. You fucking *teapot*. I resign.'

'Dia—'

'Stuff your fucking teapot job. Why would I want a teapot job? Fuck it. And fuck you. Come on, Val. We're leaving.'

Dia stands, aware of Val clambering to her feet next to her. Neil Sneed stands also, but she turns from him in disgust. As she turns she feels another gleam pass over her face – this time a flash, a spark of mirrorball brilliance. For a moment it is there, and way down at the back of it another Dia is too: a Dia who screamed in public just to hear the sound of her lungs, who raked her nails down human faces to observe the lambent patterns that resulted, who tested or exercised the powers of her body as if she feared at any second they might be taken from her. Who broke all the fingers on her left hand and thought nothing of it, never thought there was anything to think of it. Who for a whole morning engaged in telepathic battle with three policemen in a police van on a silent Hampshire byroad. There she is, a danger woman, a trouble woman, alive and trembling way down in the gleam. All or what. Do or what. Then the light fades and the other Dia does too and the only Dia left in the room is the one who knows where the buttons of her self-control are. Nice polite Dia with her head screwed on.

She is halfway to the door before she notices that Val is not following her. She looks back and sees Val standing at her desk.

'What are you doing?'

Val's glance is fragmentary. For her at least the new reality has not yet framed itself. 'Don't you want your things? In your desk?'

'Leave it. Load of crap. We're not walking out of here carrying boxes.'

'I want my things.' Val flaps a hand at her desk drawers. 'There are some nice bits in there.' She smiles. She beams. And then it appears, the new reality: beatific, angelic. 'I suppose now I have to look for a box!'

It's only when she steps outside that everything falters, the frame slips and she's thrown in X-ray against the seashell tiles of the square, the obsidian sides of the Complex buildings: under the flat blue sky she is rattling bones and tinkling blood that nothing in the universe can protect. She has lost her skin, her surface; her silhouette has been sheared from her. Her heels clack-clack on the tiles, catastrophically, apocalyptically stupid. Who is she again? Here are her veins, her frightening lungs; here is her gaudy liver. She is babble-mouthed, piss-smelling. She is the trash of the searing street.

'What's a "teapot job"?'

'As any schoolboy knows, it's a job a teapot gives you.'

Suzy laughs.

They're sitting in a booth at Vlad's, the café directly across the road from the hospital exit at which Dia has just spent two hours waiting for Suzy to appear after her shift. It wasn't even that she turned up on the off-chance: Dia called Suzy from Granby Row, caught her on a break, wailed into the phone at her, and prearranged a time to meet. But shifts are shifts, as Suzy is always telling her. They end when they end.

As it happens, Vlad's is precisely what Dia needs right now: a subpar chip shop with a sideline in any-hour fry-ups and tall mugs of milky coffee. Everything in sight pretending to be wood, chairs fixed to the floor, cutlery chained to the table. Bonnie Tyler on the radio, fat sizzle and chip steam – she loves places like this anyway, but tonight Vlad's could move her to tears. Couldn't she move in and live here? Find Vlad and ask if he needs any help with the pots? He wouldn't have to pay her; she could eat bits of fat left over from the fryer and sleep curled under a table. If she got lonely at night she could peer out through the slot in the shutters at the hospital and its swivelling lights . . .

In fact Suzy suggested they take the bus to the NQ and find somewhere there to eat. But the thought of all that mismatched cool made Dia's teeth curdle.

'Poor teapot,' Suzy says, dabbing the last of her fried bread in the last of her egg. In a light wool cardigan over the strict lineaments of her uniform, she is unrecognisable as her sourly vintage alter ego. On the contrary, she resembles some war-era ideal of pluck and patriotism. 'Must have been a nightmare for him.'

'"A nightmare for him"?'

'Well, you'd not given him much choice, had you? He had you bang to rights.'

'*Val* didn't give him much choice. Bloody Val.'

Since her peculiar turn this morning (rattling bones, tinkling blood), Dia has of course been fine. But the fear astounded her. After everything she's seen and done, after her wilderness years, trouble years, she had no idea she could be so astounded. She knows she has not lost her skin but she is no longer certain it can keep her from the wind and rain.

'Aren't there agencies for your sort of thing?' Suzy says. 'And you can temp. You only need one teapot to take a shine to you and you're quids in.'

'What am I even worrying about?'

'If you fancy something in the meantime, I could find you a gig.'

'Sorry, Suze, I don't know one end of a bedpan from the other.'

'Not at the hospital. Mate of mine, you've met him, Evan Splendid?'

'Rings a small, strange bell.'

'He's a good bloke. Owns a barber shop in Affleck's. He's always saying he could do with another pair of hands. Someone to make the tea, sweep up . . .'

Dia says she'll think about it. They settle up, head back out to the street, and as they walk arm in arm to Suzy's bus stop Dia leans against her, then into her. She has been doing so well – she has been completely fine. But now she has locked into Suzy's friendly human warmth, her simple other-bodiness, and she's saying, 'Is it weird that I want to ask if I can stay at yours tonight?'

'I don't know, honey. Is it weird that I assumed that was happening anyway?'

They wait for the bus, which heaves into the stop with the usual arthritic snorting and shaking, then join the stampede of students for the upper deck and its few empty seats among the summer-holidaying schoolchildren. The late bus into town – at this hour affectionately known as The Murder Bus – can be a torment, but tonight it's not so bad, the raucous kids an affable and even endearing bunch, and with the first tremble of the engine, the first sway of onward movement, Dia with relief feels something like the lulling of a kindly power, the hush and coo of a benevolent dictator . . .

A gentle nibbling at her side makes her aware that her phone is ringing. She snakes it out, expecting Val in blazing apology mode, but it's Sumi at Greenflowers.

'Hey Dia, just wondering, anything new happening with your contribution this month?'

'No, why?'

'Just can't see it. No bother. I drew the short straw so they've got me calling round a billion people. Fair play, it's a contribution. People go with it for as long as they can, things change, circumstances change . . .'

'Nothing's changed.'

'Okey-dokey. For that I put you in the smiley-face column.

Probably it's a bank thing, we get this every time some bright spark updates a database. Maybe give it a day or two before you start wringing necks.'

'You know me, Sumi, never sorry to be wringing necks.'

'So the telephone voice moves to the next name on the list . . .'

'I'll send the contribution. Nothing's changed.'

'All I needed to hear. She's great, by the way. Looked in on her a little while ago. Sleeping like a baby.'

6. Order of Creature

Returning to Affleck's Palace, the indoor market on Oldham Street that since time out of mind has served the lifestyle needs of the northwest's misfits, proves bittersweet. For Dia as for so many teenagers of her time and temperament, Affleck's walled city of tattooists and T-shirtists was a site of pilgrimage, the hour by train and the catcalling builders on Piccadilly Gardens redeemed by entry into a multilevel labyrinth of creaking boards, random three-stair staircases, spidery branchings and windings and recesses compacted with every imaginable article of countercultural impedimenta in a floorplan unstable as quicksand.

Now, wandering Affleck's, half an hour early for the meeting with Evan Splendid that Suzy set up for her between swallows of toast on the phone this morning, she can't help thinking the old Mosher Mecca has got dreadfully slick. The poster racks, mannequin heads, badge displays, dragon figures and white-witch shelves are all present and correct; but now there's a coffee shop that is not just Affleck's nice but real-world nice, a clean stencilling-on-glass toast café, an ambient streamlining or interlocking of identity parts that says everything you want it to say (freaks welcome; bigots try next door) but nonetheless feels a little too close for comfort to branding. Corporate Affleck's? You take that back.

At half ten, in his mirrory unit on the second floor – 'Splendid

Barbers' – she meets Evan Splendid. Far from being the mustachioed circus strongman his name suggests, Evan turns out to be a short plump fellow with thick grey hair and impish green eyes. Her faulty gaydar notwithstanding, Dia reads Evan as homosexual, possibly a first-generation Afflecker, and so again she catches a twang of what the place used to be, a refuge and a haven for the odd sods, misshapes, inverts and deviants of the shires, called forth from terrace end and cul-de-sac to be ennobled under its radical canopy. Isn't that what brought her here? But now everyone comes here. Now that feeling like a freak is no longer a pouch of acid sewn into your stomach but the preferred sensation of lower-middle-class youth, Affleck's is merely one more stop in everyone's weekend itinerary.

Get a grip, Dia. You're showing your age. You're sounding *old*.

Evan remembers her immediately (drinks in Walrus, anyone?), hugs her, makes her a cup of tea and asks her what the hell she's doing coming to a waster like him for work.

'Last I heard you were some high-powered management gal, with your spreadsheets and quarterly reports and suchlike. Not much of that here.'

'To be honest, Ev' – he has instructed her to call him Ev – 'sweeping floors and making tea all day sounds like my idea of heaven right now.'

'You been in the wars, chick?'

'Don't ask.'

Soon after which Evan says he has an opening she can take up whenever she wants, she suggests this afternoon – spot of business she could do with seeing to at the university – he says fine and then, for a while, they chat over their mugs of tea. During the time before she leaves, they see not one potential patron. She suspects they are not going to be run off their feet at Splendid Barbers.

As must happen in the Northern Quarter, talk soon turns to the Northern Quarter. 'Suze tells me there's some investment group buying everything up. Faustian pacts behind closed doors and whatnot.'

Evan laughs. 'Except they're not very closed, these doors, are they? Everyone knows. Suzy knows, and she's still here drinking her whole-grain smoothies and buying her granny frocks. Same with the rest. So long as they get the service they're used to you won't hear a peep out of this lot. They'll bob along in their bespoke, artisanal, farmhouse, save-the-planet, cool-kid fantasy and never worry where the money's coming from, or where it's going. Just so long as everything above the waves stays the same.'

'It's all in their heads.'

'A Northern Quarter of the mind, chick. Same as it always was.'

In fact she has two spots of business at the university: delaying the next instalment of her payment of tuition fees; and meeting Andrew, who replied to her letter-length text with a curt message inviting her to find him in his office at twelve.

Early again, she steps into the School of Arts, with its portico and its columns and the scrag of gold-leaf Latin – ARDUUS AD SOLEM – that you see everywhere and that she's never bothered to learn the meaning of, heads up to his office, knocks, gets no reply, tries the door, finds it locked, and waits in the corridor, standing then bouncing a hip against the wall then lying with her whole back against the wall until she has to accept that he's not about to round the corner and come sheepishly strolling towards her, hands in pockets, full of some storyline about an overrunning lecture.

She texts him, waits, tries to call him, but drops at once into the automated abysm of voicemail.

At half twelve she heads down to the faculty office and talks to Sondra, who not only knows about Dia's and Andrew's relationship but also heartily approves of it. Sondra says Professor Evert is in a meeting. Further details are not forthcoming. Meeting where? With whom? For how much longer? Couldn't tell you, Sondra says.

Dia gives up. Stalks out of the School of Arts into the glass sheet of the postgrad admin office where she is directed to a chair across from a smartly dressed and incredibly gangling young man who she keeps expecting to reveal more and more skinny pinstriped limbs from beneath his desk.

'I'd like to delay paying my tuition fees,' she tells him.

'We want to put a hold on the payment?'

'If that's what that is, yes.'

'A hold' sounds reassuring: like this is something that happens, something there's a routine for, a button, a click.

'Would this be a one-time instance or potentially a recurring arrangement?'

'I want to delay the payment just this one time.'

'Well, generally speaking, there shouldn't be any . . .' His voice trails off and she loses him to his screen.

There's nothing to do but wait. She studies the young advisor, then the noticeboard behind him with its peppy announcements and reminders.

She studies the office. Desks and chairs under hollow strip lighting, people talking round the edges of screens as if playing some quaint game. She notices an elderly man dressed in not-quite-shabby tweeds with spectacles and a neat white beard smiling at her. She glances away, glances back, but the man is still smiling at her. There is no desk in front of him, no screen, no advisor. It appears that he has taken his chair from one of the nearby consultation pods and placed it at the back of the room so he can sit with a view of the entire office. Except now she can't avoid the impression that he has positioned his chair in order that he can sit with a view of *her*.

'That's odd.'

She looks at her advisor. He is unfamiliar. Is this the same person she was just talking to? Or is it possible that, while she was worrying about that beardy weirdo, someone else came and took his place?

'What's odd?'

He turns his head to one side and holds it there. 'Excuse me,' he says and gangles up from his desk, revealing only the requisite number of limbs.

Her advisor goes to another desk and stands talking for a long time to a colleague she can't see. She waits for him to point at her or in some other way indicate her, and when he doesn't, when his arms remain stiff at his sides as if invisibly shackled there, that's when she starts to panic. At last the colleague, a middle-aged man with worn blue eyes and jagged black hair, a startling relic of punk youth, steps into view and follows her advisor back to his desk. As the two men bend to consult the screen, the younger one winks at her, the older sniffs, no eye contact, a forefinger pressed to his lip.

'Then like a *paragraph* . . .' her advisor is saying to his colleague.

Who sharply depresses his forefinger: *ssh*.

The older man stands, reading the screen. He rocks on his feet. Then he folds his arms and says, 'Miss Talwar, I'm sorry to say we can't help you today.'

'No?' It's hard to speak. Her jaw feels numbed, iced, enveloped. Like after the dentist's. 'May I ask why not?'

'We're having some issues with our system. Leave your request with us and when we're up and running again we'll process it for you as soon as possible.'

'Will you?'

Over his folded arms this fortysomething Sex Pistol eyes her with a quietly precise hostility. 'We will.'

There's nothing else to say. But even as she stands she looks again round the office, the advisors at their desks chatting with variously problematic young people, tapping and clicking at what appear to be perfectly compliant and wakeful computers. Which makes no sense, does it? Or does it?

She looks for the weird beardy codger but sees only his chair, still positioned against the back wall, empty and more than empty, as if unoccupied in hours, days.

She is almost at the door when she calls back, '"*Arduus ad solem*" – what is that?'

'It's the university motto,' the young advisor says gently.

'What does it mean?'

'"Striving towards the sun".'

Arriving back at Affleck's, not quite late for her first shift, she rackets up the stairs to Splendid Barbers and finds no one there. She scans the aisle, puts her head round the unit on either side, but catches no sight of Evan. It's the girl at the novelty-soaps stall opposite who says, 'Ev? Think I saw him putting the world to rights with the top-hat dudes.'

After several circuits of the floor above, she locates him in a cluster of men talking in a narrow satiny passage stacked from floor to ceiling on both sides with funereal head attire. The men loft their mugs, chortle conspiratorially. One of Evan's interlocutors is classic hipster, with ethnic beads and unkempt whiskers and white-boy dreads. The other, in jeans, T-shirt, Docs, could be a self-employed electrician.

For some reason she has difficulty catching Evan's eye. Even when she stands right at the entrance of the hat passage he seems unaware that she's there. Then he seems aware that she's there, just not looking at her. The man with the dreads glances her way and gives her a beautiful smile. Then the three men carry on talking.

Finally Evan begins to leave the conversation. But even this takes time: he detaches slowly, stepping out of the passage then stepping back to add a footnote, a wry addendum. The dreads man ducks out of the passage and lopes off. Evan and the electrician-looking man carry on talking.

She waits. Evan completes a lengthy sequence of farewells then turns to her. He sees her, drops his gaze and stands rubbing his eyebrow.

'Sorry I'm late,' she says. 'My spot of business kind of spiralled.'

'It happens.'

'I didn't see anyone at the shop. Should I have waited there?'

'No, no. About that, though.' He shows her eyes that have a look in them. 'Not sure I can use you, chick.'

'What's that, Ev?'

He digs a fingernail into the corner of his eye, picking at a rind of sleep that isn't there. 'Not sure I can justify the hours. I thought there were all these hours going begging, turns out there aren't. When you factor everything in.' With an embarrassed flourish he mimes a hand on an abacus, slotting, sorting, then goes back to digging nothing out of his eye. 'Sorry to disappoint, chick.'

'There's no job.'

'I'm shocked too. Hours aren't there. Hold my hand up, I made a boo-boo. Didn't do my sums properly.'

She is amazed. It doesn't make sense. Nothing today makes any sense.

'This is pretty mental, Ev,' she says slowly. 'You do know that?'

'Honest to God, I feel terrible. Stupid noggin . . .' He knocks a closed fist, hard, against the side of his head. 'Tell Suzy next time she sees me she can kick my arse, yeah?'

'Will do.'

She drifts back down the stairs, weightless with amazement. And she is outside, frowning in the afternoon sun, when she thinks again of Evan's eyes and the look that was in them. What was that? A liar's look but something else too. Almost like he was *frightened* or something.

Realising she has had nothing to eat since toast this morning with Suzy, she floats to the cash machine at the end of the street, distractedly feeds her card into the slot and stares into the hooded screen while it gulps through its decisions about her. The screen invites her to wait. It invites her to wait some more. Then she hears a faint dry snap somewhere inside the machine, the snicking of a trap, the sealing of a chamber, and the screen clears in a way she has never quite seen before and shrugs together its welcome page. As if she has done nothing, as if she's not even there.

At first none of this processes. She is about to move away, look for another machine, when she remembers that this one still has her card. With fresh horror she leans forward and claws at the keypad under the screen, tries to enter her PIN, though the screen only goes on pretending she's not there. She jabs every key in the keypad then lets out a disgusted scream and slaps the screen as hard as she can.

Still she's reluctant to move away, to abandon her card to the machine's traps. She turns to find that a queue has amassed on the stub of pavement behind her.

'Don't know what you're looking at,' she says to the queue generally. And then, as she steps from in front of the machine and starts away down the street: 'Wouldn't bother with that one if I were you, it's fucked.'

The nearest branch of her bank is on Market Street. She strides through the sliding glass up to the headset by the door. A woman whose face is, despite the fake lashes and lipstick, all dour rugged squares.

'One of your pathetic machines just swallowed my card.'

Dia gives the woman her details. More time spent staring at someone who is staring at a screen you can't see. Then the woman's expression changes – her hard face hardens – and she says, 'I can't see a record of your account. But you definitely have one, don't you? You're always in here. Look.' The woman swivels her screen so Dia can see it.

She looks. It's true; her name appears nowhere on the proffered screen. Impressed nonetheless, she glances at the woman's name-tag: Iris.

'Let me . . . Les?' Iris summons a man in a suit with his hands behind his back. 'There's a problem with this customer's account.'

'Oh,' Les says, 'I doubt there's a "problem" . . .'

'No,' Iris says, 'Miss Talwar's account should be here. Even if it's been cancelled there should be a record.'

Les wrenches the screen away from Dia towards himself. He reaches across Iris to make a few light taps at her keyboard. The way in which this happens tells Dia there is no sexual tension, no erotic texture whatever between Iris and Les. Each handles their body round the other as they would round pipes in a boiler cupboard.

After a moment Les straightens. 'I'd say you're best going to your account online—'

'How can I do that? I've no account. I've no card. I've no money.'

'In these cases the website is extremely—'

The word 'website' feels like permission to give him it with both barrels, which is what she does, if not with Iris's active support then her silent approval, for the next ten minutes. By the time she's finished with him Les' face has gained a pleasing redness and turbulence, yet his line has not substantially changed. He brings the branch manager to talk to her, a squat bear of a man who absorbs Dia's artillery without deviation from his apparent strategy of boring her to death. Because of course they don't want to help her. Their function is to *appear* to want to help her. To comprise a layer, a human shield between her and the bank's imperium. They want her to leave, and that's all. Everything they do and say is calculated simply to get her back out on the street.

While she is still talking to him, the branch manager goes

away, ostensibly to assist another customer. Then Les goes away, and once again she is alone with Iris.

'Is it just me,' Dia says, 'or is this literally a joke?'

Iris slides a slab of Post-its and a pen across the desk. 'I'm going to keep working on this. Pop your number down for me and I'll get back to you when I know what's what.'

Dia etches her phone number into the note slab. When she looks up again, Iris is staring at her.

'Have you really got no money?'

'I've got a couple of quid. I just said that for the Chuckle Brothers' benefit.'

'Don't you worry, Miss Talwar. I'm going to sort this out.'

Dia drifts back to the sliding glass. The doors chop open, chop shut again in front of her. Then she goes back to Iris's desk and says, 'Iris? Just so you know. You're the best thing that's happened to me today.'

Iris's grin illumines all those rugged squares. 'Save me from the day you're having!'

She still has not eaten. She walks into a shop and scours the food aisle for so long there is a real danger she will pass out. She checks her purse and discovers that in fact she does not have a couple of quid: she has one pound twenty-two pence. The only food she can afford is a plastic-wrapped pork pie. She buys it, staggers outside, and leaning against the shop's window wrenches the pie out of its plastic and eats it in two eye-watering mouthfuls.

Noticing that her phone's charge has sunk perilously low, she tries to call Suzy but gets no reply. She tries to call Andrew. No reply.

She stands in the street, looking at the traffic and the people.

In a distant way she thinks of Lila. She supposes it is the sense of crisis. Whatever else she was (and she was lots of things), Lila was good in a crisis. When rain came running through Sycamore House, when some arsehole of a hit-and-run driver left a kid bleeding on Sycamore Lane, Lila was first responder, first to the scene, the fissures in her face that usually gave her such a defeated look transformed into jags of authority. Even her poor, scalded voice – 'Ri-i-ight, you lot' – became the voice of a small god. There she'd be, at the crux of the emergency, laying down the law and bossing people about – and she loved that, didn't she, bossing people about, whenever she got the chance . . . But the sense of crisis recalls Lila for other reasons, too. Because half the time in Dia's memory it was Lila who was the crisis, who was herself the emergency. Because half of Dia's childhood was her mother running with crazy rain or steeped in blood in the night-glittering street.

Traffic and people. Dia teeters over the lumps of the pavement.

She approaches the tall door of Suzy's building. She knows it will not open, but tries it anyway. It does not open. She knows Suzy is at work, but punches her flat number into the keypad anyway. She takes her time, spacing each digit, before punching the 'Call' button. Is this what they do, the rough sleepers, to get through their day?

No reply. Suzy is at work.

She steps away from the door, goes to stand on the opposite pavement. Her plan is to wait until she sees another resident of the building come along and slip in after them when they open the door. It should be easy; no sweat.

Instead it's hard. Every time Dia has visited this building with Suzy, she has had the idea that people are constantly flying in and out of it – racing out to the bars, darting in with groceries. Today she sees no one. The place may as well be abandoned. She stares at the door for so long its planks seem to soften and distort, flail out in a loose web.

About half four a tiny scuttling man whom she recognises as a resident of the building comes along the street. He stops in front of the door and spends a long time finding his key, fitting it into the lock, turning it, pushing open the door. Fixed to her spot on the opposite pavement, she watches him scuttle inside.

She leans against the wall behind her. It's tempting to sit, to drop her bag and sit on it with her back against the wall, but she knows she cannot do this. If she sits she changes her position in the street entirely; with the altered sightline she is transformed into another sort of person, a different order of creature.

She stands, she leans. She is distracted for long periods of time by things that are not present on the street. With immaculate calm she watches a couple laden with shopping bags make their way into the building.

Can you believe this? Can you hear me?

There is a rush of people passing by on both pavements: young men in suits, young women in sunglasses, everyone carrying a laptop, speaking into a phone. The lights on the corner fill the street with cars. It is electric; she feels taken hold of by an ecstasy not hers. The joy of no future – of there being no future. The empty exultation of a baby, safe from all harm. Then there is a quickening, a reckless untethering, a spreading of ropes, and it is the end of the day.

A little later it's possible that she watches Suzy enter the building. She doesn't stand, doesn't move, doesn't call out. Is this despair? Or what is this?

If you can hear me, reach through the sky. Reach out your hand.

She sits. This is why they sit: if they don't, they fall over. She knows if she does not sit she will fall over. So she puts her bag on the ground on her intractably fixed spot and sits.

She lets her head rock back against the bricks. It's uncomfortable at first, then not so uncomfortable. It's tempting to close her eyes, to rest her head against the bricks and lower her lids, but she knows she cannot do this. If she closes her eyes. If she closes. If.

Reach through the sky. Unzip a panel of cloud and put your hand through. Reach out and help me.

There is a nibbling at her hip. She looks down, expecting without disgust to find she is being harassed by some small creature – a dog, a rat. But it is her phone, ringing.

'Hey Dee,' Samson says. 'How are tricks?'

'Help me,' she says.

7. Everything You Feared

He picks her up from under the blue-neon sign outside Element Bar, and it's no armoured box he sends this time but the fantasy car, the money car, coming down the street like an oil slick that attracts every bright sliver of the sign and grows scarcely more coherent even when it pauses in front of her. She senses a door opening, takes a half-wild guess and plunges from the street into a dim low chamber that seems to be made out of couches.

She smells him before she sees him: aniseed and iron filings. There are shifts of soft music, indefinite light sources, a glass-topped table covered with papers, the ergonomically sculpted couch she's sitting on and another facing it, which Samson is sitting on. Relaxed but concentrated, knees apart, leaning forward.

For some reason he's smart: a low-key sort of suit, though a suit nonetheless, open-necked silk shirt, no tie. Even his bald head looks as if it's been given a polish. So he was somewhere, attending something, no doubt bored stiff, when he called her. Then he heard the crack in her voice, and put down his champagne flute, and rose abruptly from his candle-lit table . . . 'Are you all right?'

'I'm fine. Probably I made things sound worse—'

'Tell me what's going on.'

So she does: how she lost her job at Sonata, in ignominious circumstances; how she tried to get temporary work, and failed;

and now, because of the way her contract ended or something, how her finances have gone haywire, with some bewildering uncertainty over the status of her account and its associated payments. She tells him the worst part of it is not being able to pay Greenflowers. The payment to Greenflowers isn't even a payment: it's a contribution, wholly voluntary. But that's the one that hurts, the one she can't stand. He asks her what Greenflowers is and she tells him.

No reason to think any of this would interest the CEO of Glaze Energy, but still Dia assumed she would get his mostly undivided attention. Instead while she's talking he sniffs, picks up a tablet computer she hasn't noticed lying on the table and scrapes at the screen with his thumbnail, as if trying to remove a scuff, food traces that got transferred there by his fingers the last time he consulted it. Towards the end of her tale of woe, he is barely glancing at her. Apart from his question about Greenflowers he hasn't spoken at all for nearly ten minutes.

'. . . Which is why everyone in the world is a prick who genuinely deserves to be dead. Like right-now dead,' she says, already starting to feel quite a lot better (what gets into her?). Legs crossed, hands joined on her knee, she looks at him, but he's still working on that screen scuff. And then while she's feeling better she is not yet feeling completely better and so she starts to say, 'This must be such a ballache for you. There you were, at your fancy do . . .'

'Board meeting. Not fancy. Not even a do.'

'All the same. If you knew you weren't even going to be arsed . . .'

With another sniff he puts the tablet down on the glass table, leans back and grins at her. 'What? Of course I'm arsed.'

'*You* called *me*, Samson.'

'I did. And you said "help me" and that's why I'm here.'

'Okay. So what happens now?'

'Nothing.' He grins at her. 'It's already happened. I tracked down your account, as you anticipated, locked away in the doldrums thanks to some wacko notification from your aggrieved former employers, unlocked it, completed the outstanding payments – with close and particular reference to the Greenflowers contribution, I might add – and then, what the hell, it's nearly Christmas, put another twenty grand in there so you're not grubbing round for any temporary chambermaid bullshit while you're getting back on your feet.' He rolls a hand, maybe a bit grandly, at the tablet. 'It's done.'

'It's not remotely nearly Christmas,' she says.

'At my age, Dee, Christmas is always just round the corner. Hungry?'

Without her registering any movement the car has brought them almost to the edge of the city centre. They get out into rosy twilight and Samson leads her across the street to a pizza restaurant where everyone not only knows who he is but appears to have been expecting him. They settle at a table, listen to the waiter's head-spinning recommendations (it takes everything Dia has to keep her from saying, 'Just bring me the lot'), decide to let him surprise them, and when he has retreated from sight slump companionably at either side of the wicker-wrapped bottle. Samson can't seem to stop grinning at her.

'I'm grateful,' she says. 'Of course I am. But I can't take your money. If you've paid payments there's nothing I can do about that, but I'm not accepting twenty grand from you.'

'Call it a loan.'

'Call it I'm sending it back to you first thing tomorrow. Account details, please.'

'But I'm not going to tell you.'

'Account details, please.'

They eat. She manages to observe decorum, use her knife and fork, despite a strong inclination to pick up the pizza in both hands, roll it into a tube and feed it directly into her mouth. Then the sensation of having food inside her at all – her first meal since that eye-watering pork pie approximately three and a quarter centuries ago – arrives with a thudding restorative shock. Her shoulders spread, her head rises on its unfurling stem. This is what human is: fullness, fedness; the sympathies expanded by mozzarella and chorizo.

While they eat, a stick-thin shadow rears into the room, and she sees it is Weland. It hasn't occurred to her until now that he must have been driving the car. As he passes their table Samson salutes him and Weland without any change in expression goes to sit at the next empty table. A waiter lounges over to him, slaps a menu in front of him, lounges away.

'Does he have to sit there?' she says to Samson.

'Weland? He does, apparently.'

'He's weird. Not in a good way.'

'Why not give him a chance? He's a good guy, my Weland Frost. One of the best.'

When she looks up at Samson again, her eyes are prickling.

'You've no idea how scary it was. *I* had no idea. And I've had times . . . Like you only exist while other people agree you exist. They stop agreeing and poof, you stop existing.'

'You're right there, Dee. I can see you and everything.'

She looks down at her pizza.

'I'm going to help you,' she tells the pizza.

Neither the pizza nor Samson says anything. She raises her head and tells him, 'Not because of the money. That's still coming back. But I'm going to find Reggie. I'm going to go to this farm in East Sussex and I'm going to find him and I'm going to bring him back.'

'Dia,' Samson says.

'Account details, please.'

He sits back, staring at her with narrowed eyes.

'You don't have to do that.'

'I go to this place. I go for their "visitor weekend". You forget I've met these people, I've talked with them, got pissed with them. There's a possibility I've even *danced* with a couple of them. Sweet idealist sorts. Above all, completely harmless. I get the train down Friday night, poke about, find Reggie and drag him back by the scruff of his neck. By the crinkly flesh of his ballsack, if need be.'

Samson stares at her. Does he see the other Dia now – that danger woman, that trouble woman? Then he takes a long gulp of wine, replaces his glass on the table with a deliberate air, leans towards her again and says, 'Dia, let me be clear. I do *not* want you to do that. I absolutely do *not* want you doing anything that might get you into grief with these types. If you want to visit this farm, check it out, see how Reggie's doing . . . well. I would be grateful. I would be . . . But that's all. Go down for a weekend, come straight back, fill me in. And that's all. Am I clear?'

'I could do it. You know I could.'

'With respect, Dia, what I know is you have no clue what you're talking about. If you come back saying we need to get

Reggie out of there, that's what I'll do. I'll take steps, I'll approach parties . . . There are companies that do this, extraction, deprogramming, the whole post-cult rigmarole. If you tell me I need to, I will employ such a company to get Reggie out. But you, Dia . . . you must not, must *not* do anything that might put you in harm's way.'

'Can you stop me?'

'I'm serious. Promise me.'

'Promise you what? That I'll be a good girl?'

'Promise me.'

'Christ. I promise I'll be a good girl.' And she does: she promises she will be a good girl. And as a good girl she will find Reggie and she will bring him back and when he opens the door and he sees them both there, Samson's face, Samson's *face* . . .

'Glad we've sorted that out.' At last he grins – that old off-kilter killer grin. 'You don't realise how important you are to me. I know you think "fifteen years, what the fuck" – but I never forgot you, Dee.'

'You've just been so awfully busy . . .'

'You know who I am. I'm the solar-panel guy. Despite what you may believe, there's not much downtime on this gig. Solar panels have enemies.'

'Like a load of hacked-off wind turbines?'

'Like you don't need me to tell you who. Various parties with an envious eye on all my cool shit. Who look at cool shit like my solar plant and see another future coming along to eclipse the one they had in mind.'

'The fiends, the ringwraiths of the Grid.'

'Let's just say there's a lot going on. Now maybe more than ever. But you'll see. You made me a promise, so I'll make you one: I promise one day you'll see how important you are to me. How important you've always been.'

On the drive to Granby Row her nearly dead phone rings and it's Iris, working God knows how late, saying in a happy baffled voice that her account has lurched back to life and she's not going to believe it but there's this *humungous* deposit . . . Dia calls into the car, 'Oy, Richard Branson: if you're determined to give someone a wad of your cash, allow me to make a suggestion,' and she tells Samson about Iris. 'Absurdly Early Father Christmas will call again this year,' he says.

They both get out and stand in the street, looking up at her building. He pushes the hair off her face and she rises on her toes towards him.

'You're sure?'

She only looks at him.

'I'm grateful,' he says.

He is. She can see he is. But there is something else, in his face or in the air or at her back, a sense of stalled or toppled monumentality, the huge jarring gestures that swept her life away and the dabbing dance of his fingertips by which it was restored to her (and how did that happen, and how did that work, and what, what, what?) and she is breathless with it, wide-eyed, on the tops of her toes, ready to be carried away, transformed or obliterated, whatever is possible on this bit of street at this time of night.

And she's still there, looking, as the car drips stealthily away under the street lamps.

Through the dressing-gown blurs of the earliest part of the morning she is called to her door and the unpromising figure of Samson's Weland Frost.

'What does he want?' she says.

'I'm here to see if you require any help.'

'Let me think about that.' Feeling no guilt whatsoever about leaving him there in the hallway, she showers, dresses, finally lets him in, and they sit at the table between her two spectacular timeworn views of the city.

'Did you bring the flyer?'

'Give me a minute.'

In his perma-suit (always the same one), with his sunglasses pushed up on his head, Weland crouches doing something short-sightedly with his phone. What a skinny face, what shallow temples, and what unnecessarily complicated eyelids: there seem to be three or four sets crammed into each socket, rolling on and off the eyeballs in anemone sequences. You can see why he likes sunglasses. And yet, examining his naked face, she's surprised to note that he is not nearly as old as she's assumed he is. The eerie black hair – surely dyed – and the withered look she has attributed to weight loss are deceiving, elements of a past or a persona she hasn't quite the energy this morning to start trying to imagine. It's possible he is only a few years older than she is – thirty, thirty-two.

After another quarter of an hour he pushes his phone at her across the table, showing two photographs: the front and back of the flyer.

'Let's see. "WHY THE NEXT WORLD DOESN'T NEED YOU . . . No one needs telling there's another world coming. Either you already know or you never will. The question is: what kind of world? Maybe the next world doesn't need you – and we reckon it doesn't – but we'd love to know what you think about it. And we'd love to tell you what *we* think about it. Next weekend take a break from your dying reality and come to see us, talk, listen, tell us why we're wrong, consider the possibility that we're not."'

'There's a number. Call it on this.' He gives the phone she's reading another nudge towards her. 'This is yours now. Your phone for the trip.'

'Says who?'

'It's a gift. Use it, don't use it.'

She calls the number. It rings for so long she considers hanging up, then there's some vague audio scuffle and a male voice says, 'Yello?'

'Oh, hi. I'm calling about the visitor weekend?'

'Hokay.'

'I was talking to some of your marvellous people who were up here for a recruitment event, I think they said. A gentleman called Jon, couple of ladies called Annette and Fee? Another not-very-talkative gentleman whose name escapes?'

'Yuh-huh.'

'Marvellous people. Marc, maybe? Mike or Marc? They were very inspiring, anyway, and they mentioned something about a visitor weekend?'

'Sure thing.'

'And I was thinking I'd like to come. This weekend, if possible.'

'Yuh-huh.'

'Is it possible?'

'No drama.'

'Terrific. So do I just rock up Friday night, or . . . ?'

'Yuh-huh.'

'Fantastic.' She waits. 'Should I tell you my name?'

'Hokay.'

She completes the call then says to Weland, 'Not a polished operation. Bless them. The Church of Scientology these clowns are not.'

'Whoever they are, now they know your name.'

'So what if I told them my name?'

'I suppose we'll find out.'

The bus stutters into Thursday evening. It is always like this, she remembers: the grinding stop-start progress that is the only public route now into Longsight Market.

Nothing to do but sit it out, the snorting air brakes, the clattering doors, the crowding influx of new passengers who have no other means of transit. She stares out of the window or into the phone Weland gave her, exploring it, getting to know it. A part of her brain reflects that she used to make this trip fairly frequently, and laments her fall into bad habits; the rest of her brain knows it's not true. She has never taken this bus often. It is only a story she tells herself, personal mythology, a nice thing she never did.

And why? Coming along Dickenson Road she feels it as she always does, an itch in the roof of her mouth, like the snag of a delicate hook. The spice shops, shoe shops, fruit and veg stalls, second-hand book and CD stalls, the clothes stalls with their rolling racks; the superbly aloof and inconsiderate signage; the Sivori's ice-cream van enchained by a permanent queue, a woman in a headscarf browsing an e-reader, a man in a kurtha stretching both arms in the air as he joyfully yawns; the whole strumming length of the street with its bazaar tumult and cobalt gloss – why does she always resist it, when it is so nearly irresistible?

She leaves the bus at the library, crosses a car park and enters the network of streets behind. As she goes along she tongues the roof of her mouth, trying to wipe off the itch in it.

And so she comes, for the first time this year, to Greenflowers.

She has her usual trouble with the intercom, seems to alert at least someone to her presence, then steps back from the door, from the whole squared-off, flat-roofed brick edifice that always makes her think of a converted pub. Then the inner door opens and through the graph-paper glass she spies Sumi.

'No one here has your money, bitch.'

'Looks like I'll be wringing necks after all.'

They embrace, much less clumsily than Dia thought they were going to, and as they go along the hallway Sumi gives her the weekly update. 'One not even episode on Sunday night, mild bowel-themed drama, you wouldn't thank me for the details, but otherwise completely fine and good . . .'

The room is the same. The bed, the ventilator, the same. It's the peonies in the vase on the bedside table that pull inside her chest. Because they're fresh, and she didn't bring them. She guesses Sumi.

'Give you two gals some privacy. Cup of tea for the prodigal?'

'Cup of tea, thank you.'

Left alone, Dia sits in the chair set slightly away from the bedside, sinks through its pattern of structural creaking.

Hello Lila, she thinks. Because she's not a mad person who's going to sit talking to a breathing corpse.

It's Claudia. Your daughter. Remember me? Don't have to say you do if you don't.

You look well. Actually you don't. You look dreadful. Like death's bedpan. Death's hot-water bottle. Death's electric blanket.

I've got news. Samson's back. That's right: the day you always feared has come and the grotty old devil has popped out of his genie lamp and come swishing about your daft girl again. Only he's not grotty any more; he's rich. And you like rich, don't you, a bloke with a few bob in his pocket. A moneyed gent not ungenerous at the bar, who knows that every round is his round. Don't worry, he's still wild and mad and leading me on in bad ways. We're already quite far along with our scheming and whatnot. Keeping secrets. Plotting against you. Not heard about my three wishes yet but I'll keep you posted.

Funny it was *that* you feared. Of all the things you might have feared. 'Oh, he's the king's jester, that one, when it suits him, but how about when it doesn't? You can't see it, he's thrown glitter in your eyes, but *I* see it. No sparkly tat in these eyes. Do you want me to tell you what that man is? He's a shark. With that shark sense that means he'll be circling you forever if you let him. Round and round in circles, and you'll never get rid.'

Yes, Lila, but another way of saying that is he was my friend. He was there when no one else was, when you weren't, and you hated that, didn't you? That I went to him, talked to him, listened to him. Well, of course I did. Why would I come to you? You were never there. Even when you were there you weren't there.

With him, the exact opposite. There even when he wasn't. In my head. You thought he wanted to be my dad but he didn't and I didn't want him to be that either.

Nothing scared you the way he did. Nothing and no one. Not me, not even you, and you scared everybody. Do you know that about yourself, Lila? You scared everybody. Not because you were big and strong but because you were small and weak and you did horrible things to yourself that flashed in the street like disaster. Samson with Aladdin's lamp, you with Alice's bottle: Drink Me. And Drink Me and Drink Me and Drink Me.

You scared me. Everything was my fault. I couldn't help it. I talked too much ate too much cried too much slept too much peed too much pooed too much and everything that I did and couldn't help made chains that flew up round you and tried to pull you out of the sky. You were this huge thing, like a flying saucer, and I was pulling you out of the sky. When you fell you would crush me flat. Everything would break. Sycamore House turn to dust. Ainscough curl up like old lino. Rubble where the tower used to be. A crater where the town used to be. And in a pit of ash at the very bottom the happy nothing that used to be your daughter. Drink Me Drink Me Drink Me.

Funny thing two: I never scared you. I think I should have. When I came through the door with two coppers and a cast on my left hand the size of a football, I should have scared you. When I didn't come through the door at all and the ward nurse called you in a voice like singing and you said you weren't getting a taxi, not at that time of night, not at those prices, I should have scared you. Five years, give or take, and you never thought one second of it was your fault.

And it wasn't. It wasn't, really. I just thought you might have thought it was.

I watched to see what they did to you, those years. And they made you look tired. Night after night, whatever they brought you sent away into the same guilty vector – a point in space between the tip of your chin and your scrunched-up right eye. You pulled that face and sent it away, whatever those five years brought, pushed it through a portal into a parallel universe where there was someone to accept like a parcel all that long-distance blame. The effort of transmission added width, depth, to your 'laughter lines'. Lila, you never did much laughing. Some cackling in The Kingfisher you probably didn't know about, some hooting along Sycamore Lane you certainly never heard. But those weren't laughter lines. Cracks, fissures. Your helpless rough edges.

You didn't blame me. Well, you did and didn't. Called me every name under the sun and a few unknown to any star, though in the end it was just politeness, the pub politeness that meant so much to you, the tower-block code that declareth *the goodly matron decries her girl child lest she fall further into error*. But you never blamed me. You blamed him.

How old was I? That age when you're still so young you feel ancient: older than you'll ever feel again. I was sitting on the floor, on that carpet like dark islands dissolving in a white-noise sea. I was tearing the head off something – a blonde doll, some berk of a stuffed toy. I was always happily tearing the head off something then. And I looked up and you were there and I said, 'Where is my daddy?'

Not *who*. But *where*. 'Where is my daddy?'

And you sat forward in that lovely, organising-yourself, let-the-lesson-begin way you sometimes had and you said my daddy was an important man, a medical doctor, a specialist who carried out operations no one else could and he travelled the world looking for people who needed the operations no one else could carry out. You said he loved me but his work was so important he couldn't see me, would never be able to see me. You said his name. Kuvam Talwar. Then you stood and went to your room and you were there for the longest time in the world while I sat and stared at the deforming, reforming carpet that stretched round me to the ends of the earth and then you came out and sat again and there was a photo in your hands. You showed it to me secretly, as if we were cheating at cards. It was him. Kuvam Talwar. Handsome – 'dashing', you said – with a dimple in his cheek like an ampersand.

And you lied. You kept it up for as long as you could, but you were too spiteful to keep it up forever. You weren't even angry with me that day you spat without spit: 'Your father doesn't know you exist. I never told him, did I? Some soft shite over here on his gap year? Why would I tell him? He doesn't know you *exist*, kid.' Later I looked at the photo, at Kuvam Talwar – a nice Gujarati boy smiling in The Kingfisher. And I thought: what did he see in you? In *you*?

It was then, that ghastly unangry day, I decided his name would be my name too.

And it was that day I saw Samson for the last time. Until now.

He's back, Lila, and we're thick as thieves again, plotting and planning again. That's what I came to tell you. And I'm doing the last thing you would ever want: I'm saving his life. Smoke pours from the broken window and he's trapped by fanged glass and I'm running in the street with my mask and my ladder. I'm going to the ends of the earth and I'm saving his life and now everything you feared has come to pass.

Shock Valley – II

I walk until the lake and the house and the two soft shadows on the kitchen floor are as far behind me as I can put them and then I halt on the road and I breathe. One breath: that's the ration. Another and I'd never get started again; people would find me here, years from now, a curious tree with the gnarled limbs and wrinkled features of a dirty old woman . . . I take my breath, take with it knowledge of who I am again, then move on along the road and following the ridge of the hills come to the village before noon.

The streets are empty, or not quite. Two men stand arguing outside the boarded-up chip shop. Their voices rise to shrieks; their language is improbably foul. Several times as I walk towards then past and away from them I think they are going to start taking swings at each other, but it doesn't happen, the wave of threat breaks, dissipates, regathers with fresh force, and I realise this is simply how these men speak to each other. Otherwise we are the only occupants of the gritted glare between the houses.

Days like this concentrate your attention on what's left. Why *this* spiny bush, why *that* feral cat – why did they survive, when so much didn't? The last time I talked to my sister I was in Buenos Aires, working out a commission, listening to her voice on what I had reason to believe was the last working phone in the city. It had taken me two days and all my skills of persuasion to find it. When at last she answered my call she said she was alphabetising her ex-husband's bookshelves.

'Deckchairs on the *Titanic*?' I said.

'What you don't realise, Mabel-Abel, is the deckchairs were the best bit of *Titanic*. They were the point of *Titanic*.'

He had been sick – the moronic ex-husband. She had gone to see him, intending to stay for perhaps a night or two. Then six weeks had gone by and the ex-husband was well again and my sister was still with him. She couldn't leave, couldn't get home.

'It's looking rough over there,' I said.

'What do you expect? This is Ainscough. The whole place always looks like a looted Peacocks. You know, for some of us this is just business as usual,' she said, and then we laughed and that's the last conversation we ever had, my sister and I, my baby sister and I.

Quickly I proceed through the village. Houses on each side of the road so quiet and still and in such states of disrepair – buckled roofs, collapsed eaves, walls tumbled to fragments of colourless brick – you could imagine the whole place had been abandoned, stripped to the bone and left to merge with the hardscrabble surrounding it, the slant miles of stone and thorn, of rust and ash, of plastic bottle, plastic bag. But it isn't so. The village is not deserted and every house has its occupants, keeping to the shade, keeping quiet, keeping still, holding on for night and whatever small mercies it may bring.

I was never a frequent visitor here. For a time I tried the neighbourly thing, turned up at the weekend market with a fixed grin and salted rabbit, but it didn't suit me and after a month or so I packed it in. Soon after that the weekend market became a thing of the past. I didn't mourn it. My dead sister's house by the lake was all I wanted. If not peace, then separation. If not quiet, then insulation. Well, now that's gone too. Things of the past.

The other reason I used to come to the village is the reason I come to it now: Hendrix. I would say 'my old friend Hendrix' except Hendrix isn't my friend. The last time I looked we were bitter adversaries (reeling crosshairs in an open-plan office in Newcastle: his fingertip, my earlobe). Then Helios changed everything and the next thing I knew I was living in a house by a ponging lake and Hendrix was living in a rubbly terrace in the next village. 'Keeping an eye out for you,' he said. Ten years later I finally believed he didn't mean 'keeping an eye *on* you'.

His house is as quiet as the rest until I hear a mechanical clunking that I follow along the ginnel to the back of his terrace and the sight of Hendrix attempting to repair his outdoor latrine. Covered with filth, and even bushier than I remember him, he comes out of the little brick hellhole, grins, embraces me. It's all right. He's dirty, sure enough, but then I am too.

'Not dead yet,' he says gleefully. I don't know if he means him or me. I suppose that's his point.

'You look like an alcoholic Santa Claus.'

'You look like a young Beyoncé Whatsername. Drink?'

He passes me a racy-looking flask that turns out to contain only water.

'I've had a visit,' I tell him. 'I've been visited.'

'Oh yes?'

'Peter.'

'Bet that went well.'

'Not the man himself. Couple of messenger boys.'

'Good grief, Mabel.' He flinches, the sacs of his eyes dimpling as if I've described some jaw-dropping injury. Because Hendrix knows as well as I do Peter's special attitude towards messages and messengers: that they go no further – that they reach their recipient and dissolve into air. Except they don't, of course, and in fact it is hard work making sure Peter's messages disappear as he wishes them to. Hendrix knows as well as I do how hard. 'How are you?'

'It'd been a while. But yeah. I'm fine. I know who I am.'

'You took the breath.'

'One breath. Then you know.' I remember my surprise about five years ago when Hendrix told me he used to do the same thing. It wasn't procedure or anything, but there it was: in the first helter-skelter seconds after he completed a commission, before he did anything else, before he surveyed egress or obstacle, he took a breath and allowed the air to tell him who he was again. To tell him that he was unchanged, or not essentially changed, by the work he had done.

I remember my surprise, too, at discovering they felt that way over on his side of the fence. For a couple of decades Hendrix and I executed more or less identical work on behalf of more or less diametrically opposed parties. And whatever else I doubted, I never doubted I was on the side of the bad guys. Later Hendrix would insist that the guys on his side were bad too, but I never knew how I felt about that. Certainly Hendrix and his guys were bad: both the means and the ends of the governmental agencies in whose interests they worked were impenetrably dark. Nonetheless I suspect they would have baulked at what I got up to over in corporate, working for businessmen such as Peter. Hendrix, I know, in his time shot at least three corrupt diplomats, poisoned at least two politicians on the take. But I killed the diplomats who were not corrupt, the politicians who were not on the take. For twenty years these were the disasters I averted, the miracles I worked, in exchange for Peter's money.

That name they called me, Mad Mabel – it was a joke. Bantersome male ribbing on account of my circumspection (and meticulousness, and efficiency) in the dispatch of every last one of my commissions. Along with my high tolerance for protocol, it's possible I enjoyed a further professional advantage. Overwhelmingly my colleagues were Aryan hulks padded out with thirty-odd years of expensive nutrition and five centuries of patrician breeding. That is, they looked like corporate assassins, and had to take pains to look like anything else. For me, at least, that was never a problem. If you want an inconvenient but conspicuous human being removed from the world, send in a woman, a black woman, a little black woman (all nerve and hidden sinew), because no one sees her. No one realises she's even there.

Now Hendrix takes a swig of water. 'What was the message?'

'This is Peter. You tell me.'

'Not a commission. *No.*'

'In fact yes.'

'Good grief, Mabel.' He shakes his head. 'Did you get a name?'

I did. It was one of those other words the kid had to tell me, bleeding from the back of his head into my kitchen floor: 'Lorelei.'

'Really.' There is no profound change in Hendrix's manner. Any subtlety is concealed by his bushiness.

'Is this someone I should know?'

'You haven't heard of Lorelei?'

'Can't say I'm familiar.'

'That must make you the only one.' Then he tells me about Lorelei. Who is, I gather, a sort of celebrity. A beautiful young woman who travels from town to town with her roadshow, which seems to consist largely of her talking – speaking, lecturing, Hendrix isn't sure. What he does know is she has become extravagantly popular. For the last six months no one has talked about anything else.

'Apparently she has a message of some kind. Nothing like Peter's messages, you'll be relieved to hear. People find it inspiring.'

'What kind of message?'

'Couldn't tell you. I just hear it gladdens the soul.' He laughs feebly. 'And this is who Peter wants?'

'Seems so.' In fact I don't know why either of us is surprised. A woman in the public eye, charismatic, magnetic – scattering her wavelengths. Isn't this exactly what wakes Peter in a cold sweat at night? Peter and every money reptile like him?

Even now my naivety astonishes me. After Helios, after the familiar world washed away (no: burned from its socket), one of my few consolations was the thought that if everything I'd ever known was going to vanish, then at least Peter and his kind would vanish too. And I was wrong. Oh, there was little sign of them during the initial breakdown; amid the protests, riots, coups and countercoups, uprisings and crossrisings, Peter's kind was nowhere to be seen. But even a world in flames moves on and when it did more and more certainly came proof that the money reptiles had survived. Not quite from scratch, from whatever they could, from this and from that – barbed wire, broken glass – they rebuilt their terrible network and its motley filaments spun out everywhere over the scorched earth.

Hendrix stands, peering into his brick outhouse. I assume I've lost him to the complexities of its antique plumbing, then he says with a tilt of his flask, 'You'll have your work cut out.'

'Tell me about my work.'

'This is worth knowing. Lorelei travels with a security team. Everywhere she goes. They even get up on stage with her. Always sounded excessive to me, but now I'm thinking again. They have these wonderful names . . .'

'Knew I could rely on you for first-class intel, 'Drix.'

'They're a sort of group. And they have a leader, reputedly a quite terrifying *hag* . . .' He peers again at his uncoupled pipes. 'Mrs Tooth, or something.'

'Mrs Tooth.'

'Or something.' In the heat the exposed bits of his face glare red. 'All I mean is you're going to be busy. If you're planning on doing it.'

'I thought I'd give him a hearing.'

'You thought you'd give *Peter* a hearing.'

'I thought I'd hear what he has to say.' I did think that. For reasons I did not realise until now I am disinclined to share with Hendrix. Because the kid who bled out on my kitchen floor had some additional words to tell me. He said: Peter has something. He said: Peter has something you want. And he said: I don't know what I don't know what but Peter has something for you and don't kill me please. And then I killed him and I thought about that. Peter has something you want. I don't know what he meant – no. But I have an idea. Or maybe a hope. Something as stupid as that.

Until this moment I assumed I would tell Hendrix all this. But I don't say anything, and he seems not remotely surprised or perturbed that I don't. 'Do you need anything?' A beam breaks out inside his face bush. 'Still got your trusty Sig?'

'And all her useless sisters.' In a locker in Stockholm somewhere. More things of the past. 'Not to worry. I've been finding this *very* useful.'

And I open my bag and show him my hammer. Hendrix makes a tender sound: the first half-second of a laugh, or a coo. He reaches as if to touch it, then at the last instant recalls his fingers.

'Did you get a place?'

I did. Another of the kid's words: 'Silo.'

Hendrix whistles. 'You're going to Silo – to give Peter a hearing?'

'The exercise'll do me good. I've been going to wrack and ruin.'

'Don't tell me you're going on foot.'

'I thought while we're having this glorious weather . . .'

'Wait.' He starts towards the back door of his house, then returns to press the flask into my hand. 'Drink. You're getting a look I don't like. Drink and wait.'

So I wait, and drink, and look at the sky, and after a while Hendrix comes back out of the house holding unnaturally high a long and peculiar object.

'Here you go,' he says.

'What is it? A giraffe's tibia?'

'This, Mabel my dear, is your walking companion. If you're walking to Silo you'll need all the help you can get, ropey old bag like you . . .'

'Careful. You're mixing me up with whatshername.'

'Beyoncé?'

'Mrs Tooth.'

I take it anyway – the stick, the staff. I exchange it for his flask, knowing it is empty, and leaning on the head of the stick again look at the sky. Hendrix looks too.

There was a time when people were always doing this: standing in silence, in twos or threes, looking at the sky. Then we stopped doing it, by and large. But now, for a little while, possibly for old times' sake, we do it again, Hendrix and me. We stand looking at the sky, in all its jaw-dropping injury. Vast hanging rips; puckered sheeny cascades, like the perished layers of an old shower curtain; no distance, no *depth*, but only the sense of a close and prickling void; the sense of some scruffy manufactured thing – a ripped-out oven, a fly-tipped fridge – except as big as the sky, taking up all the space where the sky used to be. Plexiglass scrapes here and there, pale enamel dents; scours, wakes.

'Is it worse than usual?' Hendrix shades his eyes with a hand. 'I can't tell any more.'

'Me neither. But that's Helios for you.'

'Hush your mouth. Don't even say it.'

'Helios,' I say.

Part Two

God's Screensaver

8. A Withering Away

On Friday she wakes early and it's already too late. She tries to call the number on the flyer to ask the questions anyone would ask (what kind of accommodation? What facilities? Will she need a hairdryer?), gets no reply, heads out with unbrushed hair and teeth and hurtles round the shops, no idea what she needs, buys a slew of travel toiletries in varieties she has never used before and even in the queue at the checkout suspects she never will use, goes into Selfridges and buys a staggeringly beautiful and expensive overnight bag, Windsor grain leather, double carry handles, top zip opening, though she knows she already owns several such items, though she knows it is Samson's money she's spending, the money she has not been able to return to him because he won't give her his account details, please.

She's stalking up an escalator in the Arndale Centre when he calls one of the phones she's carrying – the one Weland gave her or her own, in her escalator fluster she doesn't notice which – to give her something else: 'This is a number you can reach me on. Do me a favour and remember it. I'm going to say the numbers and I want you to commit them to memory. All set?'

Why not? It's already too late.

'You know you don't have to do this,' he says. 'If it's too much.'

'It's not too much,' she says, but she's only talking. Amid the folds of the escalator she has no idea whether it's too much or not.

Back at the flat she tries to call Andrew, gets no reply. Tries Suzy, no reply. She thinks about trying Sumi, then it's time to pack, check her packing, repack her packing, then run to the station.

She buys her ticket from a machine then stands for a long time, with sweating eyes, looking for her train details on the electronic boards at the centre of the concourse. To say the least of it, she's uneasy. Travelling always makes her feel as if she's left at least one arm or leg on the kitchen table but it's worse this time because, after agonised prevarication, she has brought with her only the phone that Weland gave her, leaving her phone – her real phone – charging on its cable by the bed. And so she feels as if she's left behind, oh, all her internal organs, her head.

It's not just that. People pass her like alien beings. When she got up on Monday she was the same as any of them, a normal person animated by ordinary drivers and purposes; now she has nothing in common with these lurid creatures carrying bags, reading magazines, eating pasties. They occupy one world, she another. In less than a week they have grown strange to her. More – they are almost pitiable. Almost contemptible, or something . . . Then she has to run for her train.

The journey to London should take only slightly longer than two hours but a period of inexplicable delay, the train heaving on its tracks outside Milton Keynes Central like an over-excited child taking a timeout at a party, brings her into Euston a full forty minutes later than scheduled. She reckons with moderate hustle she can still make her train from Charing Cross, until she finds the entire Tube system has been closed by a day of strike action she has managed not to notice any warning of, and furiously she boards a cab locked into the motionless traffic towards Charing Cross, and her whole trip unravels. Still, only three hours later than expected, and with none of the shouting and carrying-on she imagined might be in order, her wholly invalid ticket gets her a seat on a late departure to Hastings.

Ninety minutes later she's hauling her new bag from one end of another station to the other, looking for a train to somewhere called Born. At last she finds an elderly railwayman who knows what she's talking about. He locates the platform, says that the train she needs runs once an hour. When's the next? His moles benignly bristle. In an hour.

It's not quite dark by the time she steps down on a planky wooden platform that bears the word 'Born' on a freshly painted sign but has no station or anything else attached to it. A series of cracked stone steps, like a sink full of broken crockery, leads her precariously to a road buffeted by sea air. Fields on either side. So much open space all at once is like the booming of a gong somewhere. She looks for the sea but discovers no trace of it.

Standing by the silent road – no vehicle has passed since she arrived, but she feels an unusual desire not to take chances – she re-examines the map on the flyer in the photo still handily stored in Weland's phone, pinches the image out until its pixels start unzipping, but clearly it has no more to tell her. There is Hastings station, there is the platform at Born, there is the silent road, and there is a fat black dot joined by a line to the scrawled words: 'Guess who?' No indication how far away, or in which direction. She starts walking along the road in one direction, feels the wind pushing at her with greater animosity, after ten or fifteen minutes of this turns on her heel and starts walking in the other direction.

She passes a field with a young man in it, sixteen or so, death-metal T-shirt, knee-length shorts, sitting on a bicycle, playing a game on his phone. 'I'm looking for the farm?'

'There's a few.' The kid's face says that something about her bothers him, but what? Genitals? Melanin? Cheekbones? All or none of the above?

'The farm with the . . . group. The . . . Tarantulans.'

'Tarantula.' He points further on along the road.

Half an hour later, when it really is dark, she comes to a gate set between stone pillars in a gap in the hedges. Is this it? She looks for a sign but there isn't one. With just the fingertips of one hand, she prods the gate and it opens easily. She steps back, then forward and through.

It is a farm, at least. In the darkness she makes out its proportions: a track leading down to a long and brightly lit house surrounded by other buildings, stables maybe, maybe a barn. Much closer, to the right of the track, stands a gatehouse, a stubby stone tube like the turret of a castle gone astray during teleport. She finds its door, knocks, waits. Then a lank-haired middle-aged man appears ('Yello?') and even before he asks if she's come for the visitor weekend she sees the black cloth tied round his left bicep.

The man is called Glen. 'There wasn't a whole lot doing tonight, not even orientation, just a few heys and how-the-hell-are-yous. So you've missed *that* . . .' His mild eyes widen then soften. 'But there's a bunch of fun stuff lined up for tomorrow. I guess we need to hit you up with a room and you'll be good for a fresh start in the a.m. Hokay?'

Evidently the gatehouse is also the 'visitor centre', because that's what Glen keeps calling it, and he leads her up a short flight of stairs to one of three doors on the building's only elevated floor. 'So we're all in here? All this weekend's visitors?'

'Sure are, Dia. It's snug, but mad cosy.'

The room is small – not quite a cell but on that continuum. 'One further query before a hearty good night. Would you be packing any mobile devices?'

'I have a phone.' Settling on the bed, which accepts her soundlessly, she shows it to him.

'And would you be willing to leave that in my bodaciously safe keeping? Only we're not crazy about visitors bringing that sort of tech onto the farm.'

'You keep it bodaciously safe, and then you give it back to me?'

'The second before you leave Sunday afternoon.'

'Fine by me.' And she hands over Weland's phone.

'There's water in the jug, and under . . . *this* plate, some chow if you're feeling hungry. Anything else you need, I'm right downstairs.'

'Keeping watch at the gate,' she says.

'Seeing all are safely gathered in. Goodnight, Dia. Sweet dreams.'

Next morning, after a night's sleep that made her feel she was being slowly, softly smothered in a pit of ashes and feathers, she's woken by a tap at her door. 'Hey, sleepyhead,' Glen calls from the top of the stairs. 'Breakfast in ten.'

She finds the bathroom, such as it is, behind the door next to hers. The toilet flushes after her third yank of the chain, the shower icily dribbles, the mirror in which she does what she can with her hair and teeth is a blistered mist. Fat lot of use her fancy-pants toiletries are going to be here: she might as well have packed a Brillo pad and a bottle of Fairy. In fact Dia has known worse than this – not for some time, maybe, but she has known it. She thinks: three doors. One my room, one the bathroom. So who's behind number three?

She gets her answer at breakfast, which takes place in a small room on the ground floor not only dominated but three-quarters filled by an immense wooden table. She has to edge along the wall to make her way to a seat, and when she gets there sits facing the weekend's only other visitors, a young married couple called Blake and Hettie Ormesher. Blake is long and tense and wiry, with a red, stippled complexion she takes at first for razor rash; Hettie is short and soft and round, dutifully blonde, insistently squeak-voiced. While Glen loads the table with an array of weirdish rustic breads and treacly preserves in tall, crack-woven jars, Dia and the Ormeshers get to know each other.

'How'd you find the drive?' Blake asks her.

'Came on the train.'

'Do you like jam?' Hettie asks her.

'Not what you'd call a major jam fan.'

They eat. Then Glen takes them to the house for orientation.

Rustling with the wind of the unseen sea, they walk down the track. As they go she takes in as much as she can through the early dazzle: the rudiments of a vegetable garden, the brick and corrugated iron of storehouses, the shabby timbers of what she thinks again must be a barn. Then the farmhouse itself. At one time it must have been a stockbroker's fantasy, picturesque as a biscuit-tin lid with its striving chimneys and unquenchable tiles, rugged walls, creeping ivy. Now, the place is far from dilapidated, but it's no billionaire's weekend hideaway. It is lived in, worked in, with a faintly desperate and heroic aspect, along with the patches of green on the chimneystacks and the overgrown ivy that makes the façade appear to have five or six dead bushes attached to it.

On their way they pass people working in the vegetable garden, people talking on the path to the farmhouse. Black cloth here, black cloth there. And middle-aged Glen, she sees, is not the exception: it's not just kids here. Grown men and women.

They enter the farmhouse, with its sledgehammer reek of rotten vegetables (Hettie squeaks and pinches her nose), and Glen leads them past a wall with some sort of splashy mural on it to a room decorated with further murals by a range of hands, a heap of actual beanbags in one corner and a horseshoe of stackable white plastic chairs, amid which sits a smiling, round-shouldered young man with a face that excites a scalp snag of recognition.

'. . . Where I leave you at the mercy of our orienteer dude, Jon,' Glen says.

Jon! From The Secret Bar! She wants to kiss him and squeeze his squishy face. But with his polite smile at each of them he seems not to recognise her, and she only sits in the chair advertised to her.

'So,' Jon says, when Glen has withdrawn, 'let's get the ball rolling. My name's Jon, as you know, and this is orientation for your weekend stay with Tarantula. I'm guessing you have lots of questions, but I'm going to try to deal with some of them right off the bat.

'Probably the question I get asked most often is: what is Tarantula? And that's not surprising, because it's by no means self-evident what we're about here. And I actually used to struggle with that question, because the answer is something I know deeply and privately but when I tried to put it into words all I got was this tedious long paragraph that still didn't touch the core of it. Then one day a friend of mine here helped me out when we were talking about this and he said, and I can't take credit for this, he said, "Tarantula is the No. We are the No."' Jon sits back, hands on knees, smiling broadly at them.

'No to what?' Hettie says.

'The No to the Yes,' Blake tells her irritably.

'Well, yes,' Jon says, 'though maybe we should unpack that. We need to think, what do we mean by Yes? Whose Yes do we mean? In what context do we mean Yes? So we can begin to determine the status of No.'

'You're a discussion group,' Dia says.

'He said they're the No,' Blake cranes round to tell her.

'I heard. Tarantulans are the No, yeah thanks, got it.'

'That's right,' Jon says, some sheen appearing on his face, 'though we don't actually call ourselves "Tarantulans". We just say "Tarantula".'

'You're all called Tarantula?' Hettie says.

'In a sense, yes, we—'

'So at dinner you all go, "Hello, Tarantula, how are you?" "I'm fine, Tarantula, could you pass the salt? And would you ask Tarantula to stop hogging the butter?"'

'Of course they don't do that,' Blake says.

'They might. And is what she' – Hettie turns to Dia – 'I've forgotten your name.'

'Dia,' says Dia.

'Is what Dia said right? You just talk about stuff?'

'Talk is a part of life here, certainly. No getting away from it.

Like it says on our flyer, we try to imagine the next world. We try to think seriously about the new reality that is already taking shape round every one of us. We ask questions about this new reality. We ask: what place do people have in the new reality? Further, maybe: do people have a place in it at all? How necessary are people to the earth? For us, I think, that's a really important question. How necessary are people? To the earth.'

'So yeah,' Hettie says, 'it's basically just a load of talking.'

'We do other stuff too. You'll notice, when I hand out your schedules, we've organised a series of sessions—'

'Are you a registered charity?' asks Hettie, who is quickly becoming Dia's heroine.

'Uh, we are—'

'Do you get paid or do you work on a voluntary basis?'

'Will you let the nice man speak?' Blake says, with a disgusted stutter.

'I thought we were meant to ask questions. This is orientation, isn't it?'

'It certainly is,' Jon says.

Half an hour later Jon hands the visitors their schedules – artfully handwritten, green-inked lists on the back of squares of embossed wallpaper – the Ormeshers meander away towards their first session, and Dia hangs back while Jon, still sitting in his plastic chair, shuffles dejectedly through the remaining wallpaper squares.

'Jon? Not sure if you remember . . . ?'

'The mysterious lady from The Secret Bar? Give me some credit. I was trying to seem professional. Not that it helped.'

'I think it went well.'

'It didn't go well.'

She is about to object when Annette and Fee come through the door and, under no constraint of professionalism, at once evince their remembrance of her with anime squeeing, and then for a while everyone is throwing arms round everyone else.

'How'd he do?' Annette says. 'You should've seen him, practising in the mirror . . .'

'I made a total dick of myself.' Jon sighs heavily.

'How could you, when you're so cute?' Fee squeezes his squishy face. 'So Dia, what delights do they have in store for you?'

'Right now I'm supposed to be in' – she consults her pretty schedule – 'a session on "Economies of Power".'

'Ugh. Blow it off. Come with us, we're having a brilliant skive.'

'That's a good session,' Jon says.

'You think Dia should to go to Will's dry-as-dust boreathon instead of having a super time with us?'

'Well, I wouldn't put it like *that* . . .'

So Dia and a fractionally less enthusiastic Jon join Annette and Fee for their skive, which becomes a sort of tour, as the others take turns to point out features: the busty big roses in clay urns by the back door; the pond surrounded by rocks and covered with juicy green scum; the disastrous strawberry patch, with its messy melting fruit and unrepellable insects. They end up in a refectory housed in a small brick building next to the farmhouse where several enterprising individuals sit round the benches engaged in Socratic discourse, or writing or drawing on squares of wallpaper, or eating, or sleeping. Fee talks to one of the men working in the kitchen and five minutes later they're leaving with scrounged-up plates of more distorted rustic bread, some intensely flavoured artisanal cheese, and a can apiece of straightforwardly non-rustic, non-artisanal Coke.

They settle for their picnic in a shaggy lawn full of ladybirds. Grass so deep you feel you could pull it over your knees like a blanket.

'It's beautiful here,' Dia says. 'But is it always this windy?'

'Is it windy?' Jon looks round doubtfully.

'It's like living on the flightpath,' Annette says. 'You get used to it.'

'Those murals in the house. They're . . .'

'Fucking mad, we know.' Sitting back from her plate, Annette keeps reeling webs of hair off her face without becoming any more visible. 'Don't worry, we didn't make them, they were here when we arrived. The house, the farm, the whole estate used to belong to an artist who had some sort of "scene" here – that whole Virginia-Woolf, 1920s, experimental-living set. No one could be bothered painting over them, so there they are.'

'If anyone tried to paint over the murals, I think I would kill them,' Fee says.

'No one's going to paint over the murals.' Annette pats her arm.

'They're sort of part of the life of the place, aren't they? We laugh about those Twenties goofs, but at the same time they're precursors. What they did then mirrors what we're doing now.'

The women are interesting. More and more Dia sees how they function as a unit. Fee is sweet, dreamy, hesitating, Annette cool and quick. But there's no mistaking how these traits are shaped by their friendship, emphases created or repressed by the women's interlocking double act. Imaginably Annette without Fee would be subtler, more reflective; Fee without Annette, spikier, hotter-tempered. Dia gets it. A person alone in a room – her only example being herself – is not the first stitch of anyone.

Dia clears her throat: *Hey Jon, did you say my pal Reggie was here? Reggie Glaze? Don't suppose you know where he hangs out? Thought I might catch up* . . . But what comes out of her mouth is: 'Are there other places like this? Other chapters, branches?'

'Just us,' says Annette. 'There are plans to expand, but for now this is it. We scoot about a fair bit with the recruitment drives, couple of weeks at a time in Newcastle, Birmingham – London, obviously – Manchester, obviously . . . obviously . . . But this is our base.'

'And you like it here?'

'In the group? It's the best of the bunch. I managed six months in Friends of the Earth and let me tell you, don't bother, complete bureaucrats. Fee was in Greenpeace, about which I gather ditto—'

'They made nice soups,' Fee says.

'And Jon here, the superstar, he was in Occupy. For *two years*.'

Jon smiles, curiously transfigured: a non-military military man.

'And we all ended up here,' says Annette. 'And yeah, it's the best. By a long way.'

'Good to know.' Dia purses her lips, as if weighing a sizable purchase, at the same time registering the others' unspoken satisfaction. But it's confusing, because no one is really trying to sell her anything. For a moment she wonders if she's got this wrong, if it is not they but she who is on trial over this weekend, if it is she who ought to be selling herself to them, and rapidly she moves the conversation on by directing her gaze up at the farmhouse. 'Well, everything seems to be coming together. Look at this place! Can't imagine what it was like when you moved in!'

She laughs. For the first time, no one laughs with her. A look passes between Fee and Annette. Jon doesn't look at anyone but holds oddly stiff as he inspects his plate.

'It was like this,' he says softly.

'It's Marc's idea,' says Annette. Ah yes: Marc. Dia's been wondering where he'd got to. 'Like it's a sort of withdrawal. A withering away.'

'A withering away of what? The state?'

'Not . . . really,' Annette says.

'A withering away of the people.' Jon inspects his plate. 'Of us.'

In the afternoon she rejoins the Ormeshers for a session called 'Narratives of Capital' run by a small, bespectacled, dark-haired and deeply serious young woman called Pearl. They sit in more stackable chairs in a room on the farmhouse's third floor with a tiny skylight but without either windows or murals to divert attention from Pearl's narrative of narratives, a tale in which its teller is so fervently invested she reminds Dia of the least persuasive of her MA lecturers – critical theory bods with their suffix fixation, turning and turning in grammatical gyres of their own fashioning.

Hettie Ormesher is on excellent squeaky form, soon interrupting to call Pearl on her bullshit, but Pearl is not the easy mark Jon was and instead of getting flustered grows steadily cooler, until by its second half the session has vanished into the seething deadlock of the two women's wills. Blake and Dia roll eyes at each other, a complicity she instantly regrets, and it's then she says she needs to drain the snake and leaves the room.

She walks down through the house, past various clothbound individuals – how many of them are there? Twenty? Two hundred?

She wishes she could get everyone to stand in a line so she could count them – then outside, where a pair of men in the garden seem to recognise her and sit up on their haunches to wave to her. She waves back, keeps walking. Is anyone going to try to stop her? Doesn't look like.

She approaches the gatehouse. Slows then stops next to it, tapping the door as if in thought, but more to see if anything happens, to see if Glen will lurch out with a blunderbuss. Nothing happens. She goes on to the gate, which anyway hangs partly open, and steps out.

Once on the road, she stops to glance back. No one looking, no one following. She's left the farm and no one has noticed. She glances away and starts walking as fast as she can. It occurs to her to run but she doesn't. In her euphoria she wants to apply makeup, smoke a cigarette, sit on an older boy's motorbike.

Of course she's going to find somewhere she can call Samson from, to give him his update. Not that he asked for an update, though she finds it hard to believe he wouldn't want one. She finds it altogether unlikely that Samson wouldn't view a progress report from her as absolutely necessary and to the purpose. And of course this has been her plan right from the moment she stood in the third-floor room and made her excuses. Not at all something that's popped into her head just now, oh, dear me, no.

The road is, if anything, even emptier than it was yesterday. No traffic of any kind: no hikers with their waders and walking poles, no farm vehicles. She glances into the fields on either side but they are likewise unpopulated. And then, far sooner than she expected, she reaches the planky platform with the sign reading 'Born'. She keeps walking.

Half an hour later she comes to a village that must be Born. A wide tiled lane opens into a square with stone cottages on three sides and a pale pub on the fourth. A circle of well-kept grass behind black-painted railings, a modest war memorial. And, yes, an old-fashioned phone box, bright red with the glass panels intact. A period feature, something for the weekending investment bankers, though hopefully one that works. As she heads towards it she's already clicking the pound coins in her pocket.

She opens the phone box and it's a flower shop. Bouquets and posies and pot plants on ingeniously crafted wooden shelves. A handwritten sign on an outsize luggage tag: 'Take what you like, leave what you can. Eileen X'.

So much for calling Samson with an update (which would have been what, anyway? Beyond her listening to his voice – to the wobbly boom of his wild-man voice?). So much, for now, for calling anyone. For now.

She retraces her steps out of the square and starts back along the road. It feels like a long time since she left the farm: there is no possibility she has not been missed. But so what? Her furlough to the village, the exact type of place where she feels least at ease in the world, has reset her bearings, given her a sense of the land. It may be, as Samson would say, 'enemy' territory, but now at least she has charted it.

She passes fields. Passes the platform. A tractor goes by, stunningly. She sees the gate up ahead then passes through it. She sees the gatehouse, sees someone standing next to it, clearly waiting for her. Hardly a shock, all things considered.

She goes striding up to him, her keeper, a broad-shouldered young man in a tight black T-shirt that draws notice to the muscle development of his imperiously crossed arms. Round one of these biceps she notices, too, the knotted black cloth. Then the rest of him: blinky blue eyes, short gelatinous red hair. Oh, for pity's sake.

'Reggie Glaze, as I live and breathe!'

She goes right up to him. The last time she saw Reggie he was – what? – seven, but the bulky lineaments of this scowling twenty-two-year-old cannot conceal him. Inside all that square-jawed freckly tan, his little-boy face peeps out at her. The avid eyes, the girly bob of the nose, the small, malleable lips.

'What are you doing?' he says.

'Been for a walk. That pub any good? Didn't look much cop, but you never know.'

'What are you doing *here*?'

'Reggie. It's Dia. Remember me? Dia Talwar. You might have me in your phone as Dia Robinson.' Last try: 'Claudia Robinson?'

'I know who you are, "Dia". I want to know why you're here.'

'Down for the weekend. For the shits and giggles.' She laughs somewhat freely then goes back to examining him. 'God, Reggie, it's good to see you . . .'

'You shouldn't be here.' He takes a faltering backward step. 'You don't belong here.'

'And you do? Oh-ho, Reggie Glaze, we need a lo-ong conversation . . .'

'We don't need a conversation. I'm telling you to leave. Leave. Fucking leave.'

'Well, that's not very . . .'

But it's already too late. Reggie has turned from her, and now on the track he breaks into a slippery run, and now he disappears past that darkly timbered building on the edge of the farm that she's pretty sure must be a barn.

9. Let's Do That

After a breakfast in the gatehouse that Dia spends largely struggling to process her evening of unintelligible theoretical sessions followed by a second night in the feathery swamp of her guest bed, Glen hands Dia and each of the Ormeshers a rolled-up dusty rug and invites them to follow him outside for their morning session, which he explains will be a practical session, and which he further remarks he will be leading. Immediately suspicious, and unhappily certain that the rug she is carrying under her arm contains a whole ecosystem of antennaed and mandibled life, Dia lags as far behind as she can in the line that Glen directs along a path, over a stile and across a field, then another stile then another field, to a slack and golden meadow in which about a dozen other members of the community are already stretching and unrolling rugs. Among them she sees Fee, who returns her wave only sleepily, a suggestion maybe that at this hour she would rather be left alone.

Even if she hadn't lost it (she has), Dia would not need to consult her schedule now to see her suspicions confirmed. She unrolls her rug anyway, exposes its crackling microcosm to the early sun, as Glen says to the group, 'What better start to a day than my tried-and-tested famous coffee-shop yoga playlist?'

Better than doing yoga? Not doing yoga, that's what. Dia hates yoga, can't do it, and mostly sits the session out, leaning back on her elbows in the fluffy, dandelion-head stuff of the meadow next to her rug rather than on it, while limber Blake knots and unknots himself and soft Hettie bravely strains.

Afterwards Fee comes up full of exasperating post-exercise perkiness. 'Gosh, you look grim! Didn't you enjoy the sesh?'

'Not my thing.'

'No, sure.' For a moment Fee seems to follow a private thread. 'But then there's so much amazing stuff going on here, you sort of take the misses with the hits.'

'I can see that,' Dia says absently.

'Can you?'

'Oh yeah. This place is definitely not like anything I've experienced before.'

'I'm *so* glad to hear you say that.' Fee beams – a lake-like shimmer of exuberance. Then as they walk along she reconnects to that thread of hers. 'About the yoga. I'm just wondering, really . . . Were we doing it wrong?'

'Haven't a clue, Fee mate.'

They are almost back at the farmhouse, and out of the corner of one eye Dia is assessing the stable buildings, wondering how she can get over there to have a look for Reggie, when Fee says, 'Have you talked to Marc yet? Come on, I'll take you to him.' And Dia hasn't said anything when Fee gives a sharp titter and says, 'It's not like I'm "taking you" to him, I'm just . . . taking you to him.'

Fee leads her into the house, past the murals of the ground floor – rings of nudely capering celebrants, exotic cacti and loti, assorted avant-garde doofi – to an office in which Marc sits oppressed by trays of paper and stacks of folders and an unexpectedly modern and minimal desktop. For a few seconds he seems to have no idea why they're there, then he slowly smiles and scratches his forehead and asks if Dia would care to join him for lunch. She says why not.

According to a dynamic slightly too familiar, Fee brings in their lunch: the bread and preserves Dia is already half sick of. She's recalling that pub in Born, speculating about the quality of its bar snacks, when Marc says, 'I'm surprised to see you here.'

'Are you?'

He picks up a pencil and starts shading in a corner of the paper in front of him. 'Quite a lot of people come down here to check us out. Since giving a shit started to be cool again, started to be the organising principle in certain lifestyles, certain ways people go about distracting themselves from the crushing inevitable horror of their personal death and so on. To a number of earnest urban souls, we look like an attractive proposition. Then they come here and they hate it.'

'Now I'm surprised.'

'They hate it. When they realise we're not going to be some accessory for their on-trend conscience. When they realise we mean it.' He shifts his pencil and begins circling the hole punched out of the sheet's margin. 'How can I put this? You don't seem like the type of person who thinks she might be interested in what we're about before she comes down here. You seem like the type of person who is *absolutely certain* she's not interested before she comes anywhere near us.'

A potentially tricky moment. Because of course he's right about her. Wherever she comes from, Dia is a city girl, impatient, impervious, tightly mapped onto the glittering crenels of Inner Mancunia. She doesn't belong within a hundred miles of a place like this. The only honest reply she can give is: *True enough,*

Marc. I don't go in for this back-to-the-garden crap. I'm here under false pretences. You see there's this bloke called Samson Glaze, and I'm saving his life . . .

'Sorry, Marc, I was under the impression it was a broad church you were running here. Welcoming of all sorts and types. Even someone who seems the way I seem.' She picks up a hunk of scribble-shaped bread and brandishes it at him. 'Even, if you don't mind my saying, someone who can sit there talking about how he "means it" while I'm guessing using the local Wi-Fi hotspot to plan his next banging bar crawl.'

Dimly smiling, Marc puts down his pencil, takes a piece of bread too and starts coating it with black syrup full of seed and pith. 'Everyone needs a holiday.'

'A holiday from the death cult.'

'This isn't a death cult.'

'Is your endgame "total annihilation of humanity" or "mass suicide under siege by police"? I imagine that's always the big one for you lot.'

'Naturally we consult with our alien overlords. Have you tried the cheese?'

'On another occasion. The fruity piquancy of deep-fried earwax, I believe.'

He smiles his dim smile. Then he says, 'The human race is wiping itself out.'

'So I hear.'

'Sometimes people struggle with that. And yet it's obviously true. Whether we're talking about chemical weapons or nuclear bombs or ozone depletion or overpopulation, humankind has committed itself to a course of self-destruction. It's just a matter of time now. No more *if*. Only *when*.'

'This is a big Tarantula thing?'

'This is our core tenet. Our central belief.'

'Tell me more.'

His look sharpens – he suspects she is taking the piss. But she isn't, and he sees she isn't.

'For some people the idea of a future without people in it is simply too awful to consider. But here we accept that idea. If human beings have no future, what other futures may be possible? What other worlds may follow the End of People? Fundamentally we exist to ask these questions. To promote these questions in wider consciousness, in what I hesitate to call "the public domain".'

'You want to tell people they're doomed.'

'People know they're doomed, don't they? Deep down. In quiet moments. We all know it. But what do we do with this knowledge? Lash out and wreck everything in some furious last tantrum, burn the pub down and sleep it off in a ditch? Or do we try to think of a future without us? To accept our fate and go quietly, with a shred of dignity and not too much more damage?'

'Big message,' she says.

'Hence the emphasis we put on discussion. On finding new expressions of the radical impulse. No banners, no chants. No angry demos or shambolic sit-ins. Our aim here is to discover an entirely new radicalism.'

While they eat she watches him. His face seems loaded down with its heavy black eyebrows, almost immobilised by them. Indeed at no point in their conversation has he become particularly animated. It strikes her that Marc's defining feature may be the one she noticed about him at The Secret Bar, when he lounged against the wall with his arm over his head, staring past his friends at the earnest zithering musician: boredom. A sort of tuned or sculpted boredom. Then she realises something else: 'Holy shit. You're the leader.'

'We don't have a leader. Tarantula doesn't have a hierarchy of any kind.'

'Bollocks. You are, aren't you? You're the leader.'

She thanks him for lunch and leaves the office unopposed. What now? She has lost her schedule, doesn't know where she is meant to be. What she does know is the session she's missing is the last one. When it ends, the visitor weekend is over and there is nothing for her to do but haul her luggage out of the gatehouse and set off for the station. Which means this is her last chance to find and get through to Reggie. Unless. But no. It's her last chance.

She leaves the farmhouse and strides up the track to the timbered building that she believes is a barn. The first door she reaches stands ajar; she steps inside. And yeah, the building isn't a barn, or not any more it isn't. It's an enormous garage, with a bus suspended off the ground in an impressive system of pulleys and ropes. There are workbenches set up at each corner of the oil-streaked floor. Tyres and vehicle parts lean against the walls. Two women and two men are partly concealed by the bus's underside and doing things to it that clatter and shrill. And yeah, one of the two men is Reggie.

Reluctant to be the cause of an accident, she stands in the doorway and waits. One of the women sees her, says something to the others that she can't hear. Then Reggie looks round, sees her, looks away again. He continues working for what feels like a very long time. Then the other man unties and begins letting out a rope while Reggie and the women lower the bus to the ground with almost superhuman smoothness, until the final instant, which fills with an astonishing metallic clanging and a chaotic whoofing of rust and dust particles. Then Reggie goes to one of the workbenches, picks up a rag, wipes his face with it, throws the rag back onto the workbench and turns and walks blank-faced to her at the door.

'What do you want?'

Good question. What she wants is in fact fairly complicated. It would take time to explain, but she doesn't have any. She could do it if she had clarity of mind, but she doesn't have that either. Nothing to do with the fact that young Reggie here has been working with his shirt off. Other than the black cloth, still knotted round his cuboid right bicep, he is naked to the waist. Suddenly she's struggling to do anything but look into it, into the chromium matrix of Reggie's upper body.

Reggie Glaze. She remembers when Reggie learned about jokes. For a month all he wanted to do was pull you into a corner with him and tell you jokes. Except five-year-old Reggie had not yet worked out what they were, so his jokes always started with something like, 'Why did the tea towel cross the road?' and you had to say, 'I don't know, Reggie, why did the tea towel cross the road?' and the punchline was, 'Because the seashells had jam on their face!' or some other mad crap. He laughed his head off, because he knew at least that was what jokes were for, and everyone else laughed too. And he would go on like this ('Why did the door handle cross the road?' 'Why did the paperclip cross the road?') until Samson stuck his head up out of whatever he was doing and shouted, 'Reggie! Those jokes are *rubbish*!' And everyone laughed at that too. Even Reggie. He didn't mind. Sitting there in his mismatched pyjamas – top half ThunderCats, bottom half Strawberry Shortcake – he tipped his head back and laughed too.

That's Reggie Glaze. So who the hell is this?

'Got time for a chat?' she says.

'We don't have anything to chat about.'

'Oh, I think we do.'

His facial expressions seem exaggerated, like mime, but that may be because she's staring at them so hard. 'What would that be? Apart from what you can do to make me leave.'

'What?' Her voice is so faint she barely hears herself. But then it has to compete with the sound of all her prepared paragraphs falling out of her head. She honestly thought this part was going to be easy. *Now, young Reggie, you listen to your Auntie Dee* . . . Holding his hand while he blinked up at her, eager and freckly. When did she forget that he was twenty-two?

'That's right, isn't it? All you're interested in is what you can do, or say, to make me leave. You're here because my father sent you. He told you, it doesn't matter what he told you. I'd gone mad. I was "having problems". I was "vulnerable" and a bunch of psychos had got their hooks into me. I was being exploited, and he was so dreadfully worried . . .'

'Reggie, I've not seen your dad in fifteen years.'

'You're lying.'

'I'm not.' She is, and the sound of it – like the triangle in the school orchestra – seems to *ting ting ting* from every plane of her skin.

'You come poking round Tarantula and it's got nothing to do with my father and nothing to do with me and it's just a massive coincidence, is it?'

She opens her mouth, shuts it again. The quarter of her brain not occupied with not looking at Reggie's chest is more or less paralysed by the shockwaves still emanating from 'I've not seen your dad in fifteen years'. Where did that come from? When did that become part of the plan?

'I don't want you to leave,' she says slowly.

His blue eyes blink. His arms do something but she's not looking at them.'Why would I want you to leave?' And everything is clear. She steps towards him and says, 'I'm here, Reggie, because I want to join Tarantula.'

'Don't make me laugh.'

'I've been thinking about it for a while. You know how it is. You grow up surrounded by all that, Thin Love, the fires, the *dogs*, and nothing else compares. Like the rest of your life is finding out nothing else is going to make you that happy. Then a couple of weeks ago I ran into Jon, got talking, and he mentioned you. Told me about his pal Reggie Glaze who he bombs about with down on the farm. That's why I'm here. Yes I knew you were here, and yes I came because I want to talk to you. To get your advice. About my decision to join Tarantula.'

The mime-artist expressions on Reggie's face offer no hint that he believes her. But then, she thinks, there is a hesitant note when he says, 'My advice.'

'Get the benefit of your insider perspective and whatnot.'

He nods without quite doing that.

'If you can spare a minute, maybe we can go somewhere, and—'

'This has to happen now?'

'Why not now? We could go now—'

'Before the end of the visitor weekend.'

'I'm not saying we go *a mile*, just somewhere quiet where we can—'

'Bullshit,' Reggie says. He steps back, his eyes flickering curiously: darting all round but not at her. His friends in the garage glance up from their tasks.

'This is not bullshit, Reggie, this is me trying to *talk* to you about an important—'

'Get to fuck,' he says loudly. His eyes darting, darting.

'Everything good, Reg?' It is one of the garage women, wiping her armpits with a rag as she walks towards them.

'Well, hello, sunshine,' Dia calls to the woman. 'Me and Reggie, we're kind of talking here, so if you wouldn't mind—'

'Get to fuck, Dia.' This is Reggie, lowering the great cubes of his arms, struggling to focus on her. 'And don't come near me again, you . . . *crone*.'

'Me what?'

But it's useless. The woman is there, judging by her stance some stubbly bit of a new girlfriend, and now the other woman, and even the other man, hanging back. No question about it, these brawny young people are extremely pissed off with her. She turns and right behind her there's Fee.

'Hey, Dia!' Fee sways from side to side. 'Are you making friends?'

'More like renewing an acquaintance.'

'Oh! I didn't realise you knew people here. Oh, golly, I hate this. Because it's time to go. It's the end of the weekend and it's time to say goodbye.'

Outside the gatehouse Hettie is standing with the Ormesher suitcase while Glen with a rolling or a flattened palm directs

Blake in edging the Ormesher Vauxhall Astra back onto the track. Progress is slow. By the time Dia returns from her room with her travel bag Glen and Blake are struggling to free the car from a midtrack rut while Hettie, oblivious, unconcerned, stands gorging her eyes and thumbs on her newly restored phone.

Jon, Annette and Fee slope over, a cheerful farewell party. At last the car judders free, Blake gets out to offer everyone his disconcertingly wet and lifeless hand, Hettie bestows on each her baby-powder air kisses, then the Ormeshers meander inexorably to their car and set out with studied evenness for the road.

'Last we'll see of them,' Jon says.

'So what?' Annette smiles dazzlingly. 'They were knobs.'

'Here we go.' Glen, coming over, slaps Dia's phone into her hand. 'Take it easy the first couple of hours. No Candy Crush for a day. Mad over-stimulating.'

'It was lovely seeing you again,' Annette says to her.

'It really was,' Fee says.

Jon doesn't say anything, only stands with lowered eyes and silently moving lips.

Dia stands there for as long as it feels viable for her to do that. Then she keeps on doing that. Because of course she can't go. But of course she can't stay. What she said to Reggie was patter, a spiel to separate him from his garage cronies, get him walking, talking, imitating her body language, falling in with her rhythms. But it didn't work. And so she has to go. But she can't go. But she can't stay.

'Hey,' she says. 'Hey.'

But she can't. But she can't. Reggie said *crone*. He said *you crone*. Me what? But she can't. But Samson said *you are here for a great reason*. He always said it. He said *you will perform a great work*. But I'm not six years old any more and I don't believe in fairytales. Even if I did. What? Stay? Stay and save Reggie? Stay and usher in the end of humankind? All or none of the above? All or. But I can't.

'What if I stay?'

They look at her.

'What if I join, what if I stay?'

'Join Tarantula?' Annette seems aghast at the idea.

'Yeah. What about that?'

'People normally want to think about it.'

'Yeah. I don't think I want to think about it.'

'There's a "cooling-off period",' Jon says, 'then Glen or someone gives you a call . . .'

'Yeah. I don't think I need a call. I think I just want to join up.'

'You mean right now?' Fee says.

'Yeah. I mean right now.'

But nothing happens right now. Jon and Annette stump back to the farmhouse while Fee stands with her next to the gatehouse, as if it's school and Dia has been fighting with another girl and has to be kept in a quiet zone until the teacher arrives. Well, she doesn't care. Doesn't care? She's delighted. Ecstatic. Apoplectic. She wants to break things and fuck things. Samson will think she's gone mad. The people standing near her in the quiet zone look at her like they think she's gone mad. Let them – she wants them to look at her like that. Because after long and exhausting absence here she is once again where she should always have been, at the centre of the mirrorball, teeth bared and fists raised amid the sparkstorm of her brilliance. Because at last she is the danger woman, the trouble woman, all or nothing, do or die.

Marc comes out. Others trail after him, intrepid ones and twos, but with his owlish, admin eyes he shooes them back.

'I hear you're thinking of coming onboard.'

'That's right.' She knew it: knew he was the leader.

'Did anyone mention there's a "cooling-off"—'

'Not interested, don't need it. Sign me up.' But he only stares at her with those spreadsheet-dimmed eyes. 'Do I need to make a . . . contribution? No problem. Is it a set amount or an "all my worldly goods" sort of arrangement? Because that's not going to come to much.' Or is it? She recalls the twenty grand Samson generously added to her account.

'No,' Marc says, 'that's not how we work.'

'So how *do* you work?'

He seems to be trying to remember who she is. Then he rouses himself and says, 'I could show you . . . ?'

'Let's do that.'

He starts towards the farmhouse, waving for her to follow. With Annette, Fee and Jon she rounds the corner of the house after him and comes into the yard at the back door with the clay urns full of strumpet roses and a stump she's not noticed before, a flat cross-section of tree about the height of a Labrador. Marc moves the stump into the middle of the yard, gestures to Annette, who with a white and thin-lipped look goes into the farmhouse, then makes everyone wait a ludicrous, embarrassing, eyerolling length of time before she returns going, 'Sorry, sorry,' with something in her hands which she passes to Marc.

'This is what we ask. An exchange. We give you this' – he holds up the something Annette passed him, which is a square of pristine black cloth – 'and we ask for that.'

At first she thinks he means her hand: she thinks the price of admission to Tarantula is one human hand. Then she sees he is pointing at her phone.

'You put it there' – now he points at the stump – 'and you take this' – he picks up and shows her a brick that was lying in the yard – 'and you do what you have to.'

'I smash up my phone.'

'Or nothing. Do nothing, go away, have a hot bath, think it over . . .'

'Not necessary.' She puts the phone (her phone, as she was just starting to think of it; Weland's phone, as it is once again) on top of the stump and goes to Marc and pulls the brick from between his fingers.

She looks round. Annette smiling as if posing for a photographer at a distant cousin's wedding. Jon whispering to himself with lowered eyes. Fee, grinning, holding up discreet double thumbs. And Marc, gazing serenely into the sky, as if worried about rain.

She looks at the phone on the stump. For a moment she senses how hard this would be to do if the phone were truly her phone – how the act of smashing her own phone would enmesh her in self-violence of a sort strange and terrible to contemplate. If she were not so close to doing it she suspects she would never have realised how strange, how terrible. Like smashing a face. Not her own face, but someone's.

She brings the brick down on the phone. No visible damage. Almost disappointed, she changes her grip on the brick, brings it down again to produce blazing white scuffs on the screen. Emboldened she strikes again. The screen caves into itself. A fourth strike and the phone's innards come spilling, cells, combs, stacked intensities, as of a vandalised hive.

In the end Marc comes forward and flexes his hands between her eyes and the top of the stump. She glances up at him as if from a daze. The phone is gone, completely gone, and all that's left is this shrapnelled unnatural muck.

'That's enough,' he's saying. 'You can have this now.' She straightens and with an almost wilful absence of ceremony he hands her the black cloth.

'I'm signed up then,' she says. 'I'm one of you.'

'You're one of us. You're Tarantula. Now you just have to decide what you're going to do with that.'

He means the black cloth. She looks at it. And he's wrong: there is no decision to make. And before Fee and Annette and Jon can crowd round her she has rolled the cloth into a tube, arranged the tube in a loose knot, passed her hair through the knot then pulled the black cloth tight, tighter, tightest at the humming base of her skull.

10. Pure Thoughts Only

Lila once said, 'You know what your problem is, kid? You don't think you know all the answers – even you're not that daft. But you think you know all the questions.'

Not having the faintest idea what her mother was talking about, ten-year-old Dia just said, 'No I don't.'

'That's why you're always talking, is it?' Lila laughed. They were sitting on the concrete stub they called the 'balcony': nine floors of vacant blaze and washing-line air going down to the cracked pavements of Sycamore Lane. One of those afternoons when they lolled facing each other on garden chairs while Lila rubbed suncream into both their arms. 'You listen to me. When in doubt, shut your mouth. Chances are, the questions you need answers to are ones you've not even thought of yet. Golden rule, kid. The sound you don't make asks better questions than the one you do.'

In sunglasses and shorts, Lila stretched towards the sun. And this was the problem with Lila. If there were nothing but *off* days it would have been easy to despise her, disregard her; but there were these *on* days too, when everything about her was on, switched on, cranked to its highest setting, and she laughed and said things you'd never forget and stretched herself luxuriously into the fire of the sky.

When in doubt, shut your mouth. Lila probably had in mind

the quandaries posed by temporary work, but Dia supposes the principle may as well apply to Day One as a full member of Tarantula, a day she spends largely contending with her shock at the sleeping arrangements – her new bed in the farmhouse, an ancient rack of springs and perished down in a row of twelve such beds, all conservatively occupied by women, in a cobwebbed gallery room that extends across half the attic – and at the perfect madcap lunacy of her decision to join the group. By the time she comes clattering down for breakfast in the ragbag assortment of clothes generously loaned her by her new roommates, in wash-whipped jeans and porridgey shirt, yesterday's sparkstorm has concentrated to a pinging throat panic that keeps almost forming her lips into the words of an excuse, an apology, a simple misunderstanding easily accounted for, and now, if no one especially minds, she'll just be popping on her way . . . It is not simply that she can't imagine how she is going to explain all this to Samson (though she can't). For now she is struggling to explain it to herself.

A few days, she thinks. If joining up buys her a few days in which to talk Reggie round or otherwise devise some means of getting him out of here, then everything still makes sense. Her plan holds, her intentions cohere. She is saving Samson's life, because he saved hers. Because huge gestures came out of the sky and swept her life away – her job, her bank account, all her cover from the wind and rain – and with magic fingertips on a screen he restored it to her. Undeniably there's still the question of how did that happen, of how did that work, of what, what, what, but this is nothing but panic.

In fact half the panic turns out to be hunger, and after a breakfast of sticky bread and scalding tea she recommits herself to a scheme of keeping her mouth shut and letting other people discover the questions she needs answers to. Other people, in this case, turns out to be Jon, who has walked her through the amenities of the farm (bathrooms, mealtimes; the whimsical convention whereby everyone makes their own breakfast when it suits them in the farmhouse kitchen, while lunch and dinner are communal affairs, formally seated in the brick refectory next door) and even granted her a glimpse of the men's bedroom, which he refers to as 'the gents' quarters' and which is a gallery room taking up the other half of the attic from the women's bedroom, its mirror image in every regard, plus the raw-meat fug of male self-negligence, before it occurs to her to ask, 'So is this Orientation, Part Two?'

'Orientation . . . ?' He squints at her, his head dropped to one side. Then slowly his eyes clear. 'Oh, no. This isn't part of my job, I'm just . . .'

'You're just being nice.'

'Yeah. Yeah, goddamit. I'm just being nice.'

Day Two is the shape of things – the shapes inside the shapelessness, of which she learns there is a great deal. Mouth strategically shut, she waits for someone to introduce her to the Tarantula equivalents of cultic stricture, and yet no one does that.

It's a strange system. After lunch, after a morning of not so much playing cricket as continually losing and then spending a long time looking in the long grass everywhere for a ball with Jon, Fee, Annette and a couple of cheerful others she forgets to ask the names of, she finds herself at a loose end. She locates Marc in the refectory, alone, gloomily turning the pages of a Japanese comic. When she asks if there is anything she should be doing, he only shrugs and says, 'Do what needs doing.' Right. Thanks. But this is as much deliberate direction as in two days she sees anyone receive. Look about, see what needs doing and do it. A system so open to abuse, so frankly pleading to be abused, no one seems to abuse it.

Still the day reveals shapes. Tarantula to the idle eye may resemble a holiday camp or arts-and-crafts getaway, but on closer inspection it begins to disclose the curves of its structures. Marc may not be the leader but he has his coterie, his personal guard consisting of (who else but) Annette, Fee and Jon. They so manifestly comprise a group within and above the larger group she can only imagine she didn't recognise it as such because she herself belongs to it. Does she? It appears she does.

Then in the afternoon she comes upon them in a muralled room at the back of the ground floor, Marc seated in a stackable chair, Fee and Annette standing with folded arms, Jon making his way on all fours across a series of sheets of paper laid out across the floor, as if playing a lonely game of Twister, and the air of the muralled room refuses to shed its chill. Jon with a gulp of laughter flails up out of his Twister contortions and says, 'Hey, Dia – we're planning the next recruitment drive. Big flyer drop. We're looking at designs . . .' These are the sheets on the floor: flyer designs. Text and image seized in place by the crosshairs of publisher software. 'Any thoughts?' But only Jon's smile has any space in it; Fee's and Annette's keep passing endlessly into space, while Marc cannot raise his look from the forefinger suspended preciously over his lips. She is not wanted here, she has intruded, overstepped an invisible boundary. She sees it pretty well immediately; only poor Jon with his darting smile goes on struggling to work it out. Still she waits out their awkwardness, then finally says, 'Nah, you're all right,' and stalks away to the front of the house and the yellow grass that in the sunlight looks as though it has caught superbly aflame.

Later that afternoon she hits on a name for them, for the clique that surrounds Marc: the Marcsmen. It is a stupid name, she knows, unkind and inaccurate, but it sticks in her head even long after she has stopped being annoyed with them.

There are other groups. At dinner in the refectory, while some well-intentioned youth fails to do a lot more than publicly fail to tune his guitar, she notices Reggie sitting with his friends from the garage: the other man and the two women. As far she can tell, the four of them spend the duration of the meal silently and dourly presenting his or her profile to the room as if all auditioning for the same modelling job.

'They seem a lively bunch,' Dia says to her tablemates.

Annette follows the line of her spoon. 'The Handsomes?'

'Is that what you call them?'

'Somewhat unbelievably, it's what they call themselves.'

'We call them that as well,' Jon says, 'but when we do it we're taking the piss.'

Day Three is the police raid.

She's lying in bed in the attic when she hears the first shout. Not yet familiar enough with her new environment to know whether or not this is anything out of the ordinary, she sits up anyway. None of her roommates has stirred at the sound. She listens.

Somewhere outside, beyond the mutter of the very early morning, a conversation is in progress. The shout she heard was a crackle of heat rising out of this conversation. Voices of men;

two, then three. Then a woman's voice. She's already losing interest when another shout breaks free of the conversation, then another and another. All four voices shout. Still no one else in the room has stirred. Then there's the vast unmistakable quack of a police siren, hastily stifled, the electronic pip of police radios, and everyone else in the room sits up.

'What the hell—'

'Pete's sake—'

Fee, three beds away, yawns expressively. But it's Annette, in T-shirt and shorts, who goes with another woman to the window and looks out and says, 'Bobby on the beat.'

'How many?' Fee stretches both fists above her head.

'Too few for punch, too many for cocktails.' Grinning fixedly, Annette flaps a happy little hand at the window. 'Hel*lo*, motherfuckers.'

This and the demeanour of the women as they dress and go out – something like a fire drill in student accommodation – reassures Dia that these unfolding events have at least some precedent, and she follows her roommates down the skreeking stairs to the kitchen, where various of the men are pulling on jumpers, pushing away yawns on the back of a hand. She is heading for the door when she feels a light touch on her arm.

'Have something, won't you?' It's Pearl, the intense theorist of Saturday afternoon, this morning with a pleasant scattered quality. She gestures at the kitchen table, where bowls of cereal and pots of tea are rapidly appearing while men and women press from every side. 'May be the only chance you get!'

It seems weird, standing there in the crowded kitchen, slurping bran-based cereal and drinking tea and listening to dazed breakfast small talk while the air outside fills with shouts, further siren quacks, further radio pips. But at last the wisdom sinks in: only the amateur plod-wrangler goes roaring out of doors in his dressing gown. The professional, the expert, makes sure she is fed and watered before she crosses any threshold.

Then Tarantula goes out. Not quite together, in runs and rivulets, Dia in the lead run with the Marcsmen, though the others follow closely enough.

Up ahead Marc and Glen are shouting at two police officers standing on the other side of the gate. In the road behind the officers – a man and a woman – the bodywork of police vehicles sickly flashes. Dia cranes to see how many, but hedges block her view. She thinks four, maybe five, vans and cars. She thinks of them coming up the road, passing the village in convoy, lightless and sirenless, a state secret on wheels.

To left and right she notices people slowing, halting. She glances round: Tarantula has stopped on the track at a non-intimidating distance from the gate. Jon lets out a terrific sneeze and slings an arm across Fee's shoulders. Annette keeps going towards the gate. Dia watches her, joining Marc and Glen at the gate, then starts walking again and joins them also at the gate.

'Redefinition of piss-take,' Marc is saying hoarsely. His voice is so big and hollow she understands at once that he's furious. And his face is full of a slippery, sharkish grin she could never have imagined seeing there. 'You know that, don't you?'

'Perfectly standard procedure,' the female officer says levelly, 'we hear "drugs"—'

'You hear "drugs" where? From who? Does it even matter?'

'We have our sources,' the officer says, 'credible, material—'

'If it's that Crawley moron again, I can tell you right now he's covering for the scrota he scores weed off at school—'

'You know we can't—'

'At that scrummy, yumptious sweet shop of hegemony, the local *school*—'

'Don't start that shit,' the male officer says abruptly, with foul force. 'We're coming in so get the fuck out of our way.'

Dia's first thought is to say something ('What's the problem here?'), but her second (*When in doubt, shut your mouth*) prevails. Unhappily, almost painfully, with bursting lips and stinging gums, she keeps silent.

'Get out of the way,' the male officer roars, and shoves the gate.

'Friend,' Glen says, 'you are *mad* rude,' and he shoves the gate back.

Both officers slam at the gate, spinning Glen off it. Marc holds his hands in the air in a gesture that appears to express as much annoyance with Glen as with the officers.

'Make way, guys,' Marc calls hoarsely down the track. Then, with defeated irony: 'Make way, make way, for the Royal Hunt of the Sun.'

Dia goes to Glen; with a jarred look he waves her away. Next to them the gate has opened and the female officer stands with a hand steadying it while her male colleague leads a procession of officers onto the farm. At Marc's instruction the mass of Tarantula has begun to separate to either side of the track, allowing the officers to pass. At the sight of these officers, Tarantula gives an interesting response. Because in black padded gear, with helmets and shields and batons, here come the storm troopers, here comes the riot squad. And Tarantula, shuffling in turn to either side of the track to allow these visitors to pass, has started to laugh.

*

They stand in lines on the deep lawn in front of the farmhouse. Half a dozen of the black-clad officers patrol them while the male officer who spoke at the gate occasionally drones something into a megaphone. More officers stride about the farm, entering buildings in groups of three and four. By Dia's count nine officers have so far entered the farmhouse. Every few seconds their investigations are signalled by a crash, a muffled thump, a series of skittering smashes inside.

She glances down at her feet. They are almost completely hidden by the thick grass. She sees a ladybird making its tortuous way along the lace of one of her trainers and realises she is standing in the same spot where she sat eating a picnic with Annette, Fee and Jon in Saturday's blowy lunchtime sun.

'Everyone nice and calm,' the policeman drones into his megaphone. 'Taking a break from the midweek grind.'

She glances up and sees Glen standing in the line in front of hers, three places to her right. He keeps shaking his head, ditheringly up and down as well as from side to side. It occurs to her that the knock he took at the gate may have imparted some serious injury, tries to remember whether or not anything made contact with his head, but can't. At his sides his hands clench into fists then smartly unclench. She notices that this happens each time there comes an especially loud noise of damage from inside the farmhouse. Then he glances left, right and behind, and she locks eyes with him. Under his lank grey hair, his teeth are gritted; his stubble is in zigzags. Mild, mellow Glen of the gatehouse: he is the angriest person she has seen in her life.

'Breathe that air,' comes the megaphone drone. 'Feel that wind on your face . . .'

She scans the lines for Reggie but does not see him. At the

centre of the first line she sees Marc. Whatever sharkish life animated him at the gate, it has vanished utterly. Hands pressed to his lower back, with slumped shoulders and head, like a postgrad at a bus stop, he somehow manages to occupy precisely the position you'd expect the leader to occupy while communicating nothing of a leader's spooky presence. He looks as if at any moment his more assertive and worldly friends will summon him with a shout, and he'll lope off to take a smilingly silent role in the backseat of their conversation.

Finally the officers come out of the farmhouse. They form a line facing the first line of Tarantula. The officers who have been ruinously exploring the outbuildings march along the paths, across the grass, and join this line. For a second Dia thinks they're going to charge – thinks the armoured officers are going to raise their shields and batons and smash their way into the defenceless mass of Tarantula.

'No surprises, people. You know the routine. God help you, if you don't by now.'

And with a palpable air of relief the officers step out of formation and walk towards the first line and start to frisk the people in it.

Nothing unusual. At the officers' surly request the friskees make themselves into human stars, which the officers pat and pick at. Nothing you wouldn't see at an airport. But something is wrong. Despite the informal tone of the exercise there is a lag to it that makes Dia stiffen. She glances at Annette, standing to her immediate left, and her face is a taut white blank with a grimace erased from it or submerged in it.

When the exercise reaches her line, she sees why. One of the officers approaches Jon, who obligingly stars himself. But the policeman barely skirts Jon's silhouette with his hands before moving on to the next person. This next person is a woman, no one Dia knows. The woman makes a star and the policeman's hands explore it. Dia cannot see the face of either the woman or the officer, but she sees, as they all see, the gloved hand on the jeaned thigh. She feels the seconds tick into minutes before the officer concludes his search and moves on.

'Hey,' Dia says to Annette. 'What was that?'

But Annette doesn't reply. The officer moves to her and with the grimace squirming inside her expressionless expression she parts her legs, raises her arms, tilts her chin. The officer does not look at her face. He looks at her chest. He crouches and slides his hands over each of her feet. He begins sliding his hands over her ankles, calves. He rises into a crouch and moves his hands over her thighs. Then with a swirling gesture his hand goes between her legs. *When in doubt . . .*

'Whoa,' Dia says. 'Whoa, officer, what's this?'

There is no possibility that he hasn't heard her. And yet the officer goes on exactly as if he has not heard her. His other hand finds Annette's behind. Then he straightens and his hands scroll up her sides to her stomach, her chest. Then he steps away from her, towards Dia.

As Annette drops her arms and closes her legs the grimace that was never quite on her face leaves it. And there is only the blank – whitening, tightening.

The officer looms in front of Dia. Through the visor she tries to catch his eye. But he does not look at her face. His gaze has already passed to her body. *When in doubt . . .*

'Oy,' she says. 'Don't even think about trying that bollocks on with me.'

Still not looking at her face, the officer flicks a finger: assume the position. Her arms and legs feel welded together. He flicks again, but still she doesn't move. And now he does look up. A round bland dish of a face, rosy with health. The look in his eyes is almost one of hurt. An idiot princeling, indulged from the second he was born by his whole idiot clan.

She narrows her gaze testily. 'Okay, officer? We have an understanding?'

His eyes focus somewhere beyond her face. He nods mechanically. And, clamping her jaws together, transferring the pressure, she fans her legs and arms into the cold air.

The officer crouches and slides his hands over her feet.

'I'm serious. Don't even think. Empty your mind.'

He begins dragging his hands over her ankles, calves.

'Officer? Pure thoughts only, yeah?'

He rises into a crouch and moves his hands over her thighs. Then his hand makes a swirling motion and passes between her legs. *When in doubt, shut your mouth.* But she is not in doubt, not in doubt at all, and anyway she is not her mother's daughter and anyway she has never taken advice particularly well and so she says, '*Fuck* off,' and pushes him off her and the officer falls sharply backwards into the grass.

Dia knows police. In her trouble years she had dealings with all the kinds of officer there are, and she knows there are good ones (the ones who took her back to Sycamore House with a football-sized cast on her left hand) and bad ones (the ones in the Hampshire police van, the one with the squelching laugh, the one with the purple thumbnail, the one with the cat-litter smell of hatred); she knows there are innumerable ones in between, ones who are just people. But the officers here are unlike any she has ever encountered. And as the dish-faced prick who touched her where he had no business touching her scrambles up from the grass, she wonders if she knows why.

On the Tarantula farm there are no mobile devices. The certainty these officers have here that they have nowhere else is that, whatever they do, no one is going to take a picture, film a film. And what was it Samson said, that thing she loathed and raged at and refused to accept: 'How good are people? Let me tell you, Dee: people are as good as the pair of eyes they believe is on them. No better, no worse.' The officer lurches at her. Behind its visor his face has turned a deep shocking red. His eyes are small and flat and glossy with injury.

'*Hunh*,' he says.

The baton in his right hand goes up.

'You're fucking *joking*,' she says.

And the officer goes spiralling down into the grass.

It takes her another moment to see that Jon is lying on top of him. That Jon has run down the line and hurled himself at the officer and knocked him to the ground.

What Dia knows about police is that, good, bad, indifferent or weird, this is a poor move. But it's too late. Before she can get a hold on Jon to pull him out of harm's way, two more officers come surging down the line. She thrusts herself in front of one, shouting and flinging her arms, blocking or at least distracting him, but she can do nothing about the other, who marches straight past her and crunches his baton across the back of Jon's head.

'Line two,' drones the megaphone voice. 'Hero complex in line two.'

As the baton strikes him, Jon clasps the officer he has assaulted more tightly. Two more, then two more officers crowd round him. In a circle they go to work with their batons. She sees Jon release the man he's been clasping and curl into a ball on the grass. Then, as the officers hunker into their labour, she can't see him at all. At the edge of a helmet she notices the frisky flip of a blonde ponytail, not quite neatly tucked away.

She spins and sees Reggie. It turns out he has been standing almost directly behind her this whole time. He is snarling; he appears to be crying. And he appears to be the only Tarantula on the lawn who is trying to do something, to burst in on the circle of police officers and help Jon. But two men are holding him back. Reggie is big, and his two friends are struggling. One is kneeling next to him with both arms round his thighs; the other seems to be trying to get a grip on his chest, as if preparing to lift a barrel. Reggie snorts and weeps but his friends are true. He will not get free. He will not help Jon.

One o'clock. The raid is over. The officers have withdrawn to their vehicles on the road.

'I don't think it's as bad as it looks,' Jon says, though it indeed looks bad. A newly mellow Glen crouches in front of him, wiggling a finger in an airy loop to see if Jon can follow it – to see if Jon's eyes both still work. It's not yet clear that they do.

And again Dia is in fighting-girl quarantine, with Annette and Fee vaguely crowding her on a corner of the lawn. People keep coming over to speak to Annette, or to Fee, but not to her; they leave without having so much as looked at her.

'They do that?' She shoots her arms at her minders in a way that she realises, too late, was more alarming than she intended. 'They just come up here and do that?'

'It happens,' Fee says, with quiet firmness.

'And you let them? You just *let* them?'

'That's right, we let them.' Fee seems to be struggling to control a temper Dia didn't know about. 'But it's not "just". You shouldn't say "just".'

Annette won't look at her. Erect, arms folded, she stares into a space on the near side of the farmhouse, a lit wreath of yellow leaves.

'Fuck this.' Dia turns. If they're not letting her near the rest of the group, she can at least go to talk to the police.

She keeps expecting one of the women to call after her. Neither does.

She reaches the gate. The police have gone, with their vans and cars. But someone else is there, standing hands in pockets at the side of the road, in his black perma-suit and sunglasses, with his dyed-black hair and withered white cheeks. Weland – Weland Frost.

'What the fuck?' she says.

'Are you all right?'

'What are you doing here?'

'I'm keeping an eye out. Are you all right?'

'Fuck you and your fake concern.' It's not fake. His face is a startled bone.

'You're upset. But are you all right?'

'Did you see what those cunts did?'

'I did. So are you all right?'

'Fuck you, Weland. Why are you even here? Because of Reggie?'

'Yes. Because of Reggie.'

'Why don't you talk to him then? Go and have a lovely chat with Reggie?'

'Can't do that.'

'No? Then what's the plan, Weland? Or is this it? You lurking in the woods, popping out every once in a while to give me a heart attack or whatever?'

'I wasn't lurking.'

'Course you weren't. Come on then, come back with me and introduce yourself. Shake hands, press some flesh. Meet the gang.'

'Can't do that.'

'Oh no?'

'Can't do it.'

'Fuck you, Weland.' Because of course he is here. She has been at the farm for five days and in all that time she has communicated no word, no palliative update to Samson. And so naturally this weird henchman or sidekick has been dispatched to find out what the hell she is up to. A reasonable question. What the hell *is* she up to? And at last her disgust, with herself, her forgetfulness, her sheer wheeling ineptitude, and with him, oh yes, with him too, is enough to get her off the road, through the gate, onto the wet and skiddy track back towards the farm and Tarantula and the detritus of the day. He doesn't follow, this Weland, this woods-lurker, this whoever he is, though his voice wavers down the track after her:

'Yes. Yes. But you're all right?'

Everything is ruined. Any glance in any direction shows more of it, exhaustingly. Somehow arm in arm with Fee she ends up going through the farmhouse, the scrape of crockery under every footfall in the kitchen, with its overturned table like a gigantic dead Cubist insect; the drift of cushion innards from slashed couches in the sitting room; the reek of dumped and kicked-apart boxes in the storeroom, all smashed eggs and broken cauliflower heads; then the chaos of the bedrooms, where as if in compensation for the unbreakable bedsteads the visitors have cut every sheet and in at least three places attempted to knock a hole through the wall. Dia keeps it together until they come to the back door and the clay urns shattered on the yard tiles, the roses churned to a mud of petals, and she lets out a shout of pure fury.

Fee hugs all the different bits of Dia's back. 'Something like this happens every few months. We practically have it marked on the calendar.'

'Is it always this bad?'

'Maybe not this bad. Marc says there was a real stinker about a year ago, just after the first lot arrived here and started getting the group going. You should ask him about it, it sounds *chronic*. But you'll see. We're incredible. Two days and you won't know anything happened. We sweep and we stitch, and woodland creatures come out of the forest and they help too . . .'

Glen and Will the Economics Bore hoist Jon into a seat made of their joined arms and set off to carry him down the road to Born, where they will call an ambulance for him from the village pub. With some pale hauteur, Annette accompanies them.

Dia and Fee join two other women in the effort of clearing out the spoilt food. They fill then empty sacks onto what promises to be the largest and most noxious compost heap in history. By late afternoon they're down to walking the hallways picking up individual bits of eggshell while two singing men pirouette about them with mops and buckets. There is some collective human beatbox, in which Dia takes no more than a featuring role.

They break when the refectory team comes round with some

bulbs of ragged bread and a miraculously unscathed pallet of lager. The cheer that greets this small divinity is muted, as if the first tumult of rebel joy, the general refusal to be dispirited, has begun to fade. Sitting on the floor, eating her bread tufts and swigging from her can, Dia sees everyone stalled wherever they'd been working, sitting on the floor, eating their bread tufts, swigging from their can also.

They work in the bedrooms until evening, when Pearl comes up to tell them there's a meeting. At the bottom of the skreeking stairs they find the kitchen swept and scrubbed with the table pushed against the wall and people coming in from other rooms and outside to sit on the scuffed boards. Fee is doing a slightly irritating thing of pretending to be Dia's baby ('I'm a tiny infant, you have to carry me in your arms'), and assuming it's the day catching up with her Dia plays along, guiding Fee to the floor then sitting with Fee's head in her lap as Marc crosses to the front of the room and, leaning back against the table, addresses them:

'We're all knackered, so I'll keep this short. I just want to say I'm proud of us. I'm always proud of us but on a day like today it's pride through the roof. The way we get up, pull together, hose off the bullshit and carry on carrying on – it makes me so proud I could wave my willy at you all. I may do that. I'm tired and vulnerable, so let's see how things develop. But really, the way we put something like this behind us, the way we move on—'

'Is that what we're doing?'

With everyone else Dia cranes round to see who has spoken, but she already knows.

'Is that the plan?' Reggie says. Near the back of the room he stands from amid the dour sprawl of his garage pals, his trusty Handsomes. 'Put it behind us? Move on?'

'That's the plan for tonight.' Marc smiles dimly. The succulent black eyebrows are an almost palpable weight. 'In the morning—'

'Sorry, sorry,' Reggie says. 'I'm new, so I don't . . . get things. But do you mean we're not going to . . . do . . . anything . . . about what they did to us?'

'I don't mean that in the least. We're going to do a lot. Have you seen this place?' Turning up the wattage of his smile, Marc scans the room, no doubt seeking the support of his Marcsmen. But the Marcsmen – as a body, a consistory – are not there.

'That's not what I'm talking about,' Reggie says. 'I'm not talking about . . . housework. I'm talking about showing them they can't do that to us.' Stepping from foot to foot, he flickers curiously. He seems to be working hard to keep his eyes from darting. And for a second he appears as he did outside the garage: as if seeing people who aren't there. 'I'm talking about sending a *message*—'

Then shouts erupt from behind him, from the back of the room. People start to get up, obscuring her view, so Dia gets up too, having to raise Fee with her, keeping her head on her shoulder.

It is Glen, and Will, and Jon, back from the hospital. Jon is wearing a pair of medical-looking spectacles with a crenellated white patch inserted under the right lens, but otherwise he's grinning, opening his arms to dispense blessings on his followers.

'Look who's back!' Glen shouts. 'Oh yeah! This pimp is back on his corner!'

'Ghosting bros and schooling hos,' Jon says, before disappearing into a many-armed embrace.

Still with Fee's head on her shoulder, Dia manages to find Glen. 'He's fine. And the eye thing is hilarious. It's not an injury, it's an infection. He got some mad shit in it while he was lying on the grass. Should clear up in a day or two.'

'Nothing broken?'

'Nope. Everything A-hokay.'

The crowd keeps building, the men and women of Tarantula drawing towards Jon and softly locking in place, and for the first time she understands that if the members of this group share anything, it is the quality of the love in them. Reaching hands on every side tell her these are people in whom the bottle of love has been broken, shattered who knows when by who knows what prodigal impact, so that the heart's unpalatable wine abundantly burst and sluiced inside them, steeped their organs, coloured their faculties, ever after clotted their eyes with volatile pigments of heart's red; these are people whose hearts have leaked. And was there ever anything so unhappy, so unearthly, so absurd?

'What's happening?' Fee asks sleepily from her shoulder.

'Jon's back. He's okay.'

'That's good. I'm glad.'

Holding onto her like a drunken waltz partner, Dia sweeps round to survey the room. But there is no sign of him. Reggie has gone.

'You have to protect me,' Fee says. 'I'm your baby and you have to keep me safe from all harm.'

11. Your Father's Money

In the morning she finds Reggie.

'Christ. They went to town in here.'

'It isn't as bad as it looks.'

'You sound like Jon.'

She stands at the door of the garage, at the threshold of mechanical carnage. He is partly hidden from her by the edge of the bus that slumps in the sawdust, its bonnet raised, innards violated. He swipes a palm at the room and says, 'A lot of it's oil.'

'Jackson Pollock.'

'Scare tactics. Their heart wasn't in it.'

He steps out from behind the bus. Boots, jeans, white T-shirt. He's so clean he looks like freshly scraped copper. No one else appears: no one else is here.

'For what it's worth, I agree with you,' she says. 'With what you said last night. The bastards shouldn't get away with it.'

'But they do.'

'Then we should do something about that.'

'Who's "we"?'

'Us. All of us. Tarantula.' She frowns, hearing herself. She means it, but until this moment had no idea she did.

'Maybe we will.' He smiles, which is difficult with everything that is going on.

'We should. We *should*.' He'd forgotten what it looks like: her stance of furiousness, of total stubbornness. Like the invisible Dia has the visible one in a headlock. He waits. Then she shakes her head, shakes out of it. 'I'll let you get on. Not like you don't have anything to do . . .'

'I'm glad you joined.'

'Are you?' She pulls a face and even with everything that is happening he sees it clearly. *And what's the use?*

'It was a shock,' he says. 'I jumped to conclusions. You know me.'

'Hot-headed Reggie.'

'It's the ginger. Biological.'

'See you later, Reggie.' She steps back from him. And what is it? What's the use?

'I'm sorry I called you a crone.'

'You should be.'

'You aren't a crone. I shouldn't have said it.'

'No you shouldn't.'

The visible Dia leaves; the invisible one he's not sure. At least as he returns to his study of Ella there is less going on and he's able with fresh rage and indignation to demand of the universe: why so much? What could ever be the use of it – of so much beauty?

Because loveliness is the earth, where he started. Before anything else he was in the dark, under the mud, close to the pulse. He had a cold and he was tearing up roots. There was no time before this, no time without the sniffles and tearing roots. Then the pulse slapped him over and the roots slithered from his hands and with his face full of snot he rolled out on top of the mud. Dogs came to lick him. They were called Snowflake and Buttercup.

*

When he was small they lived on the mud. His father said it was their address. Where there's mud there's our house. His father laughed when he said this, as if he didn't really know what mud was, or what a house was, for that matter. His mother did not laugh.

He lived at the height of the dogs, in their feelings and voices. Fires made Buttercup sad. Snowflake liked the taste of batteries. You were always taking them out of her spit.

With her hands his mother desired him to be clean. She scrubbed him and scrubbed him in the dribble of serpentine hosepipe, always different, always the same: a hosepipe in the open air, a hosepipe in a hutch of breezeblocks. But no one is just one person and with her eyes his mother desired him to live always in the earth, where loveliness is. The way to the earth was down through the mud. Then her agonies, her hosepipe torments. Yet it was what she desired. He pitied her.

Snowflake told him: your mother is the earth. She is darkness, loveliness.

Buttercup told him: your father is the sun, and he is terrible – a terrible blaze.

It was all true.

There were people. There was a woman and a man. The woman was called Mama but she was not his mama. And the man was called Pi but he was not a pie.

There were other people. His father said they were family. His mother said they were friends. For a long time they scared him. They had too much life in them. Their voices did too many things and too much happened to their faces that he couldn't make sense of.

Then the man called Pi spent so long throwing him in the air he had no choice but to like him. So then he liked him, though he was still very scared of him.

There was the girl he couldn't look at. She was twenty times his size and her voice went on forever. She didn't smile, never smiled, couldn't, and she was always looking at him though she never looked at him, looked only at his father, and at the sun, and at the sun machines that his father made. Never look at the sun, his mother said. Never look at the sun, or the sun may look at you.

His mother said they were leaving. Her mouth said they were happy. Her eyes said they were being torn to small pieces.

Who wants to live in a place like this? Who wants to live in a smelly, dirty van with a lot of smelly, dirty people and smelly, dirty dogs? She went round and round, wrenching doors open, slamming drawers shut. He couldn't stop screaming.

But we have a house now, his mother said.

But we have a house *now*, he said.

The first house smelled of when he broke his arm and had to look at the prickly black hairs in the doctor's milk-white nose. It smelled of things gone wrong, going wrong forever.

He had a room. It was the hardest thing he'd ever felt. No part of it gave, yielded, returned a bounce for your bounce. No part of it knew about dogs. All it did was think about being the same size and shape forever.

Standing on tiptoes, he drew the curtains shut so he wouldn't have to look at it. Then he turned and the squeedies were there. On the floor, the walls, the shelves loaded with toys that had never belonged to anyone else, the bed he couldn't imagine ever being able to sleep in. They floated, flickered, snickered, gestured obscenely. Sun germs, sun drones, harsh crackles of light life with blinding faces and fingers and fins. They raced round the room to make sure he knew he shouldn't be here.

He went to school. School was his mother's study before lunch. After lunch it was just his mother's study.

He learned that everything is too big. His mother showed him maps, charts. The earth is too big. But Jupiter is so big 1,300 earths could fit inside it. But the sun is so big 1,000,000 earths could fit inside it. He couldn't stop thinking about them, the million earths burning inside the sun.

Do you know where you come from? his mother said.

I come from the earth.

That's right, she said. But she thought he meant *the earth*.

I came out of the earth, out of the mud, and the dogs licked me.

Not quite. She laughed. Apart from anything else, we didn't have the dogs when you were born. You were almost two when we got the dogs.

Still laughing, she showed him other pictures, other diagrams then. He learned that people aren't voices or faces but worlds of blood. This one or that one. Saturn. Mars.

He tried to listen but his head hurt. Inside it was a gory planet: Mars or Saturn. Then he asked if there was any such thing as the squeedies and she laughed and said no, no, no, and then his head stopped hurting because he knew he didn't have to believe her. He knew he didn't have to believe anything she said ever again.

*

The second house was so big men had to come to hear their voices in it. They stood on the stairs, talking louder and louder, testing how the house made them boom. They shook his hand, kissed his mother, then went upstairs to talk to his father for two weeks.

One of the men was called Gerald. He was like a gnome that had been stretched out: long bald head, long pink lips, a white beard pulled until it showed the yellow. When he came to the house his father was always saying My friend Gerald and Comrade Gerald and Brother Gerald. Everyone acted like he was a magician round him but he wasn't anything like that. He was a bored posh old man who owned a factory that made wind turbines.

You must always be very nice to Gerald, his father said.

One day he opened a book his mother had shown him and he read: ichor. A foul discharge, like blood or water. And at last he had a name for it, for what they left behind – for the stuff the squeedies left slathered on everything to make sure he knew he shouldn't be here.

The third house was so big there was no room in it for school and so he went to the school other children went to, a tall long building the shape and colour of a roof slate.

He sat in class and learned that people are two things all the time. People are always frightened and always obedient. They don't always know what they're frightened of and they don't always know what they're obedient to but it doesn't matter. They are those two things all the time. Other things also, at other times.

The boy who sat next to him was called Brandon Tallis. There were times when as well as being frightened and obedient Brandon was sad. In the middle of the lesson he closed his eyes and leaned forward slowly until his forehead touched the top of his desk. Reggie put his hand on the back of Brandon's neck and said, There, there.

There, there, Brandon said.

At school they did history and sums and they read out poems in mad, drunken voices. They read a poem about the earth and the things that click and rattle in it and the things that pant and scuttle in it and they read out the words 'red in tooth and claw' and then for a while they fell over their desks and they were all mad and drunk.

So many people came to the house that some of them never left any more. Two men lived with his father. A man and a woman lived with his mother. Three women lived with the house and each had a different relationship with it: tempestuous, long-suffering, coyly indulgent.

Men went with his father up to the attic in such numbers he began to suspect some of them never came down. He imagined them hanging in the rafters, folded into their suits and clutching their briefcases, milky-eyed, sleeping.

Gerald came to the house. Sometimes it seemed like he lived there too, sometimes not. Sometimes when he went to his room Gerald was sitting on his bed and wanted him to sit next to him and talk to him about school and about his friends and girlfriends.

Gerald said, I suppose in your world 'wind power' is farts, is it? Burps and farts?

No, he said. It's wind power.

He came in from football practice one night and his mother

and father were shouting. The house was the trembling ear trumpet of the three women who lived with it.

Since when do you care? his mother shouted.

Since always, his father shouted. Since before anything I ever did.

Then when do you plan on showing it? his mother shouted.

What? his father shouted. *What?*

The three women each had a different relationship with the house but they all had the same relationship with his mother and father.

The first time was in Brandon's house, in Brandon's parents' bed. It was the summer holiday and Brandon's parents were in Switzerland. Brandon's younger older brother was in therapy and his older older brother was in the army. The school was in his house.

He came down the stairs and Brandon was laughing.

What was it like?

(It was like hurting someone who has forgotten what being hurt is.) Not bad, he said.

Was she into it?

She seemed fairly into it.

You poor prick. Brandon was laughing so much he couldn't even be high any more. Do you think you fucked her? You didn't fuck her. You fucked your father's money.

The trick was being a body. When he was a body the squeedies couldn't find him. So he played football and basketball and volleyball and he sprinted and wrestled and boxed. After school he went to the gym but it was nothing so he found a place next to the cinema in town. The subscription was his father's name.

He loved it all, lusted after it all. The lights, the screens, the grips, the weights, the kitten weakness at midnight that left him too frail even to raise his hands to the headphones still plugging his ears. He loved the fuckoff of it: the endless reps that said: I am *meat*. Rep after rep, out of time: I am *meat*. I am *meat*. I am *meat*. I am *meat*.

His mother was ill, was dying, was dead. It had happened before it started to happen.

One of those nights that blur back to day as he came reeling in with a girl from town and it was Jeff the money bot, the bank clown, who told him. Heart attack: his mother's heart had attacked her. The girl he'd reeled in with started crying. He didn't know her name. She knew his name but it was the only thing she knew about him and there she was crying.

Where is he? He meant his father.

Jeff the cash droid just stood there.

Don't tell me. Meetings. Projections. Contracts. Money.

So Jeff didn't tell him.

And it was the girl whose name he didn't know who said to him later, No one actually knows how to grieve, do they? No one knows how it's done.

What do you think? his father said.

They were in his father's attic, looking at his father's model. The funeral was so long ago he was no longer sure it had happened. He had not been to school. He wasn't certain the school still existed.

It's the future, his father said. Not oil, not coal, not nuclear, not even Gerald's well-intentioned flatulence. One day soon this baby is going to kick out enough juice to boil every kettle in Warwick. Wash every dish, tumble every dryer from Coventry to Leamington Spa.

His father waved his arms over the dazzly model. 'Sharing his world', 'making a connection': something he'd read in a book, glanced at in a browser.

What do you think?

I think it's shit.

What?

Who wants this? No one wants this. This doesn't *help*. This doesn't help anything.

It's the future, his father said. It's what's coming, ready or not.

Fun and games, his father said.

It was the first time he'd seen him in a month. They were sitting in a prison cell in Shepherd's Bush.

It's what you did, isn't it? You and Pisces.

No, his father said, it isn't.

It wasn't. Brandon had buggered off almost straight away, though he'd stuck it out, stayed on to the last atom of junk. Now there was no one and the police and the bailiffs had flooded in and there were no more atoms.

It was Sellick who knew everything. First the oceans will rise. The sky will burn until there's nothing in it but sun, the air will grow hot, hotter, like powder on the lips. Then the earth will die. Dead rivers, dead lakes. The stink of the fields will come into the towns. The pipes will choke and their stink will rise also. Then the army will come into your street and then it will leave and there will be just the street, the empty sky, the murdering sun. He grinned and showed you his brown teeth, teeth like the oak of the world's first wood. And any movement of his head displayed the hanging rings, the opened loops of his earlobes. Then the police and the bailiffs showered in and Sellick catapulted off over a line of broken bicycles, jumped each in turn like a hurdler, an astounding feat.

I'm glad you called me, his father said now.

He nodded, though he was not at all glad he had done this. He had sworn he would not do it, had listened to himself in his head, swearing he would not do it. But after the door clang of the police van settled its true terribleness among the rims of his skull he felt the name, all its power and force, digging its way out of him. Let me call him. Let me call my father. Let me call Samson Glaze. So he had called him and his father had come, trembling with jetlag, sheeted with the environment of a conference centre on a subtropical island, sitting next to him in a prison cell in Shepherd's Bush and peering at the damage the van door had done to his face and neck and shoulder.

Never. Never again. Every feeling of it burned, like empty sky, like murdering sun. There in his wretchedness, in the constant revelation of his wretchedness, he knew he would rather die than ask his father for help, for anything, ever again.

How's the eye?

Like a spoonful of mercury.

In New York there were no women, only remotely controlled mannequins that squeaked up to you then squeaked away again on blood-clotted castors. There were no men, only coin-operated guides to the sunsets and the skyscrapers' sightlines and the other sightlines that pass inwards through brain and gut.

Your earliest memory, the doctor said.

I came out of the earth, out of the mud, and dogs licked me.

I hesitate, but are you familiar with the term 'false memory'?

All memory is false. But it's all we have, isn't it?

Let's talk about that.

So they talked about that.

My father once told me he wanted to make the future. He said he wanted to make it with his own hands.

Your father sounds like a deeply troubled individual.

It didn't matter. England, America. London, New York. Wherever he went the squeedies knew about it and they were waiting for him, waiting to slather their ichor on everything and make sure he knew he shouldn't be here.

He sold his first-class ticket on the internet and flew back between two screaming mothers and their peacefully sleeping babies.

To his astonishment, Brandon was clean too. His parents had handcuffed him to an oar in the boathouse for three weeks.

I'd like you to meet some people, Brandon said.

Not massively interested, he said.

She wasn't one of the people Brandon meant, but she was there at Brandon's house one night: the girl from town he'd reeled in with the day after his mother died, the one who started crying. She looked up open-mouthed, saw him, and did it again: burst into tears.

She was called Matilda and the Friday after next she was moving in with friends.

So which one are you sleeping with?

It was Gerald. Hands behind his back, squinting out of the

window. He meant Matilda, or Amelia, or Aidan, who had left the room as soon as he entered it. Then he turned his beardy little face, crackled out a laugh.

Oh, I see. All of them. Do they know?

They didn't, but the day had long passed when he had to be very nice to Gerald.

Would it hurt to see him? I know he'd be pleased as punch.

Hurt who? Me? Him?

Well, would it? Do you think? Or would it help?

You could stay for a couple of days, he said, but Sellick was already shaking his head.

His poor, punctured, flame-jangled head. By the time he'd got to the clinic two nurses had been pinning the patient's wrists to a wall while he gamely snapped at them and howled and laughed. Pure show, it turned out: once the notes were folded away along a succession of palms and the release papers produced in their neat cardboard folder, Sellick assumed a penitent air, subdued though amused, that lasted until the pair of them collapsed guffawing into the backseat of Matilda's car.

Be kind, Sellick said, apparently meaning the nurses. Have patience with those who have not sight of the runes.

Fascists, Reggie said, knowing this was the sort of thing that generally went down well with Sellick.

We're all looking through keyholes, chief.

Either it wasn't true or it was and the keyhole Sellick looked through was a gorgeous one-off, an artfully ornamented and ingeniously turned aperture with perspectives running in directions that no one else even knew existed. Half a lifetime pretending it wasn't so, wearing a Spider-Man tie to an office in Bedford (IT

Support), trying to blot out those parching radiances with Special Brew and *Match of the Day*. Then another half a lifetime sleeping under bridges and behind deconsecrated altar stones, undoing the blots, restoring the view. Sellick talked and talked – his friends in the music business, in the drug industry, in unlikely places high and low – but you never felt you knew the start of it. He wasn't a junkie, though he took lots of junk; wasn't a rough sleeper, though he lived nowhere, or everywhere. In the squat there had been nights when Reggie would roll over and press his head to Sellick's, hard and harder until the bones creaked, in the hope of sharing some glimpse of its inner scintillance, its bounded flame world, though he never did, though maybe sometimes he did.

It'd be no trouble, he said, and Matilda in the driving seat murmured her agreement.

Not for you, Sellick said.

His father pretended to be alone but there was the minder as soon as he opened the door – at the end of the corridor, the weird one, the Weland one.

You're upset, his father kept saying. You're upset about your mother.

I'm not upset about my mother, he said. I'm upset about my father.

On the table was his phone: the only loose thing in the room. His father threw it at the wall then he threw it at his father. Direct hit. He felt the connection in his own throat.

There, there.

I'd like you to meet some people, Brandon said.

There were four of them. A woman called Vicki and a woman

called Tori and a man called Marc. And Brandon. Though it was Marc who did the talking.

We all think like people, Marc said. But doesn't a time come when we have to try not to do that? To think not as people, think beyond people. To imagine a world without people.

People will wipe themselves out, Marc said. Take it from me, they won't need any help and nothing will stop them doing it. They may think they want to stop doing it, but they don't. The unconscious desire of people is to be annihilated and whether they know it or not they work tirelessly and ceaselessly to that end. And now, happy day, in our time that work is almost complete and that end is upon us.

What if that's okay? Marc said. What if there's a way to live that shows we're coming to the end of people – that accepts the future doesn't have people in it, and there's nothing wrong with that future, with that world? A way to live as an example: acceptance. No more struggle. No more distortion of self or environment. No more violent intervention in an effort that is both doomed and undesirable. No longer trying to shape the world to suit us, but shaping ourselves to the world. Weaning ourselves off the internet, off electricity, off indoor plumbing. Fading into the weeds. Making a good end. Withering away.

He'd never been to the countryside. He didn't know anything about it. And the squeedies didn't either. Stand outside the whole day or close every door and build the deepest dark he could build. They'd never heard of it.

Until over Ella's bonnet one afternoon Brandon said there was a visitor called Dia.

She wasn't twenty times his size any more but her voice still went on forever and she still didn't smile, never smiled, couldn't. And though they raced round her, floated, snickered, obscenely gestured – V-signs, wanker signs – he was able to wonder: what's the use? Of so much of it. So much beauty.

Vicki and Tori and Brandon arrive, in that order, and they get to work on Ella and make good progress. She's a strong girl and she helps them. In the afternoon, after lunch on the grass, they break down the engine. Police or no, they reach depths they've never reached before – Ella's secret veins, her aortas.

But it stays with him. In the night he disentangles from the others' sweat and goes through the garage to stand outside on the coldly moonlit grass. What is it? Anger, ichor. And: what would hurt, what help?

It isn't Dia. She didn't bring the squeedies, though they drip from her, hang from her. No: they followed her. Not because of who she is, but because of where she's been.

It isn't even the police. They are a layer, a human shield. Hiding behind them is the same terrible blaze hiding behind Dia, wreathing her with bright snicker life. His father.

What would hurt, what help? But he knows. If the enemy is his father, there is only one place to hurt him. And it is eight square miles in Warwick, a fallen artificial heaven, a false dropped sky of lenses and mirrors.

12. We Never Talked

Just when she thinks she has it, the routine changes. Dia has absorbed the convention that breakfast takes place in the kitchen, other meals in the brick refectory building; then on her fifth morning she comes late down the skreeking stairs and the kitchen is not merely empty but bare, stripped out. Yawing with hunger and disorientation and a queasy sense of being the only one who didn't get the memo, she stumps outside, into the white morning, crosses the green overgrowth to the refectory building, and there everyone is – packed onto the benches, talking, laughing, eating and drinking, passing things to each other or having things passed to them.

She fetches her tray and with a cracked bowl of bran-based cereal and a chipped mug of over-brewed tea she locates the Marcsmen wedged into the corner of a table halfway down the length of the room. Jon, bless his heart, has held a space for her. Before moving to take it, she slides her tray onto the table and stands behind him for a while with her arms round his neck.

'"My hero"?' he says, as he has every time she's done something like this.

'Still no.'

Shuffling past him to the free space, she notices Annette draw herself slightly more erect on the bench. Holding on to that shit, are we.

'How come we're in here?' Dia asks no one in particular.

'Marc mentioned it last night,' Fee says. 'You were there – his big "time of tribulation" speech? He said it might be nice. Sort of a bonding thing. Everyone sitting down together in the morning rather than grabbing a bowl and waltzing off with it.'

Dia considers saying something about everyone sitting down together *without her*, then relents. Annette's knickers still being in a twist may explain it; and Jon did at least save her a space.

As Fee begins her customary detailed account of her night's dreams, Dia examines the room. She spots Reggie in the midst of his Handsomes at a table near the door. They seem different this morning: rather than exhibiting their usual coordinated languor, they're puppyish with animation. The other man leans keenly forward while the women take it in turns to laugh with the same burly emphasis. Reggie is talking, quietly but continuously, shaping and reshaping a volume of air on the table between them with his hands. A loose square, containing a series of waves and, at its centre, a forefinger point.

'See you later, yeah?' Annette unwedges herself from her corner and with a general glance at the table's occupants stalks away with her tray.

'Is it just me,' Dia says, 'or does anyone else thinks it's a bit much that she's still so off with me?'

'She's embarrassed,' Fee says. 'She wishes she'd done what you did.'

'Then why didn't she?' But it is the wrong question, and hangs airlessly resonating.

When Jon goes to look for the teapot she glances again at the Handsomes. And now here's another interesting thing: the other man and the women have left, but Reggie is still there.

As Dia watches, he beckons to Pearl and gestures at the place on the bench facing his. Pearl sits and he leans forward and starts urgently talking to her. Shaping the square, the waves, the point.

Reggie and Pearl are still deep in conversation by the time Fee and Jon drain their refilled mugs. 'Back to it?' Jon wonders.

'Catch you up.' Gratuitously Dia indicates her empty mug.

She waits for Pearl to leave, for a chance to scoot over and take her place and ask Reggie what he's up to, but Pearl stays where she is even when Reggie looks up at two men who are passing and starts talking to them too. On the other side of the refectory Dia waits, with a gutful of sick foreboding, for him to start shaping that square again. Instead he stands, high-fives Pearl, and walks out of the door, still talking to the two men.

Pearl goes on sitting there. Dia waits. But Pearl is still sitting there.

'Hi, Pearl?'

'Dia! *Hi!*' Pearl in intense-theorist rather than pleasantly scattered mode this morning.

'Mind if I join you?' She drops into the wide saddle of body heat Reggie has left. 'I noticed you were chatting to Reggie just now, Reggie Glaze?'

'Reggie! Yes!'

'You know what I always think? About Reggie? What an interesting young man.'

'I'll say!' Pearl's laugh clicks through its various avid permutations. 'There was quite the stir when he first arrived here. Talk about a debacle!'

'How do you mean?'

'Well, he's famous, isn't he? Some people find that conflicting. Also, he's pretty full on. By Tarantula standards Reggie takes a conspicuously hard line. Oh, there was some "robust debate" when he first got here! All manner of jolly ructions!'

'I can imagine.' Chuckling, Dia settles her elbows on the table. 'So, what was he going on about?'

'Hmn?' Pearl's forehead shoots up. She rubs a hand over her mouth and her whole face pulls tight.

'What was he talking about? Just now? Anything interesting?'

'Oh, no. I wouldn't say so.' She's lying. Her poor little forehead writhes. Then with a cough she rises from the bench. 'Super-nice to see you again, Dia.'

'See you later, Pearl.'

After yesterday – a day she spent largely indoors and sedentary, indeed largely on the same spot of bedroom floor, learning how to stitch up holes in bedsheets and getting dismayingly good at and hypnotised by it – she decides today will be a day outdoors and moving about.

She walks round the house. It is a blinding day, all heights of white glare, and she walks with a hand over her eyes. Two women call to her from the vegetable garden; she calls back. Glen and another man are gooning in a tree/picking apples, depending on who you believe. Three men are sitting on the lawn talking – just talking, by the look of it. She has already passed them when she realises it's Reggie and the two unfamiliar men from the refectory.

She keeps walking. In one of the further fields, against a golden horizon, she makes out a line of figures engaged in some energetic agricultural activity. There is possibly the involvement of hoes; of scythes. Evidently the place to be. She starts walking towards it, then asks herself distinctly what the hell is wrong with her and turns and heads back.

By the time she reaches the lawn the group has already scattered: the two men smile as they pass on their way to the golden agricultural field – she *knew* it – while Reggie's back is retreating in the direction of the garage.

'Reggie!'

He stops on the track, looks round, crosses his arms. But he's still there, waiting for her to reach him.

'Reggie,' she says. It seems she has run to him. And now she is breathless and half blind (where did that handy hand go?) and heat is everywhere, gusting off him in sheets.

'Tell me,' she says.

To her surprise he appears genuinely pained. The hands at the end of his crossed arms scratch his sides.

'You're on a mission,' she tells him. 'I know you are because you're talking with your hands. Same as always. There you'd be in a corner with Mama or Pisces, talking with your hands, and it always meant the same thing. Reggie on a mission.'

'Don't know what you're talking about.'

'Uncross those . . . uncross your arms. Talk with your hands. *Tell* me.'

'You said we should show them they can't get away with it.'

'I absolutely did say that.'

'Well. I worked out a way we can.' The arms unhook from his sides. And as they do she is fully faced with it – the great span of his strength, of his superheroic freckly beauty. 'Through me. Through my father.'

'Okay,' she says, when what she wants to say is, why are you talking like this?

'Because it isn't the police, is it? The police are the police. Moronic thug militia protecting the interests of the wealth cartels. Of people like my father.'

'Right,' she says, when what she wants to say is, why are you here?

'He's a money reptile, same as the rest of them. Worse, actually. Worse than "the Grid". Remember them? Well, at least the Grid *know* they're criminals. While my father thinks he's such a good guy. He honestly thinks he's helping, but he isn't, he's hurting just like they are. He isn't just a part of it, he's the worst part of it, the worst part of the Grid.'

'I see,' she says, when what she wants to say is, you could have the world at your feet. With your strength, your beauty, Reggie, you could have everything. So why are you here, why are you talking like this?

'His whole operation is a smokescreen. Put up a few solar panels, tell everyone they can stop worrying, everything's going to be fine. It's a lie. Every last one of us is going to vanish from the earth and we don't need some parasitic turd saying otherwise.'

'Well, that's food for thought . . .'

'More than that. It's fuel for action.' He gives her face one final look. 'There's a thing he's working on. Massive solar plant . . .' And he shows her with his hands: the square of the perimeter, the waves of the panel arrays, the pointed watchtower.

She walks up the track. She comes to the gatehouse, which looks quiet. Not that it matters: there could be a ten-strong guard watching over the gate and she would continue walking. But no one is there and she passes the gatehouse unchallenged.

In fact she is in excellent spirits. Because the decision is no longer hers. She has to speak to Samson immediately, and that's all there is to it.

She steps past the gate onto a road she barely recognises. Now that she has to walk it at speed, the road is an assault course of traffic, of cars and vans and farm vehicles. Where did everyone come from? What day is it? What year?

There's no footpath so she hacks along in the mud and weeds at the side of the road, aware of eyes in the jammed traffic locking onto her. When she looks back at them she sees what they see: the boots and jeans; the porridge-coloured shirt; the black cloth in her hair. She is used to being looked at, though not for the reason she's being looked at now. She is a woman, non-white, non-southern and, for the moment, non-employed. But what the gawkers in the traffic see is Tarantula.

Eyes and eyes. When she was a little girl, before Samson, before the invisible portcullis that rose magically above the scrub for her every autumn, Dia made dens. She filled the flat with them: a bedsheet stretched across armchairs, couch cushions pulled from their slots and leaned sloppily together teepee-fashion. She sat in there, sometimes concentrating on the sensation of her self, sometimes just pissing about with dolls. And she remembers – one time Lila stuck her head inside. Dia was sitting in her den at the back of the living room, a tent of newspapers with a duvet snugged round it, and suddenly Lila popped her head inside. Her face with her eyes and lips in it was somehow the cleanest thing Dia had ever seen. And she said, 'I see you. Don't you worry, kid. You're real, you exist. Mummy sees you . . .'

She reaches the village and it too is a festival. Groovy middle-aged women in the tie-dyes of their youth stand at trestle tables loaded with second-hand books and third-rate watercolours. Well-to-do rural families skip and scamper. Expecting at any moment to catch sight of a maypole, or a wicker man, she comes to the unpromisingly crowded pale pub and starts up its steps.

Entering the hallway, she again feels eyes on her. But there's a difference: now she can hear her spectators as well as see them. She had almost forgotten it, the hushed word falling in her wake: 'Look alive . . . *Ranter* . . . You missed . . . *Ranter* . . . Right behind . . . *Ranters* . . .'

At the bar she meets no gruff and wary-eyed landlord but a cheerful twenty-five-year-old with the spit and polish of catering college still on him. He explains the cashback policy succinctly and humanely, swipes Dia's card and returns it to her with a clutch of pound coins and the drink of her choice. Bizarrely, it turns out that her choice is a Coke. She asks why the village is so busy and he tells her about the fair.

She finds the phone in a recessed bit of wall in the hallway. Two men stand braying at each other in front of the recess until she rolls them away from it with a frown. She puts her Coke and her pound coins on top of the antique Yellow Pages stuffed onto the ledge by the phone, picks up the receiver, taps in the number. She worries she's muddled the digits; worries she won't be able to hear anything over the noise of the pub.

Then the call connects and Samson says, 'Hello?'

'It's me,' she says.

And he says, 'Oh, thank God.'

His voice goes on sounding through her, the reverberation that catches a particular thread in her breast and makes it hum. No other sound in the world catches this thread inside her. If she had never heard Samson's voice she wouldn't know it existed, this secret filament in her breast. He says are you crying and she says grow up.

'I joined,' she tells him. 'I joined Tarantula.'

'You did what? I've been going out of my mind.'

'Didn't whatshisname tell you – Weland?'

'I haven't seen Weland. Is he there? Is he with you?'

'I thought he was with you.'

Samson is quiet in a sticky way she doesn't like. Then he says, 'Never mind. Let me worry about Weland. What do you mean, you "joined"?'

'I was going to tell you.' Was she? Or was she planning on simply swooping down on his doorstep one morning with Reggie at her side and a fabulous tale to unfold? 'Then I thought Weland must have told you. Believe it or not, I've had my hands pretty full down here.'

'It's not what we agreed. We agreed you would go down there for a weekend, scope the place out and come back. Instead you join a . . .'

'Doomsday cult. Death cult.' If he's going to be funny about it.

'Dia . . .'

'Psycho-killer cult. Murder-suicide headcase cult. Or I could tell you it's nothing like that, it's essentially a discussion group, but you don't want to hear that. You want to hear about the human sacrifices. The blood rites and whatnot. Much more fun than eschatological chin-stroking over mugs of, like, *tea*.'

'But what on earth would possess you to . . .'

'Nothing possessed me. I made a reasoned assessment and I came to a reasoned conclusion.' This is of course bollocks, but even Dia is awed by how convincing she sounds. Don't mess with the Talwar. 'If you're interested, since I joined the group I've had plenty of opportunity to catch up with Reggie. We've been talking. A lot.'

Samson is silent. Then he says, 'Reggie's there?' She doesn't say are you crying because she knows he is. '. . . Is he . . . ?'

'He's fine. Puddled, though you'd expect that. But he's completely fine.'

Samson's voice comes back a stuttering yodel. 'These Ranters, they're not mistreating him in any way?'

'Nah. They're . . .' Don't you listen? They're not like that. And they're not called 'Ranters', if you don't mind. They're called. We're called. 'Samson, listen—'

A collective roar goes along the bar that makes Samson say, 'Where are you?'

'I'm at the pub in the village. Only way I could call you. I've walked out.'

'They let you do that?'

'I don't think they're keen on it. That's why I don't have much time. Listen. It's Reggie. He's got it in for you.'

'All right,' Samson says.

'He wants to hurt you. He's trying to drum up support for an action against you.'

There it is again: that sticky, unwholesome quiet, like the hush of a failed hive. Then he clears his throat and says, 'What sort of an action?'

'He's got this plan. Sometime tomorrow he's going to call and say he wants to meet you. Talk about making up. But he won't mean it. It won't be real. He's going to say he wants to meet you at your solar plant, the one in Warwick, he'll say he'll only meet you there. And he'll say he wants to bring some people with him. He's going to ask you to give him clearance to come to the plant with some friends and then he's going to rock up with this *mob* of Tarantula and . . . I don't know. Make trouble. You see? It's a ruse.'

'I see.'

'So when he calls you have to talk to him. Worst-case scenario, make an excuse, put him off until—'

And Samson says, 'No, I don't think that will be necessary.'

'What?'

'I can't tell you how grateful I am to you for bringing this to my attention. But now you have to listen to me. I'm not putting him off. When Reggie calls, I'm telling him to come. I'm giving him clearance and I'm telling him I'll be there.'

'Did you hear what I—'

'You've done so much for me already, but I have to ask you for one more thing. Will you do one more thing for me, Dee?'

'Yes,' she says. 'Fuck. Yes. What?'

Another roar goes down the bar. She doesn't hear it – the one word he utters.

'Say again,' she says.

And he says it again: 'Nothing. You understand? You never called me. We never talked. You're a good little Ranter, doing what Ranters do.'

'You want me to stand by and—'

'Stand by. Let it happen.'

'You heard me say he wants to *hurt* you?'

'I'm sorry,' he says. 'I can't explain. It's my boy.'

She should go back. But she stands there in the recess, drinking her Coke. Then she calls Andrew.

'Dia? Where are you?'

'Let's say I'm taking a break in the country with friends.'

'Did you change your phone? I've been trying to call you . . .'

With a lovesick lurch she thinks of her phone, on the other side of the country, suckling at its cable, growing more desperate as each day passes. 'I'm sort of between phones at the moment. How are you? Anything to report?'

He pauses. 'Don't you know? I'm not at the university any more. I left last week. And I don't mean I tendered my resignation with a view to serving out a notice period. I mean I left. Told them I wasn't coming back, and walked out.'

'Holy shit. Why?'

'I'm not at the flat any more, either. I imagine that's going to take somewhat more sorting out, but . . . such is life.'

'Oh,' she says. And the rest of it she can pretty much guess.

'On a highly temporary basis I've moved back into the house. Back in with the banshee.'

The banshee: his ex-wife.

'May not come to anything. We both just got to the point where we thought we should at least give it a go. So . . . that's what we're doing. No work, no distractions. I'd say we were "clearing some space", if it didn't sound so patently wanky.'

She thinks of his flat, with its unopened boxes, and at last she understands it. Andrew left his stuff in taped stacks because he always knew the arrangement was temporary – always knew he was going back to the house and the banshee. Because that is the type of person he is: a smiling concretion of the temporary, whirling from one non-catastrophe to another in a life that equates work with distraction. Such lightness, such luxury: makes you wonder where it comes from, what it's based on . . . But all she says is, 'Good for you.'

'Not making any predictions, but the banshee does seem to be doing her bit this time. Pitching in and so forth . . . Probably I shouldn't call her that, should I?'

'The banshee? No, probably not. You should call her . . .' But she can't remember Andrew's ex-wife's name, if she has ever known it.

'It would be nice to see you sometime,' he says carefully.

'Yeah.' She runs a scan and in fact this is all right. He is a fool and a coward and a monument to the indulgences of his fatuous caste, but her feelings for Andrew contain only tenderness. 'We'll have to see what we can do.'

'One thing I meant to ask you about. Wasn't there a day we were supposed to meet up? You sent me a text, some problem at work . . . ?'

'And you were in some meeting you'd forgotten about.'

'That's the thing. I was in a meeting, but I hadn't forgotten about it. It was never scheduled, just appeared out of nowhere. And once I got there it was abundantly clear that no one had anything to talk about, there was no agenda, and it went on all day. I kept checking my phone and seeing I was getting all these texts and missed calls from you . . . and I started to get this weird feeling. Almost as if they were keeping me there on purpose. As if they were keeping me from seeing you. Isn't that weird?'

'That's really weird,' she says.

13. A Good Death

By the time she gets back a great bandwidth of afternoon is preparing to absorb the fields and a meeting in the farmhouse is already in progress. She comes through the door and there are people crowded against the kitchen murals, no one sitting cross-legged on the floor as during the meeting on Wednesday night, but everyone standing, leaning forward, straining to hear the voices projected from the front of the room as well as the mutters of commentary leaking in from either side.

Somewhat wildly she hopes that the excitement has to do with something other than Reggie's proposed attack on his father's solar plant – repair schedules, meal arrangements. But her first glance across the kitchen discovers Marc standing at one end of the room and Reggie at the other. Reggie, talking, looks highly animated: his big skullbones seem fit to burst. Marc, listening or anyway not talking, arms crossed and head down, looks dimly incensed, dimly amused.

Reggie is telling the assembled Tarantula, 'My understanding is we have a commitment to an idea that my father's work, that this plant of his, directly obstructs. It's an obstruction we have the means to remove, so why not remove it?'

'I think we need to take a breath here, Reggie,' Marc says over his crossed arms. 'Consider the language you're using: "remove". What do you mean by "remove"?'

'Shall I "define my terms"? All right, if that's how we want to spend our time. Defining terms instead of going out and doing something that actually demonstrates our beliefs . . . '

Hard to see how the meeting is going. Dia thinks of her confusion when, as a child, she first saw a TV sitcom that didn't use a laugh track: how was she supposed to know which bits were funny? Likewise this is a debate without claps or shouts or howls or whistles but only an intently listening audience.

'We're going in circles,' Marc says. 'Maybe there are more views in the room . . . ?'

Hands go up: not the full classroom arm, but a lot of forefingers raised at chest height, as at an auction. Marc gives the floor to a dark-eyed woman who querulously begins, 'Sorry if this is me being dense, but is it funny that we're talking about taking action against a solar plant? Shouldn't we be talking about fossil fuel, or fracking, or . . . ?'

Reggie grins: 'Talking about what everyone's talking about? Taking action where action's already being taken? Wasn't it you' – Marc – 'who told me, "If people are talking about it, it's no longer worth talking about"? If an issue has entered public discourse then the real debate's already over, the battle's already lost, and there's no use losing more sleep.

'Where we *can* do something is by showing people an obstruction they aren't yet aware of, revealing an evil, by tearing . . .' He mimes ripping aside a curtain. 'Solar isn't going to save us. My father isn't going to save us. Men like my father are liars who offer false hope in a time of crisis so they can line their own pockets. Isn't that something people should know?'

'If it's true,' someone says. This someone is Dia.

Her words have carried distinctly across the room. Reggie

stares at her, the plates of his head hotly pulsing. Without looking away from him she has a fair idea that everyone else is staring at her too.

'If what's true?' he says.

'If it's true that your father's a liar. If it's true that the hope he offers is false.'

'What else could it be? Any suggestion that there's hope for human beings is false. Any intimation that human beings have a future worth fighting for is false.'

'So we fight for a future *without* human beings?'

'We do.'

She glances at the faces turned towards her. 'And how do we all feel about that?'

'That's kind of what we're debating,' Marc says.

The faces are not hostile but meticulously curious. And she realises something else about the good people of Tarantula: their hearts may have leaked, but their brains certainly haven't. The room purrs with the smooth running of many minds.

'Right you are,' she says.

'We should move to a vote,' Reggie says.

Marc looks at him, and sags slightly. 'Do we think we're ready to vote?'

It seems they do. And still Dia has no idea what is going to happen.

'Votes in favour of the proposed action?'

Again hands go up. While Marc counts with a dabbing fingertip, Dia tries to get an estimate too, turning on the spot as casually as she can. Naturally Reggie has a hand up; each of the three other Handsomes, standing right by him in a bunch at the front of the room, has a hand up; Pearl with an electrically engaged expression has a hand up. There are others, but how many? A lot? Or not a lot? It seems like a lot, but she can't be sure.

She notices the Marcsmen lined against the wall on the far side of the kitchen, their hands very decidedly not up. Annette surveys the room, making a count of her own, with leadenly folded arms; Fee smiles supportively at Marc, her fingers laced in a bouncing pommel across the jut of one raised knee; Jon, with his hands stuffed deep into his pockets, stares at the floor.

'Okay,' Marc says. 'Votes against?'

More hands. A mechanically instantaneous straight swap between the Handsomes and the Marcsmen: the garage trio drop their arms as if stung while Fee, Annette and Jon reach for the ceiling with such competitive vigour they remind Dia of a ball game. Turning on her spot, she makes out other hands (is that Glen? Is that Will?) but again fails to establish a method that would allow her to calculate an actual number. Is that a lot? Or not a lot?

'Okay. Abstentions?'

Hands, though few – clearly fewer than on either of the previous occasions. Gradual, embarrassed, they come up on the air: one here, one there.

'Yeah? Abstentions, yeah?'

He is not looking at her, or anywhere near her, but Dia with a start decides that Marc is talking to her. She hasn't yet raised a hand, and somehow he knows she hasn't. And why hasn't she? Why didn't she raise a hand to oppose Reggie's proposal, as she wanted to? Or raise a hand to support it, as Samson instructed her to, as she would have done if she were a good girl? Because she is not a good girl – because she is a danger woman? But a danger woman would hardly have forgotten to raise a hand at all; she would have cast her lot for chaos and determined to live with it, whatever, whatever the consequences . . .

Too late. Furious with herself, and with ratcheting resistance of the elbow, she raises a hand high above her head and leaves it there, a wagging flag of self-disgust, long after the others have come down and the count has been taken.

'Well, that's carried,' Marc says. 'The proposed action is a go.'

At last there is a reaction: not a cheer or applause but a sudden lurch towards the speakers accompanied by a blast of talk, as if everyone in the room simultaneously strikes up a conversation with them. She skirts the flash mob of Reggie's supporters, at the edge of which she finds Marc, not especially despondent, in a huddle with his Marcsmen.

'What bullshit,' Annette is saying. 'I assume we'll challenge it?'

'Challenge it with what?' Dankly grinning, Marc lifts his shoulders.

'It was very close,' Fee says.

'Close?' Annette says. 'It was bullshit. He's no majority there.'

'We voted,' Marc says, running a hand over his glistening scalp.

'Did we, though?' Annette shifts her hip in a way that Dia feels is aimed at wagging abstention arm. 'I'm not sure we did.'

'Doesn't matter.' Marc appears to be trying to push his hair into a knot or a fin on top of his head. 'The result's the result. The only thing we can do now is get on with it.'

'Get on with what? This is such bullshit,' Annette says and still not having sent a look or a word or anything towards Dia apart from that accusatory hip she stalks across the room to the door, Fee and Jon trailing after her in their various dumb shows of commiseration and apology. Marc waves then goes back to piling up his sweat-drenched hair. He goes on doing this, seemingly having forgotten that Dia is still there, until she moves to stand directly in front of him and says, 'Are you happy about this?'

'I wouldn't say happy.' His black eyebrows glitter densely, like treacle.

'What happened to "new expressions of the radical impulse"?'

'It turns out there remains an appetite among us for the old ones.'

'And you're just going to let this happen? An attack on a solar plant, Marc?'

'It wouldn't be my choice. I think the scheme is premature and . . . foolhardy. A good way for us to get hurt without making our case.'

'You couldn't have said that during the debate?'

'I did say it. Opening statements.' In his grin there is a pass, a sinuous swish of the shark that sometimes patrols it. 'Weren't you here?'

At lunch next day Reggie comes into the refectory with the drolly exhausted look of a warrior returned triumphant from bloody battle. As he walks between the tables conversation drops, leaving only those remote continuous threads of talk that no arrival can break. With a grin he raises his arms: 'It's done.' He has been to the village, to the pub, and called his father. He has poured out his heart, sung the song of his soul, and arranged to meet his father at the solar plant in Warwick. 'One o'clock tomorrow. I said I was bringing some friends.'

Variegated laughter. Fee, with a disapproving look, gives Dia a nudge. But Dia doesn't respond. The thought of Reggie and Samson speaking on the phone to each other is so steeply appalling she feels dizzy with it.

Reggie disappears, but then when people start filtering out of the refectory the other three Handsomes are there, far perkier and more personable than Dia has seen them before, waiting to meet everyone with a smile and a light touch to the elbow and a suggestion that you might want to head over towards the garage, where there's some cool stuff going on you might want to get involved with.

They arrive to find a loose circle of people forming on the grass in front of the garage. Some sit talking; others watch Reggie, who on hands and knees at the centre of the circle appears to be assembling a very large and rudimentary jigsaw puzzle: thirty or forty squares of wallpaper that he arranges in columns and rows until the lines inked on their backs start to connect and cohere. When he is satisfied that a square has found its place, he holds it down with one hand while with the other he takes a small pale stone from a pile and drops it onto the square, pinning it against the wind.

By the time the rest of the Handsomes come to join him, presumably having swept the farm to ensure no straggler has been left behind, the jigsaw of wallpaper squares is complete and the circle is full of eagerly talking people. Reggie stands, pats his knees, and straightens smirking over his handiwork.

'No draughtsman am I, but hopefully you get the idea.' The image wavily held down in the squares is a tolerable reproduction of the model she saw in Samson's attic: the ranks of arrays, the pods and dishes. 'The main entrance is here. The site's mostly deserted, has been for a year or so, holdups with contractors and the like, so there shouldn't be more than odds and sods of security. Couple of minimum-wage guys playing Minecraft, you know. I give the clearance code, they let us in, and then we go to work.'

Questions jump out of the circle – go to work doing what?

What's the clearance code? – but Reggie holds up a hand while his fellow Handsomes return from the garage and set down on the grass a succession of dinged and spattered paint tins.

'By which I mean we make merry with these. They don't have paint in them, in case you're wondering. We gave the matter some thought, and at one stage we were inclining in favour of tinning up the compost heap, but certain practical considerations came to mind, by which I mean we realised it would fucking stink. In the end we settled on mud. We go in there and we make merry with our tins and we cover the thing with mud. We bury it. Put it back down in the earth.'

'Bury it?' someone says. 'Eight square miles of power plant, and you're suggesting that with a few tins of mud we can *bury* it?'

'I mean symbolically,' Reggie says. He looks as if he wants to speak through gritted teeth, but manages not to do that. 'It's a symbolic gesture.'

'Symbolic of what?' someone else says. 'Isn't there always the problem . . .'

There are more questions and more: how many tins? How many panels? How much mud? What kind of mud? With only the slightest shift in stance Reggie applies himself to his answers, scratching his elbows as he calls up the requested information, quantity of this, volume of that, and Dia, losing interest, notices for the first time that she is sitting next to Annette. Before she can think too much about this, she leans against her and says quietly, 'Is it bad that I want to throw something?'

Not looking at her, Annette purses her lips. 'Throw something.'

'Chuck a rock at his head. Liven things up.'

'He's such a knob. Even leaving aside the fact he's unbelievably full of himself. He's out of his mind. And daddy issues pelting from every pore. "We get it, your dad's this big millionaire industrialist. Stop being so bloody proud of him."'

'You still think Marc should challenge the vote?'

'Of course I do. That whole scene last night was laughable. If Marc had even one ounce of bollock he'd shut this mad crap down. He won't, though. Lacking as he does the requisite testicular ounce.' They both chuckle carefully.

For a while neither of them speaks; there is only the background wash of numerical crosstalk. Then Dia decides she will say something about the awkwardness there has been between them and she's considering what it will be when Annette snatches up a blade of grass and says, 'I know you think I've been rotten to you.'

'I don't know about "rotten" . . .'

'I was pissed off. But I'm not any more. I'm glad we stood up to the cops. And in the end it's not about individuals but systems. Our system against their system.'

Dia isn't sure this is the way she wants to look at it – isn't sure she wants to renounce the particular satisfaction she took in hitting that particular copper – but she only shrugs. 'All for one and all that.'

'You know him, don't you? Reggie?' Fee said.

'Just when we were kids.' So Dia tells her about that – a story about the Thin Love Collective and its seasonal trips to her town reshaped to focus on her friendship with a little boy called Reggie; barely a mention of the scruffbag patriarch, Samson Glaze.

'You know,' Annette says when she's finished, 'I see what you mean. I want nothing more than to split that man's skull in half.'

'Don't know if he'd see the funny side.' Dia tells her about that too, and when she's finished Annette raises her face with a serious look and calls, 'Reggie?'

He goes on answering the question he's midway through answering.

'Reggie?' Annette calls sternly. 'Why did the tea towel cross the road?'

Still answering the question, Reggie throbbingly reddens.

'Uh, Reggie? Why did the door handle cross the road?'

He twitches at her, twitches away.

'Why did the paperclip cross the road, Reggie? Why did the paperclip do that?'

Now finally he looks at them both, beams a sickly ironic beam, mouths 'Fuck off' and invites another question about weight, about mass, about load.

'Nicely done,' Dia tells Annette.

'We've got to be heard. What's the point of any of it, if we're not heard?'

Reggie goes on answering questions. Scratching his elbows, occasionally raking the clouds for arithmetical assistance, he seems nonetheless to be winning his questioners over. And Dia comes to two realisations. One is that Reggie is withholding something, holding back some element of his plan. The other is that Marc has been more honest with her than she has allowed. Yes, Marc is not the leader, Tarantula has not previously had a leader. But beyond doubt it has one now.

'Look at you. Overwhelmed with excitement.'

'I am a bit overwhelmed,' Fee says mildly.

Since Reggie's al fresco planning meeting they have eaten dinner in the refectory and Dia has wandered upstairs to find

Fee lying in a nest of torn blankets on the floor of one of the discussion rooms. It may be the room in which three million years ago Pearl tried to teach her and the Ormeshers about Narratives of Capital, but she can't be certain.

'I can't believe it's tomorrow,' Fee says now.

Dia sits in one of the stackable plastic chairs. 'Isn't this how it normally goes?'

'I don't know about in Tarantula. In other groups I've been in, anything like this takes a long time to come together. Weeks, months even. And we're doing this *tomorrow*.'

'Tarantula's not taken an action before?'

'Not that I know of. One or two very low-key marches, but nothing you'd call a proper action.' Sliding onto her back, Fee raises one foot into the air and gazes wistfully at her woolly white slipper. 'At least my folks will be pleased. Glad we're "getting stuck in". They were so happy when I was in Greenpeace, running about and breaking stuff and getting arrested – it made them so proud. But they knew what that was. Reminded them of their own heady days. I think Tarantula is radical in a way they can't quite get hold of.'

'Your parents are activists too?'

'Used to be. They're in publishing now. They don't really get it. Do yours?'

'My parents?' How do you explain Lila Robinson? How do you explain Kuvam Talwar? Answer: you don't. 'They're not a big part of my life.'

'Do they know you're here?'

'I don't know what they know.' Which is true. What does Lila know, in her gasping dream of bottled death?

Fee looks at the ceiling. 'Mine *are* a big part of my life. We talk about *everything*. I wish they understood, but it's difficult for them. When they stormed the student union and all that, they wanted to make things better for people. They fought for justice and dignity and decency and when you say none of that matters they just look at you. People in the end don't want justice and dignity. They want fever, and gratuity, and gorgeousness, and then death. Death for everyone. Death for themselves.

'And it's sad people are that way. Not all of us, but more of us than anyone can do anything about. And the signs are everywhere now, aren't they? Everywhere you look and everywhere you don't, there's just this . . . *pandemic* of hostility. Displacement, dissolution, Pyrrhic-victory nationalism – the rise of the "suicide state" . . . What is it Marc says? "In our time humanity is poised to fulfil its oldest, deepest dream: its own extinction."'

Fee flips her foot and the slipper jolts down so that it's suspended only by the tip of her big toe. She sways her foot, the slipper swings. They both watch it.

'This is what I think. If the human race is dying, the only question is, "How do we make this a good death?" And I think that's what Tarantula is for. To help the human race have a good death. To soothe the tears, and mop the brow, and sing soft lullabies, and provide every last consolation as the human race sinks down into death.'

A second flip and the slipper falls. Fee works her toes in the air through her sock.

Dia says, 'Maybe your parents aren't ready to give up on people.'

'They should.' Fee looks wonderingly at her moving toes. 'They should give up.'

'Are you?' Dia sits forward. 'Forgetting the ideology for a minute. Are you really ready to give up on everyone?'

'I am.'

'Even people here? Annette, Jon? You?'

'Oh, Dia. I gave up on me a long time ago.' She looks only at the air-treading toes.

'I can't see why you'd do that.'

Fee looks at the ceiling. 'You don't have to like me.'

'But I do. And you should too.'

'No . . .'

Then there's nothing for it but to get down in that nest of blankets and squeeze her until she starts to laugh and the tears collected on her eyes spill away in sticky spangles and tell her again, 'I do, and you should too.'

In the evening she goes out. *Do they know you're here?* She doesn't know what Lila knows. There was a time when Lila liked to pretend she knew everything, and certainly a good deal more than the wishful thinkers who passed for teachers at Ainscough Secondary. On the balcony of the Sycamore House flat she used to read aloud Dia's termly report, skewering the teachers' insipid comments: '"Claudia needs to believe in herself". Ha! You listen to me, kid. Never mind what these fairies tell you, there's not any such thing as "your self". Your self is just a great big hole, same as everyone else's. You want to believe in something, believe in what you like. You go out and find something you like and believe in that.'

Is that what Lila did? All Dia knows about Lila's family – a God-fearing clan in Port Talbot whose interweldings young Lila was unable to break free of soon enough – is that the only member of it she has ever met is Lila. Not one of them has ever tried to see her. And why is that? All her life she's wondered what her mother might know and not have told her about the Port Talbot Robinsons. For instance: when she left, did Lila escape them, or were they released from her? Were the Robinsons too oppressed by Lila as by a flying saucer to which they were helplessly shackled – bound by chainlinks of love and loathing? Until they weren't any more, and the only prisoner of those chains was a little girl whose father didn't know she even existed? And what else does Lila know, that Dia now never will?

Everyone's stupid except you and me.

Pausing by the track, Dia sees something: a black dot starkly outlined against that distant golden agricultural field. As she moves onto the track the dot extends into a figure. And then the figure raises an arm, and she raises an arm too.

Long before she reaches him she sees the mass and outline of his black perma-suit. No sunglasses, though. His eyes start in their pink fronds.

'You know you're trespassing, don't you?'

'I've been waiting for you. For a long time.'

'Poor you.' She glances back at the farmhouse. 'I suppose you also know what's happening tomorrow?'

'The plant. The action.'

'I've underestimated you, Weland. If this is you "keeping an eye out", I'm impressed.' She considers saying something about their last meeting, their unexpected reunion by the road amid the shockwaves that succeeded the police raid, and her maybe not entirely civil style of speech. (Fuck you, Weland. Fucking fuck . . .) But she decides against it and just says, 'I assume you spoke to Samson?'

'Did you?'

'So what if I did?'

'You told him I was here?'

'So what if I did?'

'Doesn't matter.'

'Wait. Samson sent you? You're here because he sent you?'

Eventually he says, 'I've been monitoring the situation. In case you required help.'

'Bollocks.'

'Any time you required help, I would have presented myself. It only so happens you have not required help. In fact you've given no indication that you are in any way dissatisfied with your current arrangements.'

Arrangements? He means Tarantula. For a moment she's so disgusted with him she can't speak. And then there is the ponderousness of his being right.

'I'm doing what Samson told me to do. He said let the action go ahead, so I'm letting it go ahead.'

'Then that's what you'll have to do. Go along with it. Keep Reggie safe.'

'Who'll keep me safe?'

The layers of his eyes grow still.

'Don't say it.' She shakes her head. 'Don't say *you're* keeping me safe.'

So he doesn't say it.

'Reggie's planning something else,' she says. 'Something on top of the action. I don't know what. Do you?'

'No. Earlier he disappeared for a while. I could see his little friends . . .'

'The Handsomes.'

'The boy and the girls he's regularly fucking.'

'. . . Is he?'

'He disappeared for a while. They went looking for him. I saw him go into the woods' – he points – 'over there. Then he came back.'

'So you think he's got something else in the works as well?'

'I would say that's highly likely.' A withery nuance collects at the side of his mouth. 'Reggie's a complicated young man.'

'Total fucknut is what he is.'

'Yes. I would tend to agree.'

'Mind you. They're all a bit like that here.' She thinks of her conversation with Fee. *You don't have to like me.* And the history she felt behind those words, the quiet decades of perfected acceptance. 'When did people start growing up hating themselves?'

'I imagine that that is absolutely humanly normal.'

'What? Shut up.'

'People growing up hating themselves? Yes. Absolutely humanly normal.'

They stand in the field, among the green lights of nature – of the earth's first software, God's screensaver. She considers the question that seems to keep cropping up round here: Would all this be better without people in it? And she is visited by a peculiar thought. She doesn't need it to be herself standing, looking, breathing in the night's toppled vividness, but she needs it to be someone. A witness, a soul fit for purpose and sure enough of beauty when she sees it.

Tomorrow Samson and Reggie will meet, father and son will converge and everything will end. She will have to give them up: Jon, Fee, Annette, even Glen, even Pearl. They drive into her, person after person, pang after pang. It is ridiculous, of course, but she's not ready. She's not ready to give them up.

Then Weland says, 'Is it always this windy?'

And she says, 'Is it windy?'

Coming back down from the field, she sees Marc talking to someone by the gatehouse. She goes over to say hello, but Marc's interlocutor, an elderly man with specs and a wispy white beard, moves away before she can get there. As she reaches Marc she hears a car engine start on the road, sees through the brain-branchings of the trees a wash of car headlights.

Marc has a shamefaced look. Good job she's the understanding sort.

'Did he have any advice for the big day?' She jerks a thumb in the direction of the quenching headlights. 'Your dad.'

'Hmn? Oh. That wasn't my dad. Nosy neighbour. Some of them like to check in, make sure we're not up to no good.'

'But we *are* up to no good.'

'That's what I was telling him.'

But he is so tense he can barely keep both feet on the ground.

It drives into her: Marc too. Tomorrow she will have to give him up too.

'Call it off,' she says. 'Christ, Marc, look at you. You don't want to do this. Call it off. Throw your weight about. Tell them it's not happening.'

'That's not how we work.' He drops his head. 'Even if it was – it's a bit late for that, don't you think?'

'I don't know, is it?'

'Yes,' he says. 'It's too late.'

14. Are You Cold?

It's not even first light but last dark when she realises no one will be clean today. Her bed is gone, the attic is gone, the skreeking stairs are behind her and she's standing outside with the rest of them dressed in yesterday's clothes and feeling peeled with uncleanliness. It is mere practicality: unless there are more she doesn't know about, the farm has only three small and dysfunctional bathrooms, including the one in the gatehouse, and all of them are occupied all day long. She's seen people sit down at dinner wet-haired from the shower they've just had. But today no one will enjoy even that luxury.

Is that what's wrong with everyone? Bug-eyed and scaly-fleshed, the group waiting by the track while nothing much happens is annoying in a way she has not felt before, as if the suspension of their ablutions has turned them into the worst sort of children. She supposes they are excited; they think they're going to do something dangerous and brave and good, or at least interesting and funny. Not one of them considers that behind the wall of their excitement is a man, real and injurable, and every motion of their desire is a steely consequence passing through the wall into him, a dart or a rod piercing his flesh.

Glen comes over and tries to talk to her, but he soon works out she's not in the mood for conversation and goes away again. The way his stubble grips his face tells her he is hurt. Well, she's sorry, but she can't talk to him. Today she can't talk to any of them. She stands holding herself, apart from the squawking clusters on every side, watching the sun trying to rise beyond the horizon of fields.

The garage door opens and the bus on which the Handsomes have been working gradually noses into the dark air. It seems about to launch onto the track, then stalls utterly. A shadowy Handsome woman – Dia thinks she is called Victoria – comes out to talk to the people standing nearest the garage; these people then follow her inside. After some minutes the woman she thinks is called Victoria comes back shouting, 'We're fine! We're fine now!' as if there is a mad rush of bodies scrambling for entry, which there isn't.

The people who entered the garage lurch out of it carrying the paint tins full of mud. Some grinning, some laughing, some pulling faces at their friends, with an uncommon air of lawlessness they carry the tins up the track to the gate and begin stacking them by the road. A couple of the stacks of tins spill and clang over, to roars of amusement.

Half an hour later the bus slides out of the garage and with a surprising appearance of health (and a surprising absence of engine noise) tilts up the track. It negotiates the gate and flexes onto the road. Here it pauses while volunteers load the paint tins into its storage bay. Then Victoria Handsome comes down the track waving both arms and with a whoop the rest of Tarantula piles up the track towards the bus.

Dia follows. Still holding herself, taking her time, she passes the gate to find a mass of people jostling to board the bus. It appears some wags have elected to make a game of it, pushing and pulling at each other, parodying loutish behaviour in a manner indistinguishable from loutish behaviour. High spirits: what can you do? Pinching her lips together, she stares at the road. She knows that if she looked up she would see any number of faces registering exactly her irritation, any number of fond smiles, sanely rolled eyes. But she doesn't look up, so she doesn't see anything.

The doors of the bus clear and Dia steps from the dark road into a cramped channel full of greasy yellow electric light in which new configurations are already forming. Scanning the aisle, she sees Annette and Fee sitting together and Jon holding a seat for her, but instead of doing what's she supposed to do and thanking him and dropping into the held seat she sweeps past the Marcsmen and stalks on down the bus. She finds a seat near the back next to a woman she has never spoken to and stiffly lowers herself into it.

More time passes, during which the bus doesn't leave. Dia and the woman sitting next to her smile and mutter at each other. Then they sit silently gazing out of the window, across the fields, at the luminous mess that precedes daybreak, a leak of light in the black sky running and trickling, seeking its level.

She glances down and sees the top of Reggie's head. Craning across her seatmate, she makes out Reggie and the other Handsome man – she thinks he is called Brandon – conferring in front of the open flap of the bus's storage bay. They seem to be arguing; it's hard to tell. Reggie is saying something; he is talking with his hands; he stabs a forefinger at the front of the bus. Then Reggie leans into the storage bay until Brandon Handsome flails away and walks to the front of the bus and boards it. Reggie grapples down the flap over the storage bay and walks to the front of the bus and boards it too.

She's right and Weland's right. As Reggie moves to his seat, it is all over his face: he is planning something else, something beyond a playful demonstration with tins of mud, and the thought of it makes his lips seize and his eyelids jump. For a moment she's sorry she can't just ask him what it is – can't simply stride up the aisle, slap a hand on his shoulder, tip her head to one side and look with humorous tenderness into those flicked-about eyes: *Come on, Reggie, what's this, what's on your mind . . . ?*

'Here we go,' she says.

The woman sitting next to her starts to reply, though Dia wasn't really talking to her, and though whatever it is she says is lost in the sudden subtle vibration, the engulfing noiselessness of the engine starting and the bus slipping free of the gate.

She keeps thinking the sun will rise. As they pass fields, farms, villages, she expects the sun at any moment to find its slot at the top of the sky and ignite the day with its light and heat. Then they come to the sullen concrete mouth of the motorway and the sun has still not found its slot, the day remains unignited. While the bus works through the traps of the junction, she realises it's not going to happen. The sun will not rise but linger all day in some peripheral oblivion, muffled by layers, dully present but without influence.

The bus has been in motion for almost two hours when she says to the woman sitting next to her, 'Are you cold?'

The woman thinks about it. 'I'm fucking freezing.'

They both look at the window, and it seems as their eyes move to it there appear on it fletches of black-sided rain.

Here we come, Samson. Hope you're ready, hope you're there.

*

It is early afternoon when they leave the motorway and pass onto a gloomy A road. At times rain is falling; at times it is not. Then the bus skates free of the road and inserts itself into a wedge of countryside uncannily like and unlike that which they left before daybreak this morning – just as green but somehow more intricate, as if with an added curlicue throughout the design, a sinister coil or cusp.

Without warning the bus dips smoothly into the side of the road. The engine dies; everyone waits. Reggie stands at the head of the aisle and calls down the bus. There is no problem; nothing has failed; they are not lost. On the contrary, they have arrived at their destination.

Reggie goes on talking from the front of the bus while the other Handsomes pad up and down the aisle distributing sandwiches and cans of Coke. He makes a joke she doesn't catch about the incompatibility of revolutionary acts and empty stomachs.

She studies the sandwich she's been handed. To be fair, it appears to be a thoroughly decent cheese and onion sandwich; still the idea of her eating it seems improbable. Along the aisle she sees people gulping down their food, quaffing their Coke. But she sees others like her, calmly but rigidly collected, eyeing their lunch as if it may burst into flames in their hands.

She takes a sip of Coke; then drains the can. She makes to offer her sandwich to the woman sitting next to her, then notices that she has not eaten hers either. She seems to be trying to fold it up, to be thinking of putting it in her pocket.

'I hate wasting food,' says the woman.

Marc stands at the front of the bus and starts to speak, but at once Reggie talks over him: 'Don't know about anyone else, but I quite fancy going for a chat with my father . . . ?'

People stand and shuffle into the aisle and filter off the bus and out under a stand of dripping yellow trees. As she joins them Dia can feel the difference in the mood of the group, the way the journey or the imminence of the action has muted or hardened it. At any rate, there is no jostling or shouting; there are no games at the door. The men and women of Tarantula step down off the bus and join an orderly queue, at the end of which one or other of the Handsomes is waiting to hand them two paint tins full of mud each.

When her turn comes, Dia sees that the Handsome in front of her is Reggie. He nods in a way that suggests this is how he has greeted every Tarantula who has come to him; that he is, if anything, slightly less friendly to her than he has been to everyone else. He reaches into the storage bay, lifts out two tins by their plastic handles and extends them to her with a banal, half-averted expression. She takes hold of the handles, he lets go, and the weight of the tins shoots down through her arms, almost wrenching her off her feet.

'Fuck,' she says.

'They're heavy.'

'Now you tell me.'

She glares at him. But Reggie only stands with that same banal expression, waiting for her to move along, so he can nod at and pass two more paint tins to the person standing behind her. Still she gives herself plenty of time to find her centre of gravity, to adjust to the horrible new deadweight of the tins on either side of her, and as she does she allows her gaze to pass behind him to the open storage bay, the jaggedly stacked tins waiting to be distributed, a black rucksack covered with pouches and zippers . . .

'What's that?'

He follows her gaze to the storage bay, seems about to raise a hand to pull the flap shut across it, then doesn't do that.

She tips her head at the rucksack. 'Someone going hiking?'

'Keep the tins level. Less chance of you unbalancing yourself.'

Then she goes to stand with the others who have received their allocation of tins, waiting just out of range of the dripping trees, different expressions on different faces, though all tightened by the weight of the tins that wants to pull their arms off, to drag them to the centre of the earth.

Here we come, Samson.

Don't worry. I'm still saving your life.

Because you saved mine. Because some commotion out of the sky whirled up my whole life and you moved your fingers on glass and you found it and gave it back to me.

I don't care. That's the thing. How it happened, how it worked, what, what, what.

Here we are. Now. Ready or not.

It rains. Everyone puts down their tins and for a lengthy period of misery stands there in the road, in the rain. With an ache she searches for the Marcsmen, for Annette and Fee and Jon, she searches for her friends. But she can't find them. Only the faces of human beings made strange by the ripples of water coursing down over them.

Finally the rain stops. At the far end of the crowd Reggie raises his arm in a signal of some kind, calls out something, and everyone picks up their tins and starts to shuffle towards him, then after him.

As he leads them along the road the day brightens, the rain becomes a flying varnish on the surface of things. Dia sees people smiling at each other. Glen shakes his head like the coat of a soaked dog, causing squeals of delight. The misery of earlier has vanished without trace; they are excited again, possibly more excited than before.

They are still slogging along when she hears shouts; coos, gasps. Distantly people call out, 'Look! Look!'

She looks; sees only wet road and wet fields. Then Glen knocks his shoulder into hers and turns her slightly and she sees it: an immense edge of dazzle levitated above the greenscape on their left. As they walk it comes then goes; comes again; goes again. It feels almost unbearably powerful and dangerous – like the ground zero of an extraterrestrial bomb that even now is silently and methodically devouring the earth.

Up ahead the fields give way to a gravel path. Reggie waits at the side of the road with his Handsomes, directing the rest of them onto this path. As she passes she sees that Reggie is wearing the black rucksack she noticed in the storage bay.

No question: whatever further gesture of dreadfulness Reggie is planning on top of the agreed action, it has to do with that rucksack. Which means from now on she'd better stick to him like skin. No question in the world. Except it would have been nice to have come to this realisation thirty seconds ago, because now she's passed him and has no choice but to keep going away from him along the road with the others.

They follow the path towards an electrical fence and a metal gate that grow more substantial, more spiked and barred, the closer to them they get. She can't avoid a feeling that they are being herded; glancing back, she sees the Handsomes a long way behind the rest of them, walking slowly, Reggie silent, the other three talking among themselves.

Easy now: easy does it. She halts, puts down her tins and stands rubbing the red dents left in her hands by the cruelly gouging plastic handles. Seeing her, a couple of the others do the same. She's still rubbing her hands when the Handsomes catch up to her. They halt also and regard her with bland puzzlement. Then she picks up her tins and walks along with them, slowing when they slow, allowing them no chance to fall back.

Two uniformed guards stand in front of the gate. Peaked caps, name badges, folded arms. Tarantula has gathered at the end of the path a hundred yards or so short of the gate and now Dia and the Handsomes walk past the rest of their group to approach the guards. Both of the women glower at her as if they're not quite sure who the fuck she thinks she is, but she only carries right on walking. When they reach the guards it is very tempting to put her tins down again, but she is aware she can no longer do that.

'We're here to see my father,' Reggie tells the guards.

'Are you now,' one of the guards says. 'And who might that be?'

'That might be Samson Glaze. I'm Reggie Glaze. His son.'

The guards leer at him. It is a curious performance, because surely they have been forewarned, surely they knew Reggie was coming, and bringing his radical friends with him. But the guard routine is so deeply engrained in them they cannot quite bring themselves to dispense with it.

'Well then, Reggie Glaze,' the guard says, 'I expect you'll have a code for us.'

'A word,' Reggie says. 'I have a word.'

'Let's have it then.'

'"Genevieve".'

The guards go on leering at him. Then they saunter to their hard metal gatehouse and for a second Dia is apprehended by a wild certainty that they are going to come out with machine guns and plough them all into their death and then the gate gives a single decisive clank and pours back out of their way.

Adjusting his grip on the paint tins he's carrying, Reggie steps forward onto the site of his father's solar plant. Even the Handsomes pause. Then they step forward after him, and Dia does too, her eyes fixed on the black rucksack gently rocking and changing shape as things move round inside it on Reggie's back.

Three, maybe four paces in front of her. If she caught up to him, gave him a shout – but as the group slogs past the gate his pace abruptly quickens, the Handsomes close round behind him and before she knows what has happened he has passed out of sight.

And so they are here, and this is it. This is the action.

They process onto a concrete walkway surrounding a field of dazzle so bright there is no way of looking at it directly. Briefly the group stands on the walkway as if the vast light in front of them exerts a physical force of repulsion; they harden their lips as if confronting a gale. Then a sheet of cloud rolls over the sun, the dazzle fades, and the eight square miles beyond the walkway become dully visible.

Nonetheless it is an incredible sight. A vast garden of panel arrays, flashing surfaces. Each unit a flatscreen arrangement of blue-green panels, four across and four down, how many, sixteen panels in total, an area roughly the size of a tank's treadprint.

Each planted at a regular six-foot interval from its neighbours in every direction, a vector in a sequence of columns and rows. Each suspended at a level just slightly above that of her shoulders on a meticulous steel stem conveying at once the delicacy of a fingerprint and the networked mass of intercontinental weaponry. Each a plane or a pane of sizzling light forms, of minute inner complexity (she thinks of cuckoo clocks made of glass). And yet beyond the spectacle of the individual arrays there is the difficulty of their number, of their multitude, their sheer manyness, forming sightlines and edge paths she cannot follow without vertigo.

She looks for the watchtower, with its sentinel point, and there it is, somehow forlorn in the backdrop of the arrays' rectilinear sublime. Then emerging from the paradoxical edge after edge after edge, other, more familiar, shapes: veined dishes of radio transmitters, concrete pods of maintenance buildings. The operation should remind her of the model in Samson's attic, or the wallpaper squares of Reggie's hand-drawn plan, but it doesn't. It doesn't remind her of anything she's ever seen.

There is something she's supposed to be doing. Someone catching up to, giving a shout to. Sticking to – sticking to like—

Reggie crosses from the walkway into the garden of the arrays. He drops one of his tins, slowly rotates to ensure everyone is watching (everyone is) then spins away the lid of the tin he's still holding, focuses his attention on his nearest array, swings back the tin in the crook of his arm – swings it sharply up at the array. In this gesture he performs the first strike, the first symbolic blow, and it is perfect. The contents of the tin flow blackly up into the face of the array in a three-braided ribbon that shatters and ricochets with startling fluency. The mud finding the glass is like a huge and beautiful eye suddenly put out. There is an idea that the plant, the site, the whole enterprize has been blinded and this idea passes immediately into the group, from which there comes a shout, a hard, wavering groan, not quite a cheer, not quite a jeer.

Together the remaining Handsomes cross after him. In one brawny sweep Victoria makes a similarly perfect throw: the array she chooses goes black and blind. Brandon goes next but misses his target almost completely, catching only the stem of his chosen array with a few black swipes. He tips his head back and lets out a howl of comically hyperbolic regret, and somehow this more than any symbolic gesture of Reggie's is the cue for the rest to surge laughing onto the grass, spinning away lids, swinging back tins.

There's Jon, covering an array and himself with a projectile of mud that he seems to have sent almost vertically into the air. There's Annette, making a studiedly competent hit (like the colour-negative of a scene shot in a carwash: the windscreen doused in black light). There's Fee, perplexed by the dynamics of her swing, seeming interminably to rock her tin while sprays of mud patter out onto the grass and nothing else. There too is Glen, spinning round and round with the tin he has gleefully and successfully emptied. Everywhere in sight there is a Tarantula flinging mud, waving arms, stamping feet.

Dia is settling her tins on the concrete when there comes a cracking sound, followed by hoots and shouts. Reggie has smashed one of his tins into the face of an array. The surface is not merely cracked but elaborately ruined, spooling out more and more glassy clockwork bubbles. He raises the tin, smashes it down again; the array jolts and sags perilously, reeling back on its stem. She opens her mouth to call to him then sees his face – red, seethed, gritted – and knows there is nothing she could say that would reach him.

As he raises the tin a third time it is clear that Reggie has moved somewhere inside himself and that he is acting on the world from within the cockpit of a furious dream. The tin he slams into the mess of concentrators is not a tin but an aboriginal weapon; the solar-panel array on which he wreaks his fury is not a solar-panel array but a monster. In his dream he is not an ideologue smashing capitalist technology; he is a hunter gouging the flesh of a beast. And it is worse than that. She sees wetness at his mouth and eyes and knows it is worse. Whether it is his dream or not, he is not wrecking an array, not attacking a monster, but murdering a body – a particular human body.

She starts towards him, looking round for the help she is sure is there, for the others who have understood as she has that Reggie is enacting a distress signal he cannot himself understand. But if those others are there, she does not see them. Instead she sees people following his lead, Brandon Handsome and both Handsome women and now Jon and Glen and now Annette and Fee and now others too searching the grass for discarded empty tins with which to batter, break, destroy the serene faces of the sun-tracking arrays.

Her next moments contain two observations. The first is that, as these others set to work on the arrays, they also pass into a trance like Reggie's: whatever is in their head when they first raise their tin, by the second or third time they cause broken glass to spring up their eyes have slitted and their lips peeled from their teeth in a dream of vengeance she cannot believe they comprehend. Or do they? Something about the women as they slam and bash and rip makes her think they understand the violence they are doing to a body – the body of some man, some father, some uncle, some boy all fists and tears; some dish-faced idiot of a copper who thought his hands belonged wherever he put them.

Her second observation is that she's doing it too. That from somewhere there is a tin half-filled with mud between her hands and she is beating this tin with all her force into a sheet of tiny lenses and twinkling mirrors. That her eyes are clefts of fire and her teeth are fangs interlocked tight as the teeth of a zipper. She brings the tin down and the tactile curd of the concentrators plumping to the metal edge and dripping into the grass with a thick, quick slapping sound is the most intense physical pleasure she has ever known.

Then she sees Samson.

In the widely scattered rain that has started to fall he appears small and old, and tired, and ill. He comes towards them over the grass in his trainers, jeans, T-shirt, hands in pockets, head jittering slightly as he peers from side to side at the damage they have done, the mud-slewed surfaces, the clogged and irreparable lenses, the shattered arrays hanging from cables or lying in great broken-light-bulb lumps on the wet grass. He appears as if at any instant he could lose his footing and go tragically wheeling head over tail, a fraught and frail codger humiliated by reality in front of screeching teenagers at a city bus stop. But his tread remains steady and he comes on towards them.

He is staring at Reggie, who has desisted from his vandalism and now stares at him too. She backs away from the array she has been wrecking, drops the tin. Has Samson seen her? Did he see what she did? Does he know she is here at all?

The young man stands; the old man walks towards him. In a

second the old will reach the young, they will meet, father and son will converge, and everything will end. All that has to happen is the young man keeps standing there and the old man keeps walking towards him. He stands, he walks.

'Reggie!'

Brandon runs to Reggie and with one hand grabs his arm and with the other points. Reggie looks and the rest of them do too. And what they see is that Samson is not alone – that the site is not deserted. Approaching across the grass, sifting between the arrays, a row or a column of security: a dozen, no two dozen, no three dozen men. Peaked caps, white shirts, black trousers, black boots. A personal guard, a private army.

For a while Reggie stands surveying the men. Along with the rest of Tarantula, he has come to know the police: but this is something else. Then he calls to his father – Dia can't hear what. Samson calls back, also inaudible; then he makes a gesture. It is, perhaps, not as dramatic or as symbolic as his son's, but its meaning is unmistakable: a sweep of one arm that takes in Tarantula, then a sweep of the other that takes in his approaching staff. *You brought your friends; why shouldn't I bring mine?*

Reggie calls again, but Brandon is yanking at his arm. Then Reggie turns away from his father, throws off Brandon's arm and runs away from them both between the arrays.

Samson has stopped on the grass. His gesturing arms are frozen at his sides. Dia keeps waiting for him to see her. She knows Reggie is running, running somewhere with that black rucksack on his back, and it can't mean anything good, but Samson is here, if he only moves his eyes slightly he will see her, and that will be something else, he will see her, he will know she is here too, and she only has to wait, if he only moves his eyes.

There is a noise. There is a faint but weirdly insistent squiggling of everything and then she's lying on the concrete with her head in an invisible bath. It is extremely puzzling and shocking; she feels the scandal, the impropriety of anything being so shocking. Her arms and legs are full of pins-and-needles disobedience, shouting down every command she sends them in order to go on lying stubbornly flush with the concrete of the walkway. At least there is the bath, which though invisible is highly soothing and palpable, cradling her face in its luxurious warm suspense. She is, she supposes, grateful for the invisible bath if for nothing else.

The sky has turned black. Or part of it has: a puffy, ripply, grainy black, its sediments angled by wind. Like smoke, almost. Unless it is smoke. A gigantic quantity of smoke. The possibility causes her to turn her head and that's when she sees the fire and the granulating wreckage and all the rest of it.

She needs some breath. It is hard to find. Apparently she has not been breathing. If she could she would roll her eyes, but she can't. Not breathing! Who forgets to breathe?

She finds some breath and uses it to lift her head out of the invisible bath that turns out disappointingly to be no more than a cracked monocle of her own blood and then to stand and see what else is going on apart from the smoke and the fire and the wreckage.

People are running. Their mouths are open but no sound is coming out of these mouths. It is at this juncture she notices no sound is coming out of anything and she uses some more of that breath. Ho hum. Hey ho.

She watches them run past her, all her friends: Marc and Glen and Annette and Fee. It's as if she sees them but also doesn't see them, and that's how they look at her too – their glances go through her and at the same time fall short of her. Tottering on the rickety wooden tower that has replaced the body she used to have, she turns it over. Ho hum. Her friends have left her. They have run away, every one of them. Hey ho.

More remotely the guards run too: not scattering but racing in two separate directions. Some race towards Samson and begin towing him away while he strains against them, eyes wide, mouth soundlessly open, in the direction that the other guards are racing in. She faces in that other direction and sees guards racing towards a man who is on fire. It is absurd, unbelievable. A man is on fire. He kneels down, first one knee then the other, and rolls on the ground and as he does so his peaked cap drops off but both the cap and the man carry on being on fire.

She decides to find out if she is able to walk, and she is. Brandon runs past her, a lot less interested in her ability to walk than she thinks he ought to be. She starts to walk and a scarf of ash wraps round her face. It is hard to breathe again. But she keeps going anyway. She doesn't see that she has much choice, given how interested she is now in finding out how long she is able to walk for, and where Reggie is, and where in the holy name of fuck he managed to get hold of high explosives.

Shock Valley – III

What do people say about the road to Silo? 'There's one more step in it than there is in you.' I always hated that. Who knows how many steps there are in me, or in anyone? But by nightfall I'm nowhere close. And despite the gentle warnings of my dear old friend Hendrix, I have walked too far, too long, too late.

Yet the valley road is endless. Tracking the ridgeline and its plummet of shadow, the road skirts the spiny, stony clutter at the base of the hills on one side and scorched waste on the other. Mud baked into county-sized squares. Like a vast tiled floor buckled by a minor earthquake. The heat going down – or coming up – in wiggly wires doesn't let you see much but with a good squint across the tipped planes and jarred edges you can make out the grey Impressionist daub of the far valley wall.

It is beautiful. People stop to look, to absorb its beauty, before adjusting their grip on whatever burden has brought them to the road and moving on. Day and night there is every sort. Families trudging in their force field. Lone men who cannot meet your eye, or any eye, ever again. Single-sex groups of women or men with the ribald air of stag or hen parties. Mixed groups ghostly with shared sorrow. There are those still hooked into busy-with-my-phone postures who will walk right through you if you let them, though no one has phones any more. (Perhaps the greatest gain of Helios, after the beauty: no more phones.) There are those who will fall into step with you and unfold the whole story of their lives and smilingly enfold the whole story of yours. A person could find a lifetime's friends and enemies walking the valley road to Silo.

At night the traffic doesn't especially change, the families don't throw off their rags and turn into gangs of cutthroats, but it feels like it does, and anyway by now I can feel I'm starting to go funny: specks in the eyes, and at the back of the head a sensation of solidified blood. Leaning harder on Hendrix's tibia-shaped stick than I'd prefer, I shuffle to the next set of lights that appear to belong to some broadly public building and old-lady beam my way through the clutch of etiolated men surrounding the door into the bar of what was probably once a rather nice country pub and now resembles the blood-soaked saloon of a Cheyenne frontier town. A sign I glimpse only in passing declares the name of the establishment: The [Something] Dog.

Delicately I circle a conference of sticky children to approach the publican. He is the grave and heavy sort you'd expect, with a single gorgeous jet lock hanging into his eyes from his sunburnt scalp. Early in our negotiations – spreading select contents of my bag across his bar: earring, necklace, stopped watch – I decide that luscious black lock is the man's moral centre and direct my appeals at it rather than at him. In any event we come to an agreement. He takes the watch (they always take the watch) and I follow him to a table whose surface I discover rocks freely on its central post. I reposition the stool and sit with my back to the cracked wall. I prop Hendrix's stick warningly against the wall next to me. As a further precaution I lay my hammer in my lap, out of sight under the table's skew-whiff edge.

I drink brown beer, eat black bread and the smallest portion of the driest beans I have ever seen or tasted. But the taste of a bean, however small or dry! *Eat your greens,* Mum used to tell us. *For God's sake, eat your greens.* Back then greens were food that wasn't really food, food you could take or leave. Often I left it, there on the side of the plate. And now you think: greens from the green of the world.

Now, after Helios, you think lots of things you never thought you would.

Helios. First identified as the Helios Accord, or more commonly the Accord. Later known as the Helios Event, or otherwise the Event.

'Mother.' I open my eyes and the publican is there. 'Your room's ready.'

'There must be some mistake.'

He flicks his brow at a staircase neither of us can see; the damp lock flops. 'It's ready, Mother. You can go up.'

'I didn't ask for a room. There's been a mistake . . .'

Then I feel a drifting in my lap that I'm not in charge of or part of and I look down and one of the sticky children is crouched under the table, stealing my hammer. For a second the child's face peeping at me, blank and sticky and beatific. Beautiful. Beautiful child. Then my hammer is gone and I look for Hendrix's stick and that is gone too and the publican and two other men are wrenching me up off my stool, pressing me against the wall while their hard hands go searching. I consider saying something clever – 'Get a good feel, lads' – but I don't bother and instead let these gruff and lusty fellows drag me across the bar to a hallway and a narrow staircase ascending into absolute darkness. The men shove me in a vaguely upwards direction and all at once I'm a crescent moon, tipping back against them and shouting, 'Hang on, hang on, for fuck's sake,' while I toe a foot into the slot of each step. They don't reply, don't give up their force, but don't increase it either. They are chimps trying to slide a piano upstairs. I am the piano.

I pass the top step and my foot toes empty space. I stagger forward into darkness. A reek of paraffin, soured, long spoilt. The men press me into the wood of a door. There is some scratchy trouble with a handle and then the door gives and the men and I pop through into a bedroom full of strange white electric light and Peter.

This is the thing about Peter. There's nothing to look at – he looks like no one, a man in a polo shirt – but he fills the room. In any room he occupies you're drowning, fighting for air, with Peter. Sitting on the end of the bed he opens his hands and says, 'Surprise.'

I cannot speak but it's not him. When for ten years your only light after nightfall has been the yellowy slobber of something burning, you forget how white, how arctically glaring, electric light is. It freaks you out. Hot and cold at the same time.

'Isn't this divine?' Peter says.

'I don't know if I'd say divine.'

A soft, scoffing laugh. While it dissipates I look for signs that the last decade has hurt him and find disappointingly few. Thinned hair, wrinkled eye sockets, random scar tissue. Otherwise this is the same Peter who recruited me (in the First Class lounge at Heathrow Airport) more than thirty years ago. The same nothing face and nothing frame that settled next to me and said I had a promising future. What makes you say that I said and he said the Armenian diplomat. I said which Armenian diplomat and he said the one in the gents', the one you just killed. I said

I didn't just kill anybody and he said oh, come on, and we pretty much took it from there.

One of his most obnoxious habits was incessantly talking about himself while knowing that you would never be able to establish whether or not anything he told you was true. You could look him up, using the most invasive means at humanity's disposal, and still all you got was garbled gossip – born here, educated there, this surname, that spelling of the forename (Petr, Pyotr). He liked to talk about his youth working on a Siberian pipeline, his early permafrost suffering and its hardening of his earthly ambitions. But then he also told you his parents were well-to-do Moscow intellectuals who had given him 'the exquisite childhood of a prince'. After a while I didn't believe any of it. I wasn't sure he was even Russian.

His favourite narrative was that of his entry into the international grey market, buying and selling commercial tech where it was never meant to be bought or sold, followed by his accumulation of shares, of companies, of magnitudes of wealth that began to afford him the almost unknown privileges (and almost unimaginable appetites) of postmillennial oligarchy. Did he ever say anything I believed? Perhaps one thing, once: 'There's no such thing as a grey market, or a black market, or any of that nonsense, you know, Mabel. They're all the same. All markets are red markets.'

For years I didn't hate him. I didn't hate myself, didn't hate my work, didn't hate him. I assumed that Peter and men like him were a cosmic fact, inexorable as entropy, and I could either exert his pressure or endure it. I did not care that I killed, or who, at that time thinking no further than the plain truth that if I didn't fulfil Peter's commissions someone else certainly would. A part of me still understands it: illuminati sense that one is at work among fundamentals, among the wires and screws that hold up the universe and keep all its wobbly little planets spinning and turning. But no part of me understands how for so long I could have not hated him. In the end I hated him, of course. And myself and my work and the rest of it. I couldn't believe I had ever felt any other way.

'Take a seat,' Peter says now.

'Don't think so.' I remember to smart at that 'Surprise'. He sends word for me to meet him in Silo then ambushes me on the road – and I'm supposed to be surprised? It's practically a trope. But then Peter never gave me enough credit. Even when he thought he did, when he so visibly prided himself on how much credit he was giving me, he didn't give me enough.

'Delighted to see you too, Ms Sawtrey. Is that right – "Ms Sawtrey"? Or did you finally get married?' When I go on not answering he waggles his head at me: look who's just being silly. 'You got my message then.'

'Bits and pieces. While we spoke your messenger boy was bleeding out, so I can't say for sure he communicated every nuance.'

'I want you to kill "Lorelei", so-called. I want you to smash her face in with your hammer. Would you say that's adequately nuanced?'

I give him my scaliest smile. Nonetheless I'm pleased he's heard about my hammer.

'Why?'

'Since when do you ask why?'

'Since you want me to break the face of a motivational speaker or whatever she is.'

'Oh, Mabel. You know better than that. You know it's always the same old reason.'

He's right; I do. Whatever she is, this Lorelei is an obstacle. An impediment in the flow of everything Peter likes to have flowing towards him.

'Why me?'

'It's a perfect match, surely. "Lorelei" is at present more a nuisance than anything else. Grit in the shoe. No one wants to burn down the house for the sake of a gritty shoe. That said, we do want grit-free shoes. So. A proportionate response.'

'Me and my hammer. That's your proportionate response.'

He laughs again – a sort of startled cluck. And then he smiles at me with real pleasure. I'd forgotten this about Peter, the unaccountably meek way he always enjoys me.

'A mad lady in a crowd,' he says. 'A tragic altercation at a public event.'

'Nothing to suggest a chain of command. An order from on high.'

'You flatter me. I'm not "on high".'

'No you're not. You're the order.'

In the white light he regards me oddly. No, he didn't like that. Not at all.

It's funny. You have only to glance at a man like Peter to see the network running through him, ramshackle as it may be nowadays, with its hanks of barbed wire and slivers of broken glass. Not an ideal structure but unquestionably an effective one, a slimy ditch system of protections, coercions, levies, tolls, taxes, waveforms of wealth and power and everything else that Peter likes to have flowing towards him.

But here's the funny part. Along with most people I tend to

assume it was Peter's kind (the money reptiles) who built this network and rebuilt it and always will rebuild it. Yet looking at Peter's disquieted face I am struck afresh by the possibility that has rubbed in a corner of my mind for ten years: that it was and is and always will be the other way round. That the network builds them. That it lives under the earth, under every passing extremity of weather, and occasionally and intelligently it rises to the surface to assemble these men and to embody itself in them. For a second Peter's face is the face of a man crucified on an electric fence. Then he blinks, hauls up a grin from somewhere, and the familiar nothing mask drops back into place.

Another observation: he's lying. Whatever she is, this Lorelei is far more to him than a mere nuisance. Downplay it as he might, Peter has already gone to considerable trouble to arrange this commission, and Peter was never in the habit of going to more trouble over anything than he absolutely had to. So what is this? What is she? What disaster does he need averting, what miracle working? And why does the sound of her name make his eyes fix on mine, as if there is someone else in the room he is trying desperately hard not to look at?

So the next thing I say is, 'I'll do this why?'

'Why?' He shows me how big he can make those fixed eyes. 'Because you love me and will do anything that brings me happiness.'

'I'm going to need better than that. Hard times after Helios.'

His face registers the word (a fillip of the eyelashes): *Helios*. People generally don't say it. I'm not sure why. It's not a religious thing, or even a political thing; my best guess is it's sort of a manners thing. Amid blood and ash and dust and bone, this chanticleer persistence of *manners*. I expect the phenomenon would make for a fascinating cultural study, if this were a world in which anyone still did cultural studies. But he brushes it aside – wipes the word off the air.

'Unquestionably true. Allow me to put the question another way. Do you think you have any alternative?'

Once upon a time I might have thought this was a genuine bluff. And that once again Peter failed to give me due credit, failed to appreciate how completely I could avoid him and every ferrous tendril of his network for the rest of my days, if I wanted to do that. But no: he's not even bluffing. He is only waiting for what I'm going to say next.

'I heard you have something for me.'

'Did you?' He sets his head at an interested elevation. He knows what's coming.

'Your messenger boy. Just before he'd finished bleeding in my kitchen. He said you have something I might want.'

'Is that right?'

'That's exactly right.'

'Well now, I wonder . . .' He taps a fingertip to his pouting lips. Deliberately infuriating. Then he says, 'I suppose he could always have been talking about your sister.'

And no, I didn't know – but I had an idea. A hope. Something as stupid as that. And Peter knew I did and though I keep my expression as neutral as possible his face breaks into a horrible grin.

My sister. My dead sister. It took me five years longer than it should have done for me to think of her as that – *my dead sister* – and even then there was a stiltedness in the thought, a sense of obligation or expedience. There was nothing natural for me in thinking of my sister as dead. But it was the only way I could stop waiting; the only way I could unplug myself from that couch in the house by the dead lake and take my hands from over my mouth and stop waiting for her.

She was the lively one. Against my dark deliberations she was commended on her girlish twirlingness, her hiccupping high-spiritedness, and she accepted the role as, more reluctantly, I accepted mine ('she's a deep one, that girl; one day we'll have to look out for her!'). It was the main thing we fell out about, and the only thing we fell out about more than once. 'Why do you do it?' I would say to her. 'Why do you let everyone think you're some bubblehead, when we both know there's a brain in there?'

'Well, Mabel-cable,' she would say, 'why do you let everyone think you're Sherlock Holmes when we both know half the time you're Homer Simpson?'

But her anger was never like mine, and she put on her fake lashes and makeup and kept her pens in a glittery pink pencil case and at the same time without anyone especially noticing got a degree and a job and rented a flat and managed the practical contingencies of her life with sober competence and independence. Her only stumble, perhaps, was the husband, so soon afterwards the ex-husband. Then again, perhaps not: bad as her marriage was, she left it with an outrageous settlement. I saw her bank statement one day and literally couldn't believe my eyes. 'You mean to say you got all this from that deadbeat?'

'That's why we're still friends.' However that was, she gave up her job at the bank, bought her dream house with the to-die-for lake view, and spent the next thirty years not getting married again and regularly visiting the moronic ex to console him over the scrapes financial, spiritual, sexual and other it seemed he couldn't do without getting into. And that was where she was ten years ago when the north broke down – when the aftershock of the Event entered its terrible escalatory phase and the lines of power slithered southwards and coiled themselves up behind roadblocks and machine-gun nests and the north crumpled. First the cities, then the towns, the villages, pouring to a single dense point of collapse.

When I at last scraped my way back into the country I looked for her; for six months I turned over the rubble that used to be the north and looked for her; then I went to her house by the lake and waited for her, for five years I waited for her. Then for another five years, with an air of dead theatre, of family-gathering formality, I didn't wait for her. I cut and salted rabbit and went to the market and at night I let the heat in, the heat that had refigured all the world. And I didn't leave. I remembered her and didn't leave. The way she named me, renamed me, every time we spoke: Mabel-babel. Mabel-fable . . .

'Do you think it might have been that?' Peter says now. 'Do you think he might have been talking about your sister?'

'You tell me.'

'I think he might have been. Because she's alive of course. You knew that, didn't you?'

'You tell me.'

'I can't imagine why we never got round to talking about this before. I was *so* keen to tell you. And there I was, waiting for you drop by . . .'

'Other things on my mind.'

'You were busy. We all were. It was a highly vexatious time. I understand. But you were too busy to see me – for ten years? I find that very . . . to think of the anguish you might have been spared. If you had only once come to talk to me.'

'She came out of the north.'

'Unlikely as it seems. But I congratulate myself that I took timely measures. When it was clear what was happening up there I arranged for certain individuals, friends and family shall we say, to be escorted off the ground.'

The expression on his face at this moment removes the last of my doubt. For a decade I have been telling myself that I don't know, don't know for a hard fact, that Peter had anything to do with the Event. Certainly the Helios Accord was an accord of businessmen, concerned CEOs, consternated captains of industry; but that didn't mean he was among them. No matter even that the Accord had his fingermarks – eleventh-hour, last-minute – all over it; you couldn't call that proof. Well, now I have proof. His curling eyelids tell me he was one of them. I don't imagine he had a significant role: Peter has never quite enjoyed sufficient standing among his peers for that. He would have served the Accord in some appropriately minor capacity (removing obstacles – smoothing bumps in the road) but beyond the last of my doubt he served it. Worked for the Accord; was the Accord. And now along with everything else I have another excellent reason to hate him. And myself and my work and the rest of it.

'Do you see, Mabel?' Peter says. 'We could have discussed this.'

'You have my sister.'

'She is under my care. And of course you must see her. At the first opportunity. I know she'll be oh, over the moon.'

'You'll tell me where she is.'

'I'll do better than that. I'll take you to her myself.'

I look at him. No word of what he has said is true. I know this. I know this. And yet for some reason I'm not telling him to fuck himself, not snapping the necks of his ambush chimps, leaping out of the window, sprinting away down the road . . .

Peter keeps waiting for me to say something. But I keep not saying anything. But I keep not telling him to fuck himself, either.

Because who am I kidding. For ten years I sat by a lake, cutting a rabbit (the same rabbit). After the Silo road and my joyous tussle on the stairs I grimace at the sensation of sharp points moving inside me, at the sensation of solidified blood at the back of my head. If I even attempted any of that blazing stuff – snapping, leaping, sprinting – oh what sad farce, what crackly slapstick.

'Lorelei is appearing before the masses in Silo tomorrow night,' Peter says finally. 'You'll be there.'

Is he right? But it's too soon to think about that so I go to the window I'm not leaping out of and look up at the sky and fold my arms and call to him over my shoulder: 'What about the security team? What about Mrs Tooth?'

'Mrs who?'

'The hag. The formidable hag.'

'Oh, I'm willing to bet on my own formidable hag.' He grins tightly. 'So you'll be there.'

'In the crowd. With my hammer.'

'You see, Mabel? You *do* know better.'

Part Three

Extinction Events

15. Like a Landslide

In the woods Dia looks at Reggie, bent over, fists on knees, coughing.

She wavers. With an idea of steadying herself she puts out a hand and it catches on the rugged sleeve of a tree. How had they thought they would be friendly: the trees? But they must have thought that. They knew the smoke wasn't friendly, or the fire; so much they agreed in that wordless interlude after she found him in the blackened grass. When they ran (the sirens and lights, which they established also were not friendly) they faced a choice between the road and the trees. In a heart-thud they chose the trees. Arm in arm, simultaneously holding each other up and dragging each other down, they swerved away from the line of vehicles massing at the hysterical gate and walked in between the trees. Walked and walked – pressed to the skin of the trees, to the muscle, the innards, the speckly gizzard. And what could have possessed them to do that?

She listens. Still crooked there with his fists on his knees, he is now muttering as well as coughing. She hears a repeated sound. Something like *gel*; something like *herald*. Then Reggie straightens and staggers, panting, back against another tree and he gapes at her with all the stained copper of his eyes.

'You're bloody,' he says.

'I'm bloody what?'

He flaps a hand at her. She touches her cheek and holds her fingers in front of her face. She frowns. Lumps of stiff black jam, with the grit and the seeds. He starts towards her and she holds the hand with the black jam on it palm out to him and says, 'No. No. Fuck off. Fuck off a minute, Reggie sweet.'

Then she is sitting, so she looks at the water. Dull, spiny claws holding onto the big green stones. When Reggie comes towards her again she barely notices him, the pale blur of him settling next to her on unevenly weighted haunches, until he says, 'This is going to hurt,' and he presses a fire into her head. She shouts. The claws ravel out and out over the stones but don't disappear. Somehow she keeps looking at them. 'Ouch,' he says.

Something drops into the water. Between skittering talons she glimpses it – a flip of black – then she's distracted by him suddenly sliding in front of her. The copper eyes, the map of freckles, the prickled skin. She looks at him. She considers licking his face. If she did it, if she leaned forward and licked his face, it would have nothing to do with him and nothing to do with her. It would simply be an event that occurred. Then she feels a snag at the base of her skull, a tow and a drag across the back of her head, and she shouts. Grainy black covering the sky. Darkness, folds, the end of the world.

'You do it then,' he says.

'Do what?'

He shows her. The bit of ruined sky with which it turns out he has been attempting to wrap her head, is the black cloth he has untwisted from her hair. He moves his hands at the sides of her face: taking in or letting out unseen ropes.

'Make it look like . . . you know.'

'No,' she says, 'I don't know.'

'You've got . . .' He dabs a finger at the corner of her eye. 'We need to cover you up. So we can move.'

'We don't need to cover me up.'

'We're not going to get far with you looking like . . .' He doesn't say it but the way he doesn't say it helps her see a burning man kneel down on the ground and start to roll and his burning cap falls off and rolls too.

'Then we don't move. We don't need to move.'

'We do.'

Of course she knows what he wants. The year she decided to change her name from Robinson to Talwar she went after school to the gym every Tuesday night with the other kids to listen to the beardy, scrunch-eyed imam who seemed to believe that the best way to teach teenagers about religion was by means of continuous reference to the Father Brown stories. With two girls she went round Longsight Market one Saturday morning and then for another year she wore the hijab every day, loving the sleek enclosing lines that made her all slipstream, that made her gleam and clang like a knight on his charger, loving also the shriek of horror it never failed to bring to Lila's eyes. Eventually she chucked it in, got bored, got tired, got interested in other ways of being Dia Talwar, ways that included being four-fifths naked at two o'clock in the morning with every finger of her left hand broken in a slatternly squadron of the A&E damned, but for a while . . . she tries and of course she remembers. She ties the knot under her chin and stands, veiled and veiled again in the sensations she recalls from her first ever time: not sleek, not gleaming, but as if her head has swollen to the size of a watermelon and filled with the soundtrack of a fox hunt. And this helps how?

Without touching her, as if in acknowledgement of her

obscurely changed status, he leads her out between the trees. He seems to be talking to himself; almost smirking, with his upper teeth starkly exposed. She remembers the repeated sound he was muttering earlier and says, 'Who's Gerald?'

He shakes his head.

'Was it Gerald who sorted you out with your lovely stash of whizz-bangs?'

'Don't know what you're talking about.'

'Yes you do. Your firework stash, your . . .' She looks for the black rucksack, but he is not wearing it. Then she looks for something else and sees he is not wearing that either. 'What happened to your armband? Your cloth?'

He looks at the bare space on his bicep, then shakes his head again.

They are still walking between the unfriendly trees when she remembers the thing she heard, and briefly saw, fall into the water. A flip of black, rearing then sinking, heavy with all the stuff coming out of her head like seed-thickened jam.

She nods. There is the road, there is the town. There is Reggie, standing on tiptoe, as if about to break into a dance. And it *is* a kind of dance – she sees that even sitting on a stub of brick wall with her hands in their pit of bottomless gravity in the centre of her lap. She seems to keep leaning forward. Craning down towards her joined hands. The scarf means she can see almost nothing except ruined sky and Reggie lifting onto tippy-toes on the pavement in front of the bus station, trying to talk to girls.

Probably she would call him back if it weren't for the fact he is evidently so good at it – so good at talking to girls. The ones going past in their twos and threes and fours have no reason to stop and let him talk to them, but nearly all of them do. Hooded delinquents quite as much as the lipgloss princesses pause at his rakishly opened arms, his coy half-bow, and stand and cackle or go into hot and secretive conclave with him before one finally works free an arm, prises loose an elbow, and the pack breaks and moves on. She really should be calling him back, but instead she clamps her lips at the sight of a girl spilling back out of her pack and tottering towards him, arm extended, phone proffered. He drops to a knee to take the phone, to catch the girl's hand and chastely kiss her wrist, before standing with his thumbs already weaving in the touchpane.

She nods. There is Reggie, talking on the phone. There is the girl, waiting for him, glancing at her friends and practically doubling over every time one catches her eye.

It is dark. Reggie is no longer talking on the phone, no longer standing in front of the bus station. She has to turn her whole head to be sure he is sitting next to her on the wall.

'Don't worry,' he says. 'Things are in hand.' He sniggers softly. His face when he looks at her seems held together by a tense kind of sweat. But it's not even hot.

Then she is standing, she is walking, he is carrying her over the pavement with an arm under her arm. Her head rolls forward. There is a van. One of the van's doors rumbles open and he is pushing her past it, shoving her inside. Because she has no other choice and because the scarf has folded again and blinded her she splays her hands and grabs at whatever they find, blunt edges, squeaky planes of things – metal rods, seat mechanics.

He climbs in after her. Momentarily he seems to be lying on top of her. Various parts of him press close to various parts of her. Her head feels very tight. She hears him trying to close the door. It takes him several attempts. She wonders if he is trying to do it with his feet. Then the door closes, and as they lurch away from the bus station things come right way up and she is sitting in a spongy low seat with Reggie sitting next to her on one side and someone else sitting next to her on the other side.

'Slick,' Reggie says.

'Yup,' says the someone sitting on Dia's other side.

She is expected to turn her head and look at this someone. She is expected to say: who are you? What is this? Who do you work for, who do you represent? Are you Tarantula? Is that what's happening, are we going back to Tarantula? Or going where? To who? Why? So she doesn't say a thing.

Then she does look. She pulls the scarf off her head and leans right over and looks the someone in the face and she says, 'Fuck me.'

'You're not my type, girl,' the someone says, with a flickering of the eyelids that shows he instantly regrets his own joke. But then he always was like that, wasn't he? He always was a bit like that, was old Pisces.

It does not occur to her to wonder where he is taking them – a campsite, a cluster of pariah vans, an alley between disused factory buildings – until they arrive at their destination, and it is a house. He has brought them to a house in a row of houses, narrow tenements with gates and hanging baskets. He gets out of the van and approaches the house. It doesn't make sense. What is Pisces doing at a house? Who could Pisces know who lives in a house? She waits for him to knock, but instead he reaches into a pocket and takes out a bunch of keys that he picks through before selecting one in particular and slotting and twisting it in two different parts of the door. Then he pushes and the door opens. She could laugh. Who would be fool enough to lend Pisces the keys to their house?

Pisces returns to the van. He opens the doors, hisses at Reggie, who springs from his seat and runs into the house. Then Pisces leans inside, clearly intent on getting hold of her. Shaking her head, she smacks his hands away and slides across the seat and descends from the van unaided, thank you very much. Then her embery temple seems to aim itself at the centre of the earth and she just has to bloody well go along with it as Pisces lifts her off her feet and carries her into the house.

He lays her down on a couch in a room full of yellow light. There are fireplace figurines, bookshelves lined with the glassy spines of CDs. She gazes steadily at his face while he engages in a long conversation with Reggie. And yes, it is Pisces' face. Smaller, sadder, with more texture showing; and the hair is a wholly new development. It goes without saying that Pisces was always militantly bald, yet now she spies the curling rudiments of an actual haircut. How can this be? For more than fifteen years she has preserved her image of him as one half of an immemorial duo – Samson all shagginess and psychedelia, Pisces with his scalp stubble, his wizardy beard and his leather waistcoat – and now he is *this*? Changed by a handclap of sudden time into something so poor and ordinary, so porous, so pregnable? Then he looks at her, and there are his eyes, there are his pursed and hanging lips, and she feels only startled, shivered love.

'What games have *you* been playing?'

She goes hurr hurr.

'Sorry, Dia love, we're going to have to see to your bonce.'

Gravely he pretends to knock on her head. 'Bit of a mess we've got here.'

'Hurr,' she says.

Pisces starts doing things – she hears a jar unscrewing, water sloshing, sees a big tight cloud of woollen wadding silently splinter from a plastic-wrapped package of the stuff – and as he stirs up the embers in her temple she manages to say, 'Where are we?'

'This is my house.'

It isn't possible. She gazes up at him while he concentrates on doing a thing to her temple. She clamps then unclamps her lips. 'Since when?'

'Ten years it must be now.'

'You've lived . . . in a house . . . for ten years?' The world is not what it was. The world has gone, dissolved completely in a wash of negligent rain. 'What about Thin Love? Mama Styx, everyone?'

Pisces' hanging lips smile. 'I haven't seen that crowd in a long time. Brave girl now.' He does something sudden and snappish to her temple. The sudden, snappish thing has nothing to do with the tears burning into her eyes, scorching up out of their craters. 'Good. Let's sit you up.'

She sits up. The tears fall off her face; she whacks the heel of a hand at each eye and expels the loudest, grimmest sniff she can muster. Standing over her, Pisces takes both her hands and guides her to her feet as if helping her onto stilts. 'Fancy a stroll? If Reggie's done as he's been bid, we should have a treat for you.'

He seems to want her to go up some stairs – some stairs in this house that she is being asked to believe is Pisces' house, Pisces who lives in a van or a tent or under a single sheet of dry newspaper or under the silver-bullet stare of the stars themselves, but not in a house, not like a person, a person like everyone else. And the clatter of anxiety grows loud in her head until she has to stop on the fourth or maybe fifth stair and dig her nails into his arm and say, 'Was it you?'

'Don't know what you're asking me.'

'Who helped Reggie. Helped him do whatever he did.'

'The first I've heard from Reggie in two years is he calls me up this afternoon saying can I drive halfway across the country to pick the pair of you up from a bus stop because there's been some bother I don't want to know about. Happy?'

He leads her to a bathroom and a bath with a low tideline of foam in it under a very bright white light. She sits on the toilet seat and looks hazily at the aqua-patterned tiles.

'What do you reckon?' Pisces stands by the door, a shy and grizzled schoolboy. 'It's mostly bubbles, but you should feel the benefit. Don't get your stitches wet.'

Don't get her whats what? But he has gone, drawn the door softly shut, and she's left alone with the tranquil rasp of the bubbles. Slowly she raises a hand to her temple and finds there the taped pack of woollen wadding and the thready circuit inside it: her seething new centre, the linear core now holding her together.

'You found the dressing gown? Couldn't remember if I mentioned it.'

'You didn't. But yeah. Obviously.'

In the stiff blue raincloud of a dressing gown she teeters past Reggie, lying it seems face-down asleep on the couch, to the dinner table at which Pisces is sitting with an almost comically overweight laptop, a dainty teacup and a Mars bar on a china dish. She sits across from him, negotiating the altitudes of the chair rather more easily than she was anticipating, and emboldened leans towards him with hunched shoulders and knitted fingers.

'What the fuck's going on, Pi?'

'Wish I knew, Dia love.'

'You and Reggie are pals then.'

'He's dropped in a couple of times. There's a bed he helped shift across a landing one time, but it was never a regular thing. And I always got the sense there were other wheels in motion. Not one for the simple life, Reggie, is he?'

She frowns somewhat decisively and there is pain across her eyes as if her face is collapsing, coming down in sheet after substantial sheet, like a landslide. 'Ow, *shit* . . .'

'It'll settle down. Patience, girl.'

She re-angles her shoulder hunch to include Reggie. 'Has he said anything?'

'Said he was hungry. Speaking of which.'

'You know what I mean.'

'I haven't asked, and he hasn't said.'

'Has he mentioned Samson?'

'No.' Interesting how his mouth ridges at the name.

'Do you ever see him? Samson?'

'Nope.' The ridges sharpen, steepen.

'Ten years. I'd no idea. What happened?'

'Nothing. I just left.' He smiles, awkwardly, with all those ridges in his mouth. 'It was a great scene, but it couldn't last. So I got out, got a job, got this place. I work for myself now. I paint. Paint and decorate. You got a spare room needs tarting up, you give me a ring.'

'Where are we? I know we're in your house. More generally.'

'Lancaster. Well, Galgate. Just outside. Nice little place. You'd like it.'

She is unable to take this in. Warwick to Lancaster – that's what? She has no feeling of the distance. To her unstitched (prestitched) head, it was nothing: a mouse click, a screen tap. And now she is here. Galgate: the gate of gall.

'Is there a Mrs Pisces?'

'Fish,' he says gently. 'There isn't, as it goes, but it would be a Mrs Fish. A Mrs Keith Fish.'

'You call yourself Keith.'

'I do.'

'No way. You're Pisces. Pisces to the death.'

'You need to eat.'

'Who's Gerald?' The name returns to her. 'Reggie was rambling about someone called Gerald. Ring any bells?'

Pisces snorts. 'There's Gerald Pinion.'

'Is there?'

'He was as they say "newsworthy" for a few years, never in Samson's league, but he got his beardy face in the papers every so often. You remember Gerald Pinion.'

'Maybe.' Gerald Pinion. Beardy face. There is an image that won't quite resolve.

'He was the wind bloke. It was like he and Samson wanted to form a renewables boy band. They had the solar one and the wind one, they just needed a lad with clever ideas about compost and they'd have had the set.'

'He was the Wind Man.' And the image coalesces: a tweedy toff with specs and beard grinning in front of a row of spindly turbines.

'There you go. Bluff old peer who pawned the family silver to buy a stake in alternative energy. He and Samson were mates for years. Shoulder to shoulder at this rally or that other sodding thing. Then they fell out. "Ideological differences". It was all in the papers.'

'I don't read the papers. I just fuck about online.'

'Not seen much of him lately. Now and then there's a gloomy bit on TV saying how the turbine market has dropped off. Last year he was in a documentary I watched about half of, looking sorry for himself.'

'So what, now he's a pal of Reggie's?'

'Could be. Reggie might have mentioned him. I don't remember.'

'Reggie and this Gerald Pinion. Do you think they—'

'You need to eat, Miss Marple. Then I have to show you something.'

'What?' She straightens in her stiff blue raincloud. 'Show me.'

He knows her well enough not to try to argue. With another, hollower snort, he turns the tubby laptop to face her. Its screen is a burning man rolling on the ground. Next to him a burning cap rolls also.

'Where is this?' She reaches for the keyboard but realises she has forgotten how to work one: do you push? Or do you pull?

'Where?' Pisces says softly. 'Dia love, this is everywhere. Right now this is the internet.'

16. Don't Be Deceived

The night is a storm of tiny pink flowers swirling off the walls of Pisces' mysteriously feminine second bedroom, the intricacies of her sleep superintended by two frowsy ragdolls slumped against each other on the bedside table (the flowers, the dolls: for whom are they intended?) while beyond the door she hears Pisces moving about the house, all night passing stealthily from room to room . . . In the morning she finds Reggie still snoring face-down on the couch, and no trace of Pisces. Facing the early blue light at the kitchen window, she makes coffee then returns in her dressing gown to the dining table and stirs up the unwilling laptop.

By the time Pisces slams back into the house with his carrier bag of breakfast things, she thinks she has gained an idea of the scale of Reggie's offence. The man whom the world has seen rolling in flames on the ground at the site of a privately owned experimental solar-power plant in Warwick is called Grayson James. He is twenty-eight years old and he has worked as a member of security staff with Glaze Energy for sixteen months. He has a wife (Carly, thirty-one), a son (Taylor, six) and a daughter (Giselle, three) who was born with a malformed lung. In addition to the images of him rolling and rolling in a blanket or a jacket of flames that he cannot strip off no matter how hard he tries, the world has seen pictures of Mr James on the couch with his young family, on the pitch with his Sunday-league football team, on the steps of the church with his bride in a gust of confetti. A long, blameless face full of butcher's-boy pink health; eager eyes; a faintly loony, mad-for-it grin.

In the incident at the solar-power plant Grayson James suffered second- and third-degree burns across eighty to ninety per cent of his body. He was taken to the burns facility at Coventry University Hospital where he remains in a critical condition. His doctors have not yet issued any statement on his chances of recovery.

The world seems to be aware that Mr James' injuries occurred during an 'invasion' of the plant site, during a 'violent protest by a radical activist group', though she finds nothing to suggest that either the group or its individual members have been named. She wonders about the absence of names. Where are they? Did someone lose them? Or did someone expend an immense amount of energy to ensure they were not found? And, if that's right, for how much longer can the expenditure be made – for how much longer can the energy last?

Pisces is still in the kitchen, and she's still winding back and forth through the footage from the solar plant – the opportunistic phone movie of one of Mr James' security colleagues, likewise unnamed – when she gets her first real shock. The screen with the burning man in it sweeps and banks and hangs for a second on a revolving face: speed-lined, pixel-jarred, but unmistakably the face of Reggie Glaze. Not quite a close-up, but good enough. Is it possible no one in the world is going to recognise that face, that world-famous face?

A moment later she gets her second shock. Blur bodies skitter through the edge of the screen. The screen flexes, grips. A single blur body teeters upright. A dark dot face opens and closes. That's it. But it is her. Even with cold shots of panic lancing her belly she determines pretty well immediately that no one is going to identify her from these images. But the blur body is her body. The dot face is her face.

'We can't stay here,' she tells Pisces as he slides her breakfast in front of her.

'No,' he says, sparing them a conversation neither of them needs. 'Anywhere in mind?'

'Nowhere. We just need to be . . . far. Really far.' She looks down at the bubbling plate. All her fingers crowd the brims of her face. And she feels it as she hasn't felt it since she was a little girl – the sense that she is being crushed by the elements. Worked to nothing by fire, by wind, by water, by the pestling earth.

'There might be somewhere,' Pisces says from beyond her fingers. 'Somewhere a bit out of the way.'

She looks up at him.

'Only I'm not sure you're going to like it.'

Reggie listens. At least she thinks he does: it's actually quite hard to tell what he's doing, or indeed if he's doing anything at all, apart from taking up space at the head of the dining table, the laptop open in front of him, his empty breakfast plate pushed away next to it. Some time ago, after Pisces shuffled back to the kitchen and she started talking to him, Reggie set both elbows on the table and dropped his head forward, so she has ended up talking largely to the tight coils of his hair. Now, with a clump of her hand heels against the table to indicate that she's finished talking, that she has outlined her idea and is ready to hear his response, she waits to see if he will raise his head. And he does, slightly: lifts his face enough that she can distinguish the baffled sneer of his bared teeth.

'All right. I mean, I'm going back to Tarantula. When everything

. . .' He pats down the air with both hands. 'But yeah, we can do this for now.'

He wants to go back. She doesn't blame him: she wants to go back too. Go back through space and time, reset the astronomical clock, reverse the threshing wheel of the visible until she arrives once more on a bench in the rafter-dropped refectory with Jon on this side of her, Fee on that . . . But what can they do? She says, 'We're going to have to proceed with caution. Just because your face isn't wallpapering the internet at this precise second doesn't mean it won't crop up sooner or later.'

Again his face lifts slightly. She can almost see his eyes. Freckle-blotched bones; the immaculate nakedness of his New York orthodontia.

'I don't think so,' he says. 'My father would never allow it.'

'Even Samson's reach has limits.'

Reggie sniffs, coughs. 'You don't know my father very well, do you?'

All at once the cold shots give way to blazing anger: 'Do you know what you've done, Reggie? Do you know what you've done to this man?' She slaps the yawning laptop. On its screen Grayson James (twenty-eight) is wrapped in yellow blanket fringes of fire. 'Do you know he could die?'

His face lifts fully and now she sees his eyes. And they are wrong. It is as simple as that. They are not empty, not sickly, not obviously unnatural: they're just wrong. And the idiot sneer of the teeth, sunk in their scandalous self-pity.

'Everyone dies,' Reggie says.

They agree the finer details of the idea – it is, of course, really Pisces' idea – with surprising ease. Pisces suggests they wait for night before moving; Dia counters they should go while time is on their side, while there are no names attaching to the images in the world's view. He agrees, saying only this time she and Reggie should not sit in the front of the van but ride out the journey in the back. She agrees.

As she leaves the house she ties the black cloth round her head, hijab-fashion, again. Pisces' eyes travel the edge of the scarf but he says nothing. Reggie doesn't even look at her until they are shut up in the black back of the van and he finds a torch somewhere and shines it banally into her face.

'Does your head still hurt?'

'It still does.' Not so much a landslide any more as a lake, huge and full of primordial turbulence.

'I'm sorry,' he says. 'I didn't mean for that.'

She thinks what the hell: 'What *did* you mean? What was the plan? Kill Samson? Ruin him? Kill someone else, like a security guard, say, and pin it on him?'

'You know what I meant. To send a message. To warn people not to trust my father. Not him or any of the fake saviours like him.'

'Because it's the end of the world and we're all going to die.'

'Not the end of the world. The end of *our* world. The end of our time.'

In the dark she considers him. 'Who helped you?'

'I've got friends.'

'What sort of friends?'

'Oh, you know . . .'

She releases her handhold in the van's portalled side, slides forward onto her knees in the grainy, canvasy space between

Reggie and herself, snatches the torch from him and beams it point-blank into the pink of his eyes. 'Let's say I don't. What friends?'

'Guy called Sellick. You don't know him.' And he tells her: *first the oceans will rise* . . . It takes a while. But at last she forms a picture of Reggie's connect to the crepuscular underworld of military-grade explosives: some hallucinogenic basket case and sad act whom he met in a Shepherd's Bush squat and, from the sound of it, from the trouble he's taken over the years to extricate this character from every form of incarceration yet devised, never got round to falling out of love with.

'And you asked this Sellick to find you a shitload of bombs?'

'We had a discussion.'

'Which resulted in you buying a shitload of bombs off him.'

'He gets it. Sellick's always been ahead of the rest of us. He saw what's coming long before anyone else did.'

'So this Sellick is basically a, a, basically an *arsehole*, while you, Reggie, you're just thinking about the planet. You're just so concerned about the world. Nothing to do with you having a knot in your nappies about your dad. Christ no. *Perish the thought*.'

'You have to do that, don't you? Shrink everything down so it's nice and easy and personal. Kitchen sink, soap opera. Mummies and daddies. Because that's always the answer for people like you – clever enough to know everything's fucked up but too lazy to do anything about it. Too scared to come out of your precious pose and do something.'

It's shaky ground but she can't help herself: 'I joined Tarantula . . .'

'And what was that? More posing. You joined Tarantula the

way you join a gym, or a spa. Because for all your cleverness you don't recognise a thing unless it looks like a holiday.'

'That's right, Reggie sweet. Here I am, enjoying my holiday.'

It is midday before Pisces releases them from the van. Dia unslots her legs and stretches the rust out of them on a grey stretch of roadside tarmac.

'Thought you might fancy a look,' Pisces says.

She doesn't, but she looks anyway.

And there it is: wet brick and tile, dark factory shapes, tufts of parks and, rising above all in the towny luminescence, grey concrete giants, one of which once squatted and forgot ever to straighten again.

Ainscough. Her town. Where she comes from.

But that's not why they are here. In fact she would rather be almost anywhere than here. They have come for the place inside the place, the world inside the world.

'How's it feel?' Pisces says.

Staring blankly up at the town, she supposes she owes old Pi the truth.

'Like nothing,' she says. 'Empty space.'

For the last part of the journey Dia and Reggie sit up front with Pisces ('Might look peculiar, you two popping out the back on a street in broad daylight'), so she has a direct view of the familiar roads and unfamiliar shop units, the arcades, bollards, ramps, a sense of threat less anything in their appearance than her certainty that they remember her – and remember Lila – along with the giants louring under the pavement-stone sky. She pulls the scarf tighter about her face and mutters at Pisces' pedals: 'Shithole.'

They stop on Sycamore Lane. Which means the leaning cliff of misery behind them must be Sycamore House. She doesn't turn, doesn't look. Even while she and Reggie stand in the road as Pisces locks up his van she holds her back set against it. Because if she turned, if she looked, there would be a six-year-old girl in her unforgivable soots and the girl's hilarious so-white-she's-blue mother with her alien sinews and her pterodactyl bones and her uproarious crunching swandives in that car park there, on that pub floor there, and no one needs to see that. No one needs to look; because they are always there, not in a room or at a window on the ninth floor, but blasted in the open spaces beneath and in between, the girl's hair a glittery snarl, the mother's loose throat squirming like jelly . . .

On the other side of Sycamore Lane, in the direction she can bear to face, is a park. The last time she was here it was scrub, a torn wound of earth with the town's dead fridges and ruined mattresses heaped on it. Now there's a duck pond, a couple of stands of healthy-looking trees, a play area equipped with swings and slides and tubular apparatus like modern art. It is, even she can see it is, better. Could it well have been worse?

On the far side of the park, where the landscaping peters out and the scrub weedily persists, brown and scored and cacti-like, she sees evidence that Pisces was right: old habits die hard, and constellated objects return, and in September the Thin Love Collective comes to Ainscough. And there it is too, a smudged circle of vans beyond the pinpointing rain.

'Is that it?' Languidly Reggie blinks. 'It looks fucked up.'

'What?' she says. 'No it doesn't.'

'It looks totally fucked up.'

He isn't right. The collective looks how it always looked – how it looked each morning when she pressed fearfully to her window on the ninth floor of Sycamore House and almost didn't dare look for fear that in the night it had gone and all she would see when she lifted the curtain was a wet disarrangement of the mud, a circular scrape like the bite mark of a great and starving mouth . . . But no, it was always there, September to November, the fortress of vans with its fire snaps and dog yelps and the invisible portcullis it raised only for her . . . She strides into the park.

Pisces calls after her. Maybe Reggie does too. But she keeps going past the empty and waterlogged benches, past the play area and the pond, until she reaches the wire fence partitioning off the bleak lands behind. She pulls at the wire, peers in annoyance at its thin unclenchings. If she had time she could probably take the whole thing apart, twist by weak twist, but she doesn't have time because on the other side of the fence now there's someone saying to her, 'You all right there?' Not in a way that suggests real concern over her well-being.

'Been better.' The man is mid-thirties, she supposes, with a bleached Mohawk, a nose ring and a staggering congeries of facial tattoos: zigzags, dagger points. He's wearing tight woollen trousers and a sort of woollen jerkin from which skinny white arms protrude with a freight of torcs and copper bangles. Altogether he looks exactly like the sort of person you'd expect to live in a quasi-legal road collective. Which is confusing. Because the people who live in Thin Love don't look like people who live in a collective. They look like everyone, like anyone; a bit bushier, maybe, a bit more frayed, but nothing like this fire swallower or space pirate. 'Yourself?'

'Happy as a pig, me. All I'm bothered about is what you're up to with that fence.'

'I'm just trying to get through.'

'That's what I'm bothered about.'

'Don't be. I'm a friend.'

'Oh aye? Friend from the council, is it?'

'Actually, sunbeam, I'm sort of a member.'

The man's daggery face closes. 'Don't think so.'

'This is Thin Love, yes? You're Thin Love?'

He doesn't miss a beat: 'We're Siouxsie and the Banshees for all it matters to you.'

'Christ.' One of the coils of wire has caught in the trailing end of her scarf. She pulls at the wire, at the scarf. 'Can I speak to Mama, please? Mama Styx?'

But now the space pirate has lost interest in her, is looking past her. He cups his hands round his mouth and shouts, 'Pisces! That you, mate?'

Pisces lumbers up next to Dia. 'The living flesh.'

'This one one of yours?'

'Both,' Pisces says, as Reggie laboriously joins them also. 'Ones of mine, ones of yours. Golden Age, Max love, before your time. Scylla about?'

'I'm about,' someone else says, and there is a moment of confusion, because the woman loping towards them is clearly Mama Styx, though not Mama as she should look now, more than fifteen years since Dia last saw her, but looking as she did when Dia last saw her, or no, as she did when Dia first saw her, or no—

'Scylla!' Pisces calls. 'Scylla Styx!'

The woman draws up beside Max the Space Pirate and stands

looking at them with her hands in her pockets. She is small, blonde, higgledy-piggledy with traveller ornaments of the old type (piercings, knottings) but otherwise a faultless replica or reboot of the inimitable Mama. She can't be long out of her teens. And she smiles at them, Reggie and Dia, with curious expectancy.

'Reggie,' she says. 'Dia.' And there they are: there are the lost names.

Reggie raises a hand in a noncommittal wave. Dia goes on staring.

'You pair of bastards,' says Scylla Styx evenly. 'You don't remember me, do you?'

Reggie isn't right, but the Thin Love Collective is no longer what it was. In fact the changes the collective has undergone lately are what Scylla is most keen to discuss as they pace the tight inner courtyard made by the circle of vans – tighter, more paranoid than Dia ever knew it, and containing two or three times as many vehicles: 'Excuse the overpop. We've filled out in recent years.'

'Recruitment drive?' Reggie says.

'Diametric opposite. Eighty per cent of these ballbags I'd chuck in the river with a smile on my face.'

Dia laughs; Scylla's eyes narrow on her. 'No doubt about it, we're a popular bunch these days. Can't tell you how many folk like to stroll in here, take a quick snap for the online album. Quite a few too who like to drop round and chat to us about the type of people we are. Or type of pond life, or type of something-lower-than-pond-life . . . Hence Maxie's, do I want to say, highly motivated demeanour earlier. Which reminds me.

To what exactly do we owe the pleasure? And, if I may so inquire, what species of pleasure are we down for here? Flying visit, or something more in the nature of a residential?'

'Maybe a couple of days half board,' Dia says. 'If you can stretch to it.'

'Suits me. Gives me a chance to tell you about the moral philosophers we draw to our circle. We'll grab some sleeping bags, curl up round the fire, we'll make a night of it . . .'

For a while they do sit by the fire – not the flaming drum of yore but a skeletal steel tripod with an energy-efficient grill suspended inside it. When she has exhausted the subject of the collective's council visitors, Scylla moves on to her mother's last days. 'Cancer. That thunderbolt sort. She wouldn't let you do a thing for her. Right up until she passed she was taking everyone's grocery orders. Folding her notebook over, licking her pencil. When she'd got the last order in she gave Max her notebook, walked to her van and lay down and that was how she passed. She was fifty-two.'

It's as if the world is splitting in two – as if the world split in two a long, long time ago and she's only just noticed that the lush forests and green fields have been replaced by crust and ash. She glances at Reggie and he seems to be holding himself in his folded arms, holding himself together. His face is full of pain but of course it is. He loved Mama too.

'We get by,' Scylla says. 'And we remember our friends. You're welcome to stay with us for as long as you need to. Can't promise The Ritz, but we've a couple of supply vans, maybe a pillow or two if you don't mind the smell of dog farts . . .'

Dia has been following Scylla round the puddles towards the vans when she glances back to see Pisces still sitting wide-kneed by the fire. She strides back to him and his face turns joltingly to hers.

'You're not staying.'

'Oh, Dia love. This is no place for me any more.'

She thinks of the second bedroom in the house in Galgate with its mysterious pink flowers and enigmatic ragdolls. For Pisces there is a life elsewhere, awaiting his return. Nonetheless she says, 'It's a place for me?'

'Right now I'd say so. Don't be angry with me. You know as well as I do, I can't give you the help you need. People here can do that.'

'I'm not angry.' And she isn't: ailed at the thought of his leaving, but not angry. And the way she saw Reggie do it she folds her arms round herself.

'You know how it is,' Pisces says. 'Don't be deceived. Our type never really go. We may leave the room but we're always in the building.'

17. I'm Coming Across

'. . . tell them to get . . .'

'. . . talking about? I'm not telling anyone . . .'

Other sounds, the clank of a toolbox, the coo of a child, the soft insistent pat-pat-pat that can mean only dogs in their light-footed patrols: sounds that make her eight, seven, six years old again, dawdling over afternoon scrub, looking at fire and feeling it in the clutch and lift of her rain-draggled hair . . .

Then a knocking recalls her to the space she's in, the tight fit among cardboard boxes full of the eerie screech of polystyrene packaging. She gets up past the boxes, chops at the van's flimsy door until it waggles outwards, into the air and the rain.

Scylla, hunched in a bomber jacket that has burst at both shoulder seams, grins up at her. 'Got a minute?'

'Uh oh.'

'Don't give me that. I need one minute.'

Dia finds her scarf, ties it over her hair and steps down from the van to join Scylla in the mudscape, the rainsphere. Only now, as they start trudging towards Scylla's van on the other side of the circle, she notices Max, standing glamorously wrapped in a sheet of tinfoil, as if he has just run a marathon. It is possible he is staring at them. Possibly only the dagger points tattooed round the edge of his face are staring at them.

Scylla's van is a revelation. Even from the outside it is a clear step up from what Dia remembers, a sleek cask of self-governance. Then Scylla heaves the door open and leads her briskly up over the threshold and further adjustments are necessary. No snug, ratty clutter but a pale space of pillows and cushions. They pass a modular workstation badged with Post-it notes and sit on a cool, low couch. 'Scylla, this is gorgeous . . .'

'It'd better be. Now "life on the road" has gained mass appeal and every sixth former in the land has to spend at least one summer parked up in a farmer's field. Not that I care. The mystical "road" doesn't belong to me any more than anyone else, and I was born right here on the ley line. No, I sympathise with the kids we're getting now. When you see what's on offer at the side of the road . . . a state of what you might call *total toxicity*. Everything so crazily befouled the kids think it's them. Think they must deserve all that shit. Think they must be shit themselves. Then halleluiah, they snap out of it and come knocking on our door.'

Scylla laughs. 'Conversation for another time. Just now, Dee, I'd appreciate your thoughts on something.' She takes a remote-control wand from the arm of the couch, taps it, and the TV positioned across from them quickens to life. The screen contains a still image of Reggie's face.

Dia doesn't really need to look. The still is taken from the phone footage recorded at the solar-plant protest or attack or whatever the hell that day ended up being. She would know it anywhere – the grain, the dotting, the jarred parabola of pixels . . .

'I'm not much of a sleeper,' Scylla is saying, 'and in the wee hours this morning I came across this. One of those breaking-news channels. This one's American. But it's on all the other ones too.'

'We're such pricks,' Dia says.

'I don't know about that, but you've been . . . busy, haven't you?' Scylla taps the wand again and the image on the screen swims into motion: scrolling forward into smoke and fire, then back, back, clamping onto a dot face, a blur body. Helplessly the body jerks towards one of the big panel arrays and begins smashing it back together. 'Now, Dee, I don't know for sure if that's—'

'It's me. That's me.'

'. . . Wow. You're really going for it there, aren't you?'

'Reggie's been named?'

'He has. And this group – "Tarantula"? No mention of you so far. I take it you're a member though, a –Tarantulan?'

'We just say Tarantula,' Dia says.

'Do you.'

'I wanted to tell you,' Dia says, with an airless intonation neither of them can believe. Scylla only draws slightly away from her, from the scarcely attempted deception.

'I can't promise everyone here is going to be ecstatic about this.'

'Do they know?'

'Some. Not everyone. Max.'

'Who wants you to tell us to fuck off.'

'Max wants me to tell everyone to fuck off. Not the issue. I assume you know there's a guy . . . ?'

'Grayson James. Security guard.'

'It doesn't look good for Grayson James, security guard.'

'He hasn't . . . ?'

'He hasn't. But a significant number of our boys and girls in blue are taking a more than usually professional interest in the whereabouts of Reggie Glaze.'

'Such *total* pricks.'

'Hey. Dee. As far as I'm concerned you're family – Thin Love originals, lifetime membership. I'm just saying be ready.' Scylla wags the remote-control wand at the TV. 'Reggie I get. But you . . . Isn't this Samson's solar-powered baby? I thought you liked Samson.'

'I did. I do.'

'Yeah? Then why am I looking at you knocking the crap out of his pride and joy?'

Her hands hurt. It is all she knows. As she steps down from Scylla's van moons of pain rise through her hands. There is that faintness of self that is also a fullness, an excess of one's own unwelcome presence struggling in the chains directly beneath a flying saucer. And what is there to feel then but the absurdity of one's struggle, without skin or shadow or silhouette? If she were not here, there or anywhere but only a happy nothing in a pit of ash at the very bottom of the crumbled tower block, of the levelled town . . .

Ridiculous. She sees Reggie's face on TV, her own dot face and blur body, and her first thought is to call Samson. To say what? But it's never what she says or even what he says but the wobbly boom of his voice. And yet if she thinks the number he gave her still connects to anything, let alone that reverberation that stirs to life a secret filament in her breast, she's a bigger fool and prick than she knew.

She tears through the circle of vans. No sign of Reggie. She stops where the tripod of last night's fire stood and stares at the three watery dents it has left in the mud and breathes and allows her fists to unclench, her moons to set. He has not gone. He has not been caught. I have not failed. Over and over until it loads her breathing: I have a great work great work great work.

She's walking along the fence that separates the scrub from the park, trying to think of a next move, when she sees him: in the kids' play area, sitting on a swing. In the middle of the park. As she looks she feels the publicness of the park swirl round them.

Her instinct is to run to him, wrap him in her scarf, bundle him away; instead she ducks through the fence with all the distracted dignity she can marshal and strolls laggingly towards him. When she gets there he doesn't even raise his head.

'Reggie.'

It is a discovery: how hard it is for him to raise his head. Whatever has happened has happened to him too, and it makes his head unbearably, volcanically heavy.

'Reggie. Come on. Look at me.'

At last he does. He eases the swing forward and raises his head.

'You've been named,' she says. 'You're on the telly. You're everywhere.'

He smiles. But she sees the information rolling into him, wave on terrible wave. Everything in his white face looks sick, sickened. 'I'm sitting,' he says. 'Can't I sit?'

'People are looking for you. The police.'

'Do you know I've never sat on a swing before? Never in my life.'

'Come on. We have to get you back to camp before someone sees you.'

'They won't see me. I'm not going to be here.'

'Because you're going to run back to Tarantula? They've –

we've – been named too. The farm's been raided, and not like last time. There's nothing left. It's gone.'

He goggles at her. 'Bullshit.'

'Look for yourself. Anyone who's not been arrested has vanished, buggered off . . .'

'I'll find them. We'll regroup.'

It is the maddest thing she has ever heard, and none the less so because the same wild thought flared in her brain when Scylla broke the news to her. Tarantula gone? No. *No* . . . Her impulse to go at once in search of Jon and Fee, of Annette and Marc, of Glen and Pearl and Will snatched her breath and lifted moons of pain into her hands. She'd had no idea she would miss them so, with such a scouring of her textures, of everything she humiliatingly feels herself to be. No idea the loss would be like that she felt one day when she was thirteen and Samson sat beside her on the steps of Sycamore House and said to her 'You'll see', and then nothing else for fifteen years . . . But it's mad and she knows it is. So she breathes; straightens her fingers, quenches her moons. 'Okay. But for now you're coming with me—'

'Why?' He stands abruptly, the swing saddle releasing with a crazy rattling and buckling of chains. 'Why don't you, why don't you vanish and bugger off too?'

'Sorry, Reggie, you're stuck with me. I promised.'

'Not me you didn't.'

No, Reggie, not you. She is not calm. Not angry, not afflicted with moon panic; but something in her chest feels to be continually unravelling. It's a wonder there is any of her still here. And she is not in any sense calm as she says, 'No, Reggie. Not you.'

'My father.'

'Your father.' That's all that happens. 'Who at the moment is the only person who may be able to keep you from spending the rest of your life in prison.'

'Who says I don't want to spend the rest of my life in prison?'

'Listen to me. You want to come back to camp and keep your head down and your bloody mouth shut until we can work out a way to get you to Samson, so—'

'I'm not going to him.' Reggie is not looking at her again – but not looking at nothing; looking next to, behind, in front of. 'I told you. We'll regroup, we'll go underground. Deep under the ground, under the mud, under the earth, where no one can find us. We'll be safe and we'll change ourselves. We'll be . . . we'll be nature red. Under the earth we'll sharpen our teeth and claws. We'll be nature red. Do you understand? It's a poem.'

'I know what it is.' Tennyson. *In Memoriam A.H.H.* (1849). Great sad thing about love and death and memory; about the way love screws up your memory, and the way death screws up your memory, and lastly and chiefly the way your memory screws up your memory.

'Nature red in tooth and claw. In tooth and claw. That's what we'll be.'

He starts past her, back towards camp. Maybe he means to go that way; maybe he's distracted by the things all about them only he can see. As he passes he mutters something, the same word over and over: *beady*, or *squeezy*. What's beady? What's squeezy?

He is almost at the fence when he swings back and with a churning effort of his whole face manages to focus on her. He raises his freckled sneer.

'What did he promise you? For looking after me, babysitting me.'

'He didn't promise me anything.'

'You're doing all this, and he didn't . . .' Reggie shakes his head. 'You know, Dia, that seems pretty mad. You know that, don't you? That makes you seem pretty fucking mad.'

By the time anything starts to happen she has been sitting in the doorway of the supply van that Scylla allocated her for almost two hours, elbows on knees, feet squared on the step or dangling over the mud below, scanning the circle for faces in which she hopes to identify some clue, some indication of direction or tendency, though most of the time she's looking at backs of heads or uncommunicative profiles, part-profiles, slivers of cheekbones of people engaged in conversations that do not include her. A couple of kids come over to ask her lots of questions and cheerfully take the piss out of her, though soon enough their mum bustles up and with a skeletally faint and compromised smile drags them away.

Her only other visitors are a delightfully sloppy Alsatian and a Lab mix with eyes of such melting clarity she can see every intricacy of their insides, the magnetic scanners that discern the gravitational fields of the earth. She strokes their curved heads, rubs their tightly pinned coats, wonders if either is descended from Samson's gorgeous prototypes. She looks for resemblances but gets nowhere. Dismaying how little she retains of them – lovely creatures she wrestled with in this same mud, enjoying the slosh of their scruffy bellies and the loll and wallop of their everywhere tongues. What were they called again, those old heartbreakers? Snowflake, Buttercup. Ron – Ronnie . . . ?

When not scrutinising the circle she stares at the door of the supply van that Scylla allocated Reggie, which has not opened since he bewilderedly shut it after himself more than two hours ago. He has, she supposes, a lot to take in: learning on one hand that Tarantula is gone, on the other that her place in it was no more than a promise and a favour to Samson. She imagines him asleep among cardboard boxes, sweating out the stress vectors that covered his body while they talked in the park.

By the time something starts to happen she has lost all feeling in her arms and legs. She has taken her left elbow into the palm of her right hand and is experimentally working the hinge, when Max the Space Pirate comes slapping out of his van with a low-shouldered look that can only mean trouble. Dia straightens her back, switches elbows. The tinfoil cape has gone; the face daggers appear as if newly painted. He struts across the circle and raps a fist on the door of Reggie's van. He shouts ('Glaze!') and raps again before the two men supposedly following him have dawdled even halfway across the circle.

She takes the two deep breaths she thinks she's going to need then drops onto her needling feet and crosses the muddy circle in time to swat Max's hand away from the door before he can rap it a third time.

'Hello, Max. Do me a personal favour and get fucked, will you?'

'You're here too, good. Saves me a job. *Glaze*!' He glares up at the door, then back at his two apparent companions, still dragging their feet. 'What's wrong with you?'

'Not much of a united front, sunbeam. I bet it was these arseholes put you up to this. Got you psyched. Brought out the bloke in you.'

'Shut up.' He raises his fist towards the door again, but before it can connect she delivers her own sharp rap to his forehead.

'Knock, knock,' Dia says.

Poor move. Max snarls; the daggers click and scrape on his bony face; but now as the two others belatedly pile in, from another direction comes Scylla, tightly striding in her burst jacket and shouting at everyone in a way that seems to originate in the strained pale lines of her blonde hair, in the deadly chips of her blue eyes.

'What – the fuck – is this?'

Max wheels on her, but his outrage, or his sense of theatre, cannot survive her blue-chipped glare. He steps back, shooting his arms at her. 'It's not on, Scyl.'

'I'll tell you what's not on, Maxie lad, you causing all this ruckus, disrespecting our mates—'

'They're not *my* mates.'

'Oh yes, they are. Dee and Reggie are your mates, my mates—'

'No, Scyl, they're not, they're not.' Max is shaking his head in a determined way that is immediately much more alarming than his strutting, shouting, door-rapping. 'They're trouble for us. Nothing but grief.'

'Honest question, Max, can you hear yourself?'

'No one wants them here. Ask anyone.'

Scylla laughs, tries to laugh. 'Do you know what you sound like?'

'Ask anyone. Go on.'

'I don't need to—'

She stops. No one else has spoken. But now every head turns in the same direction beyond Dia's shoulder and Scylla calls, 'How many?'

And someone from behind Dia calls back, 'At least one.'

She turns to see a boy, a tall teenager, standing by the fence.

Then there is a sense of grim general stir and everyone in the circle begins to move away towards the boy.

'What?' she says to Scylla. 'At least one what?'

But Scylla, Max and his friends have moved away towards the boy too.

She reaches the fence to find that most of the collective has arrived there before her. The tall teenager who has been set to watch it – a security measure introduced since her and Reggie's arrival, it appears – is pointing at a man who has attempted to climb the fence and ended up tangled in it. Not visibly concerned by his audience, the man works in a patient way to extricate himself. As he does so his black suit pulls and pincers about him, drawn taut at the nib of some unseen snarl.

The pointing teenager looks at Scylla expectantly. But Scylla only squints at the man.

'Problem there?' Scylla calls.

The man mumbles, continuing his work on the fence.

'I said—'

'I'm stuck,' the man shouts.

'Might be best if you head back.'

The man mumbles at his hands.

'I said—'

'Nothing would give me greater happiness than "heading back".' The man is roaring at them. 'Alas, that option is not open to me.'

He straightens. And he is Weland. The man is Weland Frost.

'Tell you what, mate.' Scylla's shoulders square. 'Might be best to piss off out of it.'

'Blood and fire, I'm coming across,' Weland roars.

Scylla flaps an arm. The pointing boy and then the half dozen women and men standing nearest the fence start towards the intruder, who pauses to regard them with disgusted, tendrilled eyes.

'What?' he says. His eyes sweep and catch on Dia. 'I'm *with* you.'

'First I've heard about it.' Still, Scylla glances at her with a confidential air: 'Is he?'

Seized in the twisty connections of the fence, his suit wrenched to rippling black forks, Weland stares. The pale creatures of his eyes reach and reach for her.

'Yeah,' Dia says. 'Shit, sorry. Yeah. He's with us.'

'Took your time there.'

'I was considering the situation.'

'Deciding whether or not to set the dogs on me.'

'Say "dogs" again.'

'I didn't mean . . . the Mamas and the Papas. I suppose you've noticed that this place is overrun with actual, literal dogs?'

He makes a revolted sound. Settling back among the boxes of the supply van, into which she just barely managed to prod him before Max's complaints about 'another one, another fucking one?' grew too loud, Weland does indeed appear revolted. It's more than his appearance of having been recently beaten up. His face seems to hang differently, more loosely, with a greater number of indignant apertures in it than a face ought to have.

'What's this?' He loops a hand through the air in a way that approximates the edge of her headscarf.

'Fashion statement. Hijab chic, it's going to be massive.' In fact she has no idea what the scarf is. She knows only that she has begun to take pleasure in being hidden, hooded.

'Aren't you going to ask me why I'm here? You should.'

'Why are you here?'

'Reggie. Is he about?'

'Reggie's about.'

The eye creatures fondle this for a while. 'I probably have to tell you some things.'

'About your travels far and wide. Your solitary mission. Your lonely adventure.'

'Yes,' he says. 'Why not.'

18. Tight, Tighter, Tightest

He went to Basra so Ruth could sit in a house of lights. It was all he cared about and he didn't care who knew. In the later days in Antwerp when the group identity crystallised he heard a lot of tasty talk about queen, country, gentlemanly ideals, and a lot of other crap besides, but no one was in any doubt about why he was going. Don't have to ask me, boys, he said. I'm going for Ruth. I'm going for the lights at night.

The only distinction Weland was careful to make was that Ruth wasn't poor; just proud. She always lifted her chin when they passed neighbours on the street, grasping his hand and rotating his whole arm so he wouldn't be tempted to return any stray greeting; on Sunday her voice at the back of St John the Martyr was never the strongest, and certainly not the most musical, but it was the steadiest, the most reedily concentrated.

Nearly everything about Ruth's pride gave him a grim sort of pleasure. Without it she would have been only pale, thin, frizz-haired and flat-featured, librarian-like (though she wasn't a librarian), spinster-like (though she had been married, passionately; and he had died, ferociously); but with it, with her pride, all those unassuming fragilities grew hard and folded and weather-bearing as the peaks of mountaintops.

Yet it was pride too that meant Ruth would not take help where everyone else did, and Sal the Batter in the video shop at the end of the arcade never once saw the whites of her ineluctable eyes. She kept her dignity while everyone else shoved it across Sal's counter and when the box on the kitchen wall clunked the flat into blackness she simply lit the candleball and wore out her eye whites trying to read by its wick-spitting flame.

He hated that candleball; that greasy agglomeration of leftover candle bits, like some multicoloured Frankenstein planet in fissured miniature, its thumbed-together lumps forever slithering apart to show the glossy snake tongues that made up its core . . . *Hated* it. But when it was gone, Ruth didn't replace it. He did schoolwork angling his book to the streetlight that came through the bedroom window and when he went into the kitchen to squeeze her hand she was still there, at the table, trying to read in pitch darkness.

There was no choice and he didn't want one. A corridor of years along every point of which Ruth was seated at the kitchen table trying to read in pitch darkness, all the white worn out of her eyes, a thin smile fixed on her lips, wasn't a choice – it was the cold-sweat nightmare that animated his days, that trundled him through the door of the recruitment office and looped his name under the officer's thumb. He was a month into basic training before he could even dream of Ruth sitting with her book in a house of lights, no box on the wall but a thousand electrically blazing bulbs sailing out, like a royal barge, into the night.

They were deployed in the last wave, the last breaker crashing over that sea of ruin. On the approach there was almost nothing to do but scroll along in their armoured depths and look. First there was the desert, in which half the globe's heat was generated; then the city, in which the concept of destruction was being refashioned for the new century. It was as if a city made entirely from tissue paper had been attacked with gigantic shears. All you could see in any direction, round any corner, along any vista, was fantastical tattering, filigree fringes lifting and trailing to the last of the light.

It was the library he couldn't take. He came to an arrangement with everything else, even those moments when the filigree streets opened to disclose this baffled flank of hostile armament, this shower of concentrated sniper fire, and with his crew he swivelled in the depths and unleashed celestially effective counterstrikes – touchpad prodigies that dissolved all opposition; even the sight of the dead and disfigured, the men and women, the boys and girls. (There were no babies. He never saw any babies. No one else did either. In Basra, you could only surmise, there were no babies, nor had there ever been.)

But the library he could find no place for. When he saw it burning he broke every regulation he'd ever heard about in Antwerp and left the depths and climbed out in the globe-generating heat and skidded down onto the street and looked. Inhuman of him – infernal. After everything he'd seen and done it was the library in its stage-villain cape of black smoke that he could not absorb because all he saw when he looked at it was Ruth at the kitchen table, her fingertip poised at the edge of the almost-read page, waiting and not waiting for the box on the wall to clunk everything black.

After the library he couldn't stick to anything. Whatever adhesive had bonded him to division and crew and armoured depths melted in the cape-swirl of those flames and he could barely bring himself to climb back in, or stay in once he had. He roamed the base then roamed his way out of it. He found himself the object of a very sharply worded verbal warning. But he didn't care, couldn't stick, and shortly afterwards found himself the object of a genially phrased written warning that more or less promised that if he broke regulations on one further occasion his career, his life would be over. He was still chortling about that as he sauntered through the marketplace one morning and a car parked on the corner of the street didn't quite fail to explode.

The doctor who treated him, a local doctor, a native of the city, spoke English with a German accent. His was the voice that came out of the darkness beyond the bandages. In his German-inflected English the doctor explained as much as was generally known: that the car in the marketplace had been seeded with a bomb as part of a coordinated attack; that the bomb mechanism had partly failed, though not entirely failed; that the defective explosive had succeeded in tearing the car open, rending its innards, but not in detonating it. So there had been no fire, no shrapnel, but only a thin shower of battery acid, the greater part of which had pattered into his patient's face. As it happened, the doctor had been passing through the marketplace that morning, and had taken the patient on himself.

He told the doctor, I'm going to be in a lot of trouble when I get back to base. The doctor laughed. Do you not realise you are already in a lot of trouble? He asked the doctor why he had not left him for base personnel to pick up and deal with, and the doctor said that his injuries were grave; he would certainly have lost his sight without immediate treatment. He sniffed, felt into the blackness beyond the bandages: the doctor's surgery, with its tinny resonance, its smell of mouthwash and machine parts. Or was it he, he himself, who smelled of the insides of an engine? So did the treatment work? he asked the doctor. Will I keep my sight? He heard his rescuer hum. We shall have to see. I am hopeful that you will retain some part of it, in some form. But it is likely there will be anomalies. We should not be surprised if we find that you no longer see things the way other people see them.

The doctor was right. Even before they came off, he started seeing things inside the bandages: cell shapes, insect outlines. Then with some Germanic formality one morning the doctor took up his scissors and swabs and he hewed and prised off the fleshy bandages and here along a steep defile of tears came the wholly new world. Things were hives; all things were variants on hives, laced and repeating geometric patterns. Sky was pink; skin was blue. All human skin was blue. The doctor examined him with his blue and bearded squint. Younger than he'd been expecting; ridges round the eyes suggested a bitterness with which the rest of the man was in permanent conflict. They will need exercise, the doctor said. Undoubtedly it was in such a spirit of exercise that the next afternoon the doctor led him out of the surgery, out of the building into his car, then drove them out of the city, into the desert, halting the vehicle as near as it was possible to get to a vast sequential spew of blue and green hexagonal fire pouring endlessly and gratuitously into the heavy pink sky. Where are we? he asked, and the doctor said, This is the crazy place. *Majnoon*. 'Crazy'. This is what everything is all about.

He understood. He no longer saw things the way other people saw them. So instead of the supergiant oilfield with its cranes and pipelines he saw a many-limbed monster lying on its back in the desert, its enormous jaws slackly open, its foul breath richly rising. He understood further that this monster put the lie to the world, the new as well as the old. It showed that the world was not what he had thought it, heavy, solid, dense with sacredness, but rather a greasy fissured shell, a thing of leftover lumps temporarily thumbed together yet determined by inertial destiny eventually to drift and slither apart, to show the glossy snake tongues that make up its core, and so end the pretence. Until that moment the monster had its foot on the candleball world. Its claws came out of the light bulbs. Its talons scraped in the box on the wall. It didn't matter whether you put money in the box or not; what mattered was that the box was there and while it was there it proved the monster had its foot on the world. All this time it had. Ruth smiled over her book and whether in darkness or a house of royal lights the monster in the desert had its foot on her throat. She smiled and the claws clicked at her jawline, next to her earlobe.

He returned to base next morning expecting interrogation, court martial, firing squad, whatever, only to find that his three-day absence without leave had gone unnoticed in the chaos following the attack pattern of which the rupturing car in the marketplace had been supposed to be a part. A wandering medic came across him and made him sit in a chair with padded plastic arms and stare at a chart made out of honeycomb. Still nothing was certain. The base thudded, the walls under sustained attack, either from without or within. Everyone he saw was a blue skeleton ravenous with paranoia. As if everyone were longing to be dead – as if everyone was longing to be dead. Then another wandering medic came at him and he was packed onto a flight with men silenced by injury and he was ejected at another base that turned out to be on the coast of

Wales. He tried to explain it to Ruth: the sense that there was no more use in him. Her counterargument was two-pronged: modern military structures were so complex they were incapable of meaningful self-awareness; and he contained inexhaustible energy, and it didn't matter how exhausted he felt, his energy wasn't used up, and it never would be. Later he tried to explain the monster in the desert to her, too, and the way her face closed he thought no counterargument was forthcoming. More fool him. Two weeks after the local quack gave him the all clear, she woke him up and pushed him into the kitchen where a new black suit was laid out on the table. Whose funeral is it? he asked. Yours, she said, if you don't get a move on. You have an interview. While he was getting the suit on (a decent fit, though since the marketplace in Basra he had lost all his muscle – had lost half his body – with wizening suddenness), he managed to extract from her the further startling fact that this interview was with the man who had made the solar panels on the roof that finally rendered obsolete the box on the kitchen wall. You'll like him, she said. He wasn't at all sure he would, and in the end he'd worked for Glaze for nearly six months before he was sure that he did. Or maybe it wasn't a case of liking so much as of respecting. Glaze was hard to respect. People said he was strange; and so he was. Except he wasn't a shaman or a mystic but merely a shambles, a fraying jumper of a crustie who had wafted on the breeze into a maze of astounding good fortune. But like him? Yes. In the end he did like him.

Not that his employer made things easy. He soon learned that if Glaze wasn't knee-deep in some trouble he'd cluelessly blundered into, he was thigh-deep, neck-deep, in some trouble of his own deliberate choosing. As time went on, the task of maintaining his bodily integrity (so nugatory, so apparently a favour to Ruth, in the early days) became a serious enterprise. By the end of the fifth year of his employment he had come to expect that every day would contain a public appearance of some kind, and each would sooner or later require him to push Glaze into some variety of protective container, car or cupboard, while groping hands or flying missiles vied to disrupt his physical equilibrium. So much he probably could have managed. It was the other stuff, the family stuff, he found hard. From almost his first day on the job he knew about the troubles with Glaze Junior, troubles that seemed to fizz and sputter like an irreparable circuit in the background of all other troubles, to the point that he, and he supposed also Glaze, stopped noticing them. Certainly they stopped noticing Junior when Cait fell ill. Cait: Cait Glaze. In some way he accepted that Glaze loved his wife. But he in no sense accepted that he loved her enough. Early on Ruth worked it out: No man could love that one enough. Not even you. Am I right? Of course she was right, but neither that nor anything else could keep Cait Glaze from dying, keep her head above the rising death waters, and then she closed her eyes and dived under and for a while after that he could look at nothing but the filth under his own fingernails. Glaze was somehow the same. At least he stopped trying to talk to him about family. What did he know about family? He'd never had a family; he'd only had Ruth, who conjured him entire out of a sheet of paper in the town hall. He knew there had been people, biological originators; and he knew Ruth had known these originators and something had happened to them when he was young (in his head the picture was a room with a ceiling of smoke) and then Ruth had had to talk to a lot of people, proudly determined, palely stubborn, before she was able to sign the sheet of paper that brought him into being and let her carry him onto the bus and back to her flat. He'd never had a family and he didn't want one. Who could blame him, when you saw the fancy new troubles Junior got himself into when he came to feel that everyone's sorrow was fixed too much on Cait, or on themselves, and not where it ought to be, which was on him, and how hard it was for him to be him. He had a hope that New York would be the end of it; but New York was not the end of it, was barely respite from it, and with the shockwaves of Cait's death still beating in his system, the concussions of grief still sounding under his skull, he found himself in that preposterous flat up north in the middle of all that shouting. He was distracted; and anyway there was no handy protective container into which to stuff Glaze on this occasion. So the phone connected with his head. The soma was breached; the psyche compromised. That, surely, had to end what New York couldn't. But it was only weeks later that Glaze had him sitting in a square between offices observing a meeting with some girl drawn up from his past, some hawkish Claudia who couldn't stand on both feet at the same time. And that waving business – Jesus. Getting completely the wrong end of the stick, Glaze said, You like her. I do not, he replied. Later Glaze said, I'm thinking we may have to reconsider our position on Miss Talwar. Oh yes? Yeah. Oh yeah. How do you mean? And Glaze said, She's not going to help Reggie. She's out . . . Except she wasn't, because the next thing he knew he was looking at the two of them talking over pizza in a restaurant that hurt all his senses. That was the night he first smelled it. Also the night he asked for two weeks' leave and was stung by the easy alacrity with which Glaze said yeah sure. Well, fair enough. The drive was a blur: motorway cells gushed by and he didn't see a single one. If Junior had joined a cult, wasn't that the actual definition of an answer to everyone's prayers? If he prayed, was not that exactly what he would pray for? If he knew what was good for him he would swerve free at the next junction and spend his leave with Sky Sport and a bottle of Glenfiddich in the first hotel he came to. But he had smelled it, and couldn't now unsmell it . . . His hands gripped tight, tighter, tightest on the wheel. She was blue, because everyone was blue, but not the blue of Glaze or Glaze Junior; not the blue of Ruth or Cait. Unaccountably she was the blue of the bearded doctor who saved what fragments of sight he still had. Midnight blue, the blue of rainclouds, with a glimmering body obscured somewhere beyond it that may be the moon . . . *You like her. I do not.* And that was right, he did not. It was something other than *like*. The sense of woundedness (his or hers), of prehistoric injury, with thorn and flail and fire – it was nothing remotely like *like*.

If he was sure of anything it was that if there had been nothing to smell, he would not have smelled it. But almost as soon he arrived it was there: the coastal blast seemed to drive it from the thatch of the tumbled pile in which the little cult wonks went about their business straight to his nostrils. A rat, a rat – its stink of grinning rat decay tracing so many loose and lacy patterns he couldn't make out the start or end of it. Pretty much on instinct he hunkered, sealed himself in. While he was figuring out what the hell was actually going on at the tumbled pile, even calls to Glaze were a risk he was not prepared to take. He switched off his phone and walked the woods until he found a beech with a sweet black hole rotted through it. Knots in the beech, here and here, were so comfortable under his palms he could remain standing for hours at a time. The sweet black hole showed him everything he wanted to see: all the Smurfs in the Smurf village. For strictly professional reasons his eye roved continually for Smurfette; for reasons that he was not yet a dehumanised monster, not yet a cousin of the slack-jawed thing in the desert, his heart thudded when he saw her. So. She was safe. The rat stink had not infected her. (And it did not come from her; the lacy patterns could not delude him so far.) Then there was that episode with the police, confusing in so many regards. After the attack itself he required a full day of investigation at locations along the coast to ascertain that it was not responsible for the rat smell – that the police of the locality were only in the ordinary way corrupt, stupid, violent, gross (the fucking *cunt* who put his hands on her), and not in any other way, not in a way that explained why he couldn't take a breath without inhaling the reek of long-expired rodent. Then there was the further distraction of that flesh-tunnelled freak Oliver Sellick, with whom he played so many happy games of hide-and-seek in the woods, games of which he was the loser on only one occasion, though admittedly it proved to be an occasion that mattered. No, young Oliver was more than a distraction. He was a disaster with brown teeth; a Neanderthal catastrophe. But he was not the source of the stench that traced back and forth over everything and it was not until Oliver's disastrousness expressed itself in fire and smoke and scorching blood that he at last determined who was. It was Gibson – the little cult wonk who looked as though he spent most of each day asleep – Marc Gibson.

When the blast sounded across the plant everything he needed was there in Gibson's face: the guilty calculus, and the retreat to another kind of knowledge. Then on the grass under pouring smoke there was a balancing up to do: because she was hurt but she was walking but she was hurt but he knew the stink came from Marc Gibson but she was hurt but he also knew – absolutely knew – where she would end up going but she was hurt but now Gibson was running (but she was hurt) and there would be only this chance to discover where he was running to. He stood, balancing it up. He knew where she was going, knew she would get there. Shuffle-footed Smurfette was the sort who always gets to where she's meaning to get to. So he angled his body slowly in the smoke until he was facing away from her, facing after Gibson, and there was no sense that he had turned from her. He had not turned from her. He was looking at Gibson's running feet and he focused on their ingenious scattergraphs and started running too. The rest was easy. From a politic distance he watched Gibson climb into a car, then climbed into his own car and followed the vehicle away from the plant, onto the motorway, back towards London.

This is the part he can tell her: this, at any rate, is the part she wants to hear about. So he sits up among the boxes crowding in on him from every corner of the van and tells her that he followed the car containing Gibson as far as the outermost edge, the scabrous crust of squamous London. Here the car veered onto a road that made up one side of a desolate square, one of those wrenched plugs of land scattered throughout the city's suburban orbit. On three sides stood the remains of incompletely demolished buildings – houses, shops, something with a lot of decorative tile that might have been swimming baths – jigsaw pieces of dusty wall teetering upwards into nothing. On the fourth stood a pub, The Sportive Dog, into which Gibson and the car's driver now hurried. He allowed a superstitious but otherwise meaningless beat to pass then hurried in after them, finding a bar empty but for a couple of sleepy-eyed codgers and a young barmaid talking brightly into her phone. He bought a pint of lager while using his other eyes, the ones embossed all over his body, to locate Gibson and his driver. By the time the barmaid handed him his change he had them: corner booth at the back of the lounge. He wandered over and dropped himself down in the next booth.

He heard the young men talking. (Wait, she says. This is Marc? *Our* Marc? This, he says patiently, is Marc Gibson. Which is to say, yes. This is your Marc.) The driver kept letting out a hysterical sneeze of a laugh while Gibson in a dreary voice said he had really thought for a moment back there his number was up, and it was true what they say, in a flash he'd reviewed the whole thing: parents, school, school disco, first kiss, first shag, uni, puddle of vomit, spotlights, spotlights, spotlights. Then the driver said something like Do you reckon he'll be much longer? and Gibson said something like You tell me. In the next booth he sucked his lips: fair enough. So Gibson was the end of the stink, not the start of it. Additionally there seemed good reason to believe that whoever was, was the start of it, was about to walk in through the door of The Sportive Dog.

From the start he had known about the Grid. In practically the same breath that he sketched his troubles with Junior, Glaze had told him all about it – Big Electric, the Masters of Dirty Power, etc. Hardly a day had passed since without some mention of the Grid and its determination to crater the earth while cutting down with the greenwoods anyone who stood up to it. For years he'd assumed it was crackpipe New Age bollocks; but in time even he had been forced to acknowledge hints, secret gleams of foul play in the rollercoaster fortunes of Glaze Energy. Now he was convinced. The stink that permeated the cult and ended with Marc Gibson could have no other origin. And here in The Sportive Dog he was about to meet it, in human form, with a human face: the Grid.

Half an hour later the men in the booth were joined by another man. The new arrival was older, slower, softer, and with archaic courtesy thanked the driver for his excellent work before dismissing him. With a final panicky sneeze the driver scuttled out and Gibson and the Gridman were left alone in the booth. The face of each man was plainly visible. But he wasn't looking at their faces. He was looking into his completely full pint glass, wondering how he was going to make himself invisible. Because his face was visible too; and it's one thing to escape the notice of people who don't know you and quite another thing to escape the notice of people who do. And the man sitting in the booth with Gibson knew him, and he knew the man. And the man wasn't a Gridman. He was Gerald Pinion.

(Wait, she says. No, he says, you wait. I'm *going to tell you.*) Gerald Pinion: the only one of Glaze's friends he'd never liked. As if the beardy bastard thought he could get away with anything just because he'd invested some fraction of his vast inheritance in wind power. As if the whole enterprise were no more than an extension of the aristo unanswerability that made up his core and that Glaze should have been able to detect and denounce. Except he didn't. Called out every plummy accent in Whitehall, but when the plums were in Pinion's throat Glaze only bowed and tugged his forelock.

It had been a relief, then, the remission of a long-standing ache, when the two parted ways. Infuriating it took Glaze so long to realise his supposed friend was not a fellow true believer but only a recreational user. He'd heard that the falling-out had led Pinion into a doomed vengeful attempt to outdo Glaze, huge further investment in and expansion of his turbine empire, leading promptly to the collapse of his interest and his own ignominious beggaring. He'd heard also that Pinion kept in touch with Junior, that Pinion and Junior had remained or become friends, possibly only out of a mutual desire to spite Glaze.

This was enough. The discovery that Pinion had manipulated Gibson, manipulated Junior in a renewed effort to hurt Glaze (and the appalling, chest-catching beauty of it: using the son, using the plant, destroying in one effort both of Glaze's most cherished offspring) was as much as he could process without forgetting altogether that he was supposed to be invisible. Still, there was more. He stood away from his completely full glass, turned towards the door, then heard Gibson and Pinion talking and had to sit down again. A crumpling of the legs so dramatic they should at least have glanced at him, though neither did.

Gibson in his dreary way was talking about regathering the group. Naturally they couldn't meet at the tumbled pile, which was no doubt being raided (reraided) as they spoke, but there were alternatives, contingencies . . . With a forbearing chuckle Pinion told Gibson not to worry himself. He then gave a queer little speech. For the duration of this speech Pinion spoke slowly and plangently. At one point he said: Tarantula is simply no longer required. At another: I believe our fantastic construction has run its course. At another still: Rest assured, dear boy, you played your part – you all played your parts – quite magnificently.

(He waits for her to say something. But she is silent, frowning at him. Does she get it? Oh yes: she gets it.) He stood and left The Sportive Dog. He was aware that what he'd heard he had not taken in, but only sort of grabbed and carried out with him. It was a cloud, a reeling stench, and he didn't want it inside him. Was it so much worse? That Pinion had not merely manipulated, but rather created? Had not merely turned the cult to his ends, but with Marc Gibson had invented it for the sole reason of his vengeances?

Outside, he saw the car that had conveyed Gibson from Warwick still parked on the square. Its driver was standing over it, holding a plastic yoghurt pot in one hand and flipping the pages of a newspaper spread over its bonnet with the other. He went up to the driver and said Hey. Hey what, the driver said. You fucking tosser, he said to the driver, who scowled at that the way you probably have to. Then they fought.

Because he never believed a word of it and Glaze was no shaman or mystic but a shambles full of salvation dreams he couldn't have believed himself and the world was a cracked candleball with snake tongues inside it and no one and nothing was going to make it any different and no one and nothing was going to mean there wasn't a monster in the desert and the monster had its foot on the world and it had only to press down.

It was the barmaid, strong as a rugby squad, who tore them apart. The driver sat on the kerb with blood running between his knuckles. The barmaid shouted at them. She was fearsome, fire breathing – he tried to imagine her parents. In his bloodied state he was oddly fascinated by the thought of the young barmaid's family. Then she told the driver and him to fuck off out of it and he crawled away towards his car.

There was nothing else to do. Glaze was broken, doubly shattered. Gerald Pinion had dreamt a cult out of whole cloth to entrap Glaze's son, to obliterate Glaze's work. The world was the world and the desert monster was starting to press its foot, starting to make the tongues come out. He reversed off the square and found his way back to the motorway and its polygonal traffic with no further difficulty.

19. It's Just Lentils

'And then you came here.'

'Then I came here.'

'How did you know where we were?'

'It wasn't hard to work out.'

'Don't be . . . insulting.'

'But it wasn't.'

She glares at him. For now this seems the safest course, or the kindest. Wouldn't want him thinking she doesn't believe him or anything.

'I made some further inquiries on my way over.' Grimacing, he lifts onto an elbow and pats his jacket pockets until one surrenders the bump of a phone. 'Do you know the problem with the name "Marc Gibson"? On the internet everyone is called Marc Gibson. "Marc Gibson" or "Mark Gibson", but you see the difficulty. To get anywhere with a name like that, you have to dig. So that's what I did. Passing the time on my way over here, you understand.'

'Well, of course.'

'I dug and I dug and in the end I managed to turn up some stuff about Marc Gibson. That is, our Marc Gibson.' He opens the phone and ditheringly sets its screen scrolling. 'Born in Willesden Green in 1987. Educated at Christ's Hospital and Rose Bruford College of Theatre and Performance. Two seasons as

Guildenstern at the Brighton Theatre Royal, Brighton. One season as Mr Smee at the Milton Keynes Theatre, Milton Keynes . . .'

'He's an actor.'

'A not very distinguished actor. No film, no TV, barely any theatre since 2011. But I suppose it wouldn't have been long after that that he was approached by Pinion.'

'About forming Tarantula.' She thinks she does a fair job of getting some disgusted spit in her voice – the sort of spit you'd expect from someone who believed a word of this.

'About creating a fake group. Something with enough obsessive appeal to draw Reggie in. The idea presumably being to take whatever animosity Reggie already felt towards his father and magnify it. To build it into an army. An exotic, eye-catching militia, with lots of media-ready imagery. To make sure Mr Glaze is not merely destroyed but destroyed by his own son, in full view of the world. With the whole world laughing at him.' He weighs the phone in his hand. 'I'm fairly sure Reggie's mate Brandon Tallis had a role in things, but I'm still putting that together.' Alarmed, she realises she has forgotten to glare at him, and tautens her arms across her chest and ignites her best ever glare. The pallid eye creatures do not appear wholly convinced. He gestures with the phone, as if it is a stone he is considering skimming across water. 'See for yourself.'

She glances at the phone. If she looked, what would she see? And would she even be seeing it for herself? Weland has, after all, already told her what to see. Aside from that, you can open any phone and read star charts of non-existent galaxies, true histories of elven battles. And when you read those things, what are you reading?

'Oh, no, you're all right.' She sees it is a mistake. The look that briefly contracts the eye creatures is not quite one of hurt, but she sees at once that she should have taken the phone, bent over its screen, scraped a fingernail through all his keenly amassed evidence. It would have appeased him, settled him, and given her a useful interval of thinking time.

'Still working also on the Sellick connection,' he says, somewhat flatly. 'Investigating how Oliver Sellick fits into the picture. No joy yet.'

She nods. She needs to think. Clearly he is not trying to deceive her. Clearly he is not aware that he is himself deceived. And can she blame him? From the outside Tarantula would look suspect. Observing it as he has, she would be suspicious too. But she has lived with the group, felt its texture and rhythm, and so she knows it is real. (Was. Is.) Has Weland met Jon? Talked to Fee, or Annette? He has not. So how can he be expected to know anything; how can she blame him for having got so utterly the wrong end of the stick?

'The interesting thing will be establishing what Reggie knew,' Weland says now, 'how far he was in on the whole fake-cult setup. My guess is he didn't know anything. But people can surprise you. They can know and not know an awful lot of stuff at the same time.'

'Tell me about it,' she says, hoping he won't.

At last the rain has stopped. She leaves the van, leaves Weland crumpled asleep among the boxes, and stands at the edge of the dripping circle. She has no idea what she is doing. Maybe she is not doing anything. She sees Reggie and Max standing by the raised bonnet of a van on the far side of the camp. Reggie seems to be working on the van's engine; Max seems to be passing him tools from a bashed-up toolbox. Neither is speaking, or showing much in the way of facial expression; nonetheless it looks like progress. Then she sees the van the pair is working on, and a weird hot shock jags upwards through her and she rushes across the circle to Reggie and says, 'Oh, my God, it's *not*.'

'It is.' Reggie doesn't look up from the exposed engine.

'How can this even be?'

'She's getting on,' Max says. 'Couple of breakdowns in the last few years that had us worried. But we wouldn't give up the old Glaze family motor without a fight.'

'Didn't he take her?'

'It was him who left. Or got chucked out or what-have-you.' Max glances at Reggie, who does not look up from his brawny tightening under the van's bonnet. 'Not her.'

'She looks great.' It's true. Genevieve looks fantastic. Wrinkled, slackened, sunken on arthritic axles, the paint job of at least one door panel out of shade with her blood-in-the-urine red, but far better than a 1972 Dodge Ram has any right to look.

Reggie withdraws his upper body from under the bonnet, grunts at Max without looking at him, and Max swaggers up into Genevieve's cabin. His Mohawk fills the windscreen as he searches for the ignition. The engine gives a rusty hack, judders, then slips back into its coma. Reggie shouts, strains and levers under the bonnet some more – as if dismantling a capstan – then shouts again and Max tries the ignition again. This time a roar, a contained blast. Dia imagines water falling in ropes from a hoisted shipwreck. But after a few seconds Genevieve once more dips her head.

'Nice one!' Max calls, joggling back down from the cabin. 'No lie, that's the best she's been since May.'

'I'll get it.' Reggie swipes up a rag out of the toolbox and starts twisting it between his fingers. 'I'll get her there.'

'Bet she brings it back, hey?' Max pats a wonky rear-view mirror. 'Happy memories.'

Reggie doesn't say anything. Only goes on twisting and twisting the rag.

Max leaves to explore their dinner options. She glances at Reggie, still making love to that rag, then strides up Genevieve's steps. Her sense is it's all here – the cupboards, the paperbacks, the perched protective intelligence – but she knows that can't be right. She sits on an only slightly ripped cushion to think about it.

When Reggie comes in she says, 'Her curtains are different.'

'So they are.'

'They used to be cream. With that pattern. Like rosehips, or wombs.'

'They weren't cream, they were white. That was fag smoke. Filth.'

He sits on the somewhat more heavily scarred cushion next to hers.

'Oy,' she says. 'You'll never guess.' It is the right thing to do: as soon as she embarks on this course she feels a surge of relief. 'Weland's here. You know Weland?' It is not intimacy between them, here on the mutilated cushions – but it is safety, it is shared ground. 'He told me your pal Gerald Pinion is behind Tarantula. He told me Gerald made Tarantula up. The whole group, everything. Just made it up.'

'Oh yeah.' Reggie grins. It is precisely the easy look of amusement she was hoping for. She could kiss him, she could . . .

'That's what I said! Well no, actually I played it a bit cool, because he was clearly quite attached to the idea. You know the drill. Nod and smile.'

'You don't smile.'

'Yes I do.'

'You don't ever smile. Never did, never do.'

'I smile. I smile when there's something to smile about. Anyway, that's what he said. Gerald Pinion made the whole thing up as a way to use you. To get back at your dad.'

'Right.' His eyes are shining – delighted. 'And why would Gerald want to do that?'

'Because of some kickoff from years back, your dad having a pop at Gerald's turbine stuff, saying he was only in it for the green glory, green props or whatever. So then there was this sort of rivalry between them, your dad and Gerald squaring up to see which of them could save more of the planet, and Gerald lost. His company tanked and he blamed your dad.' She laughs – an uninhibited porcine snort. 'Can you believe it?'

'I don't think I can.' He laughs too. She could, she could . . .

'Thought it'd give you a laugh.'

'It has,' he says.

'I mean the idea. That the group wasn't real. Does he even know what he's saying?'

'What a joke.'

'Oh, you're an expert on jokes now?'

'I wouldn't say "expert" . . .'

'Why did the tea towel cross the road, Reggie?'

'You know very well why.'

'Because the seashells . . .'

'Because the seashells had jam on their face. As you very well know.'

'Why did the door handle cross the road, Reggie?'

'Well now, that's a, that's an *entirely* different question . . .'

It is not relief any more, though she has no idea what it is. As their laughter subsides, she decides it will be whatever it will be – whatever it becomes. They look at each other then away. Reggie extends his legs, looks down at his feet, squints at them. He sighs. Then he says, 'Why did you tell me this, Dia?'

'Hmn? The Gerald stuff? I thought it was funny.'

'Did you.' His face turns towards her and it is ghastly. His face is crumbling, wearing away from the freckles. 'I'll tell you what's funny.' His face is pouring away. But terribly he staggers up from the cushions. 'All this. I think all this is hilarious.'

He is nothing but viciousness. She sits back, instantly bored, detached.

'Sorry, Reggie sweet. No idea what you're talking about.'

'Do you know what my father likes about you? You let him believe what he most wants to believe about himself. That he's everything, the whole world. No one else lets him get away with that. Ma didn't, I didn't. Gerald didn't – even *Weland* didn't. But you do. Because you believe it too. In your fucked-up, deep-down, can't-even-face-it way, you believe he's the whole fucking world.'

'Now, Reggie . . .'

'And it's so pathetic because actually you're nothing to him. And you know. That's the hilarious bit. You know you're nothing to him and still you race round doing his every dirty bidding. And you *know*. You knew all along.'

'Reggie . . .'

But there is no talking to him, no making sense of him. Running out like sand, he staggers to the door and is gone.

It is dark, and raining again, a sparse and speckling drizzle that seems to vanish on contact, when she finds Scylla, sitting outside anyway, leaning out of a garden chair to assess a tray of something placed on the white-hot grill inside the tripod.

'Fancy a bite?' Scylla calls.

'I think Max is exploring options.'

'I wouldn't hold your breath for Max. Sit with me.'

She goes through the drizzle to sit in another, apparently bone-dry, garden chair.

'Can't promise much – "Lentil Surprise", Mama called it, though it's just lentils.'

'Mama's cookouts.'

'Tragic, weren't they? That woman could burn steam.' Scylla scrapes a portion of the glistening stuff in the tray into a bowl, which she passes to Dia with a curly-tined old fork. Dia takes a cautious mouthful: granular sludge, but warming, expanding.

'Just like Mama used to make,' she says. 'Though not burned.'

'Ha!' Scylla scrapes more sludge into another bowl and begins eating it somehow with a penknife. 'I remember *your* mum. Lily? Lila? She came round here one day and scared the crap out of everyone. People going round afterwards like they'd seen the Yeti or something. The Abominable Snowwoman . . . Shit, Dee, did your mum pass?'

'Oh, no. I won't bore you.'

'You won't.' Scylla considers. 'If you want to tell me, you won't.'

Does she want to talk about Lila? She doesn't, never does. Yet now she hears herself saying, 'Well, Lila was a drinker. Whatever else she was, and Lila was lots of things, she was that. She drank. It was rough. Like – I don't know – like nothing liked you. Like everything was against you. The elements, fire, water, wind, earth, all against you. Then for years I tried to outdo her. Had the teenage rebellion phase but whacked up to full volume. I saw what the wild girls were doing and did it too. But even the wildest wild girl I knew was still tame compared to Lila, so I had to go further, wilder than wild, badder than bad.'

Is that what that was? Yes: no: maybe. Whatever she was trying to do to Lila (scare her? Impress her?), she knows the shrieking nights and crying days of her trouble years were also her teenaged self's coolly determined way of trying to get to the end of herself, to see what comes after.

'So for years I did that. Went out, went wild. Then I came in one night and Lila was on the bathroom floor. She'd fallen, hit her head. She was drunk and I was drunk and she was lying all bloody on the bathroom floor. But she was always falling, always hitting her head, always lying all bloody somewhere, and anyway as I mentioned, I was drunk. So I went to bed and slept for ten hours and when I got up she was still on the bathroom floor.

'They kept her in the hospital as long as they could. Every time I went someone with a clipboard wanted to discuss alternatives with me. But nothing sounded like alternatives. It sent me cold. Something was wrong with her. Because of my dad, I don't know. My dad was this student. And I knew what Lila was like. She had hooks. I can't say that she put her hooks in him, some poor gullible pillock over from India on a gap year, but I saw her do it so many times. Anyway, it sent me cold.

'The clipboard people at the hospital came up with a plan. They told me there was a place in town, an "appropriate unit", and Lila would be better there than anywhere else. I'd have to go to live in town to be near her. So I went to live in town and it was only when I got there I remembered the last thing I wanted was to be near Lila. So she went in the unit and I went to live in town and I didn't see her.'

'You never went?'

'I went sometimes. Not often. She's still there. Lila could be great but it was like her life was a shock to her. Like she couldn't get used to herself. Who she was, what she was. Her bones, her skin . . .'

Dia stares at the grill. But her heart is pounding – poking, prodding. She has never put the matter of her mother into these words before: Lila couldn't get used to herself. Couldn't learn herself, belong to herself. She has never had this thought before.

'Tell you what I think.' Scylla gives a flip of her forehead. 'I used to get narked at Mama because she wouldn't tell who my dad was. Didn't matter how many times I asked, she said she wasn't telling and it was for my own good she wasn't. Whatever that meant.'

Scylla leans back in her garden chair and roars laughter at the falling specks. 'One day when I'd been following her for hours like a little robot going, "Who's my dad? Who's my dad?" she sort of *whirled* round and said, "Don't you know half the trouble on this earth is caused by fathers? More than half. Mothers put you on the earth but fathers are the trouble on it. People would be better off without fathers at all. Don't you know how lucky you are?" She might as well have slapped me. I'd never felt lucky. And: mothers put you on the earth. I never forgot that. Say what you want about Lila, but it's true. No mother, no earth.'

'No mother, no Mother Earth,' Dia says, and it's so stupid this time they both lean back in their garden chairs and roar at the blackness above. She closes her eyes, feels the drizzle specks make contact with the rim of her mouth, where they magically vanish. Has it ever happened that she has longed, truly longed to see her mother? To stroke the thin stuff of her hair, press a palm to her white-blue cheek? Oh, Lila, she thinks: I have done you wrong, oh, Lila. I'm very afraid I have done you wrong.

Weland eats the lentils she takes in to him then washes his face at the box-crowded basin and pulls on his jacket.

'Don't know where you think you're going,' she says.

'Stretch the legs.'

'Are you staying or leaving? Just for information.'

'I'm staying.'

'You should talk to Scylla. She might be able to find you somewhere . . .'

'I don't need somewhere. See you in the morning.'

His leaving exasperates her far more than it should. Lying in the dark she imagines him walking the camp, occasionally stooping at a lit window, then straightening to hold the same tree-like posture for hours while the moon plumes through suburban clouds . . . and the exasperating thing is she's sure this is what he planned, her lying here, imagining that.

Then he is rocking her. All at once the van is electric with leaks of light and Weland is softly rocking her shoulder, the skinned nodules of his eyes still asleep in his face.

'Dia?' The hand that isn't rocking her shoulder hefts his phone in front of her. Images she can't make out slide precariously about its screen. 'He's died.'

The security guard: Grayson James. She can't quite bring herself to say it.

Weland goes on rocking her shoulder. For some reason she lets him. Then she stirs and sits up and he retreats from her into the electric light.

Half an hour later Scylla calls at the van. Her face tells them she already knows. She slumps between the boxes with the loose limbs of a condemned woman. She starts talking about how hard things are going to be, how hard some members of the collective are going to find the next few days, in a way that suggests she's expecting one or the other of them to jump in. Dia wants to do it but there are too many black slates heaped on top of her, too many clanking chains wrapped round her. Eventually she shakes her head. 'We're going.'

'That's not what I'm saying.'

'We'll go. It's not fair. After everything you've done. I'll find Reggie and we'll go.'

'Go where?'

'Don't worry about it.'

Leaving the van to look for Reggie, she worries about it. Is there really anywhere she can take Reggie and try to hide him from a manhunt until Samson can find them? Samson, who now has the death of Grayson James on his conscience, on the spike-point of his soul. Suzy's, maybe? No – she can't do it to her. Andrew's, then? Not the flat, which doesn't strictly exist any more, but the house, wherever that is, where he and the banshee are busy clearing space in their marriage? God, no – she can't do that to any of them. Then where? She is going round and round in the rain before she realises Reggie's not here.

We'll regroup and we'll go underground.

He's not here. Not anywhere in the circle of vans.

We'll be safe and we'll change ourselves.

She goes to the park. The swings hang empty on their chains.

We'll be nature red. Nature red in tooth and claw. In tooth and claw.

She goes back to the van, where Scylla is talking to Max. Weland sits on the bed, holding his phone between his knees as if it were a weapon of deadly force. Oh yeah, Max says: Reggie has gone. Gone when? Cleared out a few minutes ago, Max says: this is what he was coming to tell them. He and Reggie were talking, then Reggie got up all sudden and shaky and said he had to go. Go where? Max scratches his tattoos for a while – their mortal edges and cusps. Thinks he mentioned someone called Jerry? Gerard, maybe?

20. Various Stopping Places

'We want to see Gerald,' Dia says, and the woman standing on the doorstep smiles as if this is exactly what she thought she would say.

'Believe me, you're not the only ones.' The woman pauses as two waist-high girls in party dresses bump past her into the street. With each bump her smile thins to show more of the steel beneath. 'I think a few of us would like to know where Granddad's hiding himself, isn't that right, Robyn?'

She throws her voice after one of the fleeing girls, who only beeps, 'Not seen him,' before continuing her flight.

'There you go. Straight from the birthday girl herself. If we hadn't had the shed talk I'd say he was there, but he can't be there, can he? Not when we had the shed talk.' The smile is now stretched thin indeed. 'If you're in desperate need of the old piker you could look for him there. I daren't. Honestly.' She shows them the palm she would use to kill him. 'Round the back. Can't miss it. Take some cake.'

She leaves them on the doorstep with their paper plates. They look at each other, then again at the street – this street in airy Wargrave to which they have made their way through every grey phase of the morning, through the network of motorways that has replaced England's viscera, this street to which Weland has driven them with a look of mild grievance and no more explanation than that he likes to keep up with former acquaintances, it's a quirk, almost a hobby – then cross with their plates to the side of the house and the balloon-tied gate that opens onto a narrow alley and the tearing sound of children's voices. Wargrave: the grave of war.

In the garden a party is in progress, which is to say a tragedy is unfolding against cheerful scenery. More balloons are tethered to stone-filled jars at each corner of a picnic table across whose surface rolls a foam of uneaten birthday cake. Shredded metallic gift paper glints like the remains of an air disaster. A plump young woman dressed as a fairy searches politely and unsuccessfully for someone to tell the story of her wings. At least two of the little girls are wailing. A mother says 'Ooh!' as she rises out of a conversation she has transacted on her haunches and faces them with a grateful expression. They are not reinforcements, however, and Dia leads Weland across the descending levels of the garden, each an act in the doomed ballet of the party, to an innocently bucolic green-painted shed withdrawn under an eave of blistered oak at its far end. Weland raises a fist as if to knock, and for Dia that's it. A kids' party is a kids' party, but the birthday girl isn't even here. Fucked off with her best mate to blow her birthday money on sweets. (What she would do. Yes. If she'd lived like this – precisely what she would have done.) She shoves her plate at him, shouts, 'Gerald? Gerald Pinion?' and rips open the door of the shed.

There isn't much to see. Wooden walls, wooden shelves, not books but what she assumes at first must be magazines, then sees are . . . comics. American comics. X-Men, that sort of thing. There is a writing table with a notebook and a pen on it. There is a chair with a blanket and an old man in it. The old man has a small neat grey beard and spectacles and he looks at them with quivering guilt and cravenness. He makes an uncertain gesture and the blanket unrolls from under his chin, the comic drops from his hand.

'Ah,' says Gerald Pinion. Then, in a completely different way: '*Ah*.'

And he smiles. Because he is not in trouble for ducking out of his granddaughter's party, because he has not been caught.

'Weland! This is a surprise. How entirely bizarre to see you. And Miss Talwar! We meet at last.'

He sounds nothing like the supervillians populating his comics, nothing like any villain Dia has heard of. He sounds like a shaky old uncle trying and failing to give the impression that he has kept up with his niece's gabble about schoolfriends. And there is something else. The fiddly sense of the spectacles, the twist and swim of the beard: she has seen him before. Not on a screen but in the flesh. She has met with the grain of this man's physical presence before. But where, when?

She looks past him into the shed. 'Where's Reggie?'

'Reggie who?'

'Fuck off.'

'How may I be of service to you, when—'

'Reggie Glaze. We know he's here.'

'I'd be surprised if he were.' He widens his eyes: a bright boyish blue that makes you think of apple scrumping, midnight feasts, epic conker battles. 'Reggie *was* here. Came to visit his daft Uncle Jed. We talked then he left. That was all.' He shrugs woollily. And this is wrong. He's the supervillain and they've cornered him at the bottom of his garden with a dozen of his granddaughter's little pals in easy grabbing distance. It's not that he's sure of himself; more like he doesn't know he needs to be so sure. Like he doesn't know he's the supervillain.

'Where did he go?'

'I don't believe I'm at liberty to tell you that. Given the circumstances.' He shakes his head. 'Unbelievable, isn't it? You try to take it in, that poor dead boy, and you just . . .'

He carries on talking. Dia frowns. She should be slamming him into the wall, telling him that poor dead boy was called Grayson James and he is poor and dead and will now be never more than a boy because he, Gerald Pinion, couldn't resist turning people into puppets and getting these puppets on their tangling strings to drift and knock into each other until they started to fall gratifyingly apart, and the Grayson James puppet was the one that gave way first, only Grayson James wasn't a puppet, he was – she should be bellowing all this into his teeth but instead she's letting him stand there talking and she's frowning, frowning.

'What did you do, Gerald?'

'I told you, Reggie came here and—'

'Before that. With Tarantula. Why did you create Tarantula?'

'Oh, I didn't create Tarantula.' He smiles his daughter's thin smile. 'Is that what you thought? No, I didn't do that.'

'Who did?'

'Don't you know?' He presents his thin smile to each of them. 'I thought you knew.'

'Who, Gerald?'

'Who do you think? Samson.'

'*Fuck* off.'

'It was, I'm afraid. I said I thought it was a bad idea. And so, alas, it has proven.' In fact his smile is not that of his daughter. Under hers there is steel: under his only mercury. Liquid flashes, lifeless pain. 'But you know Samson. Hears what he wants to hear.'

'Fuck this.' She turns to Weland. 'Come on. The old goat's out of his mind.'

Weland ignores her. He ducks forward into the shed, with grim ceremony sets the plates he's been carrying down on the writing desk, then picks up one foamy slablet of cake and begins nibbling it. He clears his lips with his tongue quickly and frequently. Then he points the slablet at Gerald and says through his full mouth, 'Speak.'

'Speak what? It's pretty obvious, isn't it? Samson wanted Reggie to have what he'd had. You too, Miss Talwar. He spoke of you often. At least as often as he spoke of Reggie. There were times, maybe we were in Kyoto, maybe we were in Stockholm, propping up the bar in some hotel late at night, and he would talk about you in such a way . . . well. You were important to him. And in all that time it was his deep dear dream to give you both what he always held to have been the greatest gift of his life, the greatest treasure, the greatest boon.'

She stares at him. Gerald waits for her to say something like: 'And, pray tell, what was that?' She stares at him.

'Another world. Another life. Oh, in that hotel bar in Kyoto or Stockholm or wherever he told me all about it. What it had meant to him, the "Thin Love Collective"? Sounded bleak to me, cold, dirty and bleak, and he laughed and said it was, but it was mine and no one else's. I don't know if it was the success, the money, the sense of mission . . . and you know Samson has always had an acute sense of mission. But it seemed to me rather as if he were trying to account for himself. How could he be who he was? How could he have all that he had? Odd that, along with the sense of mission, there was some sense in which he held himself to be monstrous. As if he felt there was something monstrous about himself.

'In any case, he came to believe that if this collective had helped him, something similar would help his son. If Reggie was troubled, and indubitably he was, Samson believed the balm for his ills was a new life. He had similar ideas about you, Miss Talwar. I understand you were . . . not any comparison to Reggie, of course not, but . . . I understand you've had troubles.'

There is surely no way he expects her to confirm or deny this. After a moment Gerald permits his gaze to wander. He sees the blanket and comic lying on the floor, and edging round Weland's halo of personal space he goes to the chair, bends, picks up the blanket, fussily folds it and places it on the writing desk next to the paper plates. He bends again, picks up the comic and stands holding it, almost fondling it.

'Do you know, I've no idea how I got hooked on these things. Comics. Comic *books*, as the Americans say, according the material a grander status than we're inclined to permit here. One hears "graphic novel" also, but that's a stretch even for me. Still, I do love them. Not the simplicity, moral or otherwise, as you may assume, but the . . . difference. The sheer otherness. I come in here, sink into my ragbag chair, open the pages and I'm . . .' He pauses, as if on the boundary line of some extraordinary crisis. The flashing mercury grows very visible. His fingers move tenderly over the edges of his comic. And then his face is only the face of a deeply English, deeply opaque old man again.

'We talked it through. In a purely speculative spirit, as I understood the matter. If he wanted to give you that, how would he go about it? I told him it couldn't be done. Whatever this marvellous collective had given him, he'd made it himself. Samson countered by saying Reggie couldn't do that. By insisting Reggie did not enjoy certain advantages he had himself enjoyed. Perversely, it seemed to me, he argued that his own background had been an advantage to him, while Reggie's background, his childhood of millionaire ease and plenty, was somehow a handicap. Well, you can imagine. I laughed and laughed. And Samson smiled but he did not laugh. It's my fault, he said. If the boy's a fuckup, I fucked him up. He's my son and it's my duty to help him. To give him a push. To give him a *start*.'

Gerald makes a scratchy sound – a chuckle without the grandfatherly component. The rasp of a failing machine. He places the comic on top of his folded blanket and looks at it.

'Of course Reggie could have no idea what Samson was up to. Samson felt strongly that Reggie's troubles stemmed from his sense that he was his father's son, that he could never escape his father's influence. So he absolutely could not know that Samson had crafted this new world for him. He had to believe it was his own discovery. And that, as they say, is where I came in. Samson asked me if I could do it. I told him assuredly I could do it. I could *do* it, but it wouldn't *work* . . . I tried exceptionally hard to impress that point on him. But he didn't want to know. He only heard my saying I could do it . . . and that was that.'

Dia opens her mouth. She knows where she has seen him before. The night before the protest at the plant, Marc was talking by the gatehouse to an old man: a 'nosy neighbour'. It was him, Gerald Pinion. Meeting with the actor Marc Gibson. Taking a report, giving instruction. Steering, directing. But it's useless. She closes her mouth.

(And now she knows it has happened before, she has seen Pinion before even that – before the gatehouse, before the actor Marc Gibson. But when, where?)

'Why?' This is Weland. He has started on the second slablet of cake and his mouth is still full or full again. 'You and Samson fell out. Hated each other's guts.'

'I don't know about that. We had our disagreements, some more spectacular than others, then yes, an opportunity presented itself. We had one fairly photogenic bust-up, as regularly we did, then we met and made our peace in private, as again regularly we did, and on this occasion he asked that we keep the peace between ourselves. This was about the time Cait died. Samson was . . . not himself. I don't say he despaired because Samson never despaired, but he wasn't himself. And he took me back to our late-night speculative talk in Kyoto or Stockholm or some other end of the earth and he asked me if I would do it. Keep the feud stoked in public, keep Reggie thinking we hated each other's guts, in your delicate phrase, then introduce the boy to his own bespoke countercultural movement. Samson was sure it would be the making of him. You too, Miss Talwar. Only in your case he was equally sure that no push would be necessary. He said we would need only touch you against the edge of such a world and you would attach. He said, You don't know that girl, Jed. She's ready. All her life she's been ready. To attach to something. To give herself to something. Just you see.

'That's how he settled on the idea of sending you down to check on Reggie. You see the logic. Perfect way to reinforce the illusion that he has nothing to do with Tarantula – is dead against it, in fact. Drive you both away from him. Straight into that parallel universe he'd created for you.' He makes that scratching sound again: the rasping, failing chuckle. 'Not that that went exactly to plan. It transpired that you required a good deal more persuading than Samson had counted on. Wouldn't you say, Miss Talwar? In the end we had to give you quite the inducement. Quite the firm shove.'

She goggles at him. What's the old goat talking about? Inducement? Shove? She shakes her head and then she sees him, Gerald, smiling at her in a room full of hollow strip lighting. Sitting in a chair against the back wall of the postgraduate admin office. Watching her, watching her life come apart, seam by fine seam.

'Astonishing how difficult it was. Even with the reach, with the . . . truly dreadful power of Samson's money. But it was difficult. The university people were difficult. The bank people were difficult. The office-supplies people were . . . somewhat difficult. And yet, you'll enjoy this, do you know who was the biggest problem? That little queen at the barber's shop. Splendid fellow. How he wept, how he shook his silly head. Still, we got there in the end. All those moving parts, all those difficulties, merely in order that Samson could swoop down and rescue you. I'm surprised you didn't pick it up. You seem like an intelligent young woman. I would have thought you'd have noticed what we were up to.'

'Bollocks,' she says. 'This is just—'

'I told him. Right from the start I said it won't work. I said you can construct a world but you can't control it. People don't stick to the script. They improvise. They make up new lines, devise new scenes. Marc, poor thing, he didn't know what to do. You knew Marc, didn't you, Miss Talwar? Possibly it was miscasting, in which case I accept full responsibility, but evidently he wasn't up to the job. By all means, I told him, let Reggie express himself. Let him work out his feelings about Samson, but, you know, keep a fucking lid on it.

'Then there was that business with the police, in which I understand you played an unexpected role, Dia. May I call you Dia? I understand you did an exemplary job of stirring things up, fuelling Reggie's fire, overwhelming poor Marc, slowly but steadily redirecting the whole venture against its creator. And let's not forget Mr Sellick. Yet can we be surprised? Once Reggie enters the Promised Land, is it a surprise if he wants to bring some muckers along with him, even such a one as Oliver Sellick? I had no idea myself until Reggie mentioned him this morning. Ideally Marc, or even dear Brandon – you know Brandon, Dia? – would have tipped me off sooner, in which event . . . but of course I deceive myself. If it hadn't been Mr Sellick it would have been something else. Some other rot on the apple, some other snake in the garden. Because, I told Samson, that is the nature of apples. That is the nature of gardens. You see I told him. I *told* him. Right from the start.'

'No,' she says. 'You may not call me Dia.'

'As you please, Miss Talwar.'

'Where'd he go, then?' Weland is licking his fingers. The cake has gone. 'After your chat. Where did Reggie go?'

'Ah, Weland. You're discomposed. You can't grasp why the man for whom you worked so faithfully for so long would exclude you from so grand an undertaking. In your discomposure it is possible you are considering unwise courses. Let me counsel you against them. And let me add that your being kept in the dark was my idea. The sole point on which Samson seemed capable of taking advice was on the point of discretion. As few involvements as possible. The only link between Tarantula and himself was to be me. I assure you no one else on his staff or in his acquaintance knew of the scheme. It was a precaution, a safeguard. No matter that we were safeguarding what could not be saved, that—'

'Where did he go?'

'Where do you think he went? He went to see Samson.'

'You told him all that?' Dia says. 'All that bollocks you just told us?'

Gerald moves his lips to inhibit something. Then he produces his razor-thin smile and says, 'I told him what I've told you. He arrived early, before this . . . descent. We spoke in my study. For the most part I think he took the news rather well. Perhaps towards the end of our conversation . . . perhaps when there was so much mention of his father . . . I do regret that. I wish there had been some way I could have explained matters to him without making quite so much mention of his father. But there seemed to be no way round it. And so perhaps at that time he became . . . not distressed . . .'

'You told him?' Weland says. 'When the whole point was not telling him?'

'I thought under the circumstances . . .'

'He said he was going to see Samson?' Her voice sounds strange to her – flat, remote, as if coming from a speaker at the back of the shed.

'Not in so many words. Though I got the impression . . .'

'Come on,' she says to Weland. 'Oh Christ, come on.'

As they leave the shed two small girls bump past them into it. Dia doesn't need to look back to know that the birthday girl has returned, that she has hotly, even passionately embraced her grandfather (while the best mate stands to one side and – what?

Watches? Envies? Or what, what?). It turns out also that she doesn't need to slow her pace across the party-wrecked garden, between the sagging balloons and curling ribbons, under the rain-heavy sky, to distinguish the voices behind them:

'Isn't it funny that those people were here? I don't remember inviting *them*.'

'Yes, my darling. I think that's very funny indeed.'

Now nothing happens quickly enough. It is clear that Weland is driving fast – she feels the speed lines ripping out of them, ricocheting into wake – yet she barely contains her impulse to throw her hands round the wheel, stamp her feet into the pedals, to do with every part of her body whatever it is you do when you drive as fast as you can.

'Stop it,' Weland says and that's when she realises she is clattering the nails of all her fingers on the dashboard.

'You don't believe any of that?' she says.

'No. But Reggie might.'

'No,' she says. 'No.'

Then he stops the car and nothing she says or does can make him start it again and he drags her out towards cafeteria lights. In the queue with her tray and the wrapped sandwich she won't be able to eat and the black coffee she won't be able to drink she calmly considers what it would be like to set her tray down on the nearest counter and kill everyone in this place. Under the strip lights, between the hardboard partitions. She could do it easily. There are moments when she is not sure she has not already done it.

Then she eats her sandwich and drinks her coffee and sits staring out of the window at the chiselling lights, tapping her fingernails against the sides of her paper cup. All the time in the world.

She reaches to pull her headscarf round her face and it is not there – she is not wearing it. Where is it? Is it lost?

Weland starts the car again. It is night, black night, she can't guess which one.

Then there is nothing to do but stare at the road and the lights and think. She leans back in her seat, wedges her head in the headrest, laces her fingers over her belly and thinks about what you think about, a sky of ash, a sea of blood, a woman picking her way between stones in a dry place that used never to be dry, the edge of an anorak overlapping the line of her eyes and everything she owns tied into a bag at the end of a shinbone-shaped stick.

If she didn't know it before she knows it now. This is England now, this road with its various stopping places. And it is only from the road that you see the truth of these stopping places: they are not various, not different from each other in any way that matters, however they think they are, however smugly their windows beam.

She has no idea when the lights change. It could have been an hour ago, could have been this same second: Weland's anemone eyes tell her nothing. But the lights on the road go from white and orange to red and blue, red and blue – the red and blue of police car, of ambulance, in a tightly spinning hub of panic that lifts her out of her seat and sets her nails again in the dashboard.

'Stop it,' Weland says. 'Didn't I say. Stop it. Didn't I, didn't I.'

They are still miles away but the panic of the red and blue lights gets into things, into the road, into space, and at the point of their tightest spin the car slides free of emergency-banded trees and fields and enters the approach to Samson's house with its surrounding wall and its tall gate. Weland aims the car at the gate. She doesn't make a sound though it is only later she sees the gate is in fact open, is necessarily open, in order that vehicle after vehicle may pass from the road into the orbit of the imperilled estate.

They are grinding over gravel when she sees the house: a diamond of lit stone picked out of the black sky. And as she looks there is a white flash, a flap, a churning flag dropping through the zone of light, and she knows what she knew from the start, from before the start, from before they left Gerald's house, from before thcy left the collective, from before . . .

It doesn't matter. Weland stops the car in the frieze of vehicles suspended at the top of the drive. Nothing makes any difference. She kicks past the door and before her other foot touches the gravel they are on her, they have her. And so it is and always was. There are the ones who wait with you at the hospital then take you back to your mother and there are the ones who thrust a hand between your legs and there are the ones in between, same as people, same as life, and there is no way to tell until they tell you, until they come out from under or press right through the uniform and tell you and as if staring into the back of her head, turning over and over on the gravel, she waits for them to tell her. Then they tell her and they are the ones who wait with you, they are the ones who take you back.

'Where is he?'

'Miss, I'm going to have to ask you—'

'I know him. Where did he fall?'

'The young man in question, we have reason to believe—'

They show her. A sheet bunched at one side on the gravel.

'Can assure you, miss, every effort—'

'But it was just now,' she says. 'I saw it happen just now.'

'I'm afraid that's not possible. Time of death recorded at nine fifteen.'

'What time is it now?'

'It's later. It's much later, miss.'

Then he comes out. It's useless but he comes out. On the steps, on the gravel. Samson.

Here he is, in layabout jeans and roadie T-shirt. And now he is here she sees him up there, in his attic eyrie with his model of the reflecting future, listening to his Ewan MacColl, his Bob Marley, his Woody Guthrie, when in through the doors and the noise bursts the son and heir: Father, I demand to be told . . .

But Reggie doesn't talk like that. Didn't. Doesn't.

Father, what is the meaning of this? Father . . .

His lips are shaking. His eyes have the stricken look of some wholly rational concern: lost door keys, overdue library book. He walks towards her for a while then away from her.

The officers don't seem to notice him. They don't seem even to know who he is. She wants to tap one on the shoulder and say: look! Don't you know who he is?

She walks up to him. He sways and stops in front of her. Shaking lips, stricken eyes.

'What did you say to him?' She shouts it though he is barely two feet away.

He looks away from her and raises his shoulders, slowly, airlessly: search me.

'What did you say?'

He looks at her. He looks down and sighs. Then he bends

one knee then the other and he is kneeling in front of her in the gravel.

'What did you do, Samson? What did you *do*?'

He looks at her a moment longer then sighs and stands and walks past her to the car she has not noticed waiting in the driveway for him for who knows how long now.

21. The Next World

Everything is as she left it. The city, or at least the part of it between the station and Granby Row, her building, her flat – nothing has changed. She finds her phone attached to its cable by the bed, thumb in mouth, mindlessly sleeping. Well, of course she does. What was she expecting? Fiery craters, heaps of brick? Still as she goes from room to unchanged room she feels sick with it, with the stubbornness, the brute permanence of things.

She calls Sumi at Greenflowers. All is well, she hears: 'A few of our usual dramas, nothing out of the ordinary.' No change there either.

'Can I visit?'

'I'm sure we can find you a window.'

'Expect me in the next day or two.'

'Looking forward to it.'

But the next day comes and goes, then the day after that, and she does not visit.

She goes out. There is no food in her flat, but there never was food in her flat. She teeters through the supermarket like someone elderly, squinting in the light, handling the vegetables in their canted trays with their bulges and freckles and unreadable markings. She fills two carrier bags which end up somehow left on the bus and then she is somewhere dark and hot and then she is outside again, sheltering from rain, trying to focus on a keypad while stepping from foot to foot and groaning because wherever she places either of her feet it hurts, it finds a sharp thin spike of pain.

Rather than buzz her into the building as she usually does, Suzy comes down to the door. She takes one look and hustles her into a bony embrace.

'I'm fine,' Dia says, not sure if this is what Suzy needs to hear. 'Why are my feet killing me? They're *killing* me.'

'They're new.' Suzy points and in the light from the atrium now she sees them: rows and columns of metal studs set into the pavement at either side of the doorway.

'What are they?'

'Disruption studs. Studs to disrupt the thoughts of anyone planning on sitting there for any length of time. You know. The accountants.'

'Holy shit. That's . . .'

'It's disgusting. I hate it.'

Suzy makes tea and Dia hugs the pink-painted pillar. Hugs it and hugs it. She hears Suzy talking and closes her eyes and listens to the sound of her voice. Eventually her legs dissolve and let her down onto the floor. Her arms are still wound round the pillar. Her head rests against it too. Her cheek sticking to the cold metal.

'And Dry's gone,' Suzy says.

'Oh yes.'

'Dry Bar. It's closed down.'

'I love this pillar,' Dia says.

'Make the most of it, honey.' Suzy tells her she's leaving. She has had enough. The love affair is over. A nice house in the suburbs. No more Northern Quarter.

'But then you'll be just like everyone else.'

'That's right.' She smiles but her voice is full of horror.

In the morning Dia is alone with the rocks in her head. A note from Suzy walks her through the stages of a hearty breakfast she can't imagine having the energy to make. She's boiling the kettle when a knock comes at the door. No buzzer, no warning. She puts her eye to the peephole.

'What do you want?'

'You left suddenly,' Weland says.

'Not an answer.'

'Are you all right?'

'I'm fine. Fine and dandy.'

'Can I come in?'

'Oh, no.'

Through the peephole she watches him fidget. He does not remove his sunglasses: she cannot see his eyes, their respiring bulbs. It takes a long time, but finally he does leave.

The funerals take place over a weekend, Grayson James' on the Saturday, Reggie Glaze's the day after. Samson is discovered at both ceremonies. She watches on Suzy's couch in front of Suzy's TV with all her fingers barring his blue-white face. There is a bit of him getting out of a car with the groping gestures of someone who has never done this before. There is a bit of him talking to a hemisphere of light that keeps snapping at him. I am shattered. This has shattered me.

What did you do, Samson?

(you don't remember)

He has the same glutinous look that Lila used to have when she spoke to the police: the look of a drunk trying very hard not to seem drunk. And something else. As if there is a terrible figure in his peripheral vision that he is steadily ignoring in the hope that it will lose interest and go away. The seer, the clairvoyant – his whole life now reduced to peripheral vision.

Tarantula is mentioned. Only the word makes her flinch. Then Tarantula is no longer mentioned. Less than a week after the funerals the same chief constable who declared a firm intention to root out the 'secret society' responsible for the deaths of both men issues a statement confirming that Reggie Glaze had a history of mental illness and both he and Grayson James were victims of a tragic pathology, a lost private battle, a failed system.

It is after this weekend that she tries to hand herself in. She goes to the police station and tells the officer at the desk everything. No detail she mentions has the least effect on the officer's blink rate. She asks if he should be writing some of this down.

She sits at a table in a room that does not conform in any way to her expectations of an interview room. There is a window, for a start: a green view of grass at the edge of a car park. A vase on the table that reminds her of Lila's room at Greenflowers. Small touches, humane considerations. For those. For those who are about to.

An older woman with a stern face and violently disordered grey hair and a man about her own age with a lot of mummy's-boy plumpness crammed into his suit enter the room and she tells them everything while they stand side by side against the far wall. The man's face gives a sort of pulse, a sort of squeeze, every so often, possibly at moments that coincide with her expression of certain wild scurrilities, possibly not. The woman's face gives nothing. It is a wooden effigy, a carved mask. When Dia has finished telling them everything the man looks at the woman then leaves the room. The woman sits in the chair opposite hers and says the story she has told them is worrying. Dia agrees it is. The woman says she wonders if Dia is troubled in some way. She says she wonders if perhaps Dia has recently undergone some upsetting experience, some shock, some loss, some trauma. She asks Dia if she ever feels an impulse to hurt herself, or to hurt someone else. Dia says what is this. What the fuck is this.

The seated woman is a totem, a graven image. She says if she were to hear such a story again she would have no choice. She says she is confident any one of her colleagues would reach the same conclusion. Trauma. A troubled mind. Treatment.

'Do it.' Dia smacks the table with a perfectly flat palm. 'Lock me up. Drag me off to your loony bin. I want you to do it.'

She makes herself as difficult as possible. It takes a long time. Nonetheless they prise her up from the table, peel her off the walls, steer her out to the pavement. The day has got very bright. The grass next to the car park blazes an intricate formal green.

When she gets back to her flat Weland is there, as he is always there now. She is not crying but this time she lets him in anyway.

'It's not your fault.'

'How do you know?'

'It was too much for him. But it was always going to be too much for him. Sooner or later, something was always going to be too much for Reggie.'

'Yeah, but how do you know?'

The money is still in her account: Samson's thousands. She keeps checking, expecting it to disappear, but the same number comes up in the screen, day after day. She finds the details of a charity that works with rescue dogs and transfers every penny and for an hour or even longer she feels clean, light.

*

The train gets her in by mid-afternoon. With hours to kill before the show she makes a brisk circuit of the town centre then sits in a coffee shop next to the theatre until she sees a queue forming. The man who takes her ticket is as large and square as a bodyguard and he allows her to pass with visible reluctance.

It is a typical provincial production of *Death of a Salesman*: hobbled by reverence and unsteady accents. He is no worse than the rest of them, no better either. His interpretation of Happy gives the character perhaps a touch more dignity, gravity, than it deserves. When the cast comes forward for its final collective bow he is sweating heavily. He drops his head forward and a spray of dark droplets silently detaches from his hair. Then he straightens and smiles at the other actors with a shakiness that feels like her first definite proof that he really is him.

Despite the enthusiasm of the applause she is alone at the stage door. Every few minutes a cast member comes out with a demeanour that shows no expectation there will be anyone waiting for a picture or an autograph. Keeping her distance on the opposite kerb, she watches them go, Loman after Loman. Another half hour passes then he comes out too, talking to a woman she doesn't remember seeing in the production.

'Marc,' she calls from her kerb. Stepping into the road, she says it again: 'Marc.'

He looks at her. For a moment he looks away, carries on talking to the woman, then he looks at her again and stops walking. He says something to the woman, who turns to Dia, bares her teeth without malice, then takes out her phone and follows it back into the theatre. Dia reaches the pavement and she and Marc stand looking at each other.

'Good show?'

'I've had worse.'

'I hope not much worse.'

'I wanted to tell you.'

'No you didn't.'

'No. I suppose I didn't.'

'You're an actor. You were acting.'

'Not always.'

'Don't give me that.'

'Not always. Not as much as you think.'

'The whole thing was pretending.'

'It wasn't. It's difficult. It was and it wasn't.'

She looks at him. He is an actor, with an actor's deportment – that air of inexorable camp. And she understands that he wasn't bored. As the leader of Tarantula, Marc was not bored but frustrated. Abysmally, atomically frustrated. Every moment of every day he acted under the constraint of this nuclear frustration. Now, facing her across the street, he is someone else, a totally different person, evincing wholly unfamiliar complications. You meet someone and you wonder what their childhood was like. What they think about when they don't have anything to think about.

'Do you ever see them?' she says. 'The rest of the troupe, the company?'

'It wasn't like that.'

'Only I assume you actor sorts are a pretty close-knit lot.'

'We weren't all actors. Me, a couple of others. Quite a few were genuine recruits. They believed what they said they believed.'

'Oh, Christ. "What Tarantula believed". What was that – a script, a bible? Or did you get creative input?'

'You say that. But what we did was not uncreative.' He flutters his fingers over the street. 'We picked stuff up. Found what was going round. What was in the air.'

She wants to ask about Jon, about Fee, Annette – but what could he tell her? And whatever he did tell her, could she believe it? She has had no contact from any of them. She knows there is no reason why she should have done and yet she feels herself waiting for it, waiting for contact from them, every day, every minute. She has ideas about what this waiting of hers may become, may tense into, may start bitterly to concentrate, though no clear ones. So now all she says is, 'I always wondered about the name.'

'Tarantula? That was Mr Glaze. So Gerald told me, anyway. I never met him in person. But Gerald told me Mr Glaze wanted the group to be called Tarantula. He was very definite about it.'

'Did he say why?'

'At the time I assumed it was just meant to sound scary. "Scary nature". Later I did some reading. Turns out tarantulas are unusually rich in symbolism. Depending on your source, they represent stuff like knowledge, or change, or fate – all the usual suspects. But I did find that generally they're associated more strongly with one idea than any other.'

'Are you going to tell me?'

'Uh, a trick. A deception, a trick.'

Weland tries to explain it to her. But nothing he says dials down the leap of panic that keeps coming into her stomach, her throat, the ends of her hair.

'No, I *get* that,' she says through gritted teeth, 'I know what he's *saying*. I just don't know what he *means*.'

They are at Greenflowers, in Lila's room, with the peonies on the bedside table and the TV on its skinny steel arm in a corner of the ceiling. Samson is talking on the TV screen. Flashes keep draining the colour from his cheeks. It returns, the colour, but less after each flash, she thinks, can't help thinking. There is no church behind him, no power plant either. Instead there is a bar, with its coiled fairy lights and stencilled glass.

Weland tries to explain. 'You can't blame him. People have been telling him to get out for years. The renewables boom, if you can even call it that, ran out of steam long ago. It was a fad. An experiment in idealism. Conscience play. He always knew that.'

But he talks through gritted teeth too. Perhaps he is crying, leaking discreet tears, but the cold-water pulse of his eyes makes it hard to tell. All she knows is that whatever he is talking about Samson didn't know it and neither did Weland. Neither does Weland now.

'It was inevitable,' he says. 'It's a sensible move.'

On the TV screen Samson is publicly announcing the discontinuation of his work in the solar-power sector. He has given instructions for the experimental plant in Warwick to be taken offline, dismantled, dismembered. He is currently in the process of dissolving Glaze Energy. He announces the formation of a family-support bursary in the name of Grayson James, a mental health charity in the name of his son, Reggie Glaze. And he announces that his future business plans will focus exclusively on leisure and lifestyle. Will develop his existing assets in the high street – bars, delis, shops, boutiques. In the bar slantingly glimpsed behind him he is about to launch his new corporate identity: Glaze Easy.

But Reggie wasn't mad, wasn't the one who was mad. At least she thinks he wasn't. She thinks she knows what she thinks then in her head a light is turned on, turned off, and she's no idea what she's looking at.

'Can't blame him,' Weland says. 'He's moving on.'

She understands. Moving on. Giving in. So why does nothing dial it down, the surge, the jump, the somersault of panic in her guts and throat and hair?

Now there is a bed next to the bed and it is her bed. At night Lila sleeps in her bed and Dia sleeps in hers and throughout Greenflowers the pipes secretly tick and the walls creak as if withholding some force of collapse.

Sumi checks in on her. 'You should take a break. Get a change of scenery.'

She stifles a laugh. Poor Sumi! Doesn't she know everywhere blurs into everywhere else? Doesn't she know you can travel the globe and still the scenery doesn't change?

Behind Lila's room there is an alleyway that fills at night with the voices of dogs. She expects to hear fighting but never does. The dogs in the alley emit only wails, whines, sobs of canine grief. It is confusing. Sometimes in the early hours she wakes and cannot tell her own thoughts from the keening of the alleyway strays. *What were they called again, those old heart-breakers? Snowflake, Buttercup . . .*

There is a sort of emergency. People rush round Lila's bed. The other bed, Dia's bed, is at some point knocked over, swatted aside, folded up on its aluminum frame by the urgent passage of thighs and knees. There is the skirling of machines, like a fire alarm, or a car alarm. In the arc of an arm she sees Lila's face contained by a transparent mask – the bone and beak of an ancient bird rising to the shell of its spittled egg.

Dia stands by the door. Things happen, she watches, waits. What was it Lila said? *There's not any such thing as 'your self'*. Yes. And: *'Your self' is just a great big hole, same as everyone else's.* Yes, yes. And (the part she always forgets): *If you're so interested in having a 'self', my girl, you'd better get busy. Roll your sleeves up and do the graft. It's not hidden away somewhere waiting for you to believe in it. It doesn't exist until you make it exist. So make it. Use anything you like, anything you can and anything you have to. There's not a lot of choice but there's some. Make it, keep it, and remember your daft old pisshead of a mum knew a thing or two once upon a time.* And why does she always forget that? What keeps it from view?

The emergency passes. Suzy Poorman checks in on her. In a bright calm way she talks about selling her flat, about leaving her flat. Dia nods but doesn't hear much of what Suzy says because now she's working stuff out.

'I was sorry to hear about your friend,' Suzy says.

She nods. Reggie? He wasn't my friend. But we were young at the same time. He was this cool little boy who didn't understand jokes, didn't understand that not everything has to cross the road, that some things just get on the road and stay on it, then he grew up into this imperiously remarkable man, superlative in every way except that he still didn't understand jokes. He wasn't my friend but we were little together.

'Is that one always here?' Suzy means Weland.

'He's always here, yes.'

He sits in a chair outside the room. For hours he sits leaning forward over his folded arms, staring self-pityingly at the floor, or else sprawled back with his hands hanging at either side, staring into the strip lights, as if punishing his eyes with the electric glare, as if trying to burn them from their sockets.

Once she woke in the night and she and Weland were walking through Greenflowers. He was holding her arm but they were both walking. They walked to his car and he drove them to a small house behind a concrete wall and he steered her by her arm into a white bed and left her there. She didn't sleep, only lay sinking and sinking. In the morning she woke to find a neat square of black cloth lying folded on top of the pillow next to the pillow she'd slept on. Without touching it she knew the square was the one she'd worn in her hair, then over her hair. She left it on the pillow and went into the sitting room, where Weland brought her coffee and toast. After she showered he brought her back to Greenflowers and with a grunt fitted himself again into the chair outside the door. They didn't talk about it, any of it. All that night and morning they exchanged barely a dozen words.

'Creepy,' Suzy says.

'He's creepy, yes.'

But she doesn't hear much because now she's working stuff out.

I used to say you're here for a great reason.

But that's not true.

You have a great work to perform. You'll change everything. Change the world.

Not true, not true.

You either want to build up this one perfect thing or smash everything to pieces.

Yes.

Then why am I looking at you knocking the crap out of his pride and joy?

Because everyone's stupid except—

You believe he's the whole fucking world.

Because I'm the danger woman, the trouble woman, all or nothing, do or—

All her life she's been ready. To attach to something. To give herself to something.

Because 'my self' is just a great big hole, same as everyone else's, because

You know you're nothing to him.

Because yes because how did that happen how did that work what did it mean what did it MEAN what

I would have thought you'd have noticed what we were up to.

I did yes I did

You knew all along.

I knew of course I knew and yet there is the question of how my soul hangs in the universe, of the hooks and grips from which it particularly depends—

all along

I was a toy in a rich kid's playpen, a bendy mirror in the father-son funhouse – you reflecting him reflecting you reflecting him—

Not thoughts. Not thoughts but dogs. Whining, keening.

Hopes are dogs.

Tarantula is dogs.

They have run away over the fields so she will feel them leaving her, person after person, pang after pang, they have stained her with their leaking hearts, gouged her with love's broken bottle so she will know her body is a wound under spinning lights of emergency, of violence and consequence, a man with folded arms staring down at the floor.

Are they right, she wonders in agony, those lying, pretending bastards: are they right? Is it true after all that the world doesn't need people, doesn't need a witness to its beauty? That whatever beauty ever shot a frond or set ripples in tree bark is only a dream in the mind of a sleeper and when the sleeper dies the dream of beauty dies too?

Then it is night and there is a sort of emergency and when it is over she hears the gush of the pipes and the shriek of the walls as they give way at last to the unbearable force that has been exerted on them since the beginning of time and it all comes down, the whole illusion, the sky and the sea, the air and the land, and there is nothing to do but put aside the bed that is hers and crawl into the bed that is Lila's and pass her arms round the tiny cold bird that is Lila now and nothing to feel, nothing to feel at all under the bright burning wave that has swept clean the disc of the earth and nothing to think except that she is ready, that she is done with this one and she is ready for the next, ready for the next world, ready for the next life, ready for the next.

Shock Valley – IV

A night at The [Something] Dog leaves me unrefreshed but less tired. Over my breakfast of beer and beans in the empty bar the publican returns to me my hammer, my stick, and – perhaps excessively – my stopped watch. Before I can leave he approaches me again with a further gift: a thing shaped like a doorstop, wrapped in a greasy cloth. I don't have to look to know what it is. My centre pings with it, bubbles, effervesces. But outwardly I maintain decorum and with an impatient grimace pack the cloth-wrapped thing into my bag, rap my stick in a forbidding way against the threshold stone of his piss-poor establishment, and stalk back out to the road.

Which I find even busier than usual. All traffic headed the same way I am: to Silo. The few pedestrians pressing against the tide don't last long. Someone calls to them – a hen or a stag party draws them to its boisterous breast – and they are redirected towards the common destination. Towards Silo, the town at the end of the valley, at the end of the world.

'Don't tell me you don't . . .'

'People not got ears where you lot . . .'

'Slow down, words of one syllable only for these fine . . .'

And the name, everywhere, on every lip: *Lorelei* . . .

By midday the road's back is broken. According to popular wisdom this is the most arduous leg of the journey but somehow it passes with my barely noticing. I can't think it is the happy current of Lorelei supporters I can neither join nor escape, lifting me up, bearing me along, elbows invisibly and unknowingly linking mine: it may be true but I can't think it. The supporters plunge eagerly into the shadow of the ridgeline; more dubiously I follow. In the darker, cooler air the caravan grows only more animated. And soon along the road's falling perspective appears the distant smut of the town: an oil bubble whose meniscus is about to break. There is a tremendous cheer. And for me that's enough. I leave the road, hike upwards against the slope facing the valley's end and the foment of bilious Silo, track with my stick among the weeds, pebbles, carrier bags and pop cans until I find a suitably shady boulder and drop myself beneath it. I'm not tired or hungry or thirsty but the sweat is seething out of me. Time for lunch.

I have my bag in my lap when I notice I am not alone on the slope. A few feet away, grey and dry as the dry grey earth, a man sits quietly talking to a child who I assume is his granddaughter. Their postures as well as their conversation confirm they have selected the spot for its view.

'So God became angry,' the man is telling the little girl, 'because men had forgotten their purpose on this earth, which is to give him praise and to venerate him, in his might and his mystery. He saw men's only thought was to pile up gold against him, do you see, poppet, to store up gold from his gift to them, and they laughed, yes laughed, thinking only of the gift and forgetting the might and the mystery. So God grew furious and sent down his wrath and he punished them, yes he did, poppet, do you see, he evaporated them.'

The girl isn't listening. I don't blame her.

'He saw the towns here' – the man waves an arm at a scrambled corner of the valley – 'and here' – another wave, another lorn pit – 'and here too, poppet, even here, do you see' – a crumbled scree just barely holding the ashen outline of innumerable sties – 'and he said *Zammo!*, God did, and he glared his hardest glare and he evaporated them. Evaporated those towns right off the face of the earth. And all the people in them. Evaporated them to nothing. Nothing but vapour. Do you see, poppet? So that's why we what?'

She isn't listening. Her hands pat about and about in some interesting dirt. But she says anyway: 'Pray.'

'That's right. We pray. We pray and do what?'

'Bow.'

'Right again. We pray and bow our heads. And to whom do we bow our heads?'

'To God.'

'Last one, poppet. And where is God?'

'There,' the girl says, and she and her grandfather bow. They bow to the sun.

In fact I've heard of these people: sun worshippers, solar cultists. At the weekend market they were always good for a laugh. But even while they laughed people said the movement was spreading, growing. Well, why not? I'd hoped for something grander (robes, masks) but then this old berk with his berkish beliefs is in his way quite grand enough.

And what do I know? I was the little girl – patting an interesting bit of dirt. All my life growing no older or wiser but stubbornly remaining a little girl not listening to anything and pat-patting some interesting dirt with my hand. Yes, things were changing. Yes, the sun was coming hotter, lower, nearer in the sky each day. Yes, there was less sky each day. But you see, Grandpa, there was this exceptionally stimulating patch of dirt right there under my hand, and I could pat it, pat it and pat it, and when I did amazing things happened . . .

The world ends and you miss it. Because the world is always ending, never ending. Daily, hourly, it flooded your antennae: the ongoing apocalypse, here, there but never quite everywhere. The same faces deploying the same warnings with a waxy look of incredulity. Fire and flood, fire and flood. Then only fire, fire. It hit me when I saw how many flights were being cancelled. Not the tanks in the street or the checkpoints between towns or the tattered convoys outside the building. Flights: that's where it hit me. Then all flights were cancelled. By the time the faces and the warnings were appreciably different than they'd been before, it was too late. This, you see, Grandpa, is how the world ends. By the time you're ready to believe it could happen it is starting to happen is happening has happened.

Like everyone else I knew about the Helios Accord – the newly conceived corporate taskforce with its bold promise to do what no government or accord of governments had been able to do: to halt, and indeed reverse, the deterioration of the earth's climate. On TV I had seen its bonhomous representatives explaining the procedures, techniques, materials; had heard the swaggering terminology (albedo modification; geoengineering). Later I'd watched as the Accord sent up formations of planes to inject the sky with an aerosol compound that in addition to its having been rigorously lab-tested and computer-modelled had the attraction of its being 0.000,000,002 per cent diamond. I'd watched them scatter the sky with diamond – replace the old dead sky with a new diamond sky that would banish the sun and save us all.

Later still (when the flights disappeared), I watched the staggered, stop-start mutation of the Helios Accord into the Helios Event. The dispersal had worked! Had not worked! Had worked better than hoped! Had made no detectable impact! Had made a significant impact! Well: it had made a significant impact. With its diamond edge it had peeled away the sky – and vanished. Not quite without trace (several million tonnes of vaporous volatility massed in the Southern Oscillation). But there was no new sky, and now there was no old sky either. And the sun leaned low, lower, lowest, and held the earth in its panopticon glare.

It was about then that the TVs stopped working. And the phones, tablets, laptops. Still you heard things. The Helios Event and its continuing, catastrophising aftershock, its tentacular escalations. The slithering reels of power, the roadblocks, machine-gun nests. The collapse of the north, of many norths, many regions, nations. And the whispered names, in ghostly duality: El Niño and La Niña – the little boy and the little girl of the Pacific Ocean, personae of the subtropics. The little girl was cool, the little boy warm. And now and forever everything was El Niño, El Niño – little boy, little boy.

Helios. Who in their right mind calls anything Helios? (Peter and his clade of money reptiles, that's who: Helios by another name.) A deadly fantasy, a ruinous global vanity project consisting of nothing but men's pride and stupidity, it should have been named not for the sun god but for that idiot son of his – the one who tricked him out of his solar reins and burned up half the earth.

'You know, I don't completely blame them,' Hendrix said one

night not long after I moved to the house by the lake. 'Of course, those Helios buffoons did what they did because they couldn't be bothered to do anything else, anything hard, anything that might hurt. But what else was there? What happened to the climate heroes we used to hear about, the green and earthen messiahs with all their wonderful ideas, and plans, and schemes? Don't know about you, Mabel my dear, but right before Helios I don't remember seeing too many of those fellows. I don't remember there being too many of them about.'

I take out my lunch. Hard water in the canteen, crumbs of black bread. Then after as long a delay as I can manage I produce the cloth-wrapped doorstop the publican gave me. I can smell it, taste it, through the cloth. There is almost no need for me to unwrap it, though with trembling fingers I do.

Is it awful? When all is said and done, I will serve any power, any force, any tyranny, that gives me cheese.

A block about the size of a mouse: the computer sort or the other sort. Dull orange with a ridged crust like road grit. Cautiously I nip at one corner of the biscuity stuff with my teeth. The taste of it connects. I close my eyes. For this – for this I will drown villages.

When it is gone, all of it, the whole block, I look up. The man sits surveying the valley. His granddaughter is collecting stones. Not quite: she teeters over the slope, every so often dropping to her haunches, selecting a stone, briefly raising it to her lips, then with delicate care replacing it on the ground and shooting up to resume her search. I can't make it out. Does she kiss the stone? Tell it something?

It is a game of some type. I don't know which type. But I know the slope, the valley, the wreck of the evaporated towns:

none of this reminds her of anything. None of it looks to her like a lost world. It looks only like the world. What she sees is the only world there ever was. Ever was, ever will be.

'Hello, stranger.'

The man is smiling at me. His face is kindly, though heavily scarred and missing an eye. And I wonder: if I smiled back, if I went over there and shared my lunch – the last drops of water, the last crumbs of bread – how would that appear? A little girl and her grandfather and grandmother. A little family.

A little family of solar cultists.

'Hello,' I call back. I heave my bag onto my shoulder and prop my stick and raise myself against it. 'Hello, hello,' I call and then, 'goodbye, goodbye.'

And I lower myself into the gradient of the slope, into the depth of the road and the falling perspective down to Silo.

It is late afternoon, and the stream of Lorelei supporters has largely dissipated, by the time I reach the toll bridge. Naturally the bridge is a joke: a bridge over a river that doesn't exist any more, over a trench of pebbles that anyone could scale in half a minute without recourse to a bridge. However the two young men collecting tolls are not in on the joke and they take their business seriously. Waiting for my turn to be tolled, I try to remember when operations like this first started appearing – five years ago? Six? Gates and bridges and barriers where formerly there was none, young men with toll tins and a thickened look that spoke of serious business. I know Peter didn't waste time. Right from the start he was clanking together the heavy bits of his network. And so these youths on the bridge, gravely monitoring the flow of life into Silo, are no more than specks, nubs, outlying tips of a mesh at whose centre reposes the blank, the void, the polo-shirted nullity that is Peter.

The queue at least is short, and soon enough I stand in front of the young men with my earring, my necklace, my stopped watch.

'No, Mother,' one of the men says. 'What's this? No barter in Silo.'

'What do you say, lovey?'

'It is money here. Pounds and pence.'

'But I don't have any pounds. I don't have any pence. What am I to do, lovey?'

'Money only in Silo. None of your backwater ways here.'

The officious pipsqueak is actually turning me away, shifting his attention to the people stalled behind me, when his fellow toll-taker lumbers across. Big healthy young chap – sandy, freckly. Never strictly my type, though in happier days there might have been one or two. *Do you want a shower, or shall I . . . ? What's wrong with both together?* Save Water: Shower with a Friend . . . Gripping his colleague's shoulder, he winks at me. 'What brings you to Silo, Mother?'

I should say: *There is a child, terribly sick*. I should say: *My daughter nears her time*. I should say: *There is a wedding, my sister's son*. But what I say is: 'Why, I've come to see Lorelei. To hear her song.'

'Does Lorelei sing?' The big toll-taker looks at the pipsqueak then again at me. 'I thought she just talked.'

'To me, it is song.'

He nods. And, smiling, the handsome youth gives his squirty colleague's shoulder a further joshing squeeze then steps back and directs me with both hands onto the bridge.

'Welcome to Silo, Mother.'

Smiling and nodding too ('Bless you, lovey – bless you, bless you') I cross the bridge and step down into a road that leads a winding way past shuttered shops and boarded-up houses towards the centre of town. And oh, it is a dump. A demolition site, a wrecker's yard. There are places where they do nice things with the cars: fill the seats with sticks and stones and white sand, turn them into little wayside Zen gardens. Silo isn't one of those places. On every corner you pass rusted stacks, shattered skeletons. The meat colours of engine parts, smashed for the fun of smashing them. Reminds you of that fad there was for a while, when people broke their phones. In public. Like a rite. With whoops and applause and high-fives all round. *Break* that mother up! You *go*, girl! You *show* that fucker who's boss! . . . Fun that wasn't fun, but rage and despair with fun's expired passport.

The road terminates in a square between low black shop units and the larger hulks beyond – towers, office spaces, glassless and cracked. The square is full of people, some sitting quietly on the ground, others standing and talking. Without difficulty I pass through the crowd until, about halfway across the square, I discern a building on the far side. Steps, pillars: Silo Town Hall. And above the double doors of the main entrance an artfully hand-painted sign: LORELEI. TONIGHT. FREE ENTRY. ALL WELCOME.

Heading back the way I have come, I find a guesthouse of a sort (I don't know which sort) on a crockled side street just off the main road. I try to negotiate with the old man at the desk but my heart isn't in it and eventually the landlord or the clerk or whoever he is waives the no-barter policy and offers me a room for two hours in exchange for both earrings and necklace.

I sit in my two-hour room. The chair is positioned by the window, presumably to allow guests a view of the street and the near side of the square, but I move it to the other wall and sit in it with my eyes closed, my stick leaning on the chair arm, my hammer in my lap. After a moment I get up, place in the window the two squares of cardboard that serve as blinds, then sit, close my eyes again. Occasionally I open my eyes in the gloom to look at the bed, this skimpy single bed in which I will never sleep.

It wouldn't matter where I put the chair. The crowd is inescapable: less its noise than its presence, its animal aura bulking the air. A constant stream of new arrivals passes on the street below with ringing shouts, pealing laughter. I think of Peter. Is he here, right now, in Silo? Ridiculous thought. Peter is everywhere. His tide, his periphery is everywhere. It would be foolish to imagine he is not keeping close tabs on his faithful disaster-averter, his loyal miracle-worker.

Listening to the crowd, I know there is another reason why Peter wanted me for this commission. A mad lady in a crowd – a mad old black woman with a hammer. Random tragedy. And the assembly seeing its bright star fall rounds on her attacker. Rough justice. Mad lady torn apart by mob. That's the other reason. Peter is sending me into Silo Town Hall because he doesn't mind that I will never come out of it. Expendable. Disposable. Free entry but no exit.

I think of the girl on the slope. I pat my hand and amazing things happen. Do you see, Grandpa – such forks, such flukes . . .

You know he's playing you, my dead sister says. If I opened my eyes I would see her there, sitting on the end of the little bed. *This Peter. Playing you like Yahtzee.*

I know, I say.

I'm dead, Mabel-label. Been dead a long time.

I know, Iris. I know.

I open my eyes and no one is sitting on the bed and the dull cast of the room tells me night has fallen. I go to the window, remove one of the boards, and there it is. At the end of the valley the sun never sinks. At the end of the world the sun never sets.

I return to the square to find movement: with spectacular enthusiasm the crowd has begun funnelling into the town hall. I wait to one side then allow the natural drift of humanity to draw me into the immense queue and its trundling progress over the square, towards the steps, the pillars, the wide double doors.

In the queue there are many pauses. For minutes at a time we shuffle our feet and peer at the weather. A woman standing nearby, short, solid, older than I am though with a teenager's sumptuous red hair, tells me she has come to Silo with her two daughters (twin russet-haired mites, each with a finger wound in a belt loop on either side of their mother) from a village so far away I wasn't sure it existed. They have walked for three days. The woman has heard Lorelei speak twice before, though tonight is the girls' first time. I am told they are over the moon. They don't look over the moon.

'I hear it's quite a show,' I say.

'The important thing is the words. No one uses words the way Lorelei does.'

'Isn't there a sort of team that comes on stage with her . . . ?'

'Oh yes!' The woman laughs – a stout cackle. 'Look out for them!'

'I will. A friend said I should keep an eye open for Mrs Tooth.'

'Mrs Tooth? Don't think I know a . . .' Thoughtfully the woman pulls on a curl hanging over her cheek – shaping, reshaping it. Then she cackles again and says, 'Oh, I know who you mean! "Mrs Tooth" indeed! You mean *Claw*, don't you? You mean Claw.'

We come to the town hall's threshold. As we mount the steps between the pillars I'm braced for a bag check or pat down, but there is no sign of the famous security team. Towing along her tots, one of whom has begun to lean against me also, the red-haired woman bustles past the double doors into a hallway through which a wall of people in front of us is struggling to press itself. She shows how it's done. Beaming, beaming, beaming, she bustles up to the human wall and butts against it until it breaks. People skitter to either side. The red-haired woman bustles through with her girls. Before the wall can reform I bustle through too.

The hall is dangerously full. Hundreds of people packed together under the gloomy ceiling. Candles have been lit and placed in the brass candleholders along the walls which once illuminated heroic paintings where now are only oblong marks in the scuffed and faded wallpaper. At the far end of the hall is a low stage accessible by steps and ramp at either side. A wide black curtain hangs over it.

'Don't worry, it's always like this!' My red-haired friend laughs. 'Lorelei knows how to draw a crowd. Just you wait until she comes on! Not even then. Usually before . . .'

The rest of her sentence is lost in a sudden roar of metallic intensity. Everyone in the hall is shouting, cheering. I look towards the stage and see that the curtain has opened. An old woman steps from behind it and takes up what appears to be a pre-arranged position facing the crowd, the audience. An instant later an old man steps out and takes up another position. Then another old woman. Then another old man.

My friend bounces up on tiptoes so I can hear her: 'It's her guard. Lorelei's guard.'

Hendrix was right: the security team have names, like bullshit wrestlers. My friend points at each: 'That's the Net. That's the Mark. That's the Fee. And that's the Well Land.'

There used to be another, she tells me, another man – but something happened to him, he died.

There is a pause. Then a fifth figure steps from behind the curtain and takes up the final position in the defensive line at the front of the stage. An old woman in a long black hood from which appear to hang loops of chains.

'And that,' my friend says, 'that's the Claw.'

I would like to look longer at the Claw, at her theatrical hood, her hanging chains, but now the roar that has steadily filled the hall gains a tumultuous new pitch. It is as though we are all going to fall through the ceiling. The walls drum and quake. A sixth figure stands on the stage, a woman, a girl, in black boots, khaki shorts, colourless band T-shirt, her dark hair in a twisty ponytail and her dark eyes everywhere in the huge gloomy room.

She starts to speak. I listen for a while. It sounds like nice enough stuff – wry recollections of girlhood with the upbeat beats patterned in – but soon I lose interest and turn to my professional obligations. In the bad old days, with my Sig, I could have taken my time finding an elevated vantage with plenty of egress. Lining up the crosshairs, squeezing the trigger when it suited me. Those days are gone however and I have no choice but to work my way in close. It's not going to be easy and it's not going to be quick. I start forward, sidling between the people in front. No one seems to notice me. I feel a yank on my sleeve. I don't look round, keep going. The yank comes again. I glance back and there's my red-haired friend, a mite in each arm.

'What are you doing?'

'Fancy a closer look.' As I start forward again I know she is trailing after me. I pick up speed, barge my way with more force, hoping the crowd's inertia at some point will drag her back.

Lorelei's voice comes over the crowd. For long spells while I'm stuck wondering how to solve the next move forward, there is nothing to do but listen to her. So I do that. I listen to her.

There are those, she says, who want to blame you. Any number of people would like nothing more than to stand where she is standing and declare that what happened is your fault. That you yourself brought about Helios (and yes, she says it, she uses the word). By your sin or stupidity, your willed ignorance of facts of one sort or another. They always have reasons, the ones who want to blame you. They always come up with something.

Likewise there are those who want you to blame someone else. Blame those other ones! such people cry. Blame them! Hate them! Make them pay! Fetch your hacksaw and your pitchfork and we'll sort 'em out together! And the people who cry such things are surely the saddest and poorest people on earth, because they are people who are always bored. Bored by everything, especially themselves. Civilisation collapses and these people are still bored – though she puts it better than that, it gets a big laugh.

Other people still want to tell you what to do. They want to be the ones pronouncing what needs to be done, they want to hear those words in their mouths, feel those actions animating their limbs, but it's not only that. These arrangers, these organisers – Lorelei says – these are people who have an idea stuck inside them. They have no choice but to act on this idea, to act always in the interests of this idea: literally no choice. It would be easier for them to die than to cease acting in the interests of the idea that is stuck inside them with its special idea-glue. Rebuild, they say. Recover, restore. Put everything back the way it was before the Event. Because an idea about the way things were is stabbing a hole in their head. They can't not say it and they can't say anything else. Their stabbing idea about the way the world used to be is more important to them than their eyelids.

These different people, Lorelei says, have one thing in common: they are afraid we don't feel it. They are terrified by their suspicion, their well-founded suspicion, that we don't feel Helios as they feel it. Don't feel the loss, the shudder, the horror as they do. And they are right. We don't feel it. We don't because we know nothing really happened. The Event occurred and nothing really changed.

Ask yourselves: what is our predicament? We are human animals. Born of nature and partaking of nature. We make and unmake and everything we do is natural for the reason that we are natural beings. It may not always seem so. Lorelei says it is easy to believe that we are different from nature, higher or lower, but in some way separate from it. She says even people very close to her have held that belief. Oh, she's had arguments! Even with people very close to her (she glances left and right at the members of her guard while the crowd warmly resonates. A shared joke, I assume, or a shared something else). But at last they too came to recognise the truth, perhaps the most important truth of all. We never step out of nature because wherever we are nature is too. It does not follow, unfortunately, or perhaps fortunately, that wherever nature is we also are. The joins, Lorelei explains, are not fashioned in that way.

And yet there are joins. Undoubtedly there are joins. From the mountains and down through the hills and the stubble and stump where the fields and forests were and through the pebbles of riverbeds and the earth under our feet and the posts of our doorways and the flesh of our bodies and the very spectres of our dreams runs a thread. It is a part of nature too, though it hates every other part of nature. People did not make it. In ten million years of trying people could not make a thing that runs so deeply through the world and themselves. It burns inside us – in our guts. It sears until we bleed. In the mountains too, in the dead woods and meadows, in the sleeping pebbles, the same silver thread burns. Except this isn't what she says at all. The words are different. The exact words. You know exactly what she means.

If anything changed it is that this thread was jarred – shocked. For a time Helios loosened the wire in our animal bowels. (And in the pebbles and the mountains too.) Soon it will tighten, start burning again, start us bleeding again, but it has not done so yet. Perhaps for the first time in history people have the chance to push back against the inflamed, the enflamed network in our nature. Not to shake it off entirely perhaps but to snap a few links, to warp the design, to deform it and live afterwards in that magnificent deformity. To spoil it a little, this web, this grid . . .

'This grid'. The Grid. And now I know why Peter wants Lorelei dead. She is not grit in a shoe, not a nuisance. She is his opposite, his tragic annihilation. The countertide that alone the Gridman dreads. This girl with her theatrical guard, and her audience here in Silo, and her audience in the last town, and in the one before that and the one after this – she is the gathering force of heads and hands that at last will come for him, for him and all his kind, the Gridmen, the money reptiles, and sweep them from their shadows and tear them from their power lines, tear the power lines. A wave building, a terror of the earth.

And now I know why Peter wants me to fulfil this commission. Why he chose me to smash Lorelei's face and scatter her force – to shatter the wave, stifle the terror. To whom would he entrust such a task but his faithful miracle-averter, his loyal disaster-worker?

Finally I reach the front of the auditorium. I glance back but cannot see the red-haired woman: she has vanished, receded into the crowd with her girls. Good. I'm glad. I glance up at the stage.

Lorelei is still talking. Two of the guardians stand between her and me: the Well Land, and the Claw. One is hooded, the other wears sunglasses. And yet both, I notice, are looking at Lorelei in a particular way – a particular raptness, a particular toothedness . . .

They are her parents. She is their daughter. I know it as surely as I know my sister is dead.

There are the steps, and there is the ramp. I opt for the ramp. Bit of a run-up – bit of momentum.

I bend and lay my stick on the floor. It is useless to me now. By the time I straighten it has already rolled away, disappeared between the feet of the people standing behind me.

I unbutton my bag and, hanging it from the strap on one shoulder, reach inside, close my fingers round the handle of my hammer, placed in preparation on top of all the other crap I've been carrying and will now never use again. In a break with tradition I take my breath: one breath. That's the ration. I take it now rather than later because there is not going to be a later. And I know who I am.

I shrug my shoulder. The strap springs free, my bag drops to the floor. I am standing at the edge of the stage in tall and wavering candlelight in full view of several hundred people with a hammer in my hand.

I start to walk up the ramp. A section of the audience pulls uncertainly towards this fact – my walking up the ramp. I swing my hammer. And the whole audience pulls sharply, fanatically, towards this fact, towards my hammer swinging forward and back. There is a noise, active and aghast, a great thrumming like a hive breaking open.

The Well Land or whoever he is comes striding down the ramp towards me. He has something in his hand – a knife, maybe an axe – but I don't stop to look and instead draw my hammer into the first loop of an infinity symbol that passes with resounding force through the old man's jaw. He doesn't fall or crumple but only goes on juddering there in his sunglasses. As I pass he makes no attempt to stop me.

On a slope outside town a little girl kisses stones or tells stones secrets. In the hall Lorelei stares at me. Doesn't run, doesn't move. Only stares. I stare at her too then the Claw or whoever she is glides heavily between us. Nothing else can happen. All the blood inside my body is ready for all the blood inside hers. And working it out of its loop, I raise my hammer again. Swinging her chains she strides towards me. And she smiles. In the thrumming air at the end of the world. The crone, the hag. Beautifully. She smiles.

ACKNOWLEDGEMENTS

I owe a great debt of thanks to my agent, Lucy Morris, who supported this book with heroic energy and insight at every stage of its development. Likewise to Lucy's colleagues at Curtis Brown, Luke Speed and Claire Nozieres, for their generous commitment to a peculiar novel.

Profound thanks also to Emma Herdman, my editor at Sceptre: Emma not only always knows what it is I am trying to do, but also, uncannily, how I can do it better. Her meticulous reading of *Claudia* found extraordinary accomplices in Lily Cooper and Susan Opie who gave more of their time and brilliance to the text and cover than I can honestly bear to think about. Tom Duxbury, meanwhile, designed a cover of such beauty and acuity he must be suspected of unnatural powers.

Thanks to my sister Clare, and to my brothers, Phillip and Bernie.

And, always, to Gemma.